BLOODRIDGE

BOOK 1 IN THE *SPIES LIE* SERIES

D. S. KANE

For my cous Les

D. Kane

ISBN 978-0-9960591-0-7 (paperback)
ISBN 978-0-9960591-1-4 (Kindle)
ISBN 978-0-9960591-2-1 (ePub)

Cover design by Jeroen Ten Berge
[www.jeroentenberge.com]

Print layout by eBooks By Barb for
booknook.biz

For Andrea,
the most important person in my world.

Contents

In this country we manufacture bullets by the train load. No one would care if a few went missing. And, remember that Middle Eastern bank you worked at for us? Well, some of those folks are still alive. And I hear they're still looking for you. So all we'd have to do is just send them your forwarding address.

—D. S. Kane's former handler,
upon hearing about this book

Disclaimer

This is a work of fiction. All of the characters and events depicted here are the work of the author's mind. Most but not all of the places are real.

Master and servant, rich and poor, strong and feeble, wise and simple, all are equal in death.

—*Gates of Repentance*

PART I

CHAPTER 1

Abel and Natasha Sommerstein's flat,
20 Milner Street Number 14,
Cadogan Square, London
February 21, 6:19 p.m.

Jon Sommers listened, hidden in the walk-in closet of his parents' bedroom. They were speaking in a language he was just beginning to understand, one of many no one had taught him. At twelve, he could speak seven languages and read five, but the one his parents were speaking now was the hardest.

"If he tells anyone the truth, it could be the death of us all." His father, Abel Sommerstein faced his mother, his hands on her shoulders. Jon had left the closet door open just a crack, and he peeked out, watching them.

Natasha pulled away and stared at him in silence. She turned away. Looking in the mirror, she adjusted the belt of her black dress. She watched her husband fiddle with his bow tie. "We can show him the rules. Moscow rules."

Abel shook his head. "He's too young to follow any rules. Look what he did today at school. Another fight. He already knows how to lie."

"Everyone lies," said Natasha, facing her husband. We have to tell him. I'm tired of pretending to be what we aren't. It's time to show him our true selves."

"No." Abel was emphatic. "Mother has made it clear that

we remain undercover. If Crane knew, he'd tumble to the conclusion of who we work for."

"It's not fair to Jon." Natasha had switched to English. Her upper lip quivered.

Abel placed his hands once more on her shoulders. "Does he ever need to know?" The bow tie was a mess. He frowned and pulled it even. "No more talk about this now." The tie still looked messy. He unknotted it and started over.

Jon shifted his weight in the closet, still unnoticed. His father muttered, "Where's my damned dinner jacket?" Jon scuttled behind a rack of his father's suits as his mother opened the closet door, and handed Abel his white jacket.

"Thanks, my sweet."

Jon resumed his position by the closet door his mother had left ajar. He watched his father unlock the cherrywood desk's center drawer and tug out a tiny box. "Your gift for Yigdal. We're to drop it in the Ambassador's potted orchids. What's new in the tech?"

His mother closed her eyes. "I've improved its range and its speed since we used it on the Syrians."

"How does the new version work?" He placed the box in the pocket of his dinner jacket and patted it flat.

"Just arm it and place the Reaper within ten meters of any computer. Takes twenty minutes to hack in and transmit a copy of all the computer's files. But its battery lasts only three days and someone still has to retrieve it before the target discovers that the data have been compromised. I'm working on one that turns to dust when the batteries have discharged."

"It's too bad we had to use it on Crane's computer to find out about the threat. I wonder if he'll survive the shit storm." Abel turned toward the dresser and unlocked another drawer, retrieving a handgun from inside. He dropped it in his other pocket.

"Is that really necessary? There will be security everywhere at Belgrave Mews. They won't even let you carry it inside the Ambassador's residence."

"It's going into the car's glove box," Abel replied.

Natasha persisted. "It's been almost a month. Do you really expect trouble?"

He donned his trench coat. "How should I know?" he asked as he helped her into her raincoat. "Take a scarf. It's going to snow."

She pulled one off the closet shelf and took his arm.

As they walked together from the bedroom, the doorbell of their flat buzzed.

Jon opened the closet door and ducked into the hallway, heading toward his room.

He could hear his mother speaking with the sitter. "Don't let Jon stay up past eleven. And make sure he completes his algebra homework."

Jon turned back down the hallway to the living room.

The sitter, Rakhel, a young, dark-eyed, rail-thin woman, was nodding in response to Natasha's instructions.

His mother pulled him to her and kissed the top of his head, tousling his brown hair. "Why are you always making trouble?"

Jon knew, self-consciously, that the prominent black eye he'd received at school had prompted his mother's question, but he deflected her attention. "Mum, I'm not a baby." He pointed to the sitter. "I don't need her."

Abel hugged his son. "Don't argue, son. You're almost an adult. Behave like one."

Jon frowned and turned away. "My point exactly." He stood as tall as he could, close to his father, measuring how much taller he needed to be. "There were three of them. They were all bigger."

Abel turned away. Seeing Jon's homework papers on the desk, he stepped over to them and pointed to one. "Jon, this equation. What does it represent?"

Jon's eyes narrowed. "I've been reading on game theory. Someone named John von Neumann. Anyway, it's just calculus. I applied it to valence theory from a psychologist named Kurt Levin. Tried to forecast a person's or a group's intentions. I've modified it so it now shows the distance between intention and the probability of success as a separate variable."

His father scanned the page in more detail. "I see. You've been reading more math and now, social psychology." He paused over the page. "So what we have here is the beginning of a method to predict human behavior." He scanned the page, his forefinger pointing at the string of variables. "Tomorrow, I'll go through this from top to bottom." He stopped at something on the page. "Jon, I think you made a mistake here. One of the parameters. This should be a subtraction, not a division."

Jon gawked at the page.

Abel buttoned his trench coat. "Tomorrow."

With that last sentence, his parents were gone from the flat, leaving Jon alone with Rakhel.

"An urgent message from Betakill." The young operative handed an encrypted text to the gray-haired man. "Natasha Sommerstein said they were being followed by a repeater. Plate number A16-248, London. I have their location on GPS." The operative handed the older man the cell phone.

The older man pressed a few buttons. He viewed the screen and muttered, "Rats." He reached for his coat and ordered the comm officer, "Tell the team to hurry. We need to find them before it's too late."

By the time they were in the garage, the driver had the car ready and waiting.

It took less than ten minutes for their Bentley to reach the location of Jon's parents.

Jon looked up from his calculus formulas when the doorbell rang. The babysitter sat near him, listening to Tchaikovsky's Sixth Symphony playing on the stereo.

He rubbed his black eye. He thought of the battle he'd engaged in when the bully and his friends tried to take his lunch money. He had to fight, or else the bullies would pick on him every day. His mistake was fighting fair. A kick to the monster's balls would have given him a fleeting advantage. The next time, he'd be ready.

The doorbell rang a second time and he looked toward the door, expecting that his parents had arrived home much earlier than he'd expected. *What had happened at their party?*

Rakhel answered the door and let in a thin man with graying hair and a short-cropped white beard. He wore a black business suit with no necktie. Closing the door behind him, the old man whispered into the young woman's ear, his voice like the raspy crumpling of paper. His language was nothing Jon had ever heard before. The only word he understood was the sitter's name, "Rakhel."

She gasped and her face fell.

Something was wrong. Jon started for the front door where they stood to hear better what they were saying. But before he could get there, he heard another knock at the door, and Rakhel let five tall men into their flat. Their bearing indicated this was serious. No one spoke to him; they totally ignored him. He was no longer merely curious. Now, he was worried.

The visitors shut all the window shades and moved on to the bedrooms. He could hear low, urgent voices, and doors and drawers opening and closing.

A few minutes later, there was another knock at the front door of the flat. Rakhel looked through the peephole and admitted two men who announced themselves as police detectives. They spoke with her briefly, in hushed tones. She nodded grimly.

The detectives remained at the door, talking with Rakhel. He could feel his pulse quicken. What were they saying? Did this have to do with his parents? His stomach did loops.

When the detectives left, she asked him to sit next to her on the living room couch. Without any preamble, she said, "Jon, your mom and dad were in a serious car accident. I'm afraid they're never coming home."

Jon examined her face for some sign that this wasn't true, but all he saw were the reddened edges of her eyes. She'd been crying.

He shook his head. This had to be a lie. "Why are you telling me this? Where are they? Really?"

She moved closer and reached a hand out to lift his chin. "I'm so sorry."

All the elegant equations in his head dissolved into a void. His world grew smaller, containing him like a steel net. He stared at his formulas on the page, damp with his tears. He jolted as he heard himself curse. There was no way mathematics could express the deaths of his mother and father.

His fists clenched and he pounded at her. He heard a scream but it couldn't be his voice, could it? Every muscle in his body stiffened, and he bawled on and on.

She grabbed his hands. He wrenched away and stormed around the room, throwing anything he could reach through the air. He smashed a lamp, and pounded another into shards. The fragments of broken glass embedded in his hands didn't even hurt.

How could they die? He felt his heart turn from anger into a sinking sorrow at this sudden loss. He ran into their bedroom and Rakhel followed him and grasped him, hugging him to her.

The gray-haired man entered the bedroom and nodded

to her. She left the room. The older man didn't move at all. He stared at Jon and the words came in a slow rasp. "I'm so sorry. Someday you will understand. I promise." He touched Jon's head and followed the path Rakhel had taken to the front door of the flat where they whispered.

She returned and took a single step toward him and stopped. "I will stay with you, along with these others who arrived." She pointed to the younger men. The young woman's accent now was different from the voice she'd been using to talk with him before. Less British, more like that of his parents when they were rushed or argued. "Don't worry. I'll take care of you."

Jon remembered earlier this evening, the last time he ever saw his mother and father. He thought of their reprimand that he behave himself. It was the last thing they told him.

His eyes shifted down, the weight of loss heavy on him.

He'd never even had the chance to say he loved them before they were gone forever.

TWELVE YEARS LATER

CHAPTER 2

Close to Heathrow Airport, London
May 19, 11:38 a.m.

Lisa Gabriel twisted the new gold band on her left ring finger as if it were aflame. Her eyes shifted to her side, where Jon Sommers stared back. She'd been quiet since they'd climbed into the cab, thinking about this new conundrum. Drifting rain distracted her as it blew across the highway. The taxi slowed, shifting lanes as it drew within sight of Heathrow.

The cabbie's radio played an old Beatles song, "Back in the USSR." The cab was redolent of her exotic Mitsouko perfume. *I've used too much.* She reached across and stroked Jon's hand. She was sure her silence filled him with a mixture of concern and trepidation. "A lot will change now. I have to tell Mother, face to face. It's better if you don't come."

His face closed in concentration. She'd learned him so well she could almost imagine his thoughts. She knew he was about object to her traveling alone to the Middle East. She wanted to smile but crushed her lips together.

He had a temper when it came to others who pushed him too hard.

It had taken her months to break through his defenses. What she found had surprised her. The boy was naïve. The man was bright, capable of elegant solutions to complex

14

problems. This contradiction between Jon's two states was what she'd fallen in love with.

She'd known long ago he would be her undoing.

Jon faced her. "I'd intended that we spend the two weeks I have off before I start working at Dreitsbank, just the two of us at your apartment. Think of it. Pure bliss."

"You know I have to go."

"Why can't you bring me along?"

"I'll take you to see Tel Aviv soon. Mother and I need to talk alone. It's just for two weeks."

She waited, summoning thoughts to counter his inevitable reply.

The taxi pulled to the curb. He was out of time, his eyes downcast. "Yeah. I guess while you're gone, I'll work on the paper I've been writing on Islamic banking. Still, I was hoping—"

"We'll have forever after I return." She slid toward the door. His graduation ceremony was yesterday. Jon now had his MBA and, if she had her way, his life would soon be full of even bigger changes.

He shifted toward her, brushing away a lock of his brown hair that had fallen on his angular face. His eyes scanned her, as if he were searching for some change in their relationship.

She smiled to cover her lies and make her face unreadable. "While I'm gone, look into converting to Judaism. It's what you promised. And when I return, I'll tell you all my secrets."

"Secrets?" His jaw moved but she shook her head and touched his lips with her fingers.

"Not now." She kissed him goodbye and reached for her bag. *I wonder if he'll forgive me when I reveal my true self?*

When she exited the cab and stepped to the curbside, the drizzle had become a downpour.

CHAPTER 3

Mountain cave complex,
outside the village of Upper Pachir,
Nangarhar Province, Afghanistan
February 22, 8:06 a.m.

As the morning sun streaked through thin, high clouds, Tariq Houmaz walked from the limestone caves of the mountain complex that housed him and his senior officers. He closed the top button of his winter topcoat and spread the small prayer rug on top of a large flat rock. The wind blustered as he looked east.

Things had calmed down in the years since the Americans had gone home. Soon, his mujahidin would start their day of training. Muzzle flashes, the sound of gunfire, and the smell of cordite would fill the air.

He pulled a flask of water from his coat. Washing his hands, he gazed up. He prayed, chanting in Pashto the ancient rhymes and prose given to Mohammed by Allah.

When he was finished, he remained kneeling, his eyes still focused on heaven. "Please, Allah, just one wish. Save my people from the will of infidels who run our government. Keep us pure, bound to you and your land. We have suffered too long. Keep us strong to do your will."

He took a deep breath and started to rise, but stopped and settled back again. "Please, please also help my brother.

Pesi has become too fond of the conveniences offered us by the West. Help him see his error. Help him focus on our tasks."

When he rose, he saw a young boy playing with a piece of wood shaped to look like an AK-47. Houmaz smiled as the child stretched his arms. He picked up the boy and touched his lips to the boy's head. When he dropped the child, the youngster aimed the stick at Houmaz and yelled, "Pow, pow."

In the clearing, he opened the cover of the aluminum case containing the secure satellite phone Prince Hamid, his benefactor, had given him.

Standing against the wind, he keyed the number for his Bank of Trade account and checked its balance. He ended the call, and punched in Pesi's number, in Riyadh. Seconds later, he heard the connection complete.

Tariq spoke in Arabic. "Listen carefully, Pesi. As of this morning, the infidels sent us the money we need to destroy them."

"Are you sure they didn't place a tracer on the transfer?"

Tariq tightened his grip on the phone. It was too late for Pesi to beg off the mission. "The funds are in our account at the Chechnya branch of the Bank of Trade. No tracers are possible at that bank. I told the fools it's for a limited operation on the border with Pakistan."

He heard Pesi laugh.

Maybe Pesi had just wanted confirmation. He gave it. "Yes. This is what we'd hoped they'd assume. We now have enough to pay for the mission. Our friends in Vladivostok will sell us everything we need. Within six months we'll be ready."

Prince Hamid had told him that the senior management of the Russian mafiya was principally Jewish. They sold weapons from the defunct Soviet empire out of their warehouses on the wharfs in Vladivostok. The weapons he intended to buy would be used against Israel. He restrained the urge to chuckle at the irony.

The Americans were in denial about the reality of the Jewish origin of the Russian mafiya and also its arms sales to Third World governments. But even Hollywood knew. They had made it the subject of a movie starring Nicolas Cage, *Lord of War*.

His brother squawked, "Too short a time for me to find and train crews. I need more time."

Tariq stiffened. "Too late now to complain. Find us two crews. Search your list of contacts as fast as you can."

Pesi's voice faded in volume. "I'll do my best, but —"

"As fast as you can, then. Don't fail me." Tariq terminated the call and walked back toward the cave. This time when he passed the child, he had a sneer on his face.

Ever since his father had disowned him, he'd been looking for a way to make the old man regret his decision. Now he could show his father how powerful he'd become. If Allah willed it, he'd have scrubbed the world of at least a million, and possibly tens of millions of infidels. All the other attacks he'd completed were insignificant compared to this. The connections he'd worked so hard to find and exploit in the Islamic banking world would make it all come to fruition. He could finally earn the respect he deserved. It was a straightforward plan, blunt and simple.

He gritted his teeth, walking through the icy wind. Soon, he would visit his banker in New York, to arrange funding.

CHAPTER 4

Near the coast of Spain,
35,000 above sea level
February 22, 10:14 a.m.

From 35,000 feet up, Aviva Bushovsky pulled the cell phone from her purse and punched in a number. "I'm on my way. I'll see you tomorrow, as planned."

The gruff voice on the other side of the line was just above a whisper. "Good. I'm worried about your recent behavior." Aviva could hear raspy breathing. She waited, but Mother said nothing more.

Aviva idly scanned Spain's Mediterranean coast from the aircraft's window. When she couldn't take the silence any longer, she said, "I hope you can see this my way."

Mother terminated the call. *So like Mother*, Aviva thought. She wondered how much Mother knew. Would what she'd done with Crane become a problem for them all? *Sooner or later*, she thought, *Mother will find out everything, and hell will truly rain on me.*

She had been overly protective of her fiancé. How could he believe so much in things that were obvious illusions?

Mother had met Jon when he was twelve, the night his parents died. The man he'd become was so similar to the boy Mother had met so long ago.

She'd lied to Jon, telling him that her father had died in

the war with Lebanon. His response was to hug her, offering comfort. Was that what had made her fall in love with him? She shook her head, her lips forming the word "no" in silence. The person in the adjacent seat looked up, and she shook her head again.

She plucked the photo of the two of them from her purse. There was another copy of it, framed, in her apartment. She stared at his handsome face, partially covered by the locks of brown hair that were always falling in front of his eyes. She studied it intently, as if she could conjure him there beside her by doing so.

Once more, she twisted the new ring on her finger. Things had gone so far off the path Mother had directed.

She'd committed treason for her lover. Didn't MI-6 and the Mossad cooperate? It was an honest mistake. How could she make Mother understand that? Crane had threatened to have Jon "taken down" if she didn't cooperate, and she was sure her cooperation, to save Jon's life, was in the best interest of both intelligence services. She rehearsed an argument about how Jon's survival and recruitment were worth the concessions Crane demanded. Would this appease Mother?

It would be difficult to win this one. Caught between Crane and Mother, she feared what either could do to her, to Jon. She wiped the tears forming in the corners of her eyes.

At least Jon would never learn the truth.

Jon woke the next morning and went to the martial arts center for a workout. Distracted, his mind wandered. A smaller, faster man tossed him like a rag doll. He tried harder to focus, but it wasn't working. After half an hour of being thrown about, he felt hurt from hitting the mat.

He showered and took the tube to the city library. At one of the carrels, he sat at the library computer, connected to a small, private library to complete research on his Islamic banking paper. Screen after screen of banking news scrolled past.

He was fascinated. Islamic banking practices paid careful attention to religious law in the Koran. No bank could charge interest for any loan, but equivalent fees were permitted.

One bank in particular was popular with Islamic fundamentalists. The bank claimed a reputation for secrecy. He scanned the bank's financials, and drew his brows together. The Bank of Trade had an extremely low capital-to-assets ratio, since most of their work was trade finance, and such transactions were recorded "off the balance sheet." Trade finance was "travel insurance" for goods shipped to another party, and this bank dominated the Islamic market.

In one of the banking and finance blogs, someone wrote:

> The B of T is a great place to store funds to be used for purchase of weapons or drugs. Many of the world's covert services also have bank accounts there. But its cash flow seems a mystery. Just the rounding errors on its foreign exchange activities might be enough to quadruple its income. Where does the rest of the cash go? It sure doesn't show up in their P&L.

Jon's father had once told him how a bank could be used as a financial Laundromat. From the financials, he could see that unless the bank was unprofitable in every other line of business, they had over a half-billion dollars of unreported profit every year. Did other Islamic banks hide as much of their income Late in the day he returned to his tiny apartment and listened to the blues music Lisa had introduced him to. Before he'd met her all he'd liked was classical music, where he reveled in the mathematics of musical progression. But as he scanned the notes he'd taken at the library, he found his fingers tapping to the compelling, driving rhythm of a Robert Johnson tune. The verses pounded through his head:

> She's a kind hearted woman; she studies evil all the time.

The song evoked the times they'd spent making love. He closed his eyes and saw her, on top of him, moving slowly, grinding against him, her hands locked on his chest. It was too much; he opened his eyes and tried to ground himself.

What would happen if his paper were published? The possible outcomes drifted past him, and he drifted into planning what he'd do. Some outcomes lifted his spirits, especially the ones where Lisa was a prime variable in the equation. But he could hear her voice as if she were there. He imagined her pointing a finger at him, telling him, "While I'm away, don't try planning our lives."

She'd once told him, "You'll be a banker, making tons of money, and I'll create and manage a charitable trust, spending all you make to fund good causes. I want to save the world, Jon. Don't you?" He still couldn't answer her question. Now, for the first time, he wondered why.

His hands in his lap, he stared at nothing, but saw her in his head. He smiled and continued working.

Within a few hours, the rough outline was complete. He read it and made a few changes. This early version had potential. It was his best work ever, possibly even worthy of publication.

While it rained outside, he spent the hours working non stop to polish a final draft of the paper. The next morning, he wrote a cover letter and placed a printed copy of the paper and the query into an envelope addressed to one of the editors at *The Economist*.

He stretched and decided to walk to a post box, even in the rain. People walked past, under umbrellas on the shallow hills inside Hyde Park. He dropped the envelope in the post box near Speakers' Corner.

The pub where they'd met was nearby. She'd made the first move, crowding beside him, smiling as she ordered a Guinness. He'd felt unsure about himself until that moment. But, by the end of the night, he had her cell number.

Now in the dark bar without her, he needed something stronger than a Guinness. "Lagavulin, please, straight up." And looking at the chipped shot glass, he realized the single malt scotch from Islay he was sipping was her usual drink of choice.

The pub's sound system played old acoustic delta blues tunes as he savored the whisky's smoky flavor. He was struck by the realization that he knew so little about her. Why hadn't he argued harder with her about accompanying her to see Israel and her mother?

He pulled his cell phone from his pocket and called her.

"Lisa, I miss you. Have you told your mother yet?"

"Calm down, Jon. I just finished unpacking."

"Yeah. Have you told your mother yet?"

He waited through an extended silence and was about to repeat his question yet again.

"Yes. I've told Mother. As I told you before I left you at the airport, Mother has some issues."

His jaw dropped. "Can you let me fix this? I can come there tomorrow. I can—"

"No, Jon. Leave everything to me. Okay? I love you. Only eight more days and I'll be back with you." He heard a door open on her end of the phone line and then there was someone talking near her. She must have covered the phone. He heard a low, muffled voice, almost certainly a male. Then she said, "I've got to go now. Mother has a question." He felt puzzled by the voice she referred to as her mother.

He finished his drink, and walked back to his apartment. She'd told him her father died in the IDF, the Israeli Army.

The war in Lebanon. They'd both lost their fathers, but at least she still had her mother.

Aviva Bushovsky could feel the tears against her cheek. "Uncle Yig, please. I did what I thought best. There was more to lose than gain."

But the man she faced across the desk hissed back, his eyes narrowed to slits. "You will address me as Assistant Deputy Foreign Minister Ben-Levy."

Her mouth fell open. She was sure he could see the anger she wanted to hide. She staggered to her feet and hurried from his office, slammed the door and sprinted down the narrow corridor to the staircase. Before anyone could notice the tears pouring from her eyes, she raced up the stairs from the basement, eager to leave the building.

What if Mother knew everything? Her heart pounded with fear. She needed to contact Crane, but she worried they might be tapping her cell phone. *Damn them all for arranging her personal life!* It was so easy before her current assignment, where she'd lost her way. She squinted against the wall of heat and bright sunshine that met her as she emerged from the lobby.

Her wristwatch chimed, signaling her weekly lunchtime date to meet Ruth Cohen at a Mike's Place, a café near the corner of Hasadnaot Street and Hamenofim Street in downtown Herzliyya.

If she didn't show up, that might make them all the more suspicious. She didn't want the company, but she did need to eat. Maybe a decent meal would clear her head and shake off her memories of the bitter meeting she'd just experienced.

Driving there would save time. She parked in the nearby Gav Yam Parking garage, an elevated structure on Ari Shenkar Street.

Striding two blocks to the café calmed her. She thought of her fiancé, more sensitive, more logical than the Israeli men she worked with, and less driven by the emotions she knew he felt. He always tried to understand her, and often did.

At a crosswalk, she considered her dilemma. She'd have to resign. Twenty-three-years old, and after four years, her current job was all she knew how to do. What could a *bat leveyha* do if she left the Mossad? It would be best not to tell Ruth, since they both worked for Uncle Yig.

She walked through the door of the restaurant and forced a smile. "Hey, Ruth. Sorry I'm late."

Ruth nodded back, her blond hair reflecting sunlight. "I heard the ruckus as I walked by the old man's door. Are you in trouble?" Ruth's expression seemed devoid of emotion. Aviva wondered if she was being tested. It might be the case, since Ruth also worked as a *bat leveyha*.

Aviva shook her head, a thick strand of red curls falling in front of her eyes. She raked a hand through her hair. "Just a difference of opinion in how to run my current assignment. Nothing to worry about."

They both ordered falafel and cola. Ruth seemed uneasy with Aviva's obvious stress and remained subdued and watchful. She mentioned an IDF major she'd seen in the halls several times in the last week. "He's a real stud. Tall and buff. Cute face, too. But I heard he's married. Name is Avram Shimmel. Ever see him?"

Aviva nodded, happy for the distraction. "He's Yigdal's next recruit. The old man never slows down." Could she trust Ruth with her dilemma? No. This was her problem, no one else's. She forced a smile.

Ruth touched her hand. "Are you sure you're okay?"

Aviva shook her head. "No, but I can't talk about it." She reached for her purse and placed some cash on the table and rose. "I have an errand to run. See you back at the office."

Ruth nodded. "Later, then." She put down her half of the cash to pay the bill and stood.

Much calmer now, Aviva straightened and examined her reflection in the mirrored wall of the deli. Her olive-colored eyes were still red from crying. She pulled makeup from her purse and covered the redness close to her eyes before she left the restaurant.

The street was crowded to overflowing and kept her from running her usual surveillance detection route.

As she walked up the stairs to her car's space, she thought again about her fiancé, and all her lies. Even her name.

But then she was consoled by what she'd done for him. Through her, he could reclaim his real identity. She would guide him, both of them working together, just as his parents had before they died. Aviva stood a bit straighter as she walked.

She took the key from her purse. Turning it in the car door's keyhole, she heard the characteristic click of a bomb trigger.

A wall of flame burst through her, swallowing her consciousness forever.

CHAPTER 5

Heathrow Airport, El Al Terminal
February 25, 7:53 a.m.

Jon had called Lisa every day. But for the past two days she hadn't answered her cell phone, forcing him to leave voice-mail.

But tonight she was returning. An hour ago he had eagerly thrown on his raincoat and caught a cab to Heathrow as the sun set behind a curtain of frigid fog. Now he stood expectantly inside the international arrivals building, in front of the exit from customs and immigration, holding a bouquet of roses.

Smiling, he paced, rehearsing his greeting. A memory of their last kiss at the airport floated through his mind. He savored the one coming soon.

The arrivals board indicated she should have landed about a half-hour ago. He waited for her to come through the door, out of customs. And waited. After an hour she still wasn't there.

He dialed her cell. There was no answer. He cursed, counting the seconds.

And waited some more.

People swept through the door, but soon the emerging

throng dwindled. The minutes kept passing and his stomach knotted.

What had delayed her? Had she missed her flight? What if she was sick or hurt? No one ever took this long to clear customs unless...What if she'd been caught bringing something illegal back from Tel Aviv? But, she would never do that, would she? He calculated outcomes based on his worst fantasies.

When he called her cell again, once more, he dropped into voicemail. Did she call him to say she'd decided to stay over a few more days? He checked his own voicemail. There was no message from her.

How could he find out what had happened?

Jon walked to the ticket counter and waited in line, his eyes darting between the customs exit and the counter clerk. "The arrivals board shows El Al Flight 36 landed ninety minutes ago. I need to know if I've missed someone who was on the plane. Can you tell me? Her name is Lisa Gabriel."

The clerk smiled, busy with screens on a terminal. "Sorry, sir. I can't give out that information."

And then, another thought: *what were her bloody secrets?*

He whispered, "Crap." He waited another hour, but nothing changed. His hands flexing and unflexing with anger, he found a taxi home.

The next day, he called her cell and got the same result. He called the airline, asking if she had been booked on a flight from Tel Aviv. The clerk declined to answer, just like the counter clerk yesterday.

He worried about her. Israel was a dangerous place. He should have argued with her about going there. They could have arranged instead for her mother to come to London, couldn't they?

He went to the airport and spent the entire day waiting for her. She didn't return that day.

She didn't return the day after.

What were the "secrets" she had confessed to having? What, exactly, was her business in Tel Aviv? He tried without success to use mathematics to construct her world in Israel.

He wandered the streets around Hyde Park, numb, seeing her where she wasn't.

To keep himself from going berserk, he took the tube down to Leadenhall Street toward the end of rush hour and watched bankers in three-piece suits pressing their ways into their downtown offices. Soon, this would be where he would spend his workdays, too. Each building had a name. Baker House. Eddings House. Spindall House.

What would he do without her? He walked for hours, passing St. Paul's Cathedral and marching over ice-covered sidewalks, reaching Upper Thames Street. He stared at the wind-swept river, remembering when they had walked along it on a freezing day two months ago, bundled up, arm-in-arm.

It was growing dusk. He was nearly frozen when he decided to return to his apartment.

Jon slogged against the wind, back through the Middle Eastern section of town near Marble Arch, and down Oxford Street past Speaker's Corner.

He stopped at a Tunisian restaurant at the intersection of Seymour and Portman streets. She had told him she loved Middle Eastern food, so he'd taken her there for lunch the week before she'd left, and offered her the engagement ring. His heart ached as he recalled her smile. He didn't know why, but he remembered the aroma of a lamb tagine steaming on their table.

But now, nothing made him feel at ease.

A growing foreboding intersected his longing for her. It got worse when he took off his coat inside his apartment, staring at his empty bed.

What were her secrets? He had to know!

He was determined to know what she'd never told him.

He donned his coat and marched the sixteen blocks to her apartment. He knocked on the door. No answer. Then he remembered; her roommate hadn't yet returned from a business trip. Lisa had given him her spare key when she'd taken his ring. He'd never intended to use it, wanting to respect her privacy.

Now things had changed.

Hyperventilating, he unlocked the door, noting the musty smell and the steamy temperature as he walked through the doorway into her room of the suite. He flipped the light switch and blinked. He still couldn't get used to the hot-pink walls. Opening her closet, he inhaled her scent. He recalled her hands on him, guiding him into her.

He opened her dresser and searched every pocket of her clothing. Then he slid his hands under her dresser. He pulled the drawer out to see if anything had been taped under or behind it. Next, on to her closet. Nothing in her jeans pockets. Nothing in the blouses. He ran his hands in under the bed. Nothing taped there. Nothing unusual in the medicine cabinet. Nothing interesting behind the books in the bookcase, and no papers hidden between their covers.

He frowned, the ache in his heart growing every second. He saw a pile of papers on the night table and picked through the stack. But he found no indications of any contact names for her friends or relatives in Israel. And no letters from her mother.

There were more papers on the kitchen table in the suite's common area. He scanned each, but many were her roommate's and even among hers, nothing useful.

She'd taken her notebook computer with her.

His mind flailing for answers, he wondered for a moment if maybe this was her way to break it off. But when he saw on the dresser the photograph of the two of them together, he was certain a change of her heart wasn't the answer. He removed the photo from its frame and looked for a long moment at the two of them together, smiling and and happy. Then he flipped the photo over and examined its back. Scribbled in pencil was a single word with a question mark: *Crane?* It meant nothing to him. Jon knew no one with that first or last name. He dropped the picture in his pocket. Who the hell was Crane? It didn't compute.

In his growing confusion, other questions formed in his mind. How many people with the last name "Gabriel'" were there in Tel Aviv? Was there an address for her family? Could he contact her mother? Would the telephone directory service in Israel speak English? Without answers, this would drive him crazy.

He replaced her possessions, but kept the photo.

When he exited the iron gate of the old brick building, he headed to the university library. He'd never been in the nano-lab where she worked, but had met her just outside, at the library's stairs down to the subbasement. Needing answers, or at least more data points, he walked down them now, entering the supercomputer lab where she'd told him she spent so many hours.

Within the hygienic hum of the lab, he found one of the techno-geeks, an overweight man with a goatee. "Do you know a woman named Lisa Gabriel? She works here."

The man scratched his chin. "Nope. And I know every-one assigned here. I'm the techno-weenie prince. I run the place." His smile showed one chipped tooth.

Jon pursed his lips. "She's about five-six, thin, olive-green eyes, red hair pulled back and an upturned nose." Then Jon remembered the photo he'd stolen and showed it to the geek.

The man examined the picture. "No one working here looks like that. Believe me, I'd remember."

Several other geeks were working in the lab. Jon showed them her photo. No, nothing.

He found the chief geek once more, and pointed to the

computer terminals lining one wall. "Can I use the facilities?" Jon flashed his student ID, with the computer sticker and registration for last semester attached.

"Your sticker's expired, you know. And it doesn't cover this computer system."

Jon nodded. "My fiancée is a student and she's missing. I need to figure out what happened to her. Please. Help me."

The chief geek shrugged and walked him to a terminal. "Sure. But I'll have to operate the system. You can't touch."

Jon nodded. He watched the techno-weenie's fingers fly over the keyboard to search for Lisa's records within the university. He relaxed when the geek pulled up a screen showing she had indeed been a student.

Jon smiled at the geek. "My name's Jon. Thanks for helping."

The geek nodded and held out his hand. "Watson." He pointed to the bottom of the next screen. "Aha! See this?"

At the bottom of the screen, Jon read that Lisa Gabriel hadn't been enrolled for the last three semesters. His stomach roiled. Reflected in the glass walls of the nano-lab, he saw his face grow red. He watched Watson punch the buttons on the keyboard harder, faster, Googling her name. Nothing.

Watson keyed his password and scanned the administrator's screen. He shook his head. "Sorry, man. Looks as if she never had user rights here. At least not in the past year." He logged off the terminal and regarded Jon with new suspicion. "You have to leave now."

Jon felt as if someone had started wiping away her existence but hadn't yet finished. A new set of equations began forming in his head. Disturbing ones.

He took the stairs up two at a time and ran out into the street, slipping on an icy puddle just as he approached the stairs of the university library. He hit the sidewalk and bloodied his hands. Rising as fast as he could, he shook the pain from his hands and pulled his expired student ID from his pocket. He pushed the ID into the card reader at the hall inside the entryway. It still worked. He passed into the lobby.

The international newspapers were online in the basement. He stopped at the loo to wash the blood off his hands. Then down the stairs, where he occupied a cubicle. He called up the web pages of Israeli newspapers for events that might have involved her. Dizzy, he feared what he'd find.

The *Jerusalem Post* reported heightened security measures due to failing peace talks with their Arab neighbors, upcoming elections, and reports of suicide bombers. His fingers froze over the keyboard as he scanned for her name.

His jaw dropped. She was listed as the first victim—ever —of a terrorist bombing in Herzliyya. *No!* His plans, their future together, all vanished in a blink. He smothered a screaming curse. The breath left him in a gasp.

He couldn't move. He felt abandoned again, but this was more intense than losing his parents.

This time, he'd lost his future. She was gone from him forever.

Someone had engineered her death. Someone who killed Israelis. He wanted justice for Lisa. But, the more he thought about his desire, the more he realized he had no contacts and no killing skills to achieve it. He sat, seething, thinking what he would do if he could find the person who'd created the bomb that blew up her car.

He didn't know how long he'd been there, but when he left the library, he felt raw and numb, as if his knowledge of her death had frozen him to the moment. The cold winter winds beat into him with every step.

Soon he felt nothing but rage. He was incapable of mathematics or logic.

Jon staggered down the street into the Marble Arch tube stop and rode back to his apartment. He'd expected them to become old and gray together, living long lives, enjoying the exploits of their grandchildren. But the rest of her life had expended itself so abruptly.

He walked up the three flights of the tenement in a trance, his vision narrowed and his hearing dulled. On his floor, two of the hallway lights were out. He was too tired to care.

How could he live without Lisa?

As he unlocked the door to his rooms, a bearded man with short-cropped white hair emerged from the darkened staircase above him and called his name.

He opened the door and gaped at the approaching stranger, who was dressed in a dark suit and white shirt, tieless. "Yes?"

The man stared back at him, running icy blue eyes over Jon, head to toe. "I knew the woman you call 'Lisa Gabriel.' We worked together."

His visitor had a foreign accent. It sounded similar to Lisa's. Israeli. Filled with confusion, Jon flipped the light switch and pointed toward two threadbare armchairs in the suite's common room. He sat in one. "Who are you?"

The older man examined the other chair with obvious distaste but lowered himself into its seat. Leaning forward, he asked Jon, "How well did you know your fiancée?"

Jon felt his face get hot. "Who the hell are you?" When the older man remained quiet, Jon shook his head. As the silence continued, he felt obliged to speak. "She told me she was born in Tel Aviv and came to London to earn her master's degree. And that she'd accepted an internship at the nano-lab, intending to stay until I finished my MBA." His hair fell into his eyes. He swept it away, feeling his eyes grow moist. "Well? Who are you?"

The older man took a deep breath and nodded. "Your fiancée's real name was Aviva Bushovsky. Lisa Gabriel died two years ago. Aviva took over her identity for us. One of our *yaholim* hacked her identity records into the university's computers, but after her death we had him hack them back out. She was one of ours. A *bat leveyha*—"

Jon's gut lurched as if he was in a plummeting elevator with a broken cable. "A what? Who the bloody fuck are you?" His voice echoed through the room.

"My name is Yigdal Ben-Levy. I work for the Israeli government. We taught your fiancée to perform covert work. She started out as one of our *sayanim*. A helper. We trained her to be a—"

Jon raised a hand to emphasize his confusion, but Ben-Levy continued. "Yes. A spy. She would have told you everything, had she lived to marry you. I came here to tell you. I owe you that much. We have a suspect in custody now. Of course, he denied constructing and planting the bomb, but we have enough evidence to believe he was a cutout, the tool of a bomb maker. Our suspect resisted arrest and was shot by Israeli IDF. He's in a coma now. We expect he'll regain conscious, and I intend to interrogate him. I'll find the name of the bomb maker responsible for her death."

Ben-Levy seemed to be waiting for a response but Jon remained shocked and silent. "We sent Aviva to fetch you. To recruit you. But when she fell in love with you, I needed to see her, to determine her state of mind. She wasn't supposed to marry you. Just arrange for you to come back with her. But your involvement with her changed the plan. Things got complicated. A phone call just wouldn't do. I asked to see her before she told you any secrets. At the time I was too involved with other activities to spend time traveling. So, I sent for her."

Jon leaned forward and brushed a stray lock of hair out of his eyes. "You sent for her? Then tell me. Why are you really here now?"

The older man shrugged. "There are things about yourself no one ever told you. You aren't who you think you are. I came here to ask you for the help your parents provided us before they died."

Jon felt muddy-minded. All the mathematical formulas he could conjure were useless to him now. He grabbed his head with both hands, and shook it to clear it. Suddenly, everything made sense. He remembered small inconsistencies in his parents' behavior, and corresponding ones with Lisa. Their secrecy when discussing things around him, and the men who'd visited the night his parents died. The times Lisa said she needed to call her mother, arguments she had on the phone and refused to discuss with him, and a lack of stories about her friends.

He knew now he hadn't really known her, and felt stupid at not being able to see the significance of these events before now. Anger welled in him for her lies.

But in moments he felt once more his love for her. The ache was enormous, replacing his anger with a desire to seek justice for her. He now knew how to gain it. He blurted out the single obvious thing he could think of. "Why? Why me?"

The white-haired man nodded. "I also knew your parents. Their deaths were no accident."

CHAPTER 6

Jon Sommers's apartment,
26 Thames Street, London
May 31, 11:16 p.m.

Bile rose in Jon's throat. "What did you say?"

"Patience."

Jon's hands shook. "Patience my ass. You're a bloody liar. My parents died in a car accident." He remembered how, at first, he felt lost and alone, but later he'd grown to hate them for their absence. He shook his head. How could their deaths not be an accident? Then he remembered his sitter's accent. Just like Lisa's, and just like Ben-Levy's.

Ben-Levy stared at Jon. "We met, you and I, once before. The night your parents were murdered."

Jon's jaw fell as he made the connection to man who walked through their door following the accident that night. This man's white head of hair was gray then. "You! How were you connected to my parents?"

The older man took a deep breath. "Your grandparents, Eve and Ivan Sommerstein, were released from Auschwitz at the end of the war and settled in Palestine near Lake Tiberius. They were Holocaust survivors and sought a way to provide security for our new country after its formation. They worked for the Mossad and had one son, Abel."

"But my father and mother weren't Jewish. I'm not Jewish."

"Yes, you are. Your father and mother married in 1973 in Haifa. Their real names were Saul and Rebecca Sommerstein, but we gave them cover names when we asked them to resign from the IDF to enter Mossad. Abel Sommers was my best friend. We worked together for almost a decade in Israel. We gave him and Natasha new identities that established your parents as British for three generations."

Jon stared at him in shock. "My mum and dad were spies for Israel? I thought they worked for the British government in a trade delegation." He shook his head. "This has to be a lie."

Ben-Levy took a deep breath. "Your mother was an electronics specialist. Your father was a deep-cover double, reporting to me. He infiltrated MI-6 and used a tool Natasha had developed to funnel intelligence to us, intel that saved Israel during the build-up to a nuclear attack from Syria that we prevented in 2003. Our country owes them its existence."

Jon frowned, recognizing the name of the British spy agency. "If your story is true, why didn't they tell me any of this?"

But as he said this, he thought of how his parents had always been protective of their privacy and quiet about their own lives. He'd been forbidden to enter the "library" room of their flat. The night of their death, after the group of men had entered and left, he'd run inside in a rage, yanking open desk drawers and pulling books off the shelves. Nothing significant except for two pieces of handwritten script in a language whose lettering he didn't recognize. He'd watched from behind the couch when the sitter walked in and retrieved two handguns from the desk and placed them in a metal box. Could this man's story be true?

The white-haired man stroked his beard. "Abel and Natasha would have told you when you reached the age of thirteen. You would have been bar mitzvah then, a man. When they died, you were still too young. I couldn't expect you to have the sense to understand the dangers you might face. To keep you safe, I kept this knowledge from you. Until now."

Jon's brows furrowed. He sought escape, yet couldn't move. He felt the muscles of his legs tighten. "I don't believe they were murdered. I don't believe any of this. It's all lies." He struggled to rise and paced the room, his fists clenched. He stopped and faced Ben-Levy. "Who could have wanted them dead?"

Ben-Levy closed his eyes in thought. "After their last mission, the Syrians sent a Palestinian hit team to take revenge on both of them. They made it look like an accident, but I wasn't convinced. Natasha had called with a repeater's car plate. I had the Mossad conduct its own investigation. It showed that this was no accident."

Ben-Levy turned away and his voice grew softer. "We thought if we told you then, it would exacerbate the danger for you. Safer to wait until you were older. Instead, I had operatives watch over you, keeping you safe."

"You watched over me? That's impossible. I would have known."

Ben-Levy smiled. "We're good at surveillance."

"But why?"

The old man smiled. "I owed you for your parents' sacrifice and service to the state. The state funded the orphanage. I'd hoped you would have the same talents they had. Two generations of spies. You're the third. Talents we could exploit for the good of Israel."

Jon's legs wobbled and he struggled to his seat. New equations formed as his head fell back against the back of the chair. He tried ignoring them. "Bloody bullshit. Why are you telling me this? Why should I believe you?"

Ben-Levy didn't answer. He paced the room. As he drew

closer to Jon, he stopped. "We set up the scholarships you earned."

Jon frowned. He stood and approached the older man. Inches separated them now. "I don't believe anything you've said."

Yigdal Ben-Levy sighed. "What if I could prove everything?"

"Go fuck yourself. I'm not Jewish. My parents never even visited Israel. None of this is true." He realized he was shouting. Had his parents deceived him? As Lisa had? He felt dizzy and leaned against the chair.

Ben-Levy shook his head. "As you wish. But, we will find her murderer. The bomb maker."

The what? Jon shook his head. He snarled, "How do I know you didn't murder her?"

Ben-Levy's mouth opened. His face lit up, red. He sighed as he buttoned his overcoat, and retrieved a business card from his pocket. "If you change your mind, call me at this number." He pulled a paperback book from his coat pocket and handed it to Jon. "You might also need this."

The book was an English-Hebrew dictionary and phrase book. Jon dropped it on the table. He scanned the card: "Yigdal Ben-Levy, Military Affairs Liaison." The address listed was located in the subbasement of a building at 134 Hamenofim Street, Herzliyya, Israel. A phone number was listed on the bottom of the card. "When you call, ask for Mother. It's my call sign." The white-haired man rose and left him, closing the door behind him.

Mother? Oh, shit! He's the "mother" Lisa spoke about visiting in Tel Aviv! The proof of the equations he cobbled that instant were irrefutable.

He ran to the loo and dry-heaved until he was unable to stand. His head connected the dots, reassembled the mathematics. Everything the old man said fit neatly. Jon's hands shook hard as he ripped the card into pieces. He staggered to the kitchen and threw the scraps in the trash. "Crap, crap, crap!"

Jon closed his eyes, concentrating on his memories of his father, a tall, strong man. His constant silence. His mother's hectic schedule. He sat in the ratty chair, his mind swirling without direction. He imagined them talking to each other, becoming silent as he entered the living room of their flat. This had happened many times, with the surprise on their faces replaced by smiles.

The old man had told him the truth.

But, was his entire life a lie?

A few minutes later, he fished the pieces of Ben-Levy's card from the waste basket and reassembled them. When the card was Scotch-taped together, he dropped it in his pocket next to Lisa's photograph. *My entire life is a lie! What should I do?*

CHAPTER 7

Jon remained unnerved for two weeks following his meeting with the mysterious visitor. Wherever he went, he thought he was being followed.

On this day, he was surprised by the warm, late spring weather, rare in London.

To clear his head, he strolled toward Knightsbridge. Perfect weather, bright blue sky, a slight breeze. Twenty degrees Celsius, and crowds filled the park. Couples on picnic blankets shared lunch. Others, like him, walked alone.

Since Lisa's death, he'd grown used to missing her. His dreams at night still included visions of her, running away from him.

But during the days, he'd managed to devote his efforts toward preparing for his entry-level position in the money-transfer department of Dreitsbank.

Once again, he saw it as his future. He'd spent the morning reading training manuals: letters of credit, documentary collections, and foreign exchange. Just over two weeks before his start date, there were four more instruction manuals to study.

Jon took the shortcut from the city library across the

park to his apartment, his backpack containing the four manuals and his notebook computer.

As he neared the edge of the park, he saw a familiar woman in front of him. A willowy woman, with a single, thick braid of red hair swinging back and forth down her back to her waist. He picked up his pace and closed the distance. As he passed, he gazed at her, about to greet her. But it wasn't her. She could have been Lisa's twin. The breath left him, and he braced himself at a nearby concrete bird feeder.

He'd never see Lisa again. He corrected himself. He had her photo in his pocket.

He plucked it from his wallet and stared. He ached to caress her.

Once again, he remembered when she'd asked him, "Why would someone as smart as you settle for being a banker? Why not choose to save the world?" He'd almost laughed then. But he'd forgotten his answer to her. And, still, the questions remained. Had she given her life for something important?

There was nothing so important in the career he'd planned. And remembering his meeting with the man called "Mother," he now doubted his purpose.

He seemed to hear her voice. "Why not decide to do something more important? Save your people." He jumped, turning around, looking for her.

But there was no one nearby. He panicked. *Am I going crazy?*

Her voice in his head. *No, Jon. You promised we'd be together forever. We will be.*

His head spun. Clearly, he had lost his mind.

The thin, balding man wore a ratty sports jacket. He sat with Jon in a small office painted robin's egg blue, decorated with soothing images of empty pastures and closeups of flowers and waterfalls. He read the notes in his folder. "It's pretty normal. After all, you lost someone you loved."

"You sure? Hearing her disembodied voice; it's disturbing. It's happened so often in the past few days. I've lost count."

The clinical psychologist looked up from his pad. He pointed at Jon with his pen. "That's the thing about loss. Sometimes when we suffer the death of a loved one, we continue to see them for a while. It's why the Irish have wakes, the Jews sit shiva. Not to worry. These visions will fade." He wrote some notes as he spoke.

Jon shook his head. "They're not visions. I hear her voice, as if she was in my head. She isn't here anymore. I'll never touch her again. And now, I can't think. I'm losing sleep."

"Yes. But, you told me you were in love. A very strong emotion. Be patient."

"Yeah. I know. But how do I get over her?" Jon's eyes drifted to the floor for an answer. He wasn't getting one from the psychologist. That was for sure.

"Your grief is so deep it seems to me something else is at work inside you. You've felt these feelings before, haven't you?" The psychologist tapped his pen against his pad, waiting for Jon's reply.

Jon shuddered. In a flash he saw his parents, she in a black dress and he in a tux, about to leave him for the final time. "Umm, my parents died in a car accident when I was twelve. At least, I thought their deaths were an accident, but now I'm not even sure of that. It seems I lose everyone I love. But I never heard their voices. Lisa, well, she was my future, my hope."

"Your parents. Well, two losses like that. Getting to the root of your feelings of abandonment from them will take us some time. As for hearing the voice of your fiancée, your best bet is to find a way to come to terms with her death. I suggest when you hear her voice, smile to yourself and welcome her inside you. She'll become your friend, and be a part of you."

Jon shook his head. "Uh, sure, doc. I'll try that." He rose from his seat.

The psychologist shook his head. "Okay, well, maybe not. But I have another idea. Create a shrine for her."

Jon leaned closer. "Huh? A shrine? No way. I want her gone!"

The psychologist was silent for a moment. "Well, then banish her. Do you have anything she gave you?"

Jon thought of the photo he'd stolen. "Uh, yeah."

"Destroy it. The act of getting rid of it that way might work. Like voodoo."

He shuddered at the thought. He wondered if it would work.

Two days later, Jon was feeling better. He was on his way home from the grocery store and passed a newspaper stand. The headline of the *Times* was, "Suicide Bomber in Jerusalem Kills 17." He stopped and read the article.

Her voice spoke to him. *See what happens in the world while you do nothing? Our people die, corpse by corpse! You couldn't save me. But, you can save others. Innocents!*

He stood still and took several deep breaths. He longed to hold her, touch her. Was that why there was no way to get her out from his head? In a daze, he made a simple decision.

He went back to the newsstand. "Matches?"

The old man shook his head. "We sell cigarettes, sonny. Want 'em? They comes with matches."

"Sure." He tossed the pack of smokes in the trash several blocks away. In Hyde Park, he found a dry birdbath and placed a few brittle leaves in it. Then he placed the photo on top of them and struck the match. He set the fire. It was

Lisa's funeral pyre. Since her death, he no longer believed there could be a God. Too much had been taken from him.

Watching her image disappear in smoke, he waited to hear her voice. Nothing. A strange calm came over him as he tossed Ben-Levy's business card into the pyre for good measure. "I'm rid of both of you. Forever."

But then he heard her laugh back at him. His head swiveled left and right. No one was there.

Several days passed and he hadn't imagined her voice. Had she left his head for good?

His first day at Dreitsbank took his mind in a new direction. He wrote his personal information onto new-employee forms, visited two orientation sessions and met so many people he couldn't keep track of all their names.

On the morning of his second day, he met the team leader he'd work for. The man took him to the bank's training center and set him to work with the letters of credit, documentary collections, and foreign exchange that he'd been studying in textbooks.

By noon, his mind was spinning. He'd thought that banking would be easy for someone with his math skills, but all he was learning was how to fill in forms and use computer systems.

During the lunch break, Jon walked through downtown London. He found a café on Leadenhall Street across from the city library, and bought coffee and a scone. As he sipped, a woman walked by and sat at the table next to his with her coffee. She reached over and touched his hand. He turned his head, unsure if he'd done something he needed to apologize for. "Yes?"

She smiled. "I'm new in town. Where's a decent music club? Can you help?" She had an accent, but he couldn't place it. Maybe German?

"What's your name?" As soon as he asked, he that worried Lisa's voice would intrude on him. "Mine is Jon. Jon Sommers." He forced a grin.

"Ruth DeWitt." She smiled back, extending her hand.

It was the first time in months any woman beside Lisa had shown interest in him. And this one had touched his hand. "Uh, yeah. There's a free newspaper with clubs in it. What you need to do is—"

Ruth shook her head. "No. Don't explain. Show me. Can you do that?" Her voice had a husky quality, and he felt his own arousal growing.

The noise from the street muddled her words. "What did you say?"

She opened her mouth to speak, but he interrupted. "Not here. Too busy. Look, I don't have time now. Can we meet after I finish work? Then, we can go to someplace quieter."

Her smile pinned him motionless. "I don't need that long." She rose and took his hand. They stopped at a diner down the street and Jon bought her coffee. She directed them to a quiet table at the back.

She stared into his eyes. "Okay. I'm an exchange student for the summer semester. I just finished unpacking my stuff. Now I'd like to spend a night on the town. Can you help me with the name of a music club?" Her gorgeous blond hair and willowy figure captivated him.

Jon opened his notebook computer and motioned for her to sit alongside him. He tapped away at the keyboard. "Here. A list of places. Rock, folk, blues, and everything else."

She nodded and looked away from him. "Oh, of course! Google." Then she turned and looked right through him. "Why didn't I think of that?" She stared into his eyes. "Thanks. I feel I owe you." She smiled. "Can I buy you dinner tonight?"

Jon frowned, his eyes downcast, still waiting for Lisa's voice. But he was alone. "Sure. When and where?"

She smiled. "Six. I can call you. Okay?"

He nodded. "Sure." Jon wrote his cell number on a page from his pad and slid it across the table.

She picked it up. "Thanks." In a blink, she was gone. Jon noticed his palms were sweating.

As dusk settled in, Jon exited the bank's lobby. His cell buzzed. "Sommers."

"Hey, Jon. It's Ruth DeWitt. The lost student you saved earlier today. I'm afraid I won't have enough time free tonight for dinner."

Jon scanned his wristwatch. 6 p.m. "That's okay. If you decide you want company some other time, well—"

"Wait. How about if we just go dancing?"

He jaw fell open and he snapped it shut. "I, uh think maybe there's a band playing Friday night in one of the rock 'n' roll clubs. But, uh, well—"

"Do you like blues?"

This was all unexpected, but he didn't need a mathematical model to figure out where it was going. "Yes, in fact I do. But why—"

"The club you showed me downtown on your computer. Wasn't it called the Bug-Eyed Blues Club? How about that one. It's just two blocks from my apartment. Please?"

What the hell. "Yes. Sure. What time and where do I come get you?" Lisa hadn't yet made her presence known. Maybe he was free?

Ruth told him she'd meet him outside the club in an hour. When he arrived, he spotted her at the end of the line. It was just after ten. The club was a large, dirty room with a tiny raised stage, and a bar on the side opposite. Its floor was tacky and folding chairs and tiny tables lined the back.

The band, Canned Heat Redux, was loud, rhythmic, and dark-sounding. Their jump-blues renditions were adequate for dancing.

Ruth reached her hand to his shoulder. Touched him. She took Jon to the front of the stage, just below the lead singer. She pulled him close so she could speak right in his ear. "May I have this dance?"

When Ruth pulled his body against hers, it was obvious she wasn't wearing a bra underneath her blouse. His body responded, alarming him. The band played a sad, slow song, about the blow-up of a relationship. She moved against his body, drifting with him to the grinding rhythm of the verses. Midway through the song, he found it hard to move, his erection caught in his clothing.

When he tried dropping a hand under his belt to reposition his anatomy, she pulled him even closer, grinned, and whispered in his ear. "I guess I'm having a nasty effect on you." Then she hugged him and whispered into his ear. "I'd like to talk to you about something. A personal matter. Would you mind that?"

He nodded, "Umm, okay," but stared into her eyes. When Ruth backed off and took a deep breath, his concern peaked. Something didn't fit right. What was going on here?

But he withheld judgment. He had nothing yet to support his assumption that Ruth was not what she seemed to be. Instead, he took hold of her elbow and guided her back to toward their table. "You have my full attention."

She pushed him past the table. "Uh, huh. Listen, my apartment is around the corner. I have snacky things, good music, and booze. And drugs if that's what you prefer." Before he could respond, she rushed him out the door and down the street, huddling alongside him against the cold wind.

She led him through the lobby and pointed to the elevator. "It's broken." At the top of the staircase she moved him to the left, farther down the hall, and halted them both. She swung her head left and right, as if looking to see if someone was hiding in the hall. She nodded toward the door. "Here. Just a modest flat, but I'm the only one lives here." She unlocked the door and entered, her eyes scanning the interior. He stuck his head in but didn't enter as he looked around.

She turned back at him. "Just being careful. I was told we had a few burglaries last month. Come on inside. I won't bite." She chuckled. "Unless you want me to."

He marveled at how lucky he was. Not only had a beautiful woman found him interesting, but Lisa Gabriel no longer seemed to care.

He had one foot inside when she pulled him through and shut the door. "So, what do you want to talk about?"

Her face was a mask of conflict. "I have something you need to hear." She turned away from him. He heard her take a deep breath. "Damn, I can't do this."

"Do what?" Jon was getting more curious and more upset by the second. Now he needed to confirm his suspicions. "What do you want from me?" He was almost sure he knew. He touched her shoulder and she turned, facing him. In seconds she was unbuttoning his shirt and pulling his belt open. When she groped his erection, he gave up trying to make sense of what was happening.

He pulled her skirt down and she stepped out of it while they kissed. She was pulling his shirt off even as he tried to undo the buttons of her blouse. When he dropped the blouse on the floor, they faced each other.

Naked.

Her body was as gorgeous as her heart-shaped face. The hunger in her eyes compelled him to look elsewhere, and his eyes drifted down. He stared at her pert, small breasts with long pointed nipples, her narrow waist, and a thatch of amber hair in the vee of her crotch.

Spellbound, he couldn't move. But he was sure this was no coincidence. Had Ben-Levy sent her? The thought didn't shock him. In fact, he didn't care. If he could make love to her, he would. It wouldn't make him care for her.

His breathing slowed back to normal.

Ruth also seemed to cool. She stepped away. "Listen, this would just be sex, nothing more." She frowned and faced away. "But it's a bad idea. So, no, we can't. Understand?"

He nodded, almost sure now what was really happening.

She cast her eyes at the floor. "Okay then. Well, I need to talk with you about something else. Something very serious."

Jon nodded. "What?" He waited.

"I didn't intend to bed you. It just started to happen. You just look good and well—"

For Jon, the mathematical equation completed itself. "He sent you, didn't he?" Jon reached and touched her face. "Ben-Levy."

She shook her head. "I'm not supposed to be here."

"Who are you? Really?"

"My name is Ruth, just like I told you. Listen, I may have been the last person to see Aviva Bushovsky alive."

Jon's world stopped and his breath halted. "What?"

Ruth drew closer. Her face was inches away. "I had lunch with your fiancée minutes before she died."

He tried to form words. It didn't work. He tried to make a sound but nothing came from him. It took him a while to recover. "Why are you here?"

She faced him. "No one sent me. I came on my own. Please. Listen." In the dim light he could see her strain to talk.

"Right. So, start talking." He realized he was shouting.

Ruth frowned. "There was something troubling Aviva when we spoke at lunch. A few minutes before she died. I'm not sure what it was."

She closed the gap between them and her voice softened. Her lips were so close to his ear, he could feel the warmth of her words against him. "It had something to do with you. I don't know exactly what, but I'm sure. I decided you needed to know."

Jon shook his head. "No one sent you?"

She shook her head. "No one."

He was sure this was a lie. "Why were we about to have sex?"

"A mistake. I felt the attraction. Didn't you?" She said nothing more.

He walked to the window. "Just sex for the sake of it?" He waited for her to speak.

"Maybe you should leave." Her voice sounded distant. She turned her back on him and stared out the window in silence, into the alleyway below.

Ben-Levy. Lisa. The Mossad. And now, Ruth. With that last thought, another followed. He felt Lisa's presence return. *Recruitment. It's what she's really here to talk to you about. She's a* bat leveyha, *just as I was. The sex would have just been part of her assignment.* Lisa's voice was just another equation.

Recruitment. Alarm rang though him. Lisa spoke again. *Jon, we would have had a perfect life together. We'd have worked for Mother and raised our children together. And sometimes Mother would send us out as a team. Think of it, Jon.* He closed his eyes, now welling with tears.

He imagined Lisa on top of him, fucking him hard. Her hands ripped into his shoulders as she caught fire and her flesh burned away into a skeleton. His head turned to the side of the room, where he imagined he saw Yigdal Ben-Levy watching in silence, taking notes in the corner of the room.

He snarled, now sure Ruth had lied. Ben-Levy must have sent her. There seemed to be no end to what the spymaster would do to achieve his ends, and Jon refused to be manipulated.

He was hyperventilating.

He had a sudden urge to see Lisa. But, he'd burned her picture. What a stupid thing to do.

Does Ben-Levy have a photo of Lisa Gabriel? Of course he does, in his files. But, the only way he could contact Mother was through Ruth, since he'd burned the card containing Mother's phone number. But how could he ask her?

Looking outside, he saw sunrise bleeding through the window. He decided never to see Ruth again. He dressed fast and left.

He thought as he walked back toward his apartment. Did anything Mother say have any truth in it? Why else would all this be happening to him?

CHAPTER 8

Dreitsbank, London branch,
101 Leadenhall Street, London
June 19, 3:23 p.m.

In a cubicle at the bank, Jon sipped coffee during a break while he built a mathematical model of the world Ben-Levy wanted him to enter. Soon, he was second-guessing himself. Before he could commit to anything, he'd have to find out more about Aviva Bushovsky, the woman he'd loved. But, he'd no idea how.

By the time his training session ended in the late afternoon, he realized he'd need a hacker to help him. Would the techno-weenie prince be capable of this?

As he took the tube to his old campus and walked toward the nano-lab, Jon rehearsed the story and arguments he could use to enroll the geek as his accomplice.

Down the stairs to the basement, the smell of Lysol assaulted his nostrils. One of the cleaning crew pushed a broom just outside the glass doors in the basement. He tapped on the glass and a student let him in. So much for building security.

He searched among the cubicles for the chief geek. Ten minutes passed and he'd been all over the basement, but not seen his target.

Jon pulled a chair to one of the computers and sat, head

in his hands. It was just after six in the evening. Maybe the man had gone to dinner. Would he return tonight or was he already at his apartment?

Jon waited five minutes and lost patience. He went upstairs to search the cafeteria. There, in the corner by the window, sat the techno-weenie prince.

Jon forced a smile as he approached. "Hey, I'm the bloke who bothered you two weeks ago. Remember?" Jon pointed to his face.

"Uh, nope." The man pushed a juicy slice of banger onto his fork and brought it toward his mouth, stopping just before he opened wide. "Wait. You're the guy whose fiancée disappeared from campus. Right?"

"Yeah. That's me." Jon pulled out the seat across from the geek. "How've you been?"

"Uh, fine. I'll earn my master's at the end of the summer. So, I'm busy now, trying to find a job. Aren't you?"

Jon nodded. "Yeah, well I just accepted an offer from a German bank. I started this week." He wondered how best to approach the man. No ideas came to him. "Listen, could I ask one more favor of you?"

The man stopped chewing. "Depends on what you want."

Jon wiped away a few bits of food the man had spewed onto his shirtsleeve. "I need to find out what my fiancée was doing just before she disappeared. She was in Tel Aviv. Who did she meet? Did she have family there?" He leaned closer and dropped his voice a bit. "I need a hacker."

The man shook his head. "No way. That's not legal. If anyone finds out, I'll be expelled from school. Maybe even arrested."

Jon frowned. "Yeah. Well, there isn't anything illegal about teaching me how to do it, is there?"

The geek remained silent but closed his eyes. "If I tell

you but don't show you, could you do the work? I mean, it isn't easy. You know?"

Jon sighed. "If it's the best you can offer, then that's what I'll take." He looked at the geek's face, thinking about what he had to offer for the man's help. "What would you like, in return?"

The geek sat stock-still for a few seconds, his eyes closed. Then he smiled and stared into Jon's eyes. "You look like the kind of man who has an easy way with women. Tell me how to find and earn the love of someone as attractive as the one you lost."

Jon's jaw dropped. He'd never had an easy time with women. Whatever he offered would be lies. After a few seconds, he nodded. There would be a challenge here for both of them. "Right, then. We'll trade, one hour of your time for one of mine, until each of us either gives up or one of us succeeds. Then we go our separate ways." He prayed his lie wasn't obvious.

The techno-weenie prince extended his hand. "I'm Phil. Phil Watson."

Jon shook the man's hand. "Jon Sommers. Shall we get started?"

CHAPTER 9

Outside the village of Upper Pachir,
Nangarhar Province, Afghanistan
June 19, 10:23 p.m.

The cold night wind was the only sound Hashim Klovosky heard, whispering through the mountain pass. Using night goggles, he watched the team leader, Amos Gidaehl, his country's most feared assassin, as the *kidon* scurried toward a lone tree between the boulders.

Gidaehl scanned the area before venturing toward the place the team used as its dead drop for intel. This *slick* was the hollow at the bottom of the tree.

The team had hunkered just north of the town of Upper Pachir. Klovosky read a copy of the intercept they'd obtained. It had named Tariq Houmaz as the extremist behind the weapons purchases. And, it indicated their target was nearby. Now, after two months of intense covert activity, they were about to deliver the intel their government needed as rationale to terminate the bomb maker.

They'd used cutouts, and paid informers. Elli Raucher, a dark-skinned man dressed as a mujahidin, had dropped a mike and camera in the cave where Houmaz lived while the terrorist was out observing the training of his men.

Raucher was the team's *bodel*, or courier. He'd been trained as a *heth*, or logistician for the intelligence service.

The team expected him to have dead-dropped the intel for pickup earlier that day.

After Gidaehl retrieved the tiny container holding the encoded message, the team would request exfiltration. Raucher had marked the tree with a small X at its base, meaning the intel was in the slick.

Klovosky felt in his bones something was wrong. No noise at all. Every nerve in his body pulsed as if he was on speed. He gulped, trying to quiet himself.

Then, as Gidaehl grabbed the container from the tree's hollow, his head exploded in a blur of blood, skull, and brain.

Klovosky winced at the team leader's death. He was an *ayin*, or tracker, and hadn't seen any hostiles. *Shit. I must have missed one of their sentries. The aleph is down. They know we're here.* "We need to leave fast. Where there's one sniper, there are always others."

Their *qoph*, Harry Schmidt, the team's communications officer, nodded.

They moved with studied care, avoiding the branches of the bushes and weeds where they'd hid. Klovosky froze, realizing they had one vital loose end. He pulled Schmidt's face close. "Where's Elli? We need to contact him and tell him we're blown."

Schmidt placed his fingers to his lips. "Later," he whispered. He pointed toward their nearby Jeep, parked and camouflaged under a tree. "Not safe. I see movement."

Klovosky nodded. They'd have to move on foot for a long distance. He scanned the landscape for threats in front of them, then felt Schmidt tugging on his jacket. He faced the qoph. "What?"

Schmidt's eyes were wide, staring at someplace over Klovosky's shoulder. When the *ayin* turned, his jaw dropped.

There were eight of them, holding Elli Raucher with an AK-47 shoved under his chin. All of them were armed and one motioned for the pair of coverts to surrender.

It was the worst thing they could do. They'd be tortured for whatever they knew, and then executed.

Klovosky used his position behind Schmidt to hide the grenade he drew from his pants pocket. He said his death prayer in a whisper, then pulled the pin and held up his hands in surrender. He sighed. His life was over. Klovosky's mind filled with memories: his parents, his wife and daughter, all the things he wished he could change. He no longer felt the cold wind. He forced himself to release the safety lever on the device, tossing it above the heads of the mujahidin.

Seeing the grenade, one of their attackers pulled the trigger on Raucher, blowing his head clear of his body.

The other attackers fired their weapons into Schmidt and Klovosky. The last thing he saw was the explosion.

With Jon's encouragement and direction, Phillip Watson had lost a few pounds, shaved his goatee and learned to dress. From what Jon could see, the techno-weenie prince had transformed himself. Jon smiled at the irony. He'd taught someone something he didn't even know.

Since the last time they'd met, the chief geek seemed to have developed unexpected grace as he walked and moved. And although he still had no girlfriend, the geek had been on more dates than Jon ever had. Jon's suggestion that Phil always smile had worked well.

As for Jon, teaching the geek had somehow altered his own confidence level with women. And, better yet, he'd learned enough about hacking to break into the university's computer system. He hadn't done anything illegal except for that. But he'd found nothing more about Lisa, and nothing he'd tried during the past month worked to gain him entry to the government of Israel's computers.

Jon sipped a cup of coffee as he waited for Phil to show for their meeting. The liquid was cool and tasted stale.

He rose to drop the cup into the cafeteria disposal when he saw Phil enter from the street. The techno-weenie prince wasn't alone. A striking brunette held his hand. "Jon, good evening. I'd like to introduce Jennie. Jennie Stolworth. My girlfriend." His grin ran from ear-to-ear.

Jon rose and shook Jennie's hand. "Well, my word." He smiled back at his new friend.

Phil removed a large envelope from his coat pocket. "When you get home tonight, take a gander." He handed Jon the packet. "I believe we've both fulfilled our bargain. So, we're done." And with that, the couple turned and Phil led Jennie out of the cafeteria.

Jon fingered the envelope. He donned his coat and headed back to the apartment. Fifteen minutes later, he ripped it open. He found fifty pages, stapled into several sets of documents stuffed inside. He pulled the pages out and scanned the first page of the first group:

Aviva Bushovsky.
Group: *Shin Bet Liaison*
Position: *bat leveyha* operative. Promotion to *kidon* recommended.
Reports to: Yigdal Ben-Levy
Dates of Assignment: July 16, 2011 through May 23, 2013.
Current Status: Deceased.
Projects completed:
     AL11-2304
     XW23-9632
     BR01-0021
Project failure:
     JS01-0021

Jon scratched behind his ear. What did any of this mean? He pulled the second stack from the envelope:

Lisa Gabriel.
Support Group: *Sayanim*, collections division
Last Cover Position: Graduate Student at University of
    London, Mathematics Department
Work History: Helped alter registrar's database records
    to wash and backstop *kidon* and *katsa* identities
Current Status: Deceased.

He remembered Yigdal Ben-Levy using the terms *bat leveyha* and *sayanim*. What did they mean?

The third stack of papers was even more interesting. It listed covert activities the Israeli government was accused of by the United States and Great Britain. activities that had been conducted within other countries without their permission. Intelligence gathering. Penetration of Muslim extremist organizations. False-flag operations. Assassinations.

Phil had risked his graduate degree in return for Jon's help. And, in return, all Jon had done was turn Phil into a more likeable guy. How had Phil hacked the information he was reading?

Jon read every word on the pages a second time. And then a third time. They described the workings of a government pressed on all sides by countries that wanted them gone from the earth.

When he'd finished, Jon saw Lisa's deception not as despicable, but as admirable. He hadn't wanted to be a spy. He'd aspired to be a banker before Lisa's death. But now, he thought about changing his life's path. She'd died to save her people. He thought about this, remembering Ben-Levy's claim that he was Jewish. No, not just her people. *His* people. He remembered her question: *Don't you want to save the world?*

He closed his eyes, picturing her loving face. Clenching his fists, he nodded. *Yes, Lisa. I do.*

The next morning, Jon dressed in his suit and stepped out of his apartment on his way to Dreitsbank. Down in the lobby, he stopped at his mailbox and found two letters. One was from *The Economist*. He closed his eyes and grimaced, sure it was a rejection letter.

He opened the envelope and slid out several pages. The first was a letter, offering to publish his paper on Islamic banking. He dropped the page in shock. The page behind it was the cover page of an agreement he'd need to sign, and the pages after those were the descriptions of the terms of the agreement.

Now he knew he had a future in banking and finance, after all. He remembered Lisa had pushed him into writing it, encouraging him to do it before she left for her death trip to Tel Aviv. He drew his pen from his pocket, signed the agreement and placed it into the return envelope. When he sealed it, he felt pure glee. He placed the envelope in his suit pocket, ready-to-mail when he reached the lobby.

The other letter was a handwritten invitation to visit Israel, signed by Yigdal Ben-Levy. He sat motionless with the second letter in his hands. Rising, he examined it as if it were something evil, containing a dark magical curse. He walked back to his apartment and dropped the scribbled note in his trash bin.

Throughout the day, he stared at the training manuals at his desk at Dreitsbank. The words could have been in a different language. He couldn't care about trade finance.

By the end of the afternoon, he could think of nothing but Lisa. He felt her presence within him. Her voice cajoled him, pushing him: *Go to Israel.*

Long ago when she'd tried recruiting him, he'd had no

interest in the future she'd intended for him. *I hate how you lied and deceived me, even though now I understand why you did it. What did wanting to save the world get you, besides death?*

He unlocked the apartment door as the sun set and dropped his attaché case on the couch. He remembered the night he'd proposed to Lisa at the Tunisian restaurant. He still missed her.

At the same time he felt the agony of her betrayal and lies. How could he ever reconcile these feelings?

He was consumed with a thirst for gaining justice for her.

He turned on the radio in his room. The tune the station played was "Evil Is Going On," a Canned Heat tune. The singer moaned about his woman's evil deeds. Jon turned it off.

He felt compelled to salvage Ben-Levy's letter from the trash, found the phone number and punched it into the cell phone. "It's Jon Sommers. Let me speak with Mother." The call terminated, but seconds later his cell buzzed. He recognized the old man's voice. Listening intently, he wrote down the instructions the spymaster growled into the phone.

A street café in Herzliyya. The day after tomorrow. A ticket would be waiting for him at the El Al counter at Heathrow.

He reached into his suit pocket and ripped the envelope containing the acceptance letter to *The Economist* into pieces and dumped it into the trash.

Jon took his backpack from under the bed and stuffed it full of clothing, determined to do what was right, no matter where the path took him. Mathematics had no play in this decision. Mathematics would be useless to him now, and forever gone from his thinking.

He would find justice for Lisa.

There was no longer any reason for him to be in London.

CHAPTER 10

Outside the Japanika Restaurant
near the corner of Hasadnaot
and Hamenofim Streets,
Herzliyya, Israel
June 22, 12:38 p.m.

Ever since Jon debarked the flight in Jerusalem, he'd kept telling himself this was a mistake. A huge one. The banker he once yearned to be intruded, assessed the risk of what might be lost or gained. The yield fell short.

After paying the taxi driver, he walked through a wall of heat along a crowded sidewalk, past restaurants named Minato, Kyoto, Mike's Place, and a building labeled "Nuvoton," and another with a bright neon sign declaring "Reset." Next to a Union Bank branch, he found the restaurant he sought across the street from the Print House, just as Ben-Levy had told him.

The intersection was filled with people moving in all directions around him. He scanned the area to get his bearings.

Outside the café, he saw tables, and walked faster. Sitting at one, in the bright sunshine, he saw Mother's white hair. The older man faced away, wearing a dark suit similar to the one Jon had seen him wearing the last time they'd met. Ben-Levy appeared cool in his heavy clothing.

Mother turned in his chair outside the café and faced him, as if he knew Jon was closing on him. The spymaster smiled and examined him, as if inspecting an unusually large pet animal. "Finally. So, you are interested in helping us after all?"

Jon remembered how lost he'd felt the night he'd learned Lisa's car had exploded. Still standing, he nodded. "I came, didn't I? First, though, I have some questions."

The spymaster's eyebrows arched. "What?"

Jon's fists clenched, muscles straining. "Why me?"

Ben-Levy stared back at him. "I already told you. Your father was our most talented covert operative. He was my best friend. I was his best man when they married. He made me promise that if anything ever happened to him and your mother, I'd watch over you. And, he asked me to offer you the life he'd had, the values he and I shared. I keep my promises."

Jon considered this. Maybe it was true. "You say a bomb maker was responsible for Lisa's death. Have you found him?"

Ben-Levy frowned. "Don't worry. We will. When we have him captive, I will personally hear his confession. And Jon, her real name was Aviva, not Lisa."

Jon shook his head. "Aviva. What a beautiful name, but she'll always be Lisa to me. As far as the bomb maker is concerned, you've taken too long finding him. Not good enough. So, I want to be the one. I want to exact justice for her."

Ben-Levy's face remained slack, but his eyes seemed to glow. "Really? We'll see. Do you still have my business card?"

Jon shook his head. The older man handed Jon another card. "Don't lose this one. Get a cab, find a hotel nearby and be at this address tomorrow at six in the morning. Ask for the SHABEK trainer. Hand my card to the guard." He rose from the table and in seconds was gone, disappearing through the crowded street.

What the bloody hell was SHABEK?

Jon used his cell phone to find an inexpensive and convenient place to stay. He called the Okeanos Suites, not highly rated but cheap, at Ramat Yam 50, and asked if they had a room available. They quoted a higher rate than the Internet had stated, but he wasn't in any mood to argue.

He was about to fetch GPS directions into the cell to when her voice spoke to him. *Come, see where I died. Go. Go there now.*

He shivered despite the heat, realizing she was still inside his head. Jon keyed the address he remembered from the newspaper report, and glanced at the GPS map on his cell. His objective was three blocks away.

He walked two blocks to the Gav Yam parking garage, an elevated structure on Ari Shenkar Street. Traffic filled the street and pedestrians bustled down the sidewalk. There was no trace of the massacre. The story he'd read had mentioned that it was the only bombing ever in Herzliyya.

He closed his eyes, trying to imagine what had happened.

He climbed the steps to the third floor and stopped by a heap of twisted steel sticking from the concrete.

Lisa's voice rang out in his head. *Look!* He stared at the spot where her car might have been parked and saw it vanish in a bowl of flames, along with the other vehicles beside it. *I died in fire.*

The thin, dapper, middle-aged man had followed Sommers all day. He'd seen Yigdal Ben-Levy arrive at Heathrow six months ago, alerted by MI-6's tether into the ECHELON system run by the NSA. Since then, he'd followed events regarding young Sommers. The older man ran a hand through his thinning hair as he crossed the street and walked back to his hotel. Alone in his room, he pulled the secure cell phone from his pocket. "It's Crane. Our target arrived and met with the Israeli. Tell the Director. If it all works out, we'll get a seat at the table after all."

He terminated the call and walked to the window. He watched the sky turn a dusky red. It had taken him years. His patience might have finally paid off. Bushovsky had failed, but he had high hopes for Sommers.

Just after dawn, Jon took a taxi from his hotel to the address on Ben-Levy's business card. It was a drab, gray, featureless high-rise. The noise of the city felt more intrusive than London. The aromas of diesel exhaust, body odors, and deep-fried food from street-side vendors assaulted him.

As he exited the cab, he could hear Lisa's voice in his head. *Jon, you belong here.* He shivered in the heat.

As Ben-Levy had instructed him, he walked into the garage of the adjacent building. An armed guard, one of several, beckoned to him and let him approach. After saying the words "SHABEK trainer" and showing the spymaster's business card and his British driver's license to a guard, he was led through the garage into a maze of narrow gray concrete tunnels in the basement. Then up two flights of stairs, along a hallway, and back down three sets of steps. The floor and walls, florescent lighting, and staccato echo of their footsteps seemed mismatched to his recollection of the white-haired man called "Mother."

Most of the rooms they passed had the names of either people or departments imprinted in both Hebrew and English into plastic plaques on the doors. Jon noticed "LAP—Department of Psychological Warfare."

On the door of a room that must have served once as a storage closet, a piece of paper taped to the outside of the door read "Mossad Special Projects—Surveil and Terminate." Below that line was another scribbled line: "SHABEK Liaison Projects. No entry without permission. By authority of Oscar Gilead, Deputy Director."

Jon read the sign and, finally, everything made sense. These were the offices of Mossad's killers. The guard knocked on the door and it sprang open. Just within, Yigdal Ben-Levy sat behind a gray Formica desk, reading a yellow file folder.

Ben-Levy motioned toward a folding chair. The lights were dim but glared into Jon's eyes. He could see Ben-Levy's face but the blinding light kept him from making out any more than just the lower bodies of others. Six or seven. Some wore perfume or cologne and some hadn't bathed. All stood along the rear and side walls, at least ten feet away.

Jon sat. He struggled to appear calm, but his gut churned with a mix of fear for his future and anger at Lisa's unfound killer.

Ben-Levy smiled. "Given your family, two generations in Mossad as *kidon*, assassins, we think you might have potential. If you're not interested in killing, you can still work for us as a *sayan*, a helper, in London, and we'll just move down the list of candidates to find our next assassin. If you don't leave right now, we'll assume you're interested in training in the killing arts. Well?" The older man waited.

Jon pursed his lips. He was still alive but Lisa was dead. Would he ever be free of her memory and her voice inside his head? "I'm staying." He scanned the others standing in darkness. "What comes next?"

Ben-Levy shifted in his seat. "The group we work for is called Ha Mossad le Teum, 'the Institute for Intelligence and Special Operations.' We refer to ourselves as 'the Office.' Our organization liaises with all the other intelligence services of Israel."

Jon's brows rose. "What other services? I thought it was only Mossad."

Ben-Levy pressed a button on his desk and a chalkboard descended from the ceiling. A light came on, highlighting the board as the rest of the room went dark. "No. There are many others. We coordinate across them. Read."

The services were bulleted on the board. Ben-Levy recited them without turning his head and glancing at the board, "Our internal security arm is called GSS, also referred to as Shin Bet, or SHABEK. It ensures defense of our consulates, missions, and embassies abroad. Israeli military intelligence is called Aman. It is part of IDF or the Israeli Defense Force. The intelligence arm of the Israeli Air Force is called AFI. The Border Patrol is called BP. Our naval intelligence arm is called NI. And the Research and Political Planning Center, RPPC, advises our politicians on long-range strategy."

Ben-Levy pointed to the square in the center. "The Mossad serves all the other intelligence services, acquiring what each of them asks for, and does what they request. They are the brain. We are but the arm."

Jon found it impossible to understand all of this in one sitting.

Ben-Levy rose and flipped a switch. The room lit halfway. "Yes, it is confusing at first. The Mossad's primary mission is political disinformation, but we also provide black operations when instructed. I report to Deputy Director Oscar Gilead. And I liaise with SHABEK for Mossad. You will have a chance to experience what I just told you, see how it all works. For now, remember that if you can survive the training we will give you, you'll report to me. Clear?"

Jon nodded, feeling confused. He noticed he was sweating profusely in the air-conditioned room.

"Good. Now, I will introduce you to your teachers. They will take you to the *midrasa*, the Mossad's training school. The course was originally designed to run two years. But we've redesigned an accelerated program, and you will be among the first such group."

Ben-Levy leaned toward Jon. "This is not a trivial task and there are no guarantees. Over two-thirds of the trainees wash out. Some die during training. Of those who become *katsa*, or case officers, only one in five qualifies as a *kidon*, warranted to carry out assassinations. Do you understand?"

Jon nodded, his lips compressed. It had to be him. He would do anything to make it so.

Ben-Levy nodded back. "The trainers will evaluate your progress and tell me if and when you are ready."

Less than an hour later, an old school bus filled with twelve recruits arrived at a compound of drab buildings bristling with antennae. The Mossad training school.

As the bus pulled to a stop, Jon gazed at the other trainees. One was blond, athletic, and attractive, two seats away. He started to smile at her but something held him back. He tried to open his mouth and say something, anything, but his jaw wouldn't work.

As he exited the bus, Jon straightened up and steeled himself to become the best at everything he'd need to seek justice for Lisa.

His first lesson took place before dinner with all the recruits in a small classroom.

The trainer was a wiry man with a mustache, about thirty-five years old. "I'm Michel Drapoff, a hacker, a *yahol*. Years ago, we created a system called PROMIS, and it mirrors the functions that America's ECHELON system provides. It hacks into telephone systems and surveillance cameras, and uses the videocam face-detection system on Israeli streets to identify Israel's enemies and pinpoint their locations. It also monitors email and Internet usage to track the origins of suspicious messages. We've sold the system to other governments, and as you may have heard, they've discovered a backdoor we engineered into it, permitting us access to all their state secrets. When the old KGB sold a copy to Al Qaeda, we uncovered a wealth of their intelligence. And of course, there is more than one backdoor." Several of the recruits laughed.

Drapoff scanned the room. "My job also includes ensuring secure communications in our safe houses, missions, and embassies. To do that, I fumigate these facilities, sweeping them for electronic bugs. I also handle babblers, counter-bugging devices. I've crafted new dry-cleaning techniques, that is, techniques to avoid surveillance. I created electronic countermeasures for the Israel Institute for Biological Research and for the Ness Ziona research facility.

"But my purpose now is to give you an overview of the Mossad's organization, referred to as 'the Institute' by our government." He seemed to scan the audience, his eyes making contact with Jon's.

The hacker pressed a button on the podium and a screen descended from the ceiling. An organization chart appeared on the screen. "The Mossad itself is divided into several departments." He named seven.

The one Jon found intriguing was the Collections Department, performing traditional espionage, stealing intelligence from foreign governments.

If he survived killing the bomb maker, Collections seemed to be an interesting place to settle.

Drapoff indicated the Collections box on the chart with his laser pointer. He said, "This is the reason Mossad was formed. Its activities mirror Mossad's motto: 'By way of deception, thou shalt do war.'"

After dinner, Jon mixed with some of the other recruits. One, a short, stocky woman, asked him, "Aren't you Ben-Levy's pet?"

"Dunno. I didn't know he played favorites." Jon wondered if there was an active rumor mill at the spy agency. He tried to turn away but she touched his sleeve.

"Everyone has heard about you. Sort of Office gossip. He's been baby-sitting you for over a decade." She shook her head. "We work hard to prove ourselves. But not you." She turned away.

Jon's jaw tightened. Had he been marked as having an unfair advantage? How could he prove he was worthy?

It was likely none of the other recruits would help him. He arched his back and stared at her back as she walked away. *I can do this.*

His trainers included several *kidons*, or assassins, a few *sayanim*, or "helpers," and one *bat leveyha*, a female trained to seduce unfriendlies to reveal intel they guarded. So this was what Lisa was trained to do? When he thought of her bedding terrorists, his fists closed. Was there no limit to what Israel would do to defend itself? He remembered her lies. He wondered how many times she'd done just this. How could he find out for sure? Was there any way he could see more of her file than what Watson had given him in London?

What would he find? Did he really want to know?

Jon passed by a conference room where the trainers met with their team leader, a *katsa*, or case officer, named Shimon Tennenbaum. He could hear the *katsa's* assistant was a *bodel*, a courier, acknowledge the reports he would hand-carry to Ben-Levy that evening.

It was the first day of their initial training, scheduled over the next four weeks.

At the start of each day, Jon donned a 50-kilo pack and jogged until his legs buckled with pain. Then, he and the other students crawled through mud spiked with barbed wire.

The third day he ran behind the stocky woman who'd called him Ben-Levy's pet. Jon thought about catching up to run beside her. Maybe there was something he could say or do to change her perception of him. But he decided she wasn't worth the effort. No one was. After all, when training was done, they'd go their separate ways and probably never see each other.

But what if they were placed within the same team? He picked up his pace. It took him two minutes of what passed for solid sprinting under the circumstances before he caught up to her. "Hey."

She half-turned her face. "You!" And she sped up.

Jon struggled to keep his position alongside her. "You know my name, but I don't know yours."

"So?" She didn't even look his way.

"So, tell me, oh nameless one, why you want to work for the Mossad." He was tiring fast now, his legs becoming rubbery. He struggled to control his breathing.

She scowled. "You don't deserve this."

He struggled to keep his voice steady. "Yes, I agree. And I never wanted it."

Out of the corner of his eye, he saw her head twist toward him. "Then why?"

"My fiancée was Mossad. She was assassinated by a car bomb."

Her expression changed several times in seconds. Surprise, followed by thoughtful consideration and then dismissal with a scowl. "You want revenge? That's all?" She shook her head.

"Whatcha mean?"

"I'm doing this to help make Israel safe. Our existence

requires hard work from everyone. Living here is not so easy as it is in Britain. Revenge is a luxury we can't afford. It makes us choose alternatives that are risky and doubtful. If that is your goal, you should leave now. Leave us today."

He kept running but lost speed as he thought about her words. What this woman told him fit what Lisa had asked of him, demanded of him. He imagined Lisa's words: "Why do you want to be a banker? Why not save the world? Save our people." He trotted forward, deep in thought as he put the pieces of his puzzle, his life, into a new configuration.

By the time he finished running, he felt different. There was new energy surging through him.

He could still feel his desire for revenge. But there was something else driving him as well. He felt the stirrings of commitment to Israel. The survival of a tiny nation depended on people like him.

He attended classes in surveillance and counter-surveillance tradecraft, interrogation, weapons and self-defense, and Mossad history and operations.

Every day he felt exhaustion dragging him. But, when he remembered Ben-Levy telling him the training had always taken two years before now, he had to work to contain a laugh. Who could do this for two years?

The Office gossip mill let him know the need for case officers and *kidon* had recently increased. Israel had lost many of them recently.

Like most who'd attended British schools, Jon spoke French, German, and Italian, having learned them from public school. The Mossad taught him Hebrew, and he developed an ear for the strange language. His fluency bolstered his confidence for his classes in Arabic and Russian.

But the most important language he learned there was the Naka, a report-writing system used by operatives. Naka enabled covert agents to relay messages to their handlers without being decrypted by hostiles. It used keys built using several changing variables, dependent on the agent, the handler, and the date, time, and location. The various keys for a single message could be contained in a paper book, using a formula to expand the variables into a full-fledged cryptographic system.

During one of his rest periods, he hung out by an indoor pool, surrounded by attractive Sabras in bikinis who reminded him of Lisa. That night, he thought of her, sleepless, remembering a time they'd sat in her tub together, their skin slippery with soapy water. He remembered seeing a large red scar on her torso, just below her left breast. He wondered if that was a result of her work for Mossad. *But of course it was.*

From the first day on, he'd attended classes in a special branch of martial arts called Krav Maga. One of their female operatives showed him moves using his wrists, elbows, and knees.

When his trainers felt confident he could defend himself, he was introduced to a *katsa* named Shulamit Ries for his exam. Ries, a thin, blond woman with dark skin and pale blue eyes, smiled at him. "Call me Shula. Show me how you defend yourself in hand-to-hand combat."

Standing ready on the mat, he tilted his head. "What do you want me to do? Which moves?"

She grimaced. "You just keep me from pounding you into the floor. It's my specialty. You keep me away from you. If you can't, I'll hurt you. You fight dirty, using moves that mirror mine." Shula sprung her left foot into his gut, doubling him over. She finished by sending her elbow into his head, and he fell to the floor.

She shook her head. "You should have seen me change the distribution of my weight in preparation for the kick. When I start to move, you have two options. Either you step to the side to avoid being damaged, or you catch my leg and flip me over. Ready?"

He hadn't been prepared for her first attack. He rose and positioned his weight. "Ready."

After ten minutes, he hurt in places he'd never felt pain before. That night, he peered in the mirror at the damage she'd done. He was covered in black and blue marks, and she'd given him a failing grade.

In two weeks, he could see her move coming and avoid it. In three weeks he could stop her and move away. In four, he could toss her down on her back. But not often.

She taught Jon how to defeat someone holding an edged weapon, a gun, or a club. As the days passed, the work callused his hands and feet. He became proficient at stopping up to three unarmed attackers at a time.

One hot afternoon, Shula walked into the room carrying a Beretta. She glared. "This gun is loaded." She placed its barrel against his forehead. "This close to your skull, even a . 22 will blow your brains out. In five seconds I will pull the trigger. We lose many trainees with this test. Keep me from killing you."

He gulped and closed his eyes, frozen. He focused on dismissing the terror he felt. Then he opened them, focusing on her face. As fast as he could, he shifted his head away as his hands pushed the gun to the other side, and in that instant he grabbed her hand and twisted the gun from her.

Shula smiled. "Good. That was your final exam. You passed." In seconds, she'd disappeared from the hall. He later learned that four of the thirty-six trainees had failed.

Ben-Levy taught a class in Middle Eastern history, focusing on the wake of World War Two, Islamic terrorism, Mossad's growth and development, and tactics and operations for both Israel and its enemies. It seemed to Jon that Israel's friends became its enemies and then to its friends again, depending on the moment's realpolitik.

According to Ben-Levy, Israel's most frustrating relationships were with Great Britain and the United States, both of which often had ulterior motives for their dealings.

The spymaster started his first lecture with this: "We don't tolerate failure among our covert operatives, especially when a covert operation that should work on paper goes bad. We never start an operation without a thorough analysis of potential outcomes. When we fail, and especially if the failure threatens to become public, we might well decide to punish the *katsa*, the operative in charge. We'll often move them to a desk job and stop giving them responsibility for covert operations. If the failed operation exposes our hand, embarrassing us in another country, we may burn the operative. In extreme cases, we'll even execute a *kidon* who failed, before he can be identified, picked up, tortured, and forced to reveal our secrets. If we intend to execute anyone, whether it be one of our own operatives or a terrorist, the execution order is presented to the Prime Minister for his or her approval."

Jon hadn't imagined the covert world could be this twisted. It seemed to him that if you were a spy, nothing was as it seemed to the rest of the world. And then, he heard Lisa's voice proclaim his own thought: *We learn to thrive in a world filled with enemies, ambiguities, and outright lies, Jon.*

Ben-Levy claimed, "In many countries, the secret police organizations have clandestine relationships with those of other countries, including us. We buy and steal intelligence from everyone we can. For example, right now, we purchase intelligence from the Germans, the French, the Americans, the Chinese, and the British. We also sell to them. Almost twenty years ago we purchased intel convincing us the Saudi royal family, particularly Prince Hamid, funds terrorism to fend off regime change."

"How does funding terrorism postpone regime change?" Jon found that one difficult to believe.

Ben-Levy stopped speaking. He shook his head. "Self-defense, refocusing the terrorist groups on objectives outside their home country. But the wealth of the royal family has lured it into non-Islamic practices such as drinking and sometimes ignoring the call to prayer. Some of the tribal leaders no longer consider them true Wahhabi. Prince Hamid's treachery won't keep the Saud family from a bad end. He's just arming the Wahhabis with terrible weapons they'll eventually use to kill the royal family, whatever their objectives outside of Saudi Arabia might be."

One of the other students, a thick-necked man inter-rupted. "I've heard we've bought intel from the Egyptians."

Ben-Levy chuckled. "Tomorrow, you'll start our course in assassination. First, we'll cover the rules for obtaining permission for an execution. And in the coming days, you'll learn how to do it well, no matter what set of variables you must cope with."

Permission before assassination. It was a concept he'd heard the United States had copied from Israel.

They spent a week of classes on teaching him how to lie. Ben-Levy stood at the front of the classroom, pacing as he spoke. "Our operatives would rather die than be captured. This isn't because of their patriotism. No, it's because our enemies love to torture their captives to death. No one who is captured returns alive, and we've seen their corpses. Disfigured, mutilated, and destroyed. Their deaths were entertainment for those who hate us. If you are captured, a swift death is best for you. But not for us. Best for us is if you lie to them first. Tell them half-truths that lead them away from us, and send them on a chase using their valuable resources while we adjust and regroup. Also, give up any ideas that torture will not break you. You must have a hidden tool that can kill you available while their torture destroys you, so you can choose the moment of your death."

Jon sat frozen in his seat as Ben-Levy introduced Lester Dushove, and then left the room. An instructor from the Institute for Biological Research at Nez Ziona, Dushov was a medium-sized man in his late forties. He had a hooked nose but otherwise was so nondescript that from the back he seemed to disappear.

Dushov pulled several vials and syringes from his attaché case. "Right then. Let's see who of you is ready to become a field agent. First rule: never look down, and never to the left or right when speaking. This must become natural. Practice it with a partner. Now!"

The class separated into pairs for ten minutes. Then Dushov filled a syringe with a clear liquid. "I need a volunteer."

No one raised a hand. Jon knew he'd regret this. He swallowed, raising his.

Dushov motioned him to the front of the class. He pointed to a folding chair. When Jon sat, Dushov placed a clip on his index finger and another on his ear lobe. Then Dushov bound him into the chair with rope. "It's for your own safety." When Dushov smiled, Jon knew he was lying.

The injection was a mere pinch in the crook of his arm. The room swayed, or was it him? He felt his focus drift, and Dushov's voice was distant now. "What's your name?"

Jon spoke but it was as if he was watching from near the ceiling. "I'm Margaret Thatcher." He felt a grin and forced it down.

"Class, did you see the color rise on his cheeks?"

He felt his pulse racing.

"You lie!" Dushov moved from behind him to Jon's front. He slapped Jon's face. "Tell the truth or I will be forced to hurt you. Now, again. What's your name?"

The room began to glow in a liquid drip. Jon took a deep breath and focused on relaxing. The disconnect between his two objectives startled him. He counted to three to himself. "I'm David Bowie."

Dushov touched Jon's face between his eyes. "Did you notice how his eyes moved down and to the left just a bit? He's still lying." Dushov's face was inches from Jon's. "Stare at the spot between my eyes. Think of something beautiful and slow your response down. Say your answer with no inflection. Again. What's your name?"

The voice of Lisa Gabriel whispered to him. *I loved you, Jon.* He looked at the space between Dushov's eyebrows. "Winston Churchill."

"Good. Class, look at the readings on the lie detector. He told us the truth, according to the machine."

Dushov cycled through the students, working with each until they could pass.

But, the next time, he failed. So did most of the class. The questions became more personal and the threats more real. Several students were tortured during their practice sessions. It went on for a week, two hours every day.

His final exam in disinformation was to pass a lie-detector exam in front of the class. Many of the recruits failed. Jon was among them. Ben-Levy appeared in the class at its end. "This skill is vital to success in our business. Remember the Mossad motto: "through deception we wage war." But if we kept those who fail in this course from working for the Mossad, we'd have few recruits graduate from the *midrasa*." He shook his head. "All who failed must repeat this course until you pass it." He let his eyes linger on Jon for a few seconds. "You must learn to lie." Mother walked from the classroom.

Jon repeated his training in the art of lying four times before he could pass the lie-detector exam.

When he passed, Dushov clapped his hands. "Finally." He entered a note into his cell phone and shouted, "Next."

Jon left the examination room and removed the thumb tack he'd hidden in his palm. Telling lies left a bitter taste in him.

One morning, Lester Dushov visited the class. "Watch." He held up his left arm. He opened the cuff of his old tweed sport jacket. "See the button?" Jon looked and saw an indentation in the inside of the jacket's sleeve. "When I press it, see what happens." Dushov lowered his arm, touched the button with a finger, and caught a Beretta .22-caliber handgun that dropped from the inside of the sleeve. "Our fashion sense may not be good enough for Paris, but it can keep you alive." The students laughed. "We also have other special garments, including a new tee-shirt that is lightweight and cool, even in the desert. It is coated with an STF, or stress thickening fluid, that makes it bullet and blade resistant. The STF is called "Liquid Armor." A point-blank shot or something heavier than a .50 caliber can penetrate this. But nothing else, including a bladed weapon." He held up a black tee-shirt that read "Tel Aviv University" and thrust a knife against it. The fabric thickened and deflected the knife. And then it once more fell loose. "We have a second-generation model in testing now, made from a much lighter fabric. It's totally bullet proof."

Dushov smiled. "Today, an overview of poisons. I create new ones. I think they are the best weapons the Mossad has. In deciding which one to use, we need to know when and where the execution will take place. You must plan to succeed. Some lethal pathogens don't work as well in daylight. Will the kill be in an enclosed space or out in the open? Nerve agents often respond differently in either situation. Some smell like new-mown grass or spring flowers, and wouldn't work well in a place where neither of those are present to mask suspicion, such as in the desert. And how to deliver them is another issue. Aerosol or injection? Each one leaves behind a different telltale, depending whether it's delivered behind the ear, into the back of the hand, or the back or thigh." He handed each trainee a manual on poisons. "Read this and learn it. Next week we will go on a field trip where I'll show you what can go wrong."

The next week the students went to the Institute of Forensic Medical Research, Their instructor was a medical examiner who demonstrated how a suspicious pathologist might conduct an autopsy to determine if death had been the result of an execution using poison. "Pin pricks, slight discoloration of the lips or inside of the mouth and nose, even a small blemish will divulge the death was no accident." Jon watched the pathologist cut and dissect a corpse to determine how a murder had been committed. "Damage to the liver, kidneys, or brain. They tell me which poison was used."

Jon watched the ME slice into the corpse's liver. He suddenly ran to the sink, where he threw up his lunch. Several others chuckled, but he could see a few seemed to want to do the same. He wiped his mouth, took a deep breath, and returned to the group. As he watched, he realized much of a *kidon*'s work was making assassinations look like accidents.

Jon studied his notes, and learned how to make decisions on the fly as to what weapon to use: poison, gun, knife, or bare hands. He passed all his exams. He found the thinking work was easy for him. But the physical work was much harder.

Ben-Levy's handguns and knives trainer judged Jon only "adequate" at throwing and handling knives in a fight, but he graded him high in firing a handgun. And Jon preferred guns.

When it came time to select a handgun, Jon entered the

armory and tried several. He found the weight and balance of a 9mm Beretta felt best to him.

The armorer showed concern in his expression. "Most *kidon* choose .22-caliber semiautomatic Berettas."

Jon asked the armorer, "Why?"

"You don't know?"

"Haven't a bloody clue. Why .22's?"

The armorer's eyes half closed. "When we close on a target, we try to get close enough before we shoot to be sure we have the correct person, not an innocent. Then, aim for the throat and keep shooting until the target falls. You end the target's life with a shot into the eye. A .22 will kill only if you can place your shot into the eye, the ear, or the throat. That clumsy thing you carry is like a butcher's mallet. The .22 is like a scalpel, much easier to hide."

Jon scanned the weapons in the armory. The .22's looked insubstantial to him. He finally settled on a Beretta Px4 subcompact Storm 9mm, slightly bigger than the .22 but still good for concealed carry, and capable of a fourteen-shell clip.

On the firing range, his instructor told them, "The word *kidon* means "bayonet." While we prefer not to use guns, and never to use knives, we realize that in a pinch, any weapon you can find is better than dying, or worse, being caught and tortured for your information. Used properly, you can slit someone's throat with a credit card." The instructor removed a credit card from his pocket and used it to split open a grapefruit in one swift move of his index finger and thumb.

Jon walked alone from the canteen one evening after dinner, hearing only his own footsteps and the chirps of crickets. As he neared the barracks, he felt a presence behind him. He tried to turn his head, but before he could, he felt a prick on the side of his neck and in just a second, the world swirled away. The last thing he remembered was seeing stars. But it was dusk, too early for stars.

He woke in a tiny concrete room, bound by ropes onto a steel folding chair. Three men wearing ski masks surrounded him. They spoke Arabic to each other. The tallest of them drew a knife from a scabbard and asked, "What is your name?"

Jon took seconds to survey the room and try to get his bearings. "Charles Dickens."

The man examined the knife as if it could determine truth and lie. "No. Let me assure you, Mr. Dickens, we will find out the truth. We will have your secrets. It's your only chance to survive. Now, again, what's your name?" This time he didn't wait for an answer. He nodded to one of his accomplices who wore brass knuckles. The other smashed his fist into Jon's belly. "Your name!"

Jon nodded. "Okay. It's Buddy Guy."

"And what are you doing in the country of Satan, Mr. Guy?"

"I'm a door-to-door salesman." Jon steeled himself for the next blow to his body, but it came to his face instead.

"Another lie. At this rate you'll be a bag of broken bones before we even begin slicing off your toes." The big man's face was inches from Jon's and his breath was rancid. "Please, we can let you have a painless death if you tell us what we've been sent to find out. Otherwise..." He motioned to the third man who held a hammer. "Break his hand."

Jon shivered. Was this real or a test? He'd thought it a test from the *midrasa's* instructors, but if terrorists had managed to spirit him off the campus, and if this was real, what should he do? What would happen if he lied? What would happen if he told the truth? He closed his eyes and envisioned a stream of mathematical equations. It was noise and didn't help. He'd have to decide based on his gut.

Two of them wrapped his hand around a wooden two-by-four and rewrapped his bindings there. They held his hand on the plank in front of him so he could see what they were about to do. The third man drew the hammer back and prepared to strike.

Lisa's voice babbled so loud in the back of his head, he could no longer think. He felt his stomach drop like an elevator with a broken cable. "Wait. I'll talk."

The man holding the hammer stopped in mid-swing. They all removed their masks. The door to the room opened and Yigdal Ben-Levy entered.

As the terror subsided, Jon felt disappointment. He'd failed. As if he could read Jon's thoughts, Mother shook his head. "Don't be ashamed, Jon. Everyone breaks, sooner or later. No one can withstand the horrors of being caught. You haven't failed us. But you have failed yourself. If you must die to serve us, so be it."

The others left Jon alone with Mother. "We taught you to lie, and that's where you failed tonight. Your lies must convince your captors to look no further for the truth. Nothing obvious like you tried tonight. Lead your captors to believe you know truths worth preserving you for. And then, deliver subtle lies and half-truths that lead them from us. Otherwise you'll end up yielding your secrets, and still you'll die in any case. Understand?"

Jon nodded.

Ben-Levy smiled. "Weapons, disguises, poisons, and assassinations are all forms of lying. Another part of lying is to make the lie fit with the environment. The hidden hand-gun and armored clothing are about making clothes lie to the observer. Choosing a poison that fits into the environment is a lie to make the death look accidental or at least innocent. Assassination is about lying to the victim: I am harmless. Only then can a well-placed shot kill your target. A gun can only be used as a scalpel by an accomplished liar."

Jon thought about how Lisa had lied to him. He thought

about his parents, how they'd lied to him. And tonight, when he felt comfortable in the lie of a safe night walk, he was taken.

He'd joined a group whose ability to lie was its greatest asset. It made him feel dirty. But now he knew this skill would be necessary if he was to achieve his goals.

He would seek justice for Lisa. Now, his greater objective became more important; keeping Israel alive. He felt surprise as he nodded. "Yeah."

Jon worked harder as the training became more demanding.

He ran a mile in under eight minutes on the tar track of the building's roof as the sun reached its afternoon zenith. Dragging his dripping body through the doors into the training center, he headed for the showers. As he emerged and before he could don a stitch of clothing, he found Shula Ries waiting for him, wearing an IDF uniform. She handed one to him. "Dress. There's a truck waiting. Your final exam is a trip through the Tse'elim. It's the Urban Warfare Training Center in the Negev"

He nodded and donned the uniform. The other recruits sat in the back of the truck. No one spoke as the truck bumped along the desert. Two hours later he found himself part of a battalion crawling prone through a Bedouin village. The silence was overbearing. He crept into a tent and saw a young man wearing a bomb vest. Faster than he'd thought possible, he aimed and fired into the boy's head. It was a blank but the counter attached to his gun triggered another success. He searched the tiny hovel and found no other threats.

The mission continued until nightfall. He heard a whistle signaling it was over. He found the truck and took his seat in the back.

When he returned to their base, Ben-Levy was waiting

for him. "Ah, Jon. I've just reviewed the report on the recruits. I pronounce you ready. Your training took you just under three months. Not quite a record, but very good. Report to my office tomorrow morning for your first assignment."

That night, he sat at his desk thinking of a time when he held Lisa in his arms, feeling her draped on him. When he remembered his forfeited desire to be a banker, his whole body tensed. How strange this journey. He'd become collateral damage from her death. Now his road had forever changed. Jon shook himself. He was committed to his path. He turned the chair to face the window and conjured her image once more. This time, he smiled. After all, she was why he'd come here.

Relaxed in meditation, he imagined the bomb maker with a tiny bullet hole in his right eyeball. His eyes sprang open.

Just before dawn the next morning, he was eating breakfast at the Mossad cafeteria when Shula, the *kidon* responsible for martial arts training sat down across from him. "Did you hear?"

"No. What?"

She leaned closer. "Amos Gidaehl, one of our *kidon*, was compromised and disappeared a few months ago while out on an assassination mission. We just got the evidence to prove he hadn't just gone black. He was one of our best alephs. The entire assassination team disappeared. Hashim Klovosky, an ayin, or tracker. A qoph named Harry Schmidt, his communications officer. Elli Raucher, a heth, one of our best logisticians is also missing. They're all dead, probably tortured first. For safety, Ben-Levy is distributing new identity documents to all Mossad field personnel."

Jon had heard of Gidaehl. He was a skilled, ruthless

killer. Jon wondered what he and his team were doing and where they were when they were taken. He looked at Shula's face for a clue.

She looked away. "They'll be looking for a replacement for Gidaehl. I looked at the grading board. Jon, you placed first in your class."

He realized he'd moved to the top of the list of unassigned *kidon*.

CHAPTER 11

Starbucks, corner of Lexington Avenue
near 42nd Street, Manhattan
August 19, 2:41 p.m.

His first assignment, as a *sayan*, surveilling a Muslim Brotherhood moneyman, had lasted three weeks.

The second assignment was also routine, acting as a *katsa*, guarding a diplomat flying from Jerusalem to New York for a speech at the United Nations. He'd found the work mundane, but used the experience to sharpen his counter-surveillance skills.

The thought that he'd ever wanted to be a banker now left him grinning. He realized he was now impatient. But, he knew he'd have to practice self-restraint. It would be a problem for him. He thought, *I'm ready for this. Sooner or later, I'll find him.*

Jon's official reporting line went up to Ben-Levy. Mother had been promoted and was now Assistant Minister of Foreign Affairs. Jon's non-official cover as a British citizen —an NOC, a "consultant" to the State of Israel—provided them all with deniability for his actions.

He settled into using the skills he'd learned and found himself ready for something more complex. His third assignment fit the bill. Jon hadn't carried a gun until now. Just one week ago, he'd met with Ben-Levy in the basement office at Mossad.

The spymaster had handed him cash in an attaché case before he left on the mission, saying, "For living expenses and any tools you need. Here's a requisition for the high-end, high-tech gun from our armory. It's a special manufacture plastic composite 9mm Beretta using armor-piercing plastic bullets. This gun can be checked in at an airport without detection." Ben-Levy reached out and placed a pink slip of paper in Jon's hand.

"Jon, This mission is vital to Israel's interests and her survival. You'll be a "jumper" working overseas. Your target, Tariq Houmaz, is responsible for six assassinations of Israeli diplomats and operatives. He uses shaheeds as cutouts, suicide bombers to do his killing. He's the man we had you follow in your first mission."

Jon's mouth grew dry. "What do I do?"

Ben-Levy was silent for a while, his eyes downcast. When he raised his eyes, he stared into Jon's. In a voice just above a whisper, he said, "Jon, we caught the bomber who murdered Aviva Bushovsky, but nearly killed him during capture. He became conscious for just long enough to tell us. We suspected before, but weren't sure. Houmaz made the bomb."

Jon's brows furrowed. "I'm following her murderer? Just following him? Nothing more?"

Ben-Levy shook his head. "Yes. Do not kill him. Follow him. We must know his contacts and his next mission, before we execute him. Otherwise, many innocents may die. Once we've determined what he's planning, I'll decide the next step. Not you. Clear?"

Jon nodded, hearing Lisa's voice utter the single word, *justice*. He felt his head grow warm, thinking she would have wanted it for her people, not herself.

It took a week for Jon to pick up the trail of Houmaz.

Nerves twitching in his gut, Jon sat in the midtown Manhattan café, his hooded eyelids hidden under a baseball cap. The gray NYU tee-shirt he wore was drenched from the heat and oppressive humidity of the summer day. The garment was treated to make it look lightweight and feel cool. It wasn't working to spec today. His 9mm Beretta was tucked into the back of his belt and the tee-shirt draped over it. His breath came in shallow spurts, his fists stuffed into his trouser pockets. He hadn't touched the latte in front of him.

Across the street, his target exited an office building at the southwest corner of 42nd Street and headed north up Lexington Avenue toward Grand Central terminal. Houmaz crossed the street and turned west on 42nd Street. Jon rose and walked with the expanse of 42nd Street separating him from Houmaz.

He hurried past a record store. The rich tones of "A Fool No More," a blues song from an old Fleetwood Mac album, blared from the store and echoed out into the street. He kept a wall of people as a curtain, rushing along, the sidewalk between him and the target. To him, the others were lost inside the pockets of their routine lives.

His pulse quickened as he anticipated his target's counter-surveillance tradecraft. So far, Houmaz used traditional methods similar to his. Jon used the store windows on his side of the street to track the other man's progress. His constant worry was being detected if the man had a team of counter-surveillance trackers. He fought the urge to see if Houmaz had any accomplices following him. If there were, looking for one would be a definite giveaway.

He'd been tracking the bomb maker for three days, since landing at JFK from London on the same plane as his quarry. Each of his days of tailing Houmaz had ended when the bomb maker returned to his hotel, a small tourist place on Third Avenue.

His target appeared well-rested and relaxed as he walked along the exterior of Grand Central Terminal. Houmaz even smiled at another who bumped into him. The bomb maker moved sideways through a group of Asians exiting into the street from a luggage store. Jon scowled at Houmaz's casual attitude.

At the next intersection, Houmaz took a right and walked north up Vanderbilt, wading against the crowd.

Now Jon nodded, suspecting the destination where the bomb maker was headed. He slowed to increase the distance between himself and Houmaz. As he passed a hot dog vendor, he stopped and sniffed. Still watching his quarry's reflection in a store window, he tried misleading his target by ordering a dog slathered with sauerkraut and mustard. Except for candy bars from his room's honor bar, it was the first thing he'd eaten since leaving the airport. The boiled meat on a bun tasted horrid as he bit into it.

The target was now a block away, crossing 46th along with so many others that Jon strained to keep sight of him. He tossed the sour dog into the trash and followed Houmaz through the Helmsley Building's short Park Avenue tunnel.

Pulling his cell phone from his pocket, Jon punched in a number and waited for someone to answer. He continued walking as he spoke. "It's Sommers. Put Mother on." The call terminated. He waited a second for the cell phone to vibrate in his hand, and a gruff male voice with an Israeli accent asked him to report status. "I'm tracking him now. He's headed towards the Bank of Trade's headquarters building. On Park at 46th. Now what?"

"Go to your hotel and get some rest. We have a team landing now at JFK. Your work is finished. But don't leave. There might be other favors you can provide, and we'll need you refreshed. Mother out."

Jon took one last look at the glass, steel, and concrete tower fortress as Houmaz walked through its revolving doors.

He wanted to end the man's life right there, right now. But his orders forbade that.

He headed east toward the Lexington Hotel. Walking into its ragged entrance, he stopped short inside. Who were the two Arabs wearing formal white desert robes at the registration desk? He panicked, and ducked back out through the revolving door. He took a deep breath. *It must just be my paranoia. Not all Arabs are fundamentalists. And not all fundamentalists are terrorists.*

Reentering, he walked past the Arabs as they leaving the registration desk and nodded at the clerk. He was back-stopped as "William Preston," one of the many new identities Mother had handed to the *kidon, katsas,* and *sayanim.* He also carried another passport bearing the name "Adam Wallace," for use if everything fell apart. The legend for each identity was clean and simple, a British banker on a business trip. And, as usual, his identities had been washed; owned by real people who'd died.

He took the ancient wood-paneled lift up to his room on the third floor. The hotel was known as an inexpensive place for tourists to stay, not ostentatious in any way. Perfect for a cover during a covert operation.

The small piece of gray thread he'd inserted between the door and its jamb was still in place. An ancient method, but still taught because of its effectiveness, and, easy to use. Sliding in his keycard, he cracked the door open and plucked the thread from the floor at the door for reuse. Pulling the plastic-composite Beretta from under his NYU tee-shirt, he took a deep breath before entering. Using a walking shooter's stance he checked the room. No one else was there. He re-holstered the gun and took a small electronic device from one of the kangaroo pockets in his khaki pants to "fumigate" the room, searching for bugs. Nothing.

He felt the grip of disappointment from not executing

Houmaz when he was so close. He could almost imagine Lisa's voice complaining, until he shouted, "Enough!"

Jon replaced the bug detector and pulled the cell phone from his other pocket. Using its keyboard to open a document file, he entered some notes. When he finished, he went to the bar and poured himself a shot of Finlaggan Islay single malt scotch. He savored its smoky taste.

Jon took off his sodden tee-shirt and unlaced his shoes.

He would now wait to be contacted.

He turned on the television and yawned with jet lag. His eyes felt heavy, and he saw a redheaded girl with olive-colored eyes and tasted the dinner he'd cooked for her in his apartment room ten months ago, just after they'd met. A Moroccan tagine, with aroma of spicy curry. She'd fallen asleep in his arms that night, her luscious hair spread over his chest like a blanket. Was that the night she'd fallen in love with him?

His consciousness dimmed and he rolled over on the mattress. He heard a click and realized he'd sprung the fail-safe trigger on a bomb placed under the bed, probably set there by Tariq Houmaz. Just the movement of his breathing could set it off. He held his breath as long as he could, but when he did gasp, he felt the room convulse with a fiery blast.

Jon jolted awake to the memory of his own fiery death, panting from fear. He took a deep breath to clear his head of the nightmare. He looked toward the window. Darker outside now. How many hours had passed?

In the dimming light of evening, he walked into the bathroom. The shower felt good. While washing his face he heard the ringing of his cell phone in the bedroom. He ran to answer it. "Yes?"

The voice growled. "Your team just cleared customs and should arrive within the hour. Wait for them to arrive. Circumstances have changed. I prepared a new plan. Our mole at the bank reported that Houmaz took the paperwork for the money transfers but hasn't returned it yet. He must not arrange for the funds to be transmitted out, and he must not live to leave the country. Deliver the completed forms if he has them. Rimora carries the plan."

Jon remembered the *bat leveyha* he'd used for a honey trap as a part of his first mission. Rimora was a gorgeous woman, her coiled black hair accenting a pronounced widow's peak. More important, she was brilliant.

When they'd first met, Rimora told him she enjoyed fucking Islamic fundamentalists. "When I bed them, I steal their mojo."

Ben-Levy's rough voice drew him back. "When the team arrives at your hotel, finish the mission. Don't call until you return home. Not until you land at Ben Gurion, unless you have questions or the mission fails." Jon frowned as the phone went dead.

He felt a rush of adrenaline as he finished drying his body. His vision tunneled and the world seemed more focused. He pushed his gun into the back of his pants belt and pulled on a fresh liquid-armored "NYU, Stern Graduate School" tee-shirt, chilling his skin in the air-conditioned room.

He flinched when the doorbell rang. He looked through the peephole and smiled, seeing Rimora's grinning face. Opening the door, he waved the four in. She wore a Princeton University tee-shirt with a similar bulletproofing chemical treatment, and he knew there would be a weapon similar to his stuck into her waistband.

Jon motioned them to sit on the bed. He took a chair from the desk. "Welcome to the Big Apple."

Rimora shook her head. "Where is Houmaz? I want to be done with this and back home."

Their driver, a *sayan* named Axel, was blond and rail-thin. He walked in with tentative, silent footsteps, examining the room as if Jon might have brought death here with him.

Jon had heard Axel's brother died last month from a Hamas missile attack in Haifa. The *sayan* flashed a grim expression. "This city has the same nasty overcrowded vibe as the Gaza." He sat on the couch and crossed his legs, with one foot tapping.

Jon pointed out the window. "Not really. It isn't half bad if you give it a chance."

Jon guessed Shimon, a *bodel*, or courier, was a local, working at the consulate in New York. To Jon, he looked like he could stand to lose a few pounds. Jon hadn't met him before, but Ben-Levy had described him earlier on the phone. The courier smiled and nodded, standing close to the door. "Great restaurants, some even kosher. There's one downtown—"

"Enough!" Yakov, the other *kidon* in the team, looked like he might have come from an upscale corporate office. It struck Jon that Yakov's freshly pressed charcoal pinstripe suit and crisp white shirt and silk tie were incongruous for a cold-blooded killer. Jon guessed Yakov had redressed in an airport restroom just after their plane landed. His face was expressionless and remote as he nodded his head to Jon. Yakov let out a long breath. Standing ramrod straight, he paced the room, peeking in the bathroom, then in the closets.

Jon faced Rimora and nodded. "Mother said you carry a plan. Tell me."

Rimora's face went blank as she spoke from memory. "Yakov is aleph for the operation. Jon rents a van using his "William Preston" identity. Buy shovels. Follow your target. Stay covert until he is alone. The team should try to take him silently after dark using a tranq with Axel's medijector. It contains a tranquilizer combined with a truth drug. Contact with the neck is best. Get him into the rental. Interrogate him and use a cell phone to record what he knows about his network, the use of the funds he's sending, and the receiving party. Drive him to Jones Beach. Kill him silently and bury him in the sand under the boardwalk, at least five feet under.

Leave the country and report back on arrival. If something goes wrong and the plan fails, obtain new identity documents from Nomi Klein, our cobbler in the Bronx." As she uttered the last word, her eyes flashed and she grinned.

Shimon shook his head. "Jones Beach in July? A bad choice. Even at night this won't be a private burial."

Jon closed his eyes and saw a stream of mathematical projections fly through his mind. The plan was flawed. He nodded. "Yeah. Even I can see this is bad. Why not the Jersey Meadowlands?"

Yakov sneered. "Because these are Mother's orders. Until something goes wrong, we follow orders. Clear?"

Jon knew better than to complain a second time. He waited for Shimon to say something or do something.

Shimon turned away. "The plan is stupid. Might get us all killed."

Yakov stuck his face inches from Shimon's. "As I just told you. We follow orders until something goes wrong."

Jon watched, worrying. No one else challenged Yakov.

Yakov gazed at each in turn. "Ready?" They nodded. He opened the door. "Let's go." As they marched toward the elevator, Jon replaced the thread and closed the door, catching up at the lift. He wouldn't need the room again. But the plan seemed so weak. Better to keep this sanctuary clean.

Tariq Houmaz hurried down 86th Street toward Broadway, glancing over his shoulder from time to time. The day ebbed cooler and it felt good to walk. Restaurant aromas seeped through the humid air and muted pinks and blues filled the sky at dusk. The streets were crowded with people seeking a place to eat. It was the perfect time of day for him to avoid detection.

The safe house was three blocks south, next door to a Chinese restaurant. Incessant traffic noise blared, making it more difficult for him to detect the coverts he'd noticed before. He thought, *counter-surveillance is a two-way street.*

The envelope in the right-inside pocket of his brown-tweed sport jacket contained funds-transfer forms and a list of the bank codes he'd obtained earlier that day at Bank of Trade. Tomorrow, he'd return the forms and send his money on its way to the Vladivostok branch of the Bank of Trade. In four days he'd meet up with the cash in Vladivostok. What a pisshole of a city. He'd make his stay as short as possible.

The left-inside pocket of his jacket contained a snubnose Heckler & Koch and the outside pocket contained an extra clip, both purchased from a gun dealer known for supplying local gangbangers and pushers in East Harlem.

His eyes sparked in anger with the memory of the day his father had changed everything, taking him from a well-to-do college student to a penniless beggar. A time so long ago when he'd studied to become a petrochemical engineer. All he'd wanted then was to work for his father at ArabOil Corporation headquartered in Riyadh. But the "accident" at the refinery where he'd apprenticed had left him without his family.

He knew for a fact it had been no accident. He'd hidden in a lifeboat and watched, peeking from under its canvas cover as Navy SEALs destroyed the refinery's rig, trying to eliminate someone the United States thought might be a terrorist conduit. "Collateral damage," the American diplomats claimed. They'd murdered thirty-seven innocent men and women. No one told him if the terrorist they were hunting had been executed or had escaped. Or even if there had been any terrorist.

But Houmaz's father hadn't believed him. The old man blamed him. Disowned him. His father insisted that Tariq should have fought the invaders instead of hiding until the fighters had finished their work and left the rig.

Without a home, and separated from his brothers and

his father, he'd drifted until the obvious occurred to him. He wouldn't run ArabOil. But there were other uses for an engineer's skills.

As dusk deepened, the rosy sky lit 84th street. He walked from shade to shade, avoiding anyone out for an evening stroll. A cooling breeze rolled down the street, blowing his hair and clothes. It felt good. He turned off Broadway onto 83rd Street.

After doubling back twice to ensure he wasn't being followed, he saw someone he'd seen before. Before he saw the face, it was the clothes that drew him. Then he noticed a few more of them. All wore college tee-shirts, but they seemed a bit old for college.

Their heads twisted from side to side, scanning the alleyways they passed. That kind of behavior was a signal that he was being surveilled by trained operatives. Were they armed? *Of course they are.* He wondered if the tee-shirts were treated with Liquid Armor. *Of course they are.* They walked close enough to be a group. Five of them, including a woman. And then he saw the face of the man who'd been following him earlier today. Definite trouble.

As the sky faded into darkness, Houmaz sought refuge, a place where he'd have a line-of-sight advantage with no choke point. He entered a West End restaurant, the Sichuan Gourmet.

He scanned the restaurant's large room and walked to the back exit. Here, he turned and faced the entrance. Fear spiked in him. He smiled. *Love that feeling.*

Two males neared the entrance; one was the man who he'd seen before. He pulled his cell phone from his pocket, wondering if the safe house was close enough to send him backup or an exfiltration team. The call on his cell took a few seconds.

The aroma of Asian cooking was at odds with his expectation of the blood and cordite odors soon to follow.

By now, some must have positioned themselves down the street and others by the rear exit to the alleyway.

He drew his gun. *I won't get out of this unless it is Allah's will.* The clip was full. *Thirteen rounds. Every shot will have to be a headshot.*

Yakov cursed in Hebrew. "Our plan just changed. No way to do anything silently. He knows we're here. No way to get him to come out. We'll have to go in. Try to wound him so we can still complete his interrogation."

Jon didn't need mathematics to know this was even more desperate and crazy than a public beach burial. Their van was parked several blocks away and Jon hadn't any idea how they could carry a wounded captive so far. He was sure shots fired in an upscale residential neighborhood would attract swift police attention. He even doubted they could execute Houmaz without having a dozen witnesses make their descriptions public. "Are you sure this is a good idea? Mother said to keep the operation quiet."

Yakov's rage sat on his face, bright red, and his fists clenched. "My operation. You follow my orders. Jon and Axel, cover the rear exit until I tell you to enter. Then, go in with a shooter's stance. Shimon and I will enter from the front. Rimora, backstop the operation. The alleyway across the street. Go now."

Jon's pounding heartbeat pinned him near the wall. He stood in the alleyway with Axel, adjacent the rear exit of the restaurant. His palms were sweaty and his head was filled with anticipation of revenge for Lisa's murder.

They used a large garbage bin as cover, and the over-powering stench of rotting food drove Jon to move as soon as possible. He heard Yakov's voice in his ear bud. "Status?"

Jon replied. "Axel and I are outside the back exit. When

can we send him to a better world?" He kept his voice as cool as ice.

Jon could see across the street to the alleyway where Rimora stood in the shadow of a building. Her role was the safety in case something went wrong and Houmaz managed to get by the four in the assassination squad.

Jon clenched his eyes shut for just a second. This was his first black op. His first time killing a person. He and Yakov were the only trained assassins in the team. The *bodel* and the *sayan* were skilled at shooting a handgun, but, probably hadn't killed before. *And neither have I.*

What if I fail? Will I be reunited with Lisa, or will my body lie cold and alone for eternity? He felt her voice, urging him, *Kill him, Jon. For me.*

He took a deep breath as Yakov's voice whispered through his ear bud. "On my signal. Go, go, go."

As he stepped into the rear of the restaurant, the world appeared to move in slow motion. Two steps in, he saw Houmaz leave the cover of the men's room doorway, aim and fire a single shot.

The back of Axel's head exploded, raining blood and brain on Jon's face. Blinded, Jon overturned an empty table near the exit and crouched behind it. Mathematics told him he hadn't a chance of surviving. He could hear Lisa's voice babbling in his head. Fear froze him for several seconds. He felt his heartbeat pounding in his chest, heard his breathing, and felt a wall of terror close on him.

Two shots splintered the wood of the overturned table, pulling Jon back to his mission. He used his forearm and hand to wipe the blood from his face, while conjuring a set of alternatives. Move right or left?

Rising, he bolted left as he glanced at the place where he'd heard the sound of Houmaz's gun seconds before. No one was there. Jon sprinted toward the men's room. He held his Beretta in a two-handed grip, ignoring the few screaming occupants. Several pulled out their cell phones. He knew they were calling 911.

The men's room was empty. Then he heard three more rounds explode from the entrance of the restaurant. He sprinted from the bathroom and through the front door, onto the sidewalk. He found them Yakov and Shimon there, lying face down, the backs of their heads bloody. The medijector rolled away from Yakov's body. Jon realized that while he had been checking the men's room, Houmaz must have exited the back. He must have run through the alleyway and looped around to surprise Yakov and Shimon from behind at the front of the restaurant.

Houmaz had disappeared.

"Shit," Had the bomb-maker returned to the back of the restaurant? Jon ran through the alleyway along the side of the restaurant. Empty. He headed back toward the street again.

Many people were running away, some shouting and screaming. He saw a black van screech to a stop. Houmaz jumped in through the back door. Jon had no shot. He slammed his fist into the building wall.

Now he heard distant sirens closing. He looked around. Those who had been there were either gone now or running away. The adrenaline surging through him had narrowed his focus, and he felt the high it gave him. Seconds remained before the police arrived.

Shaking his head to clear it, Jon took off his bloody jacket and dropped it in a trashcan at the edge of the alley-way. He walked away from the restaurant, down the street, looking for Rimora. Jon kept his eyes focused ahead, walking with deliberation as two police cars sped past, their lights glowing, stopping where his team lay dead. He took out his cell phone and dialed Rimora's number. No answer. But he could hear its nearby ringing and followed the sound.

She lay amidst trash in one of the alleyways across the

street from the restaurant, shot in the chest, her breathing shallow. If the Liquid Armor had failed, the shot had to have come point-blank. Jon eyed the distance from the restaurant and back to where the van had been.

No, Houmaz couldn't have done this. It was too far for him to run, shoot her, and return to where the black van had picked him up. So he must have allies somewhere. Wary that he was still a target, he cupped her head and studied her wound. He was sure it was a fatal shot; blood spurted from above her breast, just below her collarbone in rhythm to her heartbeat. She was hyperventilating and her face was going gray.

There would be no way to get her to a hospital before she died. He knew she knew it. "Who shot you?"

Her lips moved as if she was talking, but he could hear nothing.

He picked up her cell and dialed 911, reporting her condition and location. It should take less than three minutes until an ambulance arrived, and by then he'd have to be far away. He forced himself to stay calm and focused. It wasn't working well. "Rimora, try again. Who shot you?"

She pulled his head to her mouth and managed to whisper a single word: "Bloodridge." A trickle of red dripped from her slack mouth. Her head fell back and her eyes began to glaze.

His team had failed. There was a heavy weight on his heart, the responsibility for all their deaths. It had all happened so fast. No time to think, no time to calculate, no data for projections. He realized mathematics was truly useless.

Lisa, love, I've failed you. Tears mixed with rage, clouding his vision. He got up and ran from the alleyway.

How could one man have decimated his entire team? Where had Houmaz gone? Who had helped him? What would he tell Mother?

And, what the hell was Bloodridge?

CHAPTER 12

Corner of 83rd Street and Broadway,
Manhattan
August 22, 7:58 p.m.

The ambulance sirens were now about a block away, closing fast. Three minutes had passed since Jon's battle in the restaurant.

He picked up his pace, his body shaking, shivering. He strained to feel his emotions and found nothing but numbness in reaction to the massacre, a function of the massive amounts of adrenaline surging through him. His vision remained scoped. He heard nothing but buzzing around him, and slowed his pace to give him time to regain his senses. He'd been trained to leave at a walking pace and find someplace from where he could call for assistance. He started north up Broadway, where he could find the subway and make his escape.

As the field of his vision widened, he saw a black limo glide to a stop in front of him. Before he could react, its doors swung open. Two suited men with bulges under their armpits hurried out. One pointed to the back seat and the other indicated the spot under his armpit where Jon knew his weapon was. "Get in, please, Mr. Sommers. We mean you no harm." The accent was Oxford through and through. He heard them but the sound was muted to his adrenalized hearing. His heart still pounded.

He moved in slow motion so as not to alarm them, raising his hands above his head. He slid into the middle of the back seat, with the two others on either side of him. As they closed the doors, he glanced at the two seated in the front. He calculated the different possible outcomes. None were good.

The driver pulled away from the curb. The passenger in the shotgun seat was turned so Jon couldn't see his face.

Jon placed his hands on his knees, palms up, so the men in the back with him could see he wasn't a threat. His ability to think, to analyze, was returning.

With this turn, the day's events had gone well past being a simple disaster.

One of the heavies seated in the back reached under Jon's tee-shirt, pulling the Beretta from his waistband.

The older man in the shotgun seat turned and nodded. Jon shifted his gaze from the two in the back seat to the man in front. "Who are you?"

The balding man in front scanned Jon. "MI-6. The man you were sent to execute is one of our assets. Just couldn't let you do that."

Jon clenched his fists. "So you killed the four in my team."

"No. We were late to the party. Just arrived from the consulate in Midtown. Damn traffic. So, no, it was the handiwork of Tariq Houmaz alone. Had you gotten closer to him, you'd have died too. He's one of the most dangerous operatives I've ever seen with a gun. We watched the entire thing." The Brit was speaking as if he were reporting a series of British football scores.

Jon assumed this was a lie. There was no way Houmaz could have executed Rimora. Not enough time before the van retrieved him. He shook his head once more to clear it. There must have been two vehicles in the operation. So, they were coordinated. Including Houmaz, the van driver, and Rimora's murderer, plus the four in this limo. A total of at least seven, and possibly more.

He stared at his palms, then out the window. His vision was back to normal for distance and close up. His pulse rate was slowing. He felt more confident now. *Be rational*, he thought. He considered their claim that Houmaz was controlled by them. *If so, then at least indirectly, they're responsible for Lisa's death. And the massacre of my teammates.* He struggled to contain his rage, taking deep breaths. As the seconds passed, he calmed once more.

For the first time Jon noticed obscure details of the four others in the limo. All wore business suits. The driver wore a fedora but Jon saw the man's blue eyes reflected in the rearview mirror. One of the two heavies he'd noticed before was blond and the other red haired. Both looked like they were in their twenties. Cut from the same mold. His sense of smell was coming back. He noticed aftershave on the older, mid-forties man in the shotgun seat. The man had a thin red scar running down his left cheek.

"Why me?"

The older man pursed his lips. "Your handler will want to make an example of you when he hears what happened. Perhaps we can help each other."

Jon struggled to keep his posture from showing any outward response. The adrenaline had dissipated. He could think this through. Formulas bloomed in his head.

It was possible they were right. During training, he'd heard Mother had a temper. Ben-Levy would be angry as hell when he found out about this mess. Jon had inherited it, not being the aleph, but the massacre still marked him. And then he'd let himself get placed in the back seat between the two heavies. So the limo men might have come to the conclusion he'd consider their proposal. He wondered if there was a way to convince them to deliver the bomb maker in return for what they wanted. He closed his eyes in concentration. "I owe you nothing. Tariq Houmaz owes me everything. Let me go."

The older man smiled and faced out the front windscreen. "We'd like closer ties with your handler in the Mossad. We'd like you to bring us to the table. Not as a mole, but as a liaison."

Jon shook his head, remembering his training class on the history of the Mossad. "You've always treated us as untouchables, a second-class operation. Whatever could you offer?"

The older man nodded. "American intelligence. We receive it every day. Albeit a bit after the date it's produced, but they have advanced technology you don't. Think your handler might be interested? In ECHELON's output?"

Jon wondered if this might soften Ben-Levy's feelings about his failure. Bringing ECHELON to Mother just might save his life. But, on the other hand, Israel had PROMIS, an equivalent technology, but not with access to equivalent networks. Representing the offer of another country's intelligence service might make it seem he was a mole and he'd planned to fail. It could seal his doom. He played out the alternatives and there was no significant difference in outcomes. He was in deep trouble either way. "Lemme think about it."

"Mr. Sommers, let me remind you, you're a British subject working for another country's secret police. That makes you a traitor. You're no better than Kim Philby, Sidney Reilly, or Mata Hari. We could bring you home and put you in a British prison. For a long time. Possibly even hang you in public. Or since this mess went down here, we could have the Yanks send you to one of their nasty rendition prisons. It's what the Israelis did to Eichmann." The older man faced forward as the driver turned onto 44th street. One of the heavies reached into Jon's pants pocket and removed his cell phone, handing it to the older man in the shotgun seat. He pressed several buttons on it. "I'm taking your cell number. I'll give you a day to consider our offer. And, just in case you were wondering, we'll have you under surveillance every second until I call."

The limo stopped. The blond opened the door and pulled him onto the street, handing him his cell phone and gun in full view of those walking by. He pocketed them both and jogged away until he was three blocks north of the spot where they'd left him.

He wondered what they'd do if he turned them down. *Probably kill me.* He swallowed hard. *They now have my cell phone number. They can monitor my phone conversations and triangulate my location. What was I thinking when I got into that limo?*

The limo sat curbside as Jon Sommers trotted away from it. In the shotgun seat, Sir Charles Crane pointed toward Jon. "Follow him." The two others in the limo's back seat were surveillance experts. They exited the car and tracked their target as he headed north on Third Avenue.

Crane scribbled a note on a pad as the driver crossed 42nd Street on the way to the British Consulate on Third Avenue near 51st Street. He looked at the busy city sidewalks, bright in the night. He'd written a question mark next to Jon Sommers's name.

The driver looked across at him while they waited for the light to change. "Whatcha think, sir?"

Crane shook his head. "Hard to say, lieutenant. Depends on what happens when he tells his handler how big a mess he helped make. They may cut him loose, in which case he's no good to us. Of course, Mossad sometimes kills operative who fail this big, to set an example." He sighed. "Damn. Wish we could have helped him out, but Houmaz is too valuable to lose. We have to have Sommers. We must know what Mossad is planning."

"Were you serious about the threats to him personally, sir?"

Crane frowned. "Whatever it takes. The Jews occupy the most dangerous piece of land on the planet. And the most valuable, too. If they play hard and lose, the whole region could go up in radioactive smoke. When one of their coverts was blown up in a bombing a few months ago, we lost our double. That agent was our window on their activities and, well, now we're blind. Sommers could be her replacement for both sides. They get a British *kidon*, we get a liaison. Fair is fair."

The driver nodded, maneuvering the limo past the security guards, into the garage. Silence reigned in the vehicle as they stopped under the consulate building. "But why Sommers, sir?"

Crane was silent. His eyes fell out of focus, recalling a time twenty years ago when he had worked on the same team as Jon Sommers's father. Before the man's death, he'd had no idea Abel was a mole. Not finding out sooner had caused Crane a demotion. It took over five years for him to discover Yigdal Ben-Levy and his role in the matter. He'd tried to explain it all to the head of MI-6, but the director refused to believe him. And it was another five years before his handlers had forgiven or forgotten. He'd been knighted last year, and MI-6 had accepted him back.

Since then, having a mole within the Mossad was his constant goal. When he found Aviva Bushovsky in London seeing Jon Sommers, he realized it was his chance to reverse his previous failure. He'd turned her, trying to get to Jon. But she had died, and he thought he'd lost. But when Ben-Levy showed up at Jon's door, he was delighted. Sommers wasn't just a mole. He was payback. The sins of the father, visited upon the son.

Crane exited the car, walked upstairs and entered through the building's lobby, filled with portraits of the royal family and the ministers of government. He breathed in the scent of flowers in vases as he passed them and smiled at the security guards. Trotting up the stairs to the second floor, he removed his Burberry trench coat, carrying it with him to the code room. Crane knocked on the door. It swung open and he nodded at the operator. "I need to send a message."

The operator, a young woman who looked to be barely past adolescence, nodded and held out her hand. He scribbled the name of his own handler as the message's recipient, and ripped out the notebook page he had written in the limo. Crane handed it over, and then left her to her work.

He walked to his office, somewhat larger than a walk-in closet with no windows. Could his mission succeed? He needed someone within Mossad soon.

Would Sommers double for MI-6?

When Jon entered the hotel elevator and ascended to his floor, he found himself unable to remember how he'd gotten there. His mind swirled, unable to focus. Exiting the elevator, he realized he'd walked two miles.

In Israel, it would be nearing sunrise soon and Ben-Levy would expect his call. Failure tainted him. Thinking about the meeting with the Brits, another wave of adrenaline coursed through his body, affecting his ability to think.

He exited the elevator, swiveled his head left and right, scanning for threats. His mind buzzed with questions of the events of his disastrous evening. He needed to understand what had happened, before he called Mother. *And the worst might not have happened yet. Who were those Brits? MI-6 or some fringe group bent on using me for terrorism? If they aren't MI-6, who are they? If they are MI-6, should I tell Ben-Levy about MI-6's involvement with Houmaz?*

Mother will be furious. I'm the remnant of my team. How to prepare? There's no way for me to tell what's coming next. What did Houmaz do yesterday afternoon at the Bank of Trade? Deposit cash or withdraw it? And why? What did Rimora mean when she uttered her last word before dying? Bloodridge. What the hell is that?

Too many unknowns. Just thinking hurt his head.

He scanned the door to his room. Had anyone entered while he was out? No, the thread he'd placed about six inches above the door's bottom was still in place. He unlocked the door and entered.

There might be blood-splatter traces on his clothing and on him. He stripped and placed the soiled items in a dry cleaning bag so he could toss them later. He took a shower and redressed. Clean, but still muddy-minded, he picked up his cell phone and took a deep breath. The Brits would want him to tell Ben-Levy. He was sure of it. Time to call.

He dialed the secure number and entered a series of keys. Then he terminated the call and pressed a button on the side of his cell to set it to secure mode. He waited mere seconds. The phone buzzed with the callback.

"Sommers here."

"It's Mother. Status?"

He gulped. "Dire. Houmaz single-handedly killed everyone except me."

"What?" Ben-Levy shouted the single word. "How could this happen?"

"I think MI-6 assisted Houmaz. They said he was their asset. They picked me up seconds after the massacre. Their *katsa* was an older man with a scar running down the left side of his face. He tried to recruit me as a double. He offered intel from the CIA if I agreed. He said as a British subject they could arrest me and send me to prison. I'm sure they were the ones who murdered Rimora." Jon steadied the shaking hand holding his cell.

"Let me think."

Jon waited, hearing the old man's ragged breathing. He wanted to hang up and flee. Mother said nothing. Jon could hear his own heartbeat accelerating.

After a long while, Mother said, "This changes everything. I'll send an exfiltration team to get you out before the police can find you. It'll take me a while to set it up. Right now I'm on my way to a meeting with the Va'adet Rashei Hasherutim, the Committee of the Heads of Service, for the next two hours. I'll get back to you by noon your time." He heard a click as the spymaster terminated the call.

Jon sat on the bed, a chill running up his spine. The committee included the deputy director of SHABEK, Oscar Gilead. He hadn't met the man but remembered Ben-Levy telling him during training that all termination orders were signed off by Gilead as well as the Prime Minister.

He felt his face go slack as he cycled through the mission plan and wondered, *what could we have done better? We did as we were trained. Followed him using standard surveillance procedures. Adjusted the plan when the target discovered us. Covered each of the exits to the building with twice the manpower of the target. Entered in a shooter's stance. We did everything right.* But then he remembered being distracted by his memories of Lisa. *Damn!*

He jumped off the bed with a sudden realization. If the Brits hadn't lied, then in order to arrive so fast, Houmaz's helpers must have been close by. Maybe the bomb maker had almost reached his safe house when Jon's team cornered him. He pounded the wall with his fist. But, it was too late now. It no longer mattered.

Ben-Levy had hinted at a retrieval team. But what if he was sending an assassination team?

The deputy director of SHABEK had pioneered many of the methods of assassination and torture developed by the Office. Jon feared his failure would place him on their "to do" list. He felt a bitter taste in his mouth. Having left Lisa's murderer alive had him feeling even worse. And the crowning glory was his freeze-up during the mission as he entered the restaurant.

He wanted to die.

If they sent a team of assassins, he'd welcome them. At least it would end his pain. Lisa's voice popped into his head. *You still love me, don't you? I gave you my heart, accepted your ring. I would have been your wife. You have to survive. You must have another chance at Tariq Houmaz. Jon, you owe me.*

He struggled to keep her out of his head, pacing the room, counting the number of individual blinds covering the window. No good.

She was running him. Ruining him. He hated her for leaving him. For leading a double life without any regard for him. It was too much.

And now she claimed she wanted justice?

PART II

CHAPTER 13

Yigdal Ben-Levy's office,
Basement of Mossad's Headquarters,
Herzliyya, Israel
August 23, 2:36 p.m.

The tiny room in the basement was crowded even though just six people were present.

The team leader, a thin young woman with dirty-blond hair and striking blue eyes, nodded and pointed to the other female member of her team. Her voice was a monotone and she closed her eyes, repeating what she'd memorized. "Esther will approach Sommers, so he suspects nothing. They haven't met. The rest of the team will assume positions with adequate visibility, but far enough away that he won't assume any are threats. She's to inject Sommers with the hypnotic solution Lester Dushov created, using the medijector. Anywhere the fluid makes skin contact will do, and no amount of it is too small to work, so Esther could even be holding the device up to eighteen inches from his skin. Once dosed, the drug will take several seconds to work. We guide him out to the van and take him to our safe house in East Meadow, New York, to debrief him. On arrival, we teleconference with you and all further orders come directly from you after you commence debrief."

Yigdal Ben-Levy surveyed the team, his eyes holding

each for far too long with an angry intensity Shulamit Ries had never seen before. "Good, Shula. You understand the nature of the mission. As for its importance, I needn't even mention that. Any questions?"

Shula scanned her team. She knew Esther wouldn't bother Mother with questions. Harry was shy; if he had questions, he'd approach Shula later. Marc would assume everything Mother said was all there could be to the mission, so, no questions from him either. Samuel was another matter. As she had the thought, he coughed.

Mother stared at him. "Samuel?"

"What if he resists? Can we send him to a better place without your debrief."

Ben-Levy stared back. "No. Absolutely not. You will not kill a *kidon* without my direct permission in advance. And I haven't given that. You may restrain him, even pound him into the ground, but not kill him. Clear?"

Samuel nodded and stared away. Abraham and Isaac just stood motionless.

Ben-Levy handed Shula an envelope and turned away from the others. He stood, facing the wall. "Your tickets are inside. I'll arrange to have him meet you. Do not fail me." The spymaster took a deep breath. "Shalom and good luck."

Shulamit Ries and her team exited what used to be a storage room and walked to the elevator. She'd heard of Mother's legendary temper, but she hadn't witnessed him losing his composure before. Was it Mother's meeting with the deputy director? Did this have to do with the public gunfight in Manhattan that left consulate personnel shot dead in the streets? She knew her team must not fail.

What a shame. She'd liked Jon.

An hour later, Ries and her team marched through the terminal of Lod Airport. Each flashed their official documents and bypassed security. Booked into first class on El Al to JFK, the group walked to the boarding area, Esther and

Marc trading jokes. Harry and Samuel argued about the possible results of the upcoming election.

Shula paced, watching the entry ramp from the terminal to the jet. She felt as if it was the *Titanic*, and she knew it would sink. She had a terrible feeling about this retrieval. Sommers would expect a hit team. What if his suspicions pinpointed Esther as a Mossad operative before she could deliver the tranq? He was still armed. And dangerous.

As they boarded the aircraft, she sifted through the nightmare of possible scenarios her team might encounter. She imagined different ways the mission could fail, and ran outcomes for permutations of the budding plan she'd crafted. A few hours later, when the pilot announced they had cleared London airspace and were over the Atlantic, she drifted off to a nightmare of suicide bombers and dismembered children on a school bus, a remnant of yesterday's television news.

It was just after dawn when she woke, jolted by the dropping of the plane's wheels in preparation for landing.

Samuel, a large man with a pockmarked face, touched her arm. "You were twitching as you slept. I thought it best not to wake you for the meal. How are you?"

She twisted her head away from him. "Fine. Has everyone in the team reviewed the plan?"

He looked out the window as the plane touched down. "Yes, of course. We know what the old man wants. But remember: no battle plan survives first contact with the enemy."

She turned and studied his face. "Sommers isn't the enemy. He's just a *kidon* who failed to complete his mission. It could happen to any of us."

He nodded and frowned. "But it hasn't. Not to any of us. Scores of missions without a failure. He blew it, the first time out the chute. His team embarrassed all of Mossad, and Mother personally."

She grimaced. "I think he'll expect termination. To be used as an example."

He frowned again. "Then, we'd best be ready for a battle."

Jon sat on the bed in his room, watching the television news. He knew it would be better if he didn't go out unless he had to. The talking head on the newscast reported on seven brutal murders, but, so far, the female reporter hadn't mentioned him or the shootings from the previous night. He guessed that with a city as violent as New York, the news editors cherry-picked which murders the reporters would focus on. But maybe there was another reason. Ben-Levy. Had the Israeli government found a way to intercede?

Jon obsessed, rethinking every second of the mission, all his movements. He remembered the smells now. Chinese cooking, ginger, garlic, sesame seed oil, meat sauté, cordite from the rounds Houmaz fired into his team, and the coppery smell of death. The faces of his dead crowded his mind, their chorus accusing him of failure.

He sprang off the bed and paced the room.

A team would arrive soon, either to exfiltrate him or terminate him. He'd no way of knowing which. After what had happened, he felt indifferent to their intention. First his parents. Next, Lisa. Then his team. Everyone who got close to him, everyone who worked with him or loved him. All dead now.

It had been almost thirty hours. All that happened was his fault. He should have been better prepared. Maybe, if—

His cell buzzed, and he jumped like a cat at the sound of a vacuum cleaner. "Sommers."

"My name is Esther. Mother says hello. If you wish, we can come to your hotel room, but if you'd prefer, we can meet somewhere more public, like the New York Public Library.

Your choice." He could hear street noise coming through the connection along with her voice. They were close by.

So, they were catering to his sense of paranoia. Maybe it was an exfiltration mission after all.

He walked to the hotel room's window, to see if he could find her on the street below. "Yes, the Public Library. There's a park on its west side, Bryant Park. The corner of Sixth Avenue and 42nd Street. Go to the north corner nearest the library. Do you know where it is?"

"No, but we'll find it. Twenty minutes." The call terminated.

He pulled on his tee-shirt and stuck the Beretta into his belt. The shirt stank of last night, but he didn't care; clothing odors wouldn't be a problem if they murdered him. As an afterthought, he took a thin Swiss Army knife from his backpack and placed it in his sneaker sock above his ankle. He'd bought it at a store near Grand Central when he was tracking Houmaz right after he landed in New York. Now, it seemed so long ago.

He would have prayed, but since Lisa Gabriel died, Jon no longer believed in God.

CHAPTER 14

Bryant Park, west of the New York Public Library,
corner of Sixth Avenue and 42nd Street
August 23, 12:22 p.m.

Shula Ries shifted to pull away the tee-shirt sticking to her skin as she waited in the humidity and heat, scanning the park. Each member of her team was walking a different corner of the vest-pocket park, far enough away from the others that they wouldn't call attention to themselves as a group.

Ries set Esther, a dark, delicate woman, at the northwest corner of the library. The young woman wore a sport jacket constructed by the Office's tradecraft department. It included a specially designed sleeve within its left arm, rigged with a button taped to her palm. Touching the button would cause the medijector to drop into her hand. She sat at a picnic table facing into the park. Waiting, like the rest of them.

Ries had placed Samuel at the corner of 41st and Sixth, farthest away from the where she expected Sommers to appear. His position was designed to give him a clear view of the other two members of their team, Abraham and Isaac. They covered the two corners nearest the library.

At this time of day, the park was crowded. The weather was perfect for a New York summer's day Under a blue cloudless sky, a mild breeze reduced the effect of the sticky humidity. The lunch-hour throng was thick around them. Cookie vendors and taco stands dotted the perimeter of the park. Children played tag near Samuel. Ries had told him if things went wrong, it would be his job to pound Sommers into unconsciousness, but not kill him.

Ries was the first to see him and she turned to face away as she spoke into her ear bud. "He's on the south side of 42nd, walking west. Near the end of the library. Entering the park. He's yours, Esther."

Esther stood up from the bench where she'd sat and smiled as Sommers approached the center of the park. "Jon?"

He stopped and turned, then stood still, ten feet away. "Yeah. Listen, I'll go with you. No drugs necessary. Okay?"

She looked back to Ries for confirmation, and Shula shrugged. Esther nodded. "Okay. We have a van parked in the garage under the Sheraton, a few blocks away. Walk with me. The others will follow."

Jon nodded. He didn't know if he was headed toward his freedom or his death.

"Once again, thanks for your cooperation. You have my personal word that our agreement will remain secret, Sir Charles." Yigdal Ben-Levy hung up the phone. Could his position on the twisty road of lies he's crafted withstand the shitstorm bearing down on him, the Mossad and Israel?

His phone rang. "What?"

"I have the Prime Minister for you as you requested. He hasn't time for a meeting, but he can give you five minutes on the phone."

"Thank you, Sarah." Ben-Levy stared at the clock on the wall. "Put him on now. I'll only need two minutes."

Jon was wedged between two others in the back seat of their

van. Surrounded by the SHABEK *kidon* team, he steeled himself to his fate. The man called Samuel steered the van across the Queensboro Bridge and east onto the Long Island Expressway.

He was sure they were all *kidon*, even Shula, their *katsa*, or case officer. They had the aura of murder on them. Why would they send so many ruthless killers if this were an exfiltration mission? He began to doubt their intentions.

He'd had a choice: live and work as a double for MI-6, or die and send a message of the consequences of failure to other Mossad coverts.

For the first time since he watched his team die around him, he realized he wanted to live. Even if it meant being haunted by Lisa's voice until he reached a ripe age, he didn't want to die with Houmaz still alive. Maybe agreeing to meet them and come in from the cold was a mistake.

He was sure this would be the final hour of his life. A bad time to have second thoughts about dying. He sought to craft a plan to escape. At least it would give him an alternative to focus on.

As they passed into the suburbs, he watched the green and orange early autumn foliage on the roadside of the Grand Central Parkway. The van exited onto the Meadowbrook Parkway, much less crowded with traffic. He memorized the turns they made as the van left the highway at the Hempstead Turnpike exit. Here he saw the sign marking East Meadow. He watched as they made a left on Merrick Avenue. If he somehow escaped, he'd need to know how to return to the city.

Jon remembered the flat penknife wedged into his sock. He carried no other weapon, having handed his Beretta to Shula when he met them in Bryant Park. The plan he'd fabricated required he palm the penknife, but with Ries watching him that wouldn't work. His gut churned with panic, perspiration soaked through his tee-shirt and now he could smell his fear fixed within its odors.

The van pulled up the driveway of a split-level house on Eric Lane, looking like it was built about fifty years ago. Shula touched his shoulder. "Out. And be hasty. We don't want neighbors getting curious."

Sommers nodded and moved among the throng of hitters. They pulled him through the door of the safe house and into the living room where the blinds were drawn. She motioned to a lone wingback chair and an ottoman, both right behind him. "Sit."

Jon gulped. "I already told you I'd cooperate."

Samuel shoved him into the chair and used his knee to brace him while one of the others tied his hands behind the back of the chair and another bound his feet together, and then knotted the rope to the legs of the ottoman.

Jon shook his head. "Shula, that wasn't necessary."

Ries pulled a cell phone from her pocket and plugged it into a speaker sitting on a small table next to a lamp. She punched in a number.

Jon knew she was calling Ben-Levy. He squirmed in his seat, growing surer by the second he'd made a fatal mistake.

The phone was answered before the first ring ended.

The growling voice of Yigdal Ben-Levy boomed through the room. "You have him? Can he hear us?"

Shula was facing away from Jon. "Yeah. We tied him into a chair."

"Jon, you disappointed us and caused us international embarrassment. An entire team lost in a public gunfight. The FBI called our Prime Minister with a formal complaint just an hour ago. I was called to meet with several members of the government. They were clear on what they want. You left me no alternatives." Jon heard the old man sigh. "Shula, we need to talk privately. Turn off the speakerphone and leave the room."

Jon raised his head. "Wait! Yakov was the leader, not me. The plan. It was flawed. I wasn't the *katsa*. I'm just a remnant! MI-6 was involved. They offered us CIA intel. Isn't that worth something?"

The voice from the telephone was silent.

Jon watched as she left him alone with Samuel and the other killers. He could feel the presence of death as if it stalked him in the room.

In less than two minutes she returned. "We have to leave for a while. Samuel, stay and watch him. Make sure his bindings are tight."

When Samuel protested, she shook her head, facing away from Jon and toward the tall hit man. "My orders, Samuel. We'll return in a half hour. Need some tools."

With that, all except Samuel left the house. Jon heard the van's engine start and its sound gradually diminished.

He wondered if something he'd said had set his fate. How had the police identified his team members?

Tools? It was now obvious Shula's team hadn't been prepared when they called Ben-Levy. If they'd been ordered to bury him after killing him, they'd need shovels.

The thought of dying was exhilarating. All his failures, gone. He smiled and closed his eyes, drifting off... to the voice of his dead lover, shouting within his head. *Find a way to get out of here. You're not done. Get out of here or I'll haunt you in Hell!* He lurched back into consciousness.

As Samuel turned to peer out the window, Jon worked the bindings. Too tight, and he couldn't reach the knife in his sock. He shifted and struggled without result. Panic set within him.

Samuel turned away from the window and faced him, raking his thinning blond hair. "You don't deserve this. You weren't the team leader."

Jon nodded. "Yes! And it was Ben-Levy's plan, not mine. Please don't let me die. Help me."

"No. Orders." Samuel shook his head. "Sorry."

Jon heard a noise at the front door, metal on metal and almost silent.

He braced himself for the return of Ries's team and his execution. And Lisa's voice began to scream. *You aren't done with me yet.* He wondered if there was a Hell where he'd hear her voice forever.

The door popped open and the two Brits he'd sat between in the limo entered in a walking shooter's stance. Each fired a Taser at Samuel as he drew his handgun. The Israeli assassin fell, groaning.

The redheaded Brit cuffed Samuel, then looked at him and smiled. "He's just dizzy. He'll be okay in an hour." The blond Brit checked the house, returned, and untied Jon's bindings. "Hurry. They'll be back any minute."

Samuel shouted after Jon as he ran behind his rescuer out to the street where the limo's motor was running. At least the Brits hadn't killed Samuel. Maybe this was a message to Mossad. Or maybe Samuel was a double for the Brits?

Jon jumped into the back seat and the car sped away. He was now coated in perspiration. "Why'd you rescue me?"

The blond Brit didn't answer from his seat alongside Jon in the back. The redheaded Brit sat beside him on his other side.

Jon rubbed his wrists where the bindings had cut his circulation. "You tracked me through my cell?"

No one responded.

Jon shook his head. He remembered his conversation with Mother. "My handler isn't interested in your offer." His stare shifted across each of the four others.

The older man in the shotgun seat turned. "Change in plans. Seems you've no future with the Israelis, so how about working for us?"

Jon blinked as his world changed. "First, tell me who the fuck you are. And don't lie to me again."

"Calm down. We just saved your life, so you owe us. We're from MI-6." He flashed his ID. Jon wondered if it was real. "I think you can be useful in basic espionage activities. Specifically, I need intel from within the Bank of Trade."

Jon thought about Lisa. About her murderer. "Forget it! I joined Mossad to kill your asset."

"Yes, yes. But look, we need to know _about_ Tariq Houmaz. Specifically, did he get to transfer out $200 million? If so, where'd he send it? You've an MBA in economics and global banking. Bank of Trade is looking to hire. We have a mole in their human-resources department. Do this and you may have a future within MI-6 instead of in a British prison for treason or an unmarked grave somewhere."

The bank Jon had been researching during the Christmas break was the Bank of Trade, the linchpin in the Islamic banking world. He'd heard rumors they had an enforcement arm. Infiltrating them would be dangerous and to do it, he'd need a lot of cash to change his appearance and craft a backstopped identity. _No way I'm going in looking like Jon Sommers_, he decided. _Any way I do this, it's more dangerous than being_ kidon. Then again, nothing in his world was safe anymore.

In his head, Jon imagined Lisa caressing him, whispering. _You might find intel within the bank's records that gives you another chance at Houmaz._ He wondered if the cash Houmaz wanted to transfer came from MI-6? He guessed it did.

There was no other future for him. Lisa's voice whispered, _don't you still love me? Isn't that a good reason to do the bidding of MI-6?_

In that moment he realized no sane person houses ghosts within. Maybe prison would be better. A place where he couldn't do damage to himself or others. Maybe he deserved death for all those he'd left dead.

Jon shook his head to clear it. "What makes you think you can trust me?"

The man in the shotgun seat chuckled. "My name is Charles Crane. I'm something of a gambler when it comes to evaluating talent. We'll give you a chance, albeit with a short leash. Will you work with us?"

There was something familiar about the man's name but Jon couldn't remember what. He drifted, trying to concentrate on where he'd heard it. And came up empty. He sighed. "I've nothing left to lose." *Not true if Lisa can haunt me in Hell.* Jon reached his hand out and Crane took it in a handshake. "I'll need cash to work my way into the Bank. Lots of it."

Crane handed across an envelope. "Everything you'll need is in this envelope."

Jon ripped it open. He found a British passport, a debit card from First Manhattan, and a bank statement indicating a balance of US$100,000.

Crane smiled at him. "You're Michael O'Hara from now on."

Jon stuffed the envelope into his pants pocket. The limo was rounding the Queensboro Bridge onto Second Avenue. "Stop here."

He realized how close to death he'd come. Yet, he'd escaped. He knew what would happen to him if Ben-Levy's *kidons* found him again. *I should feel like an action hero. Like James Bond. I survived by the barest of margins, just like he always does. Not bad for a day's work. At least I should feel alive.*

But he felt tired and filthy as he walked away from the Brits.

CHAPTER 15

Corner of Second Avenue at 60th Street,
Manhattan
August 25, 6:22 a.m.

From the moment they dropped him off, Jon knew the Brits owned him. And he couldn't return to the hotel; Mother would have it surveilled as soon as he found out what had happened in East Meadow.

In lobby of the Waldorf Astoria Hotel, he found a dark place under an antique wall mural. He crafted a plan to recover his life, but it had holes he couldn't find any way to fill.

No matter, he needed to act. And soon.

The photos on his new British passport and the extra one Mossad had provided looked too much like him. If he used either identity, he'd be marked for the rest of his short life. No, not good. He'd need another identity, one he could assume for an indefinite period, one looking unlike himself. If he grew a beard, identity software could still find him, but it was the best he could do.

What was the name of the cobbler Mother told them to use if he needed a forged identity, just in case his cover was blown and he couldn't be exfiltrated? He was sure they hadn't had time to inform all the lower-tier *sayanim* about his burn notice. Didn't Rimora say the cobbler lived in the Bronx? Where?

Jon walked to the E train station at 53rd and Fifth, and rode it downtown to Seventh Avenue where he transferred lines and waited for half an hour on the steamy platform. He took the D north into the Bronx, exiting at Tremont Avenue. The Grand Concourse. As he walked to the corner, he saw four gangbangers walking in a tight-knit group, their tats and weapons bulges identifying them. He crossed the street. At the next corner, he saw a drug dealer, peddling his merchandise to several locals.

He knew the old woman lived nearby. But he couldn't remember the exact address.

He wondered how long it would take for his name and description to filter down to all the cobblers? A while, perhaps days.

She would tell Mossad about his new identity, but, for the time being, he needed an identity the Brits wouldn't know about. Just in case he failed in his work for them.

By now, Jon remembered everything he needed. Her name was Nomi Klein. He knew there would be security arrangements the Mossad would've installed at her office residence. Cameras, of course. Mundane but effective. He'd have to figure out some way to fool the cameras recording the woman's customers. But not disable them. If he did that, it might alert Mossad.

The sun was rising, bright and hot, as he walked down 177th Street toward Morris Avenue. No stores open yet. He was hungry, thirsty, tired and felt like hell. *A brush with death will make you feel that way.* Jon found a phone booth next to a bus stop and looked Klein up in the telephone directory. He sat on a bench waiting there until 8 a.m., when stores would open.

He found a First Manhattan branch and withdrew $4,000. There was a bodega at the next corner. He scanned its shelves. Bought himself a black coffee, a ski mask, a large brimmed cap, and some women's cosmetics, including eye shadow.

The forger's little shop of horrors was on East 177th Street near the corner of Walton Street. In minutes he was around the corner from her building. He donned the ski mask and placed the cap over it, covering his head. Entering the building lobby, he rang her apartment. "My name is Harry Schwartz. I need some documents."

The voice coming from the outer speaker was high-pitched and tinny. "Who sent you?"

"Mother. I'll pay you three large for a passport, Ms. Klein."

The outer door buzzed and he entered. Knocking on her door, he heard feet shuffling. He clenched his fists. Was he up for this?

The door cracked open, but not enough for him to see Klein's face. He heard the click of a handgun's trigger, chambering a round.

The door sprang open and she thrust the gun forward into his gut in a shooter's stance. She looked to be about seventy years old. She might be a senior citizen, but she moved like a woman in her prime. "Enter." The old woman drew a few feet away and pointed with the pistol toward a metal folding chair in the center of the living room.

Jon sat and she used plastic cuffs, binding him to the chair. "I have cash."

"What's your real name?" She didn't sound happy.

This was a test. He couldn't divulge his true identity; no one from Mossad would. So he stuck with the lie. "I told you. Harry Schwartz. Ben-Levy sent me. You're *sayan* to Mossad and so am I. My cover was blown and one of the American intelligence agencies is looking for me." This time, it felt good to lie.

She scanned his face. Then she nodded, uncuffing him. "Cash please."

He pulled his wallet out and handed her the cash. "I want a washed Pakistani passport with a clean legend. How long?"

"Less than twenty minutes. You wait while I work. Believe me, I want you gone fast." She turned and walked to the bedroom door. "Come here and stand against the wall. I have to take your picture."

Jon removed the cap and ski mask. He held up a finger and pulled the cosmetics from a bag in his pocket. Soon his face was a few shades darker and the skin where his beard was beginning to grow was much darker. "Take the picture now." He stood against the white wall. He noted she held an early model digital camera.

Twenty minutes later he had a Pakistani passport for a man named Salim al-Muhammed. "Destroy the photos in your camera."

She shrugged and deleted the images while he watched.

He donned the mask and cap and rushed out the door. After speed-walking just over a block, he took off the ski mask, stopped and stood in the shade, hyperventilating.

When he'd cooled, he bought a taco from a vendor and scanned the area for a sign indicating apartments for rent. The food tasted rancid, but he was so very hungry.

An hour later, a man named Salim al-Muhammed handed a landlord $1,000 total for the first month and security deposit to rent a run-down furnished studio on 177th Street.

Jon signed the lease in his new name. He smiled while shaking the hand of the landlord. Wondered if his British accent would work for the man. "I'll need a set of phone books."

The landlord nodded and disappeared for a minute, returning with copies of the white and yellow pages. "Rent's due on the first of the month."

So, his accent would suit his Pakistani passport after all. "Of course."

After the landlord left, he sat on the ratty couch. This place made his London flat look like a palace. The odor from the furniture and walls of the room was a mix of ancient untended garbage and stale urine. The couch and the fabric covered chair were both torn and stained. The table had food scraps caked onto it, now part of the finish. The seat of the wooden chair was cracked and it looked unstable. He looked at the bed and shook his head. Who would live like this?

Jon closed and locked the apartment door. He entered the shower and washed off the makeup using a combination of cold cream and soap from the bodega. He'd have to perform for the Brits. At least until he could get something on them he could use. A plan formed in his mind, and he smiled. Soon, he was gone from the hovel and marching out onto the sidewalk.

He strolled toward the concourse, his head shifting left and right, scanning for the MI-6 trackers. No sign of them. Taking the steps down to the subway platform, he boarded the IND heading south to West Fourth Street.

On McDougal Street near Broadway, he found a discount clothing store where he bought a cheap business suit, collared shirt, and tie. After he paid the clerk, he used their fitting room to don the suit.

Jon walked to the Stern School of Business at NYU on West 4th Street in the West Village, and used his identity card for "Jon Sommers, London School of Business" to get him a guest pass into their computer center. He figured neither the Mossad nor MI-6 could have found a way to track his use of the expired school ID in the United States. It felt good to do something he'd trained for in Graduate Business School. He smiled at the irony that his real task was to set up a covert cover.

He remembered studying the Bank of Trade, its branch

locations, operations, and financial results, when he wrote the paper for *The Economist*. Its operations headquarters were in Karachi. He took note of the branch address there and the limited list of names of personnel at the location.

He called Crane from the Stern library. "I'll need to find a contact at the Bank of Trade's operations center in Karachi. Do you know of anyone there I can use?"

Crane said, "Hang on a sec." Jon could hear file drawers opening and a computer keyboard clinking. "Yes, old boy, you're in luck. We follow all their personnel when they travel. So, one of their low-level operations staff is returning to Karachi from Cleveland. She's in play right now. On her way to JFK, where she'll change planes after a stopover. I'm sending you the details." Jon heard the email beep as it entered his cell. He thanked Crane. *I'll have to move fast.*

Jon used the library's Internet connection to book "Michael O'Hara," the identity the Brits had given him, on his target's flight on Pakistani International Airlines to Karachi for later that evening. He scanned her photo. *Attractive woman.*

He bought a small spinner suitcase and some clothes at a nearby store, and packed fast, standing on the street. Just after noon, he took the stairway down to the IND station on West 4th Street. He caught the subway to JFK, carrying passports for all his identities in the jacket pocket of his business suit.

It was just after lunch hour and the subway car was crowded with workers. As the train left Manhattan and entered Brooklyn, it emptied to just a few passengers headed home. He recognized no one in his car or the ones adjacent to his.

When the train entered the station near the airport, he boarded a bus and took it to Terminal 4. The arrivals and departure board for PIA listed his flight, PK 722, leaving at 8:05 p.m. for Karachi.

Near the counter, he inserted his Michael O'Hara debit card and printed a boarding pass. At an airport traveler's shop he bought a sewing kit, more clothing, and sundries. On the other side of the security gate, he went to the men's room and used the sewing kit and an undershirt to craft a pouch. He dethreaded the spinner's cloth lining, placed the spare passports in the pouch, and placed the pouch within the lining, then re-sewed the interior of his suitcase.

He placed the remainder of the clothing into the suitcase to fill it. Then he pulled the suitcase behind him as he strolled to his gate, where the final few passengers were waiting in line.

His objective was to find the contact Crane had given him. He scanned the photo once more; a woman in her late twenties, dark skin, ebony hair, thin face. Crane had her working in the bank's operations headquarters. Could he convince her to help him? The math told him the odds were steep against him. Bad odds to find her. Worse to convince her.

Several of those in front were wearing Western garb, but most were dressed in Middle Eastern and Far Eastern clothing. The odors wafting off several of them were offensive, reminding him that soon, he'd smell just like them. Then it occurred to him body odor could be used as a disguise.

He found his target and sat next to her, not caring that his assigned seat was two rows further back. The aircraft wasn't even half-full. No perfume. She resembled her photo. Straight raven hair and dark skin. He nodded at her as he sat, but said nothing. When the aircraft taxied into position, he noticed her hands, rigid on the armrests. "You don't like flying?"

The woman stared straight ahead. He worried he'd upset her more by speaking to her without a chaperone present. As the plane lifted off the ground, one of her hands left the seat, closing over her mouth to smother a scream. He touched the other hand, next to him with a death-grip on the armrest. "Nothing bad will happen. Have faith."

Now her piercing brown eyes settled on his. "If it is Allah's will." She smiled, then averted her gaze.

The plane crawled through a cloud layer lighting them with the afterglow of a rosy dusk. It leveled and Jon picked an in-flight magazine from the seatback. As he opened it to its first page, his companion faced him. "I am Sandhia Sorab."

"What a pretty name. I'm Michael O'Hara. Is your destination to home or for a visit?" Jon felt his face split in a smile.

She brushed her hair off her face. "Karachi is home. I am returning from a visit to my brother in Cleveland."

Jon smiled. "Ah. And it was a pleasant trip?"

"No. He isn't a pleasant man." She looked away.

"Home is a better place for you?"

"Yes. The rest of my family is gone now. But I have managed on my own. I'm a banker. I have friends there."

"Which bank?"

"Bank of Trade. I'm one of the supervisors in the money transfer area."

"It sounds like an important job."

She smiled back and shook her head. "No, not actually so. Hard hours. I've been there since school."

He thought hard how to reel her in. A slew of equations streamed through his consciousness. *Pick the right approach. Not too fast. Careful. Ask questions.*

"Which school?"

"Just a school for women, in Pakistan. Nothing you'd ever have heard of."

He dropped the magazine back into the seatback. He remembered his non-credit banking coursework at Dreitsbank, and his internship the previous summer at Bank of London, in foreign exchange. In his head he conjured the organization chart for a typical money-center bank and determined Crane had struck gold. "Money transfer. Sounds important. What's a day there like? Can you tell me?"

Sandhia seemed to focus on something in front of her he couldn't see. "The bank is nothing like anything else in Karachi. So modern, so clean. And everyone is polite. I arrive at eight in the morning."

"You seem so Western."

Her eyes looked startled. "Well, I am. I was educated in the West." She turned face away.

"Are you devout?"

"No. Too long in the West. London, Amsterdam." She picked the in-flight magazine from the seatback.

Jon sought to force her attention back to him. "What do you do?" He wished he could take notes. It was possible she could provide him with all the knowledge he'd ever need about Bank of Trade's money transfer accounts and transactions.

By the time the aircraft touched down, he'd arranged a date with her the next night. And for the entire air voyage, the voice of Lisa Gabriel remained silent.

Jon entered Sandhia's address into his cell from the slip of paper she'd given him, and followed his GPS to her home. Just as she'd said, it was near the market. *Ah, here.* He knocked on the door. Her footsteps within grew louder and the door opened. She was dressed in a traditional Pakistani purple sari with gold threads in an ancient paisley pattern. A plain black silk scarf covered her hair.

Her smile was demure as she stepped outside and locked the door behind her. "There's a good restaurant two blocks away."

He smiled back. Lucky she didn't invite him in. He wanted to keep this as "professional" as he could.

The restaurant was dim, and Jon felt uncomfortable in its romantic atmosphere. The tables were brass trays, leaving Sandhia closer to him than he'd wanted.

He waited until they had finished a shashlik appetizer. The skewered chunks of marinated spiced lamb, roasted onion, and red pepper reminded him of a dinner he'd had with Lisa in the Marble Arch area of London. Also a Pakistani restaurant. Now, for the first time in over a day, her ghost inside his head shrieked. *Don't you still love me?* He needed to act soon. "I'm a banker, just like you."

Her face reflected surprise. "Which bank?"

"First Manhattan. I work in foreign exchange." He waited for her reaction to his lie.

"I thought you might be a professional." She smiled.

She pulled back and looked down and to the left. Bingo. Her body language said she was lying. He guessed she thought he was a rake, a raconteur. If she thought that, it wouldn't be easy to enroll her in his project. "What do you do in funds transfer?"

"I supervise. I told you that on the plane."

Wrong question. Now she's wondering about me. "No, I mean, local or global transactions."

He watched her face relax. Now she stared into his eyes. "Oh. Global. About 50-50 incoming and outgoing."

The waiter arrived with their entrées and a plate of saffron rice.

He wondered how to get her to describe the area. "It must be like a factory there. All those transactions. A machine could do all the work."

She shook her head. "No. Things go wrong and our job is to handle them, making them right."

"How?" He thought, *I've got you now.*

"We have repair stations where workers research incorrect information entered by the sender, such as a receiving bank's name or the format of its account numbers."

For a few seconds they remained silent.

"Do you supervise the repair stations?" He remembered that one-off transactions, not to be repeated, often contained errors, since the customer might misspell something or enter incorrect information. Repetitive transactions almost never failed, since they were corrected and then stored in the computer for future use. He was sure Houmaz hadn't set up a repetitive transaction, since this was likely to be his only chance at funding his project. Besides, one-offs were easy to trace. Therefore, the queue of one-off transfers was more likely to contain the bomb maker's among them.

She nodded. "Yes. By the time I arrive, the outgoing repair queue of funds transfers with missing or incorrect data is filling. So, it appears you know much about the global money transfer function."

"Just what I learned in school, and at the bank. Electronic funds transfers, foreign exchange. And, come to think of it, we might share a client. Some guy who sends money to your center from First Manhattan every so often. Tariq Houmaz."

He watched her face tighten and her hands clench. "Who are you?"

"Huh? I told you."

She rose from the cushion. "Take me home. Now."

He touched her hand. "If I've offended you, it wasn't intentional. Please. I meant no harm. I was just curious."

He watched a war of emotions waging within her. She sat. "How do I know you don't work for my government? If they thought I was loose-mouthed, they'd hurt me."

"I'm a Brit." He plucked his Michael O'Hara passport from his pocket. "Not a Pakistani." He opened it, displaying every page for her.

Then she amazed him by picking up one of the skewers and chewing off a piece of lamb. As if nothing had alarmed her. She seemed capable of changing in an instant.

"Sandhia, I don't work for your government. Promise." Jon locked his eyes to hers, no smile this time.

"Are you even a banker?" The corners of her mouth tightened. She wasn't convinced. Never would be. No lie would work this time. He could see her gathering herself and preparing to rise from the table.

He sighed, dropping to the next equation bubbling up in his head. "No. I graduated college, majoring in global banking and economics from Cambridge. Then earned my MBA from the University of London." He watched her face relax as his lies fell away. But not enough. She still clenched her legs. This wasn't going well. "Just graduated. And I'm unemployed. My girlfriend was killed by a bomb manu-factured by Tariq Houmaz when she was in Tel Aviv. I want to know as much as I can about her murderer."

Her face melted. She settled back on the seat and reached out. She touched his hand. "I'm so sorry." He watched and saw the disappointment in her body, her legs crossing. She was no longer interested in his body, and Lisa's voice remained silent.

He remembered Ben-Levy teaching them that assets became what the handler wanted because it was what *they* wanted. What would her motivation be if he convinced her to help him? Who in her life had tormented her? She either had lost someone close to her or was worried it might happen. He recalculated his subsequent moves in this chess game, and decided her brother was at risk.

He took a deep breath. "Thanks. Look, I came here to find out all I can about her murderer. And, on the plane ride here, I found you. Perhaps it was the will of Allah. We'll see if it was. You see, I'm begging for your help. Can you see if he's wired money into or out of the bank during the last four months?"

"What will you do to him if you find him?"

"Murder the son of a bitch." As soon as the words left his mouth, he regretted them.

She nodded but he could see her stiffen. He wondered if she was shocked. But she bent toward him and uncrossed her legs. In seconds, she seemed to relax and soften, and he suspected she was aroused. Her head cocked to the side as she examined him. She moistened her lips, dragging the lower across the upper one. "If I do this, can I ask a favor in return?"

He grinned. "Anything," he lied. Jon doubted she'd succeed. He also worried what she'd ask him to do. He didn't want to spend more time than necessary in Karachi. He worried about his exposure here to the same government officials she feared. "Let's order the next course and you can tell me what you want from me in return."

The waiter arrived with gulab jamun, a sweet dessert. Over a glass of wine, she told him about her family. "My brother, Ravi, got a student visa to go to the University of Ohio. He studied electronic engineering but couldn't find a job. They hire Americans first. After six months he was homeless and started dealing drugs and guns to make money to survive. He's been on the run since his visa expired three years ago. He's bitter about how he's been treated."

Jon nodded. "I can't say I blame him. Bloody rough. We have the same problem all over Europe and Great Britain as well. He's the one you were visiting?"

She nodded. "I think he'd have been better off if he'd returned to Karachi after earning his degree. But by that time, he was becoming an evil man."

"Why did you visit him?"

Her eyes drifted away from him to the food. "He hadn't written for many months. No emails. I was concerned. The bank owed me three weeks of holiday. I used all of them." Tears formed in the corners of her eyes. "He's the last of my family. He needs me. I want to move to Cleveland. Get me a visa. I don't care which country. When I leave here I'm never returning. I'll fly to Toronto and find a way to get inside the border of the United States. From there I'll find my way to Cleveland."

Jon's brows arched. "A visa? That's the favor you want from me in return for the information I asked for?"

"Yes. Only that. Can you? Will you?"

What about his deal with Crane? But, if he'd been a student, he'd have no power to arrange it. "My uncle works in the government of Great Britain. I'm sure he has the connections to arrange it."

An hour later, they were standing at the doorway to her apartment. After she unlocked her door, he reached for her hand, to shake on the deal. But she pulled him close and then within the apartment. She used her foot to close the door. He was surprised when she kissed him.

He tried to draw away but she gripped his shoulders. She stared into his eyes. "More."

Jon's jaw dropped in surprise. She'd seemed so cold. He wondered if she felt nothing and wanted sex for its own sake. "But it's against your religion, isn't it? And it's our first date. Surely—"

"More." Her voice was conversational yet insistent. And she pulled his face to hers.

The kiss was sweet and hard, but the danger of her offer and the complications ran hard against his arousal. And Lisa's voice cursed through the back of his head. He gulped. "Are you sure? Isn't this against Islamic law?"

She nodded and unbuttoned his shirt. "I'm as Western as you. Too long in your world. As long as no one ever finds out. If they do and I manage to escape, I'll find you and kill you." And, in one quick move, her sari flew off her shoulders. Confused, he ran a new set of equations. The math offered no resolution, and he fought against panic.

His eyes snapped to her body. She wore no bra and was

gorgeous. *Oh God. What can I do to escape?* But before he could react, she'd unbuckled his belt and his pants were dropping to the floor. She pulled off the rest of his clothing. Exposed.

Frozen on the spot where he stood.

She walked him out of his clothing, towing him further into the apartment. Her bed was in the corner of the single room. She pushed him down and knelt between his legs, her hand fondling his erection. Her lips gripped it and he felt her teeth nuzzle against him. Losing control, he reached for her breasts, thumbs rubbing the stems of her nipples. Before he realized it, she was atop him, and he was inside her.

All the while, as she moaned with pleasure, Lisa's voice screamed inside his head. For every instant his flesh responded to her heat and ecstasy, his dead fiancée's sadness and jealousy draped over him in a corresponding wave. All he could do to stop it was to ejaculate. But, so distracted, it took him forever.

Their deal was simple. In two days he had a thumb-drive containing the records he sought, and she had a promise that he'd get her a passport and a visa within two weeks, to any country in Europe or Canada or the United States. If he needed additional data on the transactions, he would contact her. He was sure Crane could accommodate the passport request in exchange for the intel. If she turned him over to the authorities, it would implicate her as well. And while the Pakistani secret police would kill him, the tortures they could inflict on her were unimaginable. No, he was safe with her.

He ticketed himself on British Air and met with her one last time. His intention was a pleasant evening where he and his asset could bond.

She said very little over dinner. At her door, she pulled

him inside and shut it behind him with her foot. "I'm not letting you go without a little payment to seal our deal."

He sighed. "Yeah. Well, I thought we'd be better off with a business arrangement, not—"

She pulled his necktie to draw him close. "Nonsense. Not negotiable." She unbuttoned his white oxford's top button, then the next. And kept on.

Jon nodded and pulled her sari off, baring her breasts. Lisa's voice howled inside his head

Sandia unbuckled his belt and his pants dropped to the floor. "Come to my bed."

Jon followed her meekly. He'd no choice if he wanted to keep her as an asset.

Before he could think of another argument, she was atop him, riding him, her voice growling as she climaxed. And she didn't stop, just kept going again and again as if he wasn't even there.

After a night where he'd pleased Sandhia more times than he'd thought possible, Jon slept for most of the ride to JFK.

By now his growing beard was obvious. He looked like his alter ego, Salim al-Muhammed. Jon drifted with the humming of jet engines and rubber-band jet lag.

The female flight attendant wore a sari similar to the one Sandhia had worn the night she'd first bedded him. She touched his shoulder and asked him a question, but he didn't understand the language. When he opened his mouth to ask her to speak English, his words came out in Hebrew. She frowned and then unwrapped the top of her sari, exposing her breasts. He tried to move further into his seat, but she was on him, straddling him in the seat, ripping off his clothing. Her face reshaped itself into Lisa's. Then they were both naked, her crotch grinding against his penis, and then she held a knife to his throat. "*Never do that with anyone else. Ever! Understand?*"

He nodded. The skin and muscle dropped off her corpse leaving her skeleton gripping his shoulders.

He gasped, waking. The flight attendant walked by, offering him water. He nodded and took a cup.

Looking out the window, the lights of city buildings blinked far away in the darkness.

The plane touched down. Jon stretched. If all went according to plan, he was close to completing his mission for MI-6. If all went according to plan, he might have the leverage to reinsert himself into the Mossad.

But, his mind filled with a sudden, disturbing thought: as his trainers had told him in Tel Aviv, *no battle plan survives first contact with the enemy.*

CHAPTER 16

William Wing's apartment,
Ascot Heights, Block A, 21 Lok Lam Road,
New Territories, Hong Kong
August 28, 8:22 a.m.

The short young man wore glasses so thick his eyes looked like they floated in tiny fishbowls. The screen, inches from his face, displayed fields requesting user identification and a password. His fingers hovered above the Enter key. He licked his lips, trying to decide. Seconds passed but then he smiled and slammed the key.

The computer echoed back "ID Approved." He grinned. "CryptoMonger is the best!" The screen shifted. William Wing entered a string of numbers before pressing the Enter key once more. He printed the screen, showing his SWIFT MT-100 transfer of $26,000 from his client's bank account to another account. His. Well, one he owned but under another name. Untraceable. His client had reneged on the fee, so Wing took the cash anyway.

He logged out and placed his purloined copy of the 200-page SWIFT Procedure Manual back on the tiny bookshelf in the guest bedroom of the apartment that served as his Hong Kong office. The codes in the manual listed the electronic addresses and specifications for the automatic handshake codes of over 3,000 banks that were members of the Society

147

for Worldwide Interbank Financial Telecommunication, as well as details of each field in every possible transaction type.

William had searched for months for someone inside a major bank who'd sell him a copy. Howard Shin, an AVP in the Bank of Shanghai, hadn't trusted William, thinking he might be a spy for the bank itself, but relented when William offered the low-level, money-transfer bank officer over $25,000 to make him an unauthorized copy.

He switched Internet pages and watched the balance of his bank account swell with the inclusion of his hacked fee. In ten minutes more, he'd wiped all traces of his hack from both the sending and receiving banks' computers.

Grinning, he decided to celebrate by going out for breakfast at a dim sum palace near Hong Kong's harbor. He was hungry for char siu bau, a sweet, steamed pork pastry. William considered the short list of restaurants, trying to decide which made the best one. He programmed the security cameras in his apartment to surveil while he was gone. Although not in the harbor, Yung Kee specialized in roast goose with delectable crisp skin, but the place was also well known for dim sum. Maybe. Xiao Nan Guo had a serious following, particularly for dim sum, such as its magnificent flavored soup dumplings and fatty "Lion's Head" meatballs. The Dim Sum Bar was a gourmet delight. His mouth watered as he made his decision. The thought of goose made him smile. So, he'd be heading toward central Hong Kong, and on to Fook Lam Moon in Wan Chai, a ferry and a bus ride away.

But as he reached for the keys to his apartment, his cell phone buzzed. Wing pulled it from his pocket and examined the screen for the caller's name. He hit the button to reject the call, wondering what his father wanted.

His father was the director of internal security for China's CSIS. His cover title was senior director at the Ministry of Foreign Affairs. Six years ago the old man had disowned William and expelled him from their house in

Beijing for his thefts as a hacker. He hadn't tried to call or contact William until last week. Now the tally was six vain attempts.

William opened the apartment door and retrieved the newspaper, its headline about the government in Beijing and his father's role in some crisis taking place on the border with Russia. He tossed it into the kitchen trash.

He exited, locked the door, and walked toward the elevator. The hallway aromas of a mélange of Asian cooking increased his hunger. Sesame seed oil, ginger, roasted Tai Chen peppers. And boiling soy sauce. He licked his lips.

And as the elevator doors closed, the cell buzzed once more. He plucked it back out and examined its screen. "Damn." Giving up, he flipped it open. "Yes, father?"

The voice he heard was oh so familiar, and, as it always had been, soft without inflection. "Son, you are still impossible. But, I need you to return home, as soon as you can."

Wing shouted. "Why should I? And why now?"

"There are certain things happening. I cannot handle them without your special talents. And I cannot discuss them on an unencrypted line."

William frowned. "Why should I help the most esteemed senior director of the Ministry of Foreign Affairs? What can be so serious for you to feel obliged to contact a criminal like me? And even if I wanted to, what help could your miserable son provide?"

"Please. Stop. It is a different world now. I now acknowledge your usefulness. Our government has agreed that your skills will be prized. Just come. Son, I need you."

He claims me now? This is so much bullshit. "So, now that I might be useful to your masters, I can return? After so many years of being unworthy in your eyes?"

But William felt surprise as he considered his father's request. There was one thing he did want. He could regain face with his father by helping the man save face with his own masters. "So when you want me, you call. Where were you when I needed you? For twelve years I heard nothing!"

"Yes. I felt you had done evil things. But things have changed. I need you now."

He sighed as he came to a decision. "Okay, father, I will help you. I'll be there as soon as I can." There was a bitter tone in his voice as he terminated the call. He pressed the button for the elevator to return to the third floor so he could pack a suitcase.

At Beijing Capital International Airport, Wing walked from the aircraft wearing a blue business suit, silk tie, and prescription sunglasses with fishbowl lenses. He carried a notebook computer in a black leather briefcase that also held several eBooks on international banking, foreign exchange, and trade finance. These would supplement his career talents in computer hacking, and constituted the skill base he assumed his father needed.

He concentrated on keeping all emotion off his face, but flinched at the noises around him one second, and felt disgust at the familiarity of the city of his birth the next second.

As he took the escalator to the baggage claim, someone behind him tapped his shoulder. He stopped short, shock holding him still as he swiveled to face the interloper.

It was his father's driver, a man in his late seventies, wearing the uniform of a captain in the Chinese army. He remembered the man from when he was a child. The driver had worked for his family for over thirty years. He seemed to find William as disgusting as William found this country. "Your father awaits. I'll have staff pick up your luggage. Please follow." With that, the driver led him out through the front of the airport where a limousine waited curbside.

As he took a seat in the back, Wing heard the trunk open and close. The ancient driver sped from the curb. William coughed. The pollution that he hadn't noticed when he was young had intensified to the point of making him choke. He pulled a handkerchief from his suit pocket and hawked into it. William watched the rural countryside flash by under a brownish sky. He saw peasants using ancient farming tools. "Captain Sung, can you tell me why I have been summoned?"

The driver remained silent. William shrugged. *In China, nothing ever changes.*

The car approached the home office of Xian Wing, Senior Director of State Security, at the north side of Fourth Ring Road near Jingping Road. The driver flashed an ID card and the compound's outer gate swung open.

They entered through the inner gate whose high wall was topped with barbed wire and guarded by armed soldiers. The limo pulled to a stop adjacent to the front door of his father's home, a twenty-eight room mansion.

The driver opened the door and William marched up a few stairs to the entryway. A soldier opened the front door for him, calling into a two-way as William passed. William's shirt stuck to his back, but inside, it was cool.

He knew where to find his father. William barged through the bamboo library doors.

A soldier unshouldered his weapon but, as William's father rose, smiling, the soldier stepped back and resumed his position at ease. His father's hair was thinning and white. His posture was stooped. "My wayward son, home at last."

William frowned. "Why am I here, father?"

His father motioned to the others in the room. "Leave. Now." As the door closed, the old man ran his fingers through his hair, sinking back into the seat behind the desk. William could imagine the thoughts cycling through his father's head. The words came as if he were uncertain of how much to tell his son. "We have a possible crisis. I need a professional to investigate. Someone is drawing our country into a needless war with our Russian neighbors. Find out who it is."

William felt the air gush from his lungs. He fell into the seat behind him. Both countries were well-stocked with nuclear weapons. And, Hong Kong was so close to the mainland. If this was true, it could be as catastrophic for him as for a billion others. "Find out who?"

Xiang Wing frowned, nodding. "I wish to use your criminal skills to hack into the Russian government's computers. And you must do it without being detected."

William doubted he or anyone he knew could do this without leaving traces. Both countries had extensive anti-cybercrime programs. He knew he could easily hack into the Pentagon of the United States without leaving any traces, but he knew from firsthand experience that Russia was the most difficult hack of all.

If he claimed he could be successful, that would be a lie. But even though his father still thought of him as a thief, here was his best chance to win back his father's respect. He sat, trapped within the web of deceit his mind was spinning. "A most difficult task. But I'm a master at this. If I can't, no one else can. You'll have to get me resources. Hardware and people."

The old man rose from his seat and shuffled toward his son. "It can be done? I can offer you a team of the 6000s, our best hackers." His father nodded. "Thank you, son."

William moved into the largest unoccupied room of the mansion. Soldiers carried furniture inside, including a bed, a teak desk, and several solid-teak bookcases. He admired the quality of life senior government officials could demand. The bed was a Sleep Number 5000, an upscale bed sold in the

United States. He wondered if it were genuine or a knock off. Either way, it was made in China, of course.

When the room was set up to his specifications, he exited and went to the smaller of the two libraries to interview his hacker team. He doubted they could be half as good at their work as he was.

He'd need to figure out how to please his father. If he succeeded, maybe he could return now, and the scorn and retribution his computer hacking had brought on his father would be forgotten. *I've wandered long enough.*

When he entered the room, the others stood up, at attention. Each wore an army uniform. William scanned their stiff resolve. "Who's in charge?"

A thin young man with sallow skin faced him. "I'm Lieutenant Chan."

Wing frowned. "What's your experience in hacking?"

The officer's face remained rigid. "I have a PhD in computer science from Stanford University. I pay our covert agents in seventy countries with bank transactions from nonexistent accounts that I create and wipe out after the funds are delivered. I have stolen commercial software from Microsoft's computers in Redmond before they are released for DVD production. I—"

Wing waved his hands. "Yeah. Okay. What about the others?"

Chan nodded. "I trained them. My fellow students at the University of Shanghai." He stood rigid, waiting.

Wing paced the room. He expected they'd be useless. He was sure no one outside the hacker community had the capabilities to supplement him. People like the Butterfly.

But he'd give them a chance before dismissing them. "Okay. I need a spec sheet for current version of the FSB's security system," he demanded, referring to the Russian security organization that had succeeded the old KGB. "And the details of the personnel of their cybercrime unit. Their training, and copies of their software tools. Everything. You can find what I want on one of their mainframes in Moscow center. Get it for me."

Chan smiled. He turned and gave orders to the other three soldiers.

William shook his head. He'd end up doing everything himself. He turned away and muttered, "Bullshit."

CHAPTER 17

IRT Subway Stop, 179th Street, the Bronx
August 28, 10:47 a.m.

A bank of pay phones stood on the Grand Concourse near the apartment, just across the street from the subway entrance. Only one of the phones worked. Jon wore his shabbiest clothing. He'd made his hair greasy and wild. Looking like a homeless person, he called Crane. "It's O'Hara. I have what you wanted. I'll need a favor from you in return."

He heard voices in the background. The voice of Crane sounded distant. "I'm busy now. What do you need?"

Jon rushed the words. "A UK visa and passport in the name of 'Sandhia Sorab.' She got us the intel and it's her payment."

"We don't pay informers without a prior agreement."

Jon had expected this. "Your agreement is with me. I can sell the information if you aren't interested. Will you provide the docs?"

"Okay, but only if the intelligence is what we need. We'll examine the contents and then decide."

Jon considered this complication. "Okay. There's a tree with a slot carved out of its trunk in Bryant Park, near the northwest corner of the library. Call me when the docs are ready and I'll make a dead drop in the slick."

"Excellent. I'll have her docs by the end of today. I'll send someone to pick up the drop. They'll arrive at noon, so make your drop about 11:45. If the intel is solid, I'll have them leave the docs in your slick the same time tomorrow, but only if the intel is what we need." Crane's voice sounded distracted. Jon wondered why as he walked from the IRT station, on his way to the apartment. He could think of no answer.

Having to wait for the intel to be vetted before getting her docs gave him an uneasy feeling. Crane didn't trust him. And Jon didn't trust Crane.

He took the subway to Bryant Park and walked past the slick, scanning the area to his south. No one seemed out of place. So far, so good. Another pass in the opposite direction ten minutes later, and nothing suspicious. He waited in the lobby of one of the glass and concrete towers—the Grace—for ten minutes, scanning all the traffic. When he was sure it was safe, he dropped the intel at the slick as instructed.

Almost time for phase two. Running from the Mossad was a headache he needed to end. Maybe, the intel could give him leverage to have Mother call off the *kidons* hunting him. After lunch, he called Mother from the bank of pay phones. "It's your long-lost son. I have something you'd bloody well kill for. Call the cell phone you sent with me when I followed Houmaz to New York. We'll set up a blind date, and no *kidons* this time or you'll get nothing from me."

William's eyes were downcast. "So, you see, father, there is nothing in the Russian computers ordering their soldiers to violate our borders. But, there are records of reports of our own soldiers crossing theirs. And, also recommendations regarding what they should do in response. If we continue these claimed violations, their intentions are violent in the extreme." He handed a thumb-drive to his father. "It's confusing."

The old man scratched his head, rose from his desk and paced the room. "Why?"

"I haven't any idea. My guess is a third party. Some kind of false flag operation. Although I couldn't identify the party provoking both them and us, whoever it is, well, they're very competent." William faced his father. "But that's just a guess. I'll keep looking, and I'll stay in touch with the men you've assigned me. Please, father, I'm of no further use here. I want to go home. When I've solved the mystery, I'll return here, to you." The unsaid desire for his father to request he remain here came to naught.

His father's face sagged and he turned away. "I understand. I'll arrange a jet back to Hong Kong. But before you leave, say goodbye to your mother."

As he rode in the back seat of the limo, all William could think of was, *I've failed my father. I'm still an outcast.* His mind drifted over his failure like a seagull hunting aimlessly for lunch as it glided over the water. *Who is provoking the border skirmishes? And why?*

This summer day in Manhattan was ideal for a walk. Jon strolled along wearing a collared shirt, a tie, and dark suit. He carried an umbrella, swinging it more to impose his sense of being the essential Brit than to protect him from the rain that had stopped long before the lunch hour. His beard was trimmed close and he knew he could pass for a Wall Street executive out for his lunch hour. Entering the pub on Washington Street just north of Wall Street, he sought a dark booth in the back. The pub had survived 9/11 and now thrived as a place where bankers and brokers lunched when they weren't scamming their customers.

The man waiting for him looked like an older version of

himself. Both were dressed in well-tailored conservative clothing. But Sommers wore a necktie, and where his facial hair was brown, his companion's was white, matching that on the top of his head.

The older man didn't extend his hand. In English with a slight Israeli accent, Yigdal Ben-Levy whispered, "Why have you requested this meeting? We still have a burn notice out on you. Not to mention a terminate-with-prejudice order."

Sommers examined his hands as if they held the secret he was here to offer. "Yeah. Well, I hope to change all that. Look, I've no desire to continue being your target. So, I've got a tidbit for you. Bank of Trade. I recruited someone within their operations center in Karachi." He beckoned the waiter. "What can I get you?"

Ben-Levy waved his hand. "Whatever you're drinking."

Sommers nodded. His formulas had forecasted Ben-Levy would be compliant. As the waiter approached, Jon held up two fingers. "Guinness, please, one cold and one at room temp." As the waiter turned away, Sommers pulled a thumb-drive from his pocket. "Courtesy of their money-transfer department." He held up the thumb-drive where Mother could see it, but he didn't offer it.

The waiter brought two bottles with glasses overturned, and uncapped them. Both men waved him off and poured their own brews. Sommers tasted his lukewarm brew with relish. "The Yanks don't understand beer. It should always be drunk at room temperature."

Ben-Levy's expression remained distant. "Are the results in the thumb-drive?"

Sommers nodded. "Some are here, but there may be more to come."

Mother took another sip. "When will you know the quality of the product?"

"I'm having it vetted right now. I should receive a report

in the next day or so. If needed, I'll request more intel from my asset. If so, it might take a week or more."

Mother reached for the drive but Jon pulled his hand back. "I'll give you this tomorrow. We'll play by my rules. You don't get this until I have some assurances. Call off your killers."

Ben-Levy nodded, frowning. "I know you don't trust me. I did what I felt best. Your death would have served as a warning to our *kidons*." He clenched his lips tight. "I'll call off the hit team."

Jon let out a breath. "Let me know when it's official. After your call, I'll do a dead drop for you. A real drop, not the multiplayer online computer game crap the Muslim Brotherhood is using now. Bryant Park, the northeast tree has a carved slot probably left over from the Cold War, maybe used by the Russians. Have Shula do the pick-up from the slick. I know her. I trust her."

"After her team tried to terminate you?" His smile was grim.

"Send her alone."

Ben-Levy nodded. He took another sip of beer, rose, and left the booth.

Jon turned away from the door as it opened to keep the sudden daylight from blinding him. He called the waiter. "Steak and kidney pie. And another room temp Guinness."

So far, the math underlying his plan was working.

Jon stood inside the lobby of the W. R. Grace Building on the north side of 42nd Street across from Bryant Park. He wore a zippered NYU hoodie with a cap under its hood and sunglasses over his eyes. Eating a candy bar from the newsstand, he watched Shula Ries approach the tree and walk past going north, swinging her head east-west. He scanned for another *kidon* and saw no one suspicious. Twenty minutes later she repeated the pass going west from the library, this time scanning north-south. Still no one nearby was following her, and no one standing still to rouse his fears. He waited for the third pass. As she approached, he left the lobby, crossed the street and followed behind. He could feel his pulse quicken in anticipation. When she reached into the slick for the thumb-drive, he placed his left hand in his pants pocket with his finger pointing through the pants to mimic a gun. "How good to see you again, Ms. Ries."

Shula's hands rose in a martial arts move. Jon slipped back a few steps. Her expression was priceless: tanned face gone white as she noticed the pointy object in his pocket. "Jon! A pleasure for me as well." Her right hand shifted toward her shoulder and he saw her fingers twitch.

"Wouldn't do that. Listen, I've no intention of hurting you. Just wanted to say, I understand why you tried to kill me. Mother calls the shots. Oh, such a bad pun. Well, consider this: We might work together again if circumstances require. Tell Mother the gift was free this time, per our deal. Next time, cash up front. Got it?"

She frowned, her hand dropping back to her waist. The other hand now held the thumb-drive.

He turned and vanished into the crowd. Phase two of the plan was complete.

Jon needed to change his appearance, so his face would match his passport. On his way from the tanning salon, the throw-away cell Crane had given Sommers beeped. "Yes?"

"It's Crane. The intel you delivered is a good down payment, but it's missing crucial details we absolutely require. Get a pen and paper."

Sommers flipped on the Record Call app of his cell phone. No paper necessary. "Yes?"

"We need transaction details. The files you gave us

contain only bank SWIFT numbers. My people say the transactions look suspicious, possibly even dangerous, but we can't tell what he bought or exactly which account he sent the money to—only the sending bank's codes. We need details for the sending party and receiving party, and the transaction details on the actual outgoing money transfer. They're probably in the Bank of Trade's accounting computer, but it's likely the machine has no telecommunications transmission port. If so, then someone will need to be inside the bank to complete the job. Tell your asset to grab them. We'll hold her passport and visa until you're ready to deliver." The line went dead.

Jon grimaced and pounded his fist against the nearest building's wall. "Bloody twit!" And threw his arms into the air. "Ah, shit." His entire plan had unraveled. What could he do now?

The Mossad would be back on his trail. He thought, trying to construct a formula that would save him from death. There was a missing variable. He needed someone's help, someone with access to the bank's accounting records.

The obvious person was sweet Sandhia. But, she wasn't in accounting. Might it still work? Nothing to lose. He'd try her first.

Sandhia Sorab swept the hair from her face and stared at the notebook computer on the desk of her Karachi apartment. The smell of curry filled the night but she ignored it in the dry, hot air as she read the email:

Sandhia, dearest,

I need a bit more information regarding our target. It appears there are no transaction details for the in-coming and outgoing transfers. Could you kindly please research and send me the additional details. I have the gift ready to send to you, right after I receive what I require.

Yours,
Michael O'Hara

She felt panic. She'd delivered what she'd promised. And now he wanted more. He'd promised to deliver the passport and visa she needed. His email implied the threat he might not, unless she helped him again. Worse, she thought, emails can be traced. She knew the Pakistani government had a cybercrimes division doing this, and now she felt unsafe. Her fear morphed into frustration, and then transformed to rage. She pounded out a reply:

> To help you, I requested a transfer to the station where I hoped to see the intel you want. I told you I found no details in the incoming and outgoing transactions.
> Therefore, the transactions you seek must be "on us" and belong to accounts where the source and destination of funds are both within my bank. No details would reach the stations. Ever. If this assumption proves true, the incoming and outgoing transactions are for very large amounts originating in hand-carried cash deposits and withdrawals at a teller window.
> I cannot ask for reassignment to the accounting department where the records of the "on us" are kept. Please send me what we agreed to. And, after you send it, I expect never to hear from you.

She prayed her message was oblique enough not to be obvious to the Pakistani secret police. She hit the Send button and then erased everything on the notebook relating to her work for O'Hara. Now, even receiving the passport and visa might be dangerous. But she needed them anyway, and right now, since the government might soon be looking for her.

Although she didn't follow Islam when it was inconvenient, she did believe in Allah. Her behavior with Jon was nothing unusual for her. What did matter was family. She longed to see her brother Ravi, even though he'd carried an undeniable rage within him since their parents' death. If he was planning what she suspected, he might not be alive much longer.

Reading the email, Jon's face tensed into a frown. This plan had also failed. He sat back down at the tiny table in his apartment and put his hands below his chin. He thought, *I need another plan, a better one.* He felt numb.

Hours passed while he sat on the couch and pondered things he might try. Most were more dangerous than performing an assassination, such as gaining employment at the Bank of Trade and infiltrating the accounting department so he could steal the data himself. Others had low probabilities of success, such as pleading with Crane to offer a covert to do the dirty work. A covert specializing in pure espionage, with a knowledge of banking? Unlikely. Worse, he didn't even have the skills of a pure spy. The apartment got dark. He gazed at his wristwatch. 7:25 p.m. He was hungry. Maybe food would fix his head.

He walked the staircase out through the lobby. As he exited onto 179th Street, he made a decision. The one tactic left to him had a low-probability outcome. He needed to have someone present within the Bank of Trade's accounting department, doing the dirty work. Someone besides the lovely Ms. Sorab. And, he'd no interest in exposing himself. No, no bloody chance of that. He'd find a hacker and see if they could find a way.

He entered the Irish pub on 173rd Street and sat down at the bar. He shouted to the bartender, "Six bottles of unrefrigerated Guinness."

The bartender approached him partway, staying a comfortable distance from Jon. "You sure?" Jon nodded. The bartender shook his head. "Forty-two dollars."

Jon raised his head. "Yeah." He tapped the space in front of him with the debit card for Michael O'Hara. "Here." He drummed his fingers against the Formica bar top.

The bartender disappeared through a doorway for a few seconds and returned carrying a carton. He whispered "Your funeral," uncapping the first of the six.

Jon sipped the amber liquid. If he didn't come up with something soon, it would be his funeral.

He remembered the techno-weenie prince from the University of London. Plucking his cell phone from his pocket, he called London's telephone information and asked, "Phillip Watson. Either London or very close by." The operator gave him a number, and he entered it into the cell phone.

It rang several times. Must be about 6:30 a.m. there. A familiar male voice answered, "Yes? Bloody early, isn't it? I'm not due in until noon today."

"Phil, it's Jon Sommers. Sorry for the sunrise call, but I wanted to make sure I got you and not your voicemail."

"Jon? From University of London? Long time since we last saw each other. You in London? We could meet for a drink."

"Uh, no, sorry. I'm across the pond, in Manhattan. Listen, I need to ask you a question. Can you spare me just a few minutes right now?"

Phil took some time before answering. "Sorry, didn't want to wake Jenn. Okay, what's the matter?"

Jon nodded to himself. "How'd you hack the Israeli government's computers? I'm in need of a hacker."

"Huh? No, Jon, I couldn't make it through their firewall. I never got further than cracking the backdoor with a ubiquitous user ID and password. There was another series of codes based on location and something else. I couldn't ever figure it out."

Jon sat straight up, wondering if what he thought was indeed true. No, couldn't be. But he had to ask. "Phil, you gave me an envelope. It contained—"

"Don't tell me. I don't want to know." Phil's voice verged on panic.

Jon took a deep breath. "Okay. Just tell me, where'd the information come from?"

"I dunno. The envelope just appeared in my apartment mailbox, with a sticky pasted to it. The note said, "Please give this envelope to Jon Sommers. And, that's what I did."

So, it was Mother after all. One of his *sayanim*. Jon shook his head. He'd been set up. "Ah, so that ends the mystery. Thanks, so very much. Well, as long as I've gotten you up so early, tell me, how are you and Jenn doing?"

"We're planning the wedding. Probably late autumn. Say, will you be in London then? I'd like it if you could attend."

Jon smiled. "But of course I'll come."

"Great. I'll send you an invitation. Got an address?"

Jon thought for a while. Where did he live? What address would work? "Send it to me, care of 34 King Saul Boulevard, Tel Aviv." This was where the Mossad had been located until their new building had been completed in Herzliyya. They still maintained a postal address there.

"Sure." There was a long silence. "You're working for them, aren't you?"

"Maybe. Just send it there, and I'll get it."

"Okay. Lemme go back to bed now. Looking forward to our next meeting, Jon." Phil terminated the call.

Jon tried to focus on his problem. But the thought of Mother's having set him up to recruit him kept bothering him.

He sipped a bottle of the beer to its end. Then another. And another.

As the hours passed, another plan began to hatch in his head.

For over two hours, he continued mulling the burgeoning plan. Yes, it might work. And maybe he could keep himself from being exposed. He just needed someone with the right skills. Could he find someone brave enough or stupid enough to try his plan? There were a few *sayanim* Mossad used as hackers, cash only, work for hire. Non-official covers, NOCs, like himself.

There was one hacker in particular whom Mother had mentioned to him before sending him out on his last mission. He tried to remember the man's name. Wong? Wang? No. It was Wing. William Wing. He concentrated on what Ben-Levy had told the class about the hacker. Jon had always been better with numbers and addresses than people's names. And then he remembered the man's phone number and email address. He hoped Wing hadn't changed either.

He smiled and left the remains of the last bottle's contents on the bar as he walked out. Maybe there was some way to postpone Ben-Levy's raging disappointment at his failure, and the hit team that would follow. Wing might be his last resort.

CHAPTER 18

Ascot Heights, Block A,
21 Lok Lam Road,
New Territories, Hong Kong
August 30, 4:16 p.m.

William Wing sat in the tiny kitchen overlooking Hong Kong's harbor. As he admired the view of boats outside, his cell phone chirped with an incoming email. He set down his char siu bau and pulled the phone from the leather case strapped to his belt. When he examined the screen, he frowned. William punched the phone number in the email into his cell. "Yes?"

"Ah, Mr. Wing. Is this a good time? I need a few minutes."

Wing frowned. "For what? Who are you?"

"I'm an independent, a stringer for Mossad. Michael O'Hara. Believe you've done quite a bit of work for us in the past. We're willing to pay, of course. Handsomely."

William's mouth curled as if he'd eaten something bitter. He thought of hanging up. But fear froze him. Mossad. It had more than paid his bills. The work he'd done for them was challenging, leaving him with a feeling he'd helped make the world safer. But, he always felt at risk helping them. He tried to say something, felt his lips move in silence. His hands shook with the feeling of exposure in an icy wind. This was far past his personal point of comfort. The sound of the man's voice made him feel this spy wanted him for something dangerous.

"William? You there?"

He shook himself out of his fear. "Uh, I, uh—"

"God's sake. I need help. Please say you'll at least hear me out."

Wing nodded to himself. "All right." He remembered cell phones were easy to trace and bug. For them to contact him this way, it must be important. And, he had a few days free. Whoever this man was, his caller would have to travel. Wing said, "Not over the phone. Face-to-face. Fly to Hong Kong and contact me from the airport."

After several seconds of silence, the caller spoke. "Why can't we do this some other way?"

"I won't do business with an intelligence officer I haven't met. It must be face-to-face. If you can't come, I'm not your guy. Remember to bring your creds. I've got to see them."

Two days later, Jon had waited in line to debark American Airlines Flight AA6124. Takeoff was 8:05 p.m. from JFK, and now, two hours after dawn, the flight touched down. With no checked luggage, he made his way through customs, on his way out of Chek Lap Kok International Airport.

He was unsure how to convince Wing. There might be risk in working with the hacker, given their joint relationships with the Mossad. He knew he was grasping at low-level probabilities. Even worse, the stress of jet lag was dulling his thinking and might easily become a more extreme danger. Time was running out. Soon, either MI-6 or the Mossad, or both might express their disappointment with lethal intentions.

As he approached the taxi line, he pulled out his cell phone and dialed Wing. His call was sent to voicemail. An instant later, his cell buzzed with an incoming text message:

Find Hing Fat Restaurant at 810 Ashley Rd., Tsim Sha Tsui, Kowloon, Hong Kong. It's near lower Nathan Road. If you get lost, call them for directions, but only if you speak Cantonese.

Jon flagged a taxi. He showed the screen to the driver, who nodded and pulled away from the curbside.

An hour later, he walked in and saw a short, pudgy man wearing thick black plastic-rimmed glasses and prominently holding the morning's *Washington Post*. He sat down at the man's table. "Why here?"

Wing pointed to the bowl of soup in front of him. "Try the soup dumplings or any of the Cantonese-style roast meats. Probably worth the trip from the States." He handed a menu to Jon.

Jon wore a hooded black sweatshirt. "William, Mossad needs help. Now. Please."

William's shoulders folded inward. In a voice just above a whisper, he said, "Yeah. Shit. Uh, no way. Last time, even though you paid me well, there was danger. To me! I hate danger." He faced Jon.

Sommers nodded. "Ah. Well, I wasn't about to pay you to go with me to the bloody opera. But, done right, it isn't dangerous."

Wing shook his head. "That's what one of your *kidons* told me last time. Look, when I got home after that disaster, I looked up the meaning of *kidon*. It means bayonet. A fucking weapon. So, why should I trust you this time?"

Jon remembered the history course Ben-Levy taught the recruits. "My mission is critical. Listen, I have a story to tell you. And it's ugly. See, about twenty years ago, Prince Hamid in Arabia saw the obvious. The more orthodox Wahhabis would overthrow the Saud family because of their obvious excesses and abuses of Islamic law, the *Sharia*. And when he approached his peers to urge them to reform, he was rebuffed. Too low in the line of succession for his opinion to be considered, I suspect. So, he did the one thing he could to accomplish his objectives. He funded the creation of the Bank of Trade. He used a bank where he was the plurality investor in common stock—American Bank and Trust—to provide capital and cover. They supplied the personnel and ostensibly invested in the bank's capital structure, selling its stock to individuals and pension funds. But most of the funds American Bank and Trust supplied actually came from his own very deep pockets. To relieve the pressure from the Wahhabi leaders, the prince told them the bank would fund terrorism, including the Muslim Brotherhood and its sister organizations. And that worked, taking the heat off the Saud family. But the prince also dropped much of his own net worth into the bank, hoping the bank would provide a safe haven, just in case things in the kingdom went south."

William looked away. "Yeah, well so what? A history lesson. Big deal. What has this got to do with me?" He picked up his bamboo chopsticks and examined the ends, soy sauce dripping off them.

Sommers was losing the argument. He raised his voice a tad. "This is serious. The bank is a danger to the world. Especially Israel. And if something happens to Israel, Mossad won't be around to make you rich. I need you to get me intel showing me who gets the cash from Hamid's account. Which terrorists are hooked to the prince's teat? Most urgently, a bomb maker named Tariq Houmaz. See, these are internal accounts at the bank. They're not on a computer hooked into any network, so, you can't hack your way in. I need your feet on the ground in their back office."

Wing's brows rose. "I thought you wanted a simple hack,

but what you want is crazy. I'm not built like that. No can do. I don't even speak their language! I speak Russian and German, but not any of theirs."

Sommers nodded, his eyes focused on something within. "Yes. There is that. But, as difficult as the language barrier might be, you're my only hope." Jon realized it hadn't occurred to him that language might be an issue. After all, in less than two months of classes with the Mossad he'd learned Arabic, Hebrew, Urdu, Dari, and Pashtu well enough to survive And, like most Europeans, Jon knew most of the Continental languages from his schooling.

Wing shook his head. "Mr. O'Hara, you're shit out of luck today." He rose from his seat.

Jon stared at the food on the table. This had been a waste of time, and time was his most precious commodity. "You're right, of course. I'll have to find another way. But when I have the files, could you—"

Wing nodded. "Sure. Call me when you've got the intel. I can hack through the files easily enough" He walked out the restaurant's door.

Jon sat at the table, dumbstruck as the waiter delivered a huge bowl of war won ton soup.

This plan had also failed. He'd have the trip back to New York to think about a new one. Crane would soon put him in prison, or worse, Ben-Levy would have him executed.

But, one thing was sure. His list of safer options was at an end. The next step would put him in real danger. He'd no alternatives left.

CHAPTER 19

The Middle Eastern clothing store near Sixth Avenue and 32nd Street provided everything Jon needed. A seedy-looking business suit, a traditional Pakistani hat, and several tribal dress shirts. Once again, he'd withdrawn cash from an ATM and handed the shopkeeper several bills. Cash leaves no footprint.

Across the street he found an electronics boutique and bought several burner phones with prepaid minutes for each of his three identities, and four additional 64-gigabyte thumb-drives. He wasn't sure what he'd need, but over-supplying himself was safer than finding out too late that he had guessed wrong.

Before heading on to his apartment, he stopped at the Stern library and used their computers to craft a résumé for Salim al-Muhammed. The legend for the document had him born in London as Harry Schmidt. His family moved to Pakistan for business when he was a teenager, and he'd arrived in the United States about two years ago on a student visa. He'd never attended college, and, he was an illegal. No responsible bank would hire someone with his creds. But, the Bank of Trade might. He printed out several copies. Then he copied the files from Sandhia's thumb-drive onto two of the spares he'd bought, leaving the other two empty.

While on campus, he called Crane. "I have an identity for Salim al-Muhammed. An illegal, with a tad of work part-time as a bookkeeper. See that your mole in the Bank of Trade calls Salim for an interview, but not for about a week. And there's one more thing I need you to do before I meet with them."

"What, Jon?"

"Get the bloody docs into Sorab's hands as we agreed. Then I'll risk my life." He waited for the spymaster's response for a minute.

"Agreed. So, you'll be infiltrating the bank. I was wondering what you'd do next. Call me when you're ready." Crane terminated their call.

As soon as he returned to the apartment, Jon scanned the yellow pages for a local doctor. A Jewish surgeon.

He asked for an appointment that afternoon. "No, I've no medical insurance. It'll be cash up front. Yes, that's right. I'm marrying a Jew and need to be circumcised before the ceremony."

When he woke in his own bed the next morning, he didn't remember the surgery. But as the anesthesia wore off, his entire groin became a wall of pain. He peeked under the covers to find his bandaged penis black and blue down to its base, the bandage bloody. Jon winced. The sight was even worse than the sensation.

Smarting, he regretted his plan. But, playing an Arab, he needed to be circumcised for the pre-employment physical. His week at Dreitsbank had shown him what an employer would require. But Dreitsbank had turned into a very temporary position. An irony occurred to him: his first real job after college was for a cover assignment.

The painkillers weren't powerful enough. It was two days before he could walk without showing signs of pain. He worried that evidence of the surgery would prompt questions in the minds of his employer. He needed to get his task completed as soon as he could. Every day he was closer to a Mossad hit team or prison in Great Britain.

When he could walk without wincing, he called Crane. "I'm ready now. Have your inside man set up the interview. And make sure you brief me about everything before I set foot in the bank."

The tanning parlor on West 61st Street offered a modicum of privacy. Jon undressed and examined his body. His penis was still red. Thinking about sex with Sandhia, the heartache he'd forced himself to ignore, the rush of pleasure; all led to an erection. The pain from his engorged penis was overwhelming. He closed the lid of the tanning bed and waited for the beep signaling he'd been properly cooked. It was his third visit in two days. He looked like the passport picture of his alter ego, Salim al-Muhammed.

In two more days, Jon's body had tanned to a medium dark brown. Even his circumcised penis was a golden color, except for the long, thin red circumcision scar running along its tip. He gathered a cheap-looking suit and a stained white shirt from his closet and donned them, along with an out-of-fashion necktie and scuffed brown shoes.

Nodding, he smiled into the mirror. His teeth were a perfect white, and there was nothing he could do about it. Except remember not to smile. Not enough time to stain them dark. He tried turning his smile into a near sneer, not exposing his teeth. That worked better. He practiced sneering until he could conjure it without thinking.

His English accent wouldn't be a problem. Many Middle Easterners had been schooled in Great Britain and then emigrated to New York. He'd have to modify his accent so it didn't sound so "Cambridge."

He pulled a cheap attaché case from under his desk and reviewed the résumé of Salim al-Muhammed, his alter ego.

He'd committed it to memory after he received the Bank of Trade's snail mail reply to his résumé for their accounting clerk position. The same day, he also received a blank envelope shoved under his door containing a single sheet of paper with the typed words "Docs delivered to SS today." Was this a lie?

It was time to go. Jon's hands were shaking. He took a deep breath and searched every pocket, and his wallet to ensure the papers he carried identified him as al-Muhammed, not Sommers or O'Hara. Jon donned the Islamic cap and took one last look in the mirror. He was good to go.

After locking the door on his way out, he took the stairs to the lobby of his apartment building. Just a forty-minute subway ride to the Bank of Trade's Park Avenue office for his job interview.

What in the world was he thinking when he thought he could find justice for Lisa, let alone change the world?

The interviewer wore a long-sleeved, ankle-length cotton garment called a *thobe*. Folded across his head was a square cotton scarf called a *ghutra*. Under that was a *tagiyah* joining the *thobe* to the *ghutra*. The *agal*, a thick, doubled, black cord on top of the *ghutra*, held it in place. It was formal Wahhabi garb for a business environment.

The bank officer extended his hand. "Mr. al-Muhammed?"

Sommers smiled and nodded. "Ah, Mr. Sambol. It is indeed an honor." He extended his own hand and they shook.

The other man handed Sommers a business card: "Aziz Sambol, Manager, Personnel and Staffing." Sommers continued standing as the Arab sat behind his desk, until Sambol pointed to a chair across from his desk. "Please."

Sommers sat and waited while Sambol read the résumé Jon had sent him via email several days ago. Two minutes passed before the Arab raised his eyes. "You have no college degree?" he said in Urdu.

Sommers raised a rueful expression. Concentrating, he replied in Urdu. "Allah has not seen fit to grant me the opportunity."

Sambol nodded. "The bank offers college tuition reimbursement."

Sommers cast his gaze down with deference. "If you hire me I will begin a degree program as soon as I can qualify!"

The banker nodded and read a single sheet of paper on his desk. "I have a list of questions. When we are done, you may be offered the chance to meet Zamid al-Ramen, our accounting manager. They need someone to start within a week. Would that fit your plans?"

Sommers took a deep breath to steady himself. "Yes. If chosen, I can start on your choice of dates."

His new plan was working!

His legend had worked just fine with Sambol. As for Zamid al-Ramen, his prospective new boss, Jon thought the man was an idiot. But he was enormous, and it wasn't fat. He shuddered at the thought of what al-Ramen could do to him if he ever found out who Jon really was or what he was there to do.

Al-Ramen stared into Jon's eyes. "Why did you leave Pakistan?" His English was excellent.

"I wanted an education. And I was offered admission to NYU."

"But you never attended?"

Jon shook his head. "After arriving in New York, my father died and left me penniless. He'd told me he had money, but the government took it all."

The accounting manager nodded. "Ah, and that left you angry?"

Jon sneered as he nodded back. "Very."

The Arab folded his hands in front of him. "Many here dislike those now running our country. You will be among friends. You have one more stop today. Dr. Zabor will administer a complete physical exam. We offer health insurance."

And, at that moment, Jon realized he'd be hired. He was closer to obtaining the intel he needed to save his own life.

The four-floor walkup was a struggle tonight, even though Jon was in good shape. Conjuring a new identity for the interviews had exhausted him, and his breathing was heavy as he puffed his way through the apartment door. He wondered how long it would take him to suck out their secrets? Three, maybe four weeks? And then he'd resign and disappear with a copy of the bank's records, no one the wiser.

He took a box of frozen dinner from the ancient refrigerator and popped it into the microwave. But when he hit the button to heat it, nothing happened. A mix of anger and disappointment filled him. It would be a bloody long three weeks, to be sure.

How long until he could snatch and grab the intel?

Jon opened his desk drawer, dropped in the training manuals for his job in the bank's Suspense-Accounting department, and ate a peanut-butter and jelly sandwich. He'd taken a few accounting courses, but learning how a real bank accounting system worked excited him. Even if it was the Bank of Trade, known for the filthy acts of terror it supported.

He still had thirty minutes left in the lunch break, and took a brief walk outside on Park Avenue. The smells of nearby restaurants were savory and delicious, but the man he was pretending to be could not afford to eat at those places.

He thought about the emerging plan he'd developed as

he walked across 49th Street toward Madison Avenue. From what he'd seen, the staff disappeared at 5 p.m. like rabbits running from a hunting dog. But Zamid al-Ramen, ambitious and stolid junior bank officer that he was, would watch them all crowd the elevator. The man was always last to leave. And when Jon waited across the street to see just how late it was before his manager left, he stood there until after 11 p.m. The man had no life. Shit!

When he scouted the floor, Jon had found a closet to hide in. At day's end, he planned to get inside there and wait until after midnight before he let himself out to poach the intel.

He worked at a computer terminal, entering general ledger journal entries, something he hadn't done before. With ten minutes remaining in the workday, he lifted his gaze and saw al-Ramen staring at the clerks to ensure that they maintained their attention on the assignments in front of them. He stared at the screen he was tending just before al-Ramen's gaze shifted his way.

At five in the evening, the clock chimed, and people rose from their desks as they finished the transactions they were processing. Jon walked toward the elevator but, with cover provided by the departing throng to hide him, he took a sharp turn into the tiny employee kitchen.

From there, he headed down another hallway just beyond its entryway. He opened the closet door just wide enough for him to slip within. For a few minutes, he left the door ajar to ensure he hadn't been noticed. Closing it behind him, he stood waiting among office supplies. And took a deep breath.

He'd need to wait until after the cleaning crew came by and they turned off the motion alarms. He set his wrist alarm to 11:59 p.m. when the cleaners would be long gone. Despite his fear, he drifted off to sleep.

When the wrist alarm beeped, he turned it off and

cracked open the door and looked into the supply room. The lights were out. No sounds, but he had no idea when the private security force walked their routes. Edging into the office proper, he was met with the surprise of motion detectors triggering the room lights.

Falling to the floor, he looked around for cameras and found several, but none pointed in his direction.

He pulled himself along the carpet until he reached al-Ramen's desk. The computer box on the desk had a USB port, one he'd seen during his interview with the heavyset Arab. He crawled into the desk well and let his fingers wander, until they found the port. He slipped the USB cable in and tucked the other end into the cell phone Wing had told him to buy. As he switched on the cell, the room lights fell dark. He waited while al-Ramen's computer installed the drivers for his cell. Jon felt incongruously calm.

As he'd hoped, the cell phone's operating system had bypassed the personal computer's security system. He couldn't use the PC's keyboard or screen, but the cell phone found a side-door into the PC.

He scanned the cell's screen, studying its image of the desktop's file structure until he'd found the accounting directories on the PC. He copied them to the 64 gigabyte micro-SD memory card embedded within the cell. He now had copies of every file al-Ramen had.

Then he crawled along the carpet to the stairs leading down to the lobby. Cracking the door, he dragged himself into the stairwell. No lights. He let his eyes adjust and saw there were no cameras. He rose and descended the stairs one floor past the lobby into the parking garage. There was no alarm on the exit door into the garage. He felt like laughing.

Still alone, he walked to the exit door leading onto 47th Street. He saw the security camera as he approached it, and pulled his jacket over his head, leaving his eyes peeking through the tiny gap he made. He faced away from the camera as he moved to the door, pushed it open and hurried away down the street.

He'd done it!

He imagined leaving New York, finding some less threatening place, and working there as a banker. It was what he'd planned to do after Lisa and he were married.

But an hour later, after he'd locked the door to his apartment behind him, he found his exuberance unjustified.

The files wanted passwords, and his own didn't work. He tried other passwords, Mohammad, Muhammad, Allah, Admin, and a litany of more obscure ones often used by systems-security administrators. None worked. He kept trying, making up far-fetched possibilities as panic welled inside him.

It was after 4 a.m. when he gave up, but frustration from his failure to anticipate the need for a working password kept him from falling asleep.

Time was running out.

CHAPTER 20

Sommers's apartment,
177th Street, the Bronx
September 4, 4:13 a.m.

Jon paced the room. The odors of greasy food and garbage from the street outside assaulted him through the open window. He cursed.

There was only one way to fill the missing variable in his plan. Only one choice open to him. One person with the skills to help him. But it was someone who'd rejected him once before.

He pulled a throwaway cell phone from his pants pocket and punched in the number.

A woman answered the phone. Jon had no idea William had a girlfriend. "Get me Wing, please."

"Call heem tomorrow. We are sleepeenk now." She terminated the call.

Jon cursed. So, William had a girlfriend. He wondered if this was the reason the hacker wanted to avoid anything dangerous.

Well, tomorrow would have to bloody well do. He undressed and climbed into the ratty bed for a few scant hours of sleep. He remembered Ben-Levy saying no battle plan survived first contact with the enemy. He kept thinking how convoluted his plans got before they failed. Sleep eluded him until his wrist alarm rang.

At noon, Jon left for lunch. Using the counter-surveillance tradecraft procedures he'd learned from Mossad, he walked several blocks and stopped at a small Lebanese restaurant on Second Avenue and 44th Street. Once more he sat in a secluded booth where he felt safe. He ordered a lamb tagine. He scanned the bar's entrance and the tunnel toward the rest rooms. Soon, he was sure no one had followed him.

He punched the number into his cell. "William, it's O'Hara. I have a problem. Need a password for several files. Can you help? I'll pay. The Mossad will send you the money, whatever you want."

"Really? Yeah. Well, I'll just charge ten thousand in USD this time, as an intro to the services I like to provide. So, look, FedEx a thumb-drive containing the files to me and I'll remove the security. In three days you'll have it back, and if I find anything encrypted, I'll take care of that too."

Jon breathed a sigh. "Can't I download this to you and save us a day?"

"No, you idiot. You do that and every spy agency on the planet will be all over both our asses in a split second. FedEx."

Jon raked his hair. "At least two days round-trip. There's no other way?"

"Nope."

Jon took a deep breath. "Right. Thanks. I'll have it in your capable hands with tomorrow's overnight FedEx delivery." Wing gave him the address of a post office box in the New Territories in Hong Kong.

After he finished lunch, he headed for the East Midtown FedEx. Jon wrote the address of his apartment on a piece of paper and stuffed it into the FedEx box. He shivered with the knowledge that he'd have to continue in his cover assignment until he was sure he had all the intel he needed to end his nightmare.

William opened the envelope and fished a tiny micro-SD chip from the thumb-drive's housing. He hummed a Kitaro tune from the *Silk Road* album as he popped the chip into a reader plugged into his desktop computer. Then he viewed details of its files and copied them all to a work directory on his hard drive. When the copy finished, he pulled the chip out. *Hmmm. One hundred seventeen files. Sixteen types of encryption, nine of which involve some kind of password. The guy who created this is definitely paranoid. No one needs all that security. Except me.*

He ran several programs to raw-read the guts of the files, searching for the passwords encrypted within each. It took several hours before he'd decrypted the files and removed the password protection.

He smiled. "CryptoMonger is the best!" Sealing the envelope, he walked to the local FedEx. He spoke Cantonese. "Please get this out before the last pick up." The man at the counter nodded. William had made it there just before the cutoff.

But when he returned to his apartment, he was curious about the contents of the files he'd copied. Wing didn't even think about how dangerous it might be to know what they contained. Since he'd decrypted them, they were now as much his product as O'Hara's.

At his desk, he opened his copy of the files and read them one-by-one. His eyes bulged at the intel O'Hara had asked him to get. But as he examined their contents with increased focus, he found several pieces of crucial data were missing. Simply not in the files. He called O'Hara and found himself dumped into voice mail. "Michael, the return mail is on its way, but I think you'll be disappointed. If you want, I can send this to someone who can tell you what's not there, and how and where you might be able to find the missing pieces. Call me back ASAP."

When the coffee wagon reached Jon's floor and staff lined up for a break, he went to the restroom and downloaded email into his cell phone.

There was an email from Wing. He also saw Wing's voicemail message, and listened to it. "Damn." There was something else wrong. Jon would have to take a break. He'd need to leave the building and find somewhere safe to talk to the hacker.

But al-Ramen dropped by his desk just before lunch break. "Please rekey these. Errors in the transactions. I marked your corrections. It's urgent, so skip lunch." The Arab handed him a stack of paper.

It was after 3 p.m. when he was able to take his next coffee break. He headed onto Park Avenue and walked east at a brisk pace, looking in windows for the reflection of someone who might be following him. After several blocks, he took a deep breath and entered a bookstore. In the men's room he called Wing.

He heard someone in the stall next to him flush and run the water. Afraid of being overheard, he waited a few seconds until the restroom door opened and closed. "William, it's me. I got your email and your voice message. What's it mean?"

"I scanned the contents off the chip. What you want isn't in those files."

Jon frowned. "How the bloody hell do you know what I'm looking for?" He realized he'd just shouted.

He heard a sigh on the other end of the line. "I'm not stupid. Want help or not?"

Jon thought for a few seconds. "What kind of help?"

"I know a hacker whose expertise is global banking. One of the best on the planet."

He thought a bit more. "Right. Well, what's his name?"

Wing chuckled just loud enough for Jon to hear it. "It's a her. Betsy the Butterfly. She'll call you tonight on your cell. After eleven your time. And, this will cost you."

"How much?"

The silence went on for about twenty seconds. "Thirty thousand USD."

That much would exhaust his cash. "No. Twenty thousand."

Wing waited even longer. "Twenty-five. Agreed?"

Jon barked "Yes," into the phone and terminated the call, wondering, *what kind of name is "Betsy the Butterfly?"* Leaving the bathroom, he walked back to the office, shaking his head.

The short, rail-thin woman with hollow cheeks and a hawk nose was humming "Fame," from the movie, while her chicken-filled Hot Pocket dinner cooked in the microwave. Behind her, a computer's screensaver depicted a psychedelic butterfly's flashing wings. Her cell phone buzzed and she removed it from the leather case strapped to her belt.

Betsy "Butterfly" Brown smiled when she heard Wing's voice. But within seconds, she wondered, *what the fuck is wrong with him now?* She listened to William and tapped her fingers in rhythm to his words, waiting for a chance to break into his nonstop chatter. *Damn*, she thought, *he must be nervous.*

"Anyway, it's a simple thing. Just examine what he has and listen to what he needs. Tell him how to find the missing data. A simple favor." Wing spoke so fast the words all jammed together.

"No, Little Wing! I don't just do favors without knowing what I'm getting myself into. What's so important, anyway?"

"Butterfly, I have a friend who needs help ASAP. I tried, but banking isn't my best area of knowledge. Of course, I know tons, but you know more in this one tiny area. Please. I'll owe you, and you know what that means."

She scowled, listening to him diss her. Then she thought about the last time he'd requested her help. They hadn't ever met face-to-face, and that was the last thing she wanted. "Not interested. You already owe me big."

Wing's voice went up half an octave. "Crap. You want me to beg? Okay, I'm begging."

She smiled once again. "Just tell me, oh holy Crypto-Monger: Who's the best hacker on planet Earth? Eh? Say it, damn you!"

She could hear Wing hesitate. *Oh, this is going to be good.* "Say it or I'm hanging up."

"Shit. Okay, you are."

But his tone wasn't convincing. "Who is?"

"Butterfly is."

Kick him while he'd down. Make him remember this moment forever! "Is what, you idiot?"

"Okay! Butterfly is the best hacker on Earth. There. Now, will you help me?"

She smiled. "I'll be your humble servant this time. Twenty thousand USD. When I'm done, I'll call you back. And you better be sweet on the phone to me, Little Wing. I expect at least a half-hour of your sweet voice guiding me to nirvana."

The microwave's bell chimed. But she wasn't hungry anymore. "Now, for the details. Call me back on a secure Internet phone line. And I'll want to know everything, Little Wing." She terminated the call and walked to the microwave. She picked up the Hot Pocket and carried it to her computer, where she initiated a secure link to his own computer.

Brown listened to him describe his friend's problem and agreed to do his bidding. As she hung up, she remembered the last time they competed in a hacking contest. *Wing won, but only because he cheated. Butterfly is the best!*

She made the next phone call as instructed. When the voice on the other end picked up, she took a deep breath. "I'm the Butterfly. Wing asked me to call you."

"Uh, Betsy? Butterfly?" She heard the upscale British accent. No one she knew. Kinda sexy voice though. Sweeter than Little Wing's.

She nodded to herself. "Yes. Correct. Do you have a throwaway cell?"

"Ah, yes."

"Good. Give me the number."

Three minutes later she connected her notebook computer to his cell. "William told me you're looking for certain bank accounts at the Bank of Trade, and the funds aren't being electronically transferred in or out. Correct?"

"I'm tracking a series of payments. Ah, large amounts but not electronic. Some kind of book entry. So, yes, that seems to be it in a bloody nutshell. I've reviewed the documents William sent back and there's nothing helpful. What can you tell me?"

She almost smiled. Not a total idiot, he had some banking knowledge. "Here's what I think is happening. The cash you want to follow is being deposited at a branch somewhere else. Possibly in New York, but not necessarily. More likely in the Middle East. It doesn't matter where. You can't hack those cash transactions. Probably large amounts."

She took a deep breath. Needed to make this simple enough for an idiot to understand. "And from there the funds are being sent with trade transactions as their cover, using letters of credit, cash collateral, or documentary collections. Got it so far?"

The Brit said, "Yeah. Got it."

She sat at the table in the kitchen. "So, you aren't seeing them because they're maintained in off-balance-sheet accounts, sort of like footnotes to the bank's general ledger. But no details for them in the general ledger. You need to get the transactions from a terminal but not in accounting. In the bank's trade finance area. A separate computer. Understand?"

The voice on the other side of the line was silent for a while. Then: "Uh, yes. So, I'm not working in the right department. Correct?" He didn't wait for her to confirm. "Blast the bloody bankers."

"So sorry, but that's the path you must travel. Would you like me to send you an email explaining this in enough detail to make it easier?"

"Ah, Betsy. I'd appreciate that. Yes." He gave her an untraceable hushmail address.

She smiled. "Consider it done." And with that, she terminated the call. She crafted the email and her forefinger hovered over the send key:

> Read this carefully. Your life may depend on not leaving any trace behind. Do your work after the bank empties, and be watchful of security cams and laser alarms. Know where the stairs are, because if you are seen, or if you set off an alarm, it will take minutes at most for security to get to you. Do NOT use the elevators after the workday ends. There will be security cams in those for sure.
> Study all the rest of this. Don't print it. I know it's dry, but you must know it!
>
> Transfers for terrorism are usually done as internal "on us" transfers between branches of the same bank located in different countries. It's the safest way to deliver money, since, if done right, no

external record of the sender's identity remains within the bank's online systems.

To do this, the vendors (arms dealers and governments) and consumers (terrorists) must have accounts at the same bank as the customer who makes the deposit.

The transfer mechanism will always be a cash collateral delivery, a letter of credit, or a documentary collection. These accounts and their "trade finance transactions" are maintained "off balance sheet." They are recorded on a separate computer system for added protection against government regulators and, of course, hackers. This makes it difficult to trace the money as it flows through the bank from those who fund terrorism to those who buy the tools to do the task.

It works this way: funds transferred for payment of weapons are moved via book entry to the vendor's account without funds ever leaving the bank. Funds moving on and off the trade-finance computer are transferred once a night in a batch run. Non-account-holding terrorists deposit bearer bonds with the bank to fund their transaction. They can also borrow (using their trade-finance collateral) to fund their activities.

Any bank will have its most impenetrable security in this department. The floor may have a door requiring entry of a key-code to maintain security. Find a way to get the code. Once inside the area, look for a single terminal on a raised platform at the back of the area. This will be where the supervisor sits. The terminal is used for approval of any modifications to the transactions, and more important, for load leveling. It is the only terminal with access to all the records.

As for passwords to the files, try "Mohammad," "Allah," and the name of the supervisor who sits there. If there's a picture of the supervisor's family, try their names if you can find them. Also try "admin." If they don't work, copy all the encrypted files anyway, and call Wing. He has software to crack most password protection.

Happy hunting,

Butterfly Brown.

She'd made it as plain as possible. Of course, this was a dark art, something most people in banking wouldn't even know.

Now, as she pressed the Enter key to send out the email, her question was, what would happen to the man she'd spoken to? He'd sounded to her as if he felt defeated.

She realized he was in a dangerous position. Then her mind drifted into an area that was none of her business. She wondered, *what's at stake here? Could some of that danger rub off on me?*

At his first coffee break during the next workday, Sommers crafted a plan. The probability of its working was low, but none of the others he manufactured looked better. He searched the company phone directory Sambol had given him on his first day on the job. Non-credit Financial Services was on the floor beneath his. On his way to lunch an hour later, he stopped the elevator on the fifth floor and took a long, detailed look as the doors opened.

The area Jon sought was behind thick Plexiglas walls. He could see the supervisor for data entry of off-balance-sheet transactions sitting at a Formica desk. Jon saw the supervisor's terminal serving as the control unit for letters of credit and documentary collections—just where Betsy's email had stated it would be, along the back wall and elevated by a platform, one foot above the other desks. He walked toward a bookcase and pretended to be searching for a reference text while he watched the keypad until someone used it to enter the secured area. From his viewpoint, he memorized the key sequence.

How does the Butterfly know this, he wondered. *Are all banks set up the same way? What if she's wrong?* He reentered the lift just as the elevator doors closed. Jon swallowed hard. There was no way to know. He'd have to risk it.

As he worked through the afternoon, he kept running scenarios through his mind. While he worked, two huge men wearing suits walked the hall for over ten minutes. Jon noticed the bulges in their jackets. Shoulder holsters. He'd heard the bank had an enforcement arm, but he'd assumed it was for delinquent borrowers. The idea that security policed the staff was a new twist on the concept.

At a deliberate pace, he eliminated the plans with obvious flaws. Soon, he'd processed all his ideas and found that none was without a large risk of detection. If his assumption about the heavies prowling the floor was correct, detection meant death.

He walked from the bookcase to the supply cabinet on the floor and pulled a fresh pad and pen from it, hoping no one would worry about his true intentions. When he got back on the elevator, his hands were shaking.

He forced his posture to a more confident pose. *Don't fear. You're so close now!* But as he walked past a window, he could see terror reflected in his face. *What else can go wrong?*

When the day ended, he pressed the lift's buttons for the lobby and the fifth floor. The doors opened on five, and before anyone could get on, he got off, walking to the men's room. Best to make it look like an emergency.

Inside, he chose the stall farthest from the entrance, closed its door, and sat inside. Someone entered just behind him. Sommers pretended to retch. The other man asked if he was okay. Jon said, "No. I'm sick. Probably bad samosa from the cafeteria." He pretended to throw up again. "Ugh, I'll be here a while. Don't worry, I'll be okay." The other man let the restroom door close as he exited.

Sommers unlocked his end stall's door and let it drift open just a crack, so no one entering the restroom would think it was occupied. He prayed nobody coming in would select his far-away stall for use.

He closed the toilet seat and knelt on top of it. Anyone who passed by would see no sign that the stall wasn't empty. He remained silent as he waited for everyone to be gone, a matter of at least five hours. All the time he knelt there, his legs cramping, he heard that cursed voice, telling him what he must do. He wanted peace from her demands. *I must be crazy. At least if I die, eternity will be restful.* He sighed.

No, Jon, it won't.

No one else entered the men's room.

Just after midnight, his wrist alarm buzzed. He opened the restroom door. From his last time doing this, he knew to crawl into the operations unit. The lights didn't trigger as he left the safety of the restroom.

It took him two minutes to slither to the door of the Plexiglas room, punch the entry code into the keypad, and crawl to the elevated supervisor's station. Breathing hard more from fear than exertion, he reached around the computer for its USB port. Her voice whispered to him, *push the cable into the port.* He fumbled with its other end trying to insert it into his cell phone. This was the easiest thing he had to do tonight, yet it took him so long that perspiration ran down his face in the cool room. The cable kept slipping in his sweat-drenched hands. Just before he gave up, he heard the satisfying snap of the connection.

Good, Jon!

Then he realized he hadn't taken a breath in almost thirty seconds. He sucked air while he ran the program to copy the computer's contents onto the micro-SD card of his cell.

He thought, *don't make any noise.* He waited under the desk as his cell processed the drive. An hour later, he heard a beep signaling its completion.

He crawled to the stairs and reached up for the door handle.

Almost done! Jon smiled; his plan had worked. The bank's data was his now, and soon he could recover his life.

He made as little noise as possible as he took the stairs down floor after floor and passed below the lobby.

But just before he could make the turn through the door into the parking level, he heard the door squeak open behind him.

He turned to see who it was, and halfway into his head-turn realized it was a mistake.

He and the man behind him saw each other.

Bloody shit! It was Sambol!

CHAPTER 21

Bank of Trade headquarters branch,
47th Street at Park Avenue, Manhattan
September 10, 3:47 a.m.

Jon tore down the stairs into the garage, and dashed, breathless, to the street exit.

His cover was blown.

He sprinted as far as he could, fear fueling him. How had he let this happen? Shit! Now, the worst thing he could do would be to go back to the apartment. His address was on his résumé and job application, and he was sure it had been stored in their computers for easy access by bank staff. And now, for the bank's enforcers. No, he'd need a safe place. He knew of only one.

The look on Sambol's face as he saw Jon—first confusion, then understanding, and last, a desperate rage—had Jon sprinting as fast as he could, until he was winded. He was already sure the enforcers carried weapons.

He constructed a plan as he ran south toward Penn Station. First, he'd need a safe place to wait until the early morning Long Island Railroad trains started their rush hour.

He stopped every block or two at the entrance to a store, to look at the reflections from street lights against store windows. He didn't see the same face twice, but he knew it didn't mean anything. If Sambol had called in for enforcers, they might be difficult to see at night until it was too late.

He stopped to catch his breath at the entrance to an office building on Seventh Avenue just north of 36th Street. As he scanned the way he was headed, he saw a tall man walking toward him, north on Seventh, sneering. The man's right wrist flicked and a knife blade appeared in his hand. Jon felt confusion. The bank's enforcers would be coming south, wouldn't they? He turned, ready to spring north and stopped dead. Two more were walking south toward him. Surrounded by hostiles, he concluded they were probably gangbangers.

He took a deep breath and turned toward the man with the knife. *Mossad trained you with Krav Maga. Three should be easy.* He ran toward the man with the knife and used his right hand to grab the surprised man's wrist while his left hand twisted the knife from him. As he slammed the man down to the pavement, he turned, knowing the other two would be on him in less than two seconds. Jon held the knife against the disarmed attacker's throat. "Come closer and he's dead."

The other two stopped. One had a Jersey accent. "What?"

Jon looked over their shoulders, toward the north. He saw a black SUV speeding down the street, still three blocks away. Possibly the bank's enforcers. And there was no way for him to know. "You guys have guns?"

"If we did, you'd be dead," snarled the shortest of the three, likely their leader.

Jon nodded. "Come here. Now, or I'll turn your friend into a spiral ham. Now!" They complied, forming a moving cover, hiding him as the SUV barreled past continuing south.

He positioned the three closest to the street and had them surround him. They strolled the last three blocks in a tight grouping.

Once outside Penn Station, he stopped and faced the three. "Guys, thanks for the help. I'm bloody grateful." He pushed his original attacker back and pulled out his wallet. "Enjoy the remainder of your night, and next time, be more careful judging your victims."

He tossed a few bills from his wallet into the air, turned and ran to the escalator, down into the labyrinth of interconnecting tunnels with their collection of railroad platforms. Many of the people on the lower floor of the station at this time of night were homeless. Seeing their ragged state depressed him.

He found a wooden bench near a gate to one of the platforms. It was midway down a hall and there were multiple staircases. He'd hoped he'd be safe here for a while. But only if he was gone with the rush hour.

He set his wrist alarm for 6 a.m., time for the early train to Roslyn, where he could find a cab to East Meadow. *The safe house is the last place where the Mossad will look for me*, he thought. *Safe for a few days and that's all I'll need. If the intel is good, things will change for me. Mossad and MI-6 will think I'm a hero. If the intel is bad, I'm out of options.*

As the gate to the platform ground open at 6:07, Jon marched through it and down the stairs. He found a spot to hide, behind a staircase on the nearly empty platform, and jumped with every strange sound he heard.

His clothing stuck to his skin and his palms were sweaty.

Where could he go after he delivered the intel? He needed a new plan.

There were only a few equations he needed to solve. Where could he find safety? What other hurdles might threaten him? The plan would have to solve these problems. And, he doubted he could do it alone. He'd need a team to fix this. Who to choose? Would MI-6 help him? What about Mossad? No, he wasn't that important to either intelligence agency. But maybe he could find another way to improve his odds. A fellow stringer might be the best way. Jon pulled his cell phone from his pocket. *Time to get William Wing involved up to his bloody hip boots. Even if I have to threaten his tiny neck. What can I use to draw him here? A promise of money? Maybe. But whatever it takes, I must have his help.*

At 6:11 a.m., an empty Long Island Railroad train glided to a stop at the platform. Jon entered and sat facing the entrance. As the train's doors closed, he thought through his new plan until it was ready. When he arrived at the Roslyn stop, he'd need to steal a car to get him to East Meadow. A taxi would keep a record of his travel, and that might lead to him before he was gone from the safe house. He remembered seeing surveillance cameras outside the Mossad safe house, and crafted a plan to disable them. No one would suspect he'd use the safe house.

From the moment O'Hara threatened him, William Wing thought how tenuous his life had always been. The thought of having his work for Mossad made public was enough to get him to agree to help. His father would have him killed if he found out he'd helped Israel. He'd need to do this task face-to-face. In his assessment, the urgency O'Hara had claimed did not outweigh the risks posed by using the insecure Internet. Wing left his apartment in a hurry, grabbing a handful of clothes and squeezing them into a suitcase. Pushing more clothing and several patch cords for his notebook computer into its case, Wing ran from the elevator and out through the lobby, looking for a cab to the airport.

Dawn broke as the plane landed two days later. He took a taxi from JFK airport to the address O'Hara had given him in East Meadow. O'Hara responded to his furious knocking at the front door. William slammed the door shut behind him, his suitcase dragging behind him, his notebook computer case in his other hand.

He sneered at Michael. "I'm here as you ordered. What the fuck's up?" William dropped his suitcase, carried the notebook computer into the living room and put it on the desk.

O'Hara looked ragged. His suit emitted a pungent odor. His beard was gone and the skin around his eyes was much darker than William remembered. Wing laughed. "You look like shit. Smell like shit, too."

O'Hara reached into his suit pocket, and the movement of his hand, sweeping open his jacket, caused Wing to flinch. But the odor that came out with Jon's hand forced William to hold his nose.

O'Hara handed a thumb-drive to him. "My cover's blown. But I wasn't leaving until I passed this to you. It's the recording of the off-balance-sheet accounts for the Bank of Trade."

Wing nodded. "And you want me to crack the files."

O'Hara grimaced. "As fast as you can. My only hope of living through all this is to trade the intel to my handlers for their help. I need to become someone else. Fast. How soon can you decrypt the files?"

Wing examined the chip. "Before the end of today."

O'Hara waved his hand. "Please, William."

Wing nodded. "Take a fucking shower before I throw up."

O'Hara nodded. "Sure. But, I need to disappear for a while. Somewhere very far away, with spots not covered by ECHELON. I'm thinking of a trip to China for a few months. Would I be safe there?"

Wing considered the covert agent. He shrugged. "How fast can you learn a language?"

"I'm a natural. Is that my only problem? And can I rely on your help if I'm there?"

Wing sighed. "Sure. I can help you for a price."

O'Hara smiled and padded off to the bathroom.

His work completed, Wing had left the house without saying goodbye. Jon wondered if he'd ever see the hacker again. Wing had copied the decoded files onto two thumb-drives, and a left behind a stack of pages holding a listing of their contents. He also had fabricated a visa page that was ready to glue into any passport Jon wanted, on the spot where he showed Jon.

Jon completed reading decrypted intel as the sun set. He felt alarm spread through his gut, realizing the importance of his discoveries. Then he punched a number into his cell phone.

The voice on the other side sounded gruff and annoyed.

"Hello, Mother. It's Sommers."

"I don't have time for you. A crisis."

"Wait! You must make time. I have what I promised." Jon's hands shook.

"That's what you said last time. It was worthless."

"This time I have the details of every transaction Houmaz sent or received with the Bank of Trade. Everything."

There was silence on the other end of the line. Mother's voice softened. "Really? And what do you want in exchange?" This time the voice was less rushed.

Jon nodded to himself. "I want you to drop the terminate-with-prejudice order. And have Klein craft an Israeli passport for me right away. I'll pick them up on my way to the airport. And cash. Say, two hundred large. I'll drop the intel in a thumb-drive with Klein on my way out of the country."

The spymaster sighed. "I'll gamble on you one more time. Don't disappoint. The passport will be ready with your Mossad photo in two hours. Nomi will also have the cash when you arrive. Give the intel to her and tell her to send it to the Office, my attention. You've wasted too much of my time. This better be good or we'll hunt you. And I'll kill you myself. Painfully.

Jon felt the hard edge in Ben-Levy's voice. He squirmed. "Yeah. Thanks."

As night fell, he exited the safe house for the last time. Streetlights winked on. He walked to the car he'd stolen at the Long Island Railroad's Roslyn stop when he'd first arrived, scanning his path and the area around him.

The drive to the Bronx took about an hour. He parked the car in an alleyway and walked the area several times to be sure no one was following him. He wondered what he'd do if the bank's enforcers followed him? He'd have to kill them. Or at least try. He'd not killed anyone, ever, and wondered if he even could.

Jon knocked on Klein's door. She must have seen him through the peephole, because she handed him a small canvas bag and held out her hand. He dropped the thumb-drive in her hand. She slammed the door in his face. He headed back to the car, and noted with relief that no one had as yet stripped its tires or stolen the vehicle.

The bag contained one Israeli passport in the name of Jon Sommers, plus lots of rubber-banded cash. Jon looked at his watch. He'd have to call Crane after arriving at the airport. He'd bought glue at a dollar store, and glued the visa onto its page.

Now it was time for him to disappear forever, a much richer man. His best odds of success were to use his new passport to leave the United States and fly to his new home in Shanghai, where it would safe for him to be Michael O'Hara once again.

He called China Airlines while he sat in traffic on the Cross Bronx Expressway and paid for a ticket using his

O'Hara debit card. Now, all he had to do was get to JFK and leave this wretched city.

At the parking lot of a car rental, he dropped off the stolen car and took their bus to JFK's International Terminal.

Once inside, his first glance in a store window reflected a huge Middle Eastern man wearing a business suit and holding a newspaper. The man stared over it, at Jon, less than fifteen meters away.

Jon panicked and scanned the corridor for a place where he could disappear. There was none that would work. His legs threatened to buckle. Jon took a deep breath to steady himself. Gradually the adrenaline in his system diminished and he walked through the throng, trying to outpace his follower.

With his second check in a window reflection he saw four of them, all wearing suits and no longer disguising their pursuit. His face dripped sweat and he broke into a sprint.

As he ran at full speed, he thought about Lisa and his yearning to find justice for her. Lisa's voice rang out inside him. *If they take you, they'll kill you, but even worse, they'll find out who your handlers and fellow coverts are. Every one.* He was shocked to realize his sense of honor wouldn't let him permit it.

He bolted through the door and saw a bus filling curbside and strained to reach it. He banged the window as it started moving away from the curb. It rolled to a stop. When its doors opened for him, he jumped in. Standing and facing away from the terminal, he waited as it picked up speed, and then found a seat. Five minutes later, he dropped down the stairs to the subway station and headed to the platform where the crowd was thickest. He tried blending in while watching the staircase he'd just descended. A train slowed into the station, crammed full. He could now smell the stench of his own fear.

He pushed his way into the nearest car, sure he'd not

been spotted. When the doors closed, he sighed, hyperventilating. Could he escape?

He looked at his wristwatch. He'd need to be at the ticket counter for China Airlines at JFK in less than an hour if he was to make his flight. He rode the subway one stop and got out in Brooklyn to find a taxi.

How had the bank's enforcers tracked him? The cell phone! He wondered if they'd traced his previous calls or triangulated his position? It didn't matter which. It was possible they now knew his plans, including where he planned to go. He'd need a new destination. Lisa's voice uttered a single word. *Singapore.* He didn't know why, but it sounded good enough.

The phrase he'd heard during his training one afternoon hunting terrorists in the Tze'elim, in the Negev, echoed inside him: *No battle plan survives first contact with the enemy.*

Mathematics had failed him too many times. He decided to make it simple: He needed a destination country whose visa was easy to obtain.

As the aircraft took off for Hong Kong, William Wing felt glad he was done with O'Hara, the Israeli spy with a British accent. He seemed full of lies. Wing shook his head and clenched his eyes shut.

As the attendant handed him a beer, he read the email from Lieutenant Chan. It was a basic progress report from his father's head hacker, containing endless details with nothing of any substance. The team had made no progress. Neither China nor Russia seemed to have any national interest in a war that wasn't winnable by either country without the other's total destruction. And whose interest would be served by that? He was sure a third party was responsible, but who?

Not a student of national politics, William didn't have an answer. He'd told his father all he knew. Until he had proof of the hidden party and its motives, the prudent thing for him to do was stay silent.

But silence wouldn't earn his father's respect. And after his last visit, he realized he still wanted that.

He'd need to keep looking for a trail of evidence, hacking the trash from the computer systems of both governments.

But, what if his father found out about his work for O'Hara and the Mossad? This thought kept him wired as the plane sped toward home.

Jon had obtained a tourist visa when he checked his bags at the airport counter. Now, at 35,000 feet, he punched a series of digits into the pay-per-call cell phone he'd bought at JFK. "Charles Crane, please. It's Michael O'Hara." He waited several minutes.

The older man's voice seemed agitated. "Where the bloody fuck are you?"

"On my way to Singapore. I have the intel you wanted. Have one of your in-country locals there call this number to arrange delivery."

The man's words were clipped. "Why'd you leave the US?"

Jon grimaced. "Cover's blown. The bank's enforcers followed me somehow."

"Singapore. Right, then. Can you tell me where you'll be staying?"

Jon had the in-flight magazine in front of him. He saw the hotel's picture. "Mandarin Oriental."

"And what's your intention?"

Jon's eyes closed as he imagined being free. "A long vacation. And in exchange for the intel, have your men deliver a long-term Singapore visa to customs at the airport in the name of Jon Sommers."

Crane's voice went up a notch. "Why would you expect it to be safe for you there?"

Jon's eyebrows arched. "Why not?"

"If they've a mind to, they can hack your trail. Their enforcers are as good as any intelligence service's hackers. Some say they're even better."

Jon considered this. The math confirmed Crane's warning. "Well, maybe. But I'm on my way, and I'm sure they didn't follow me onto the aircraft. So how would they hack my destination?"

"Right. Well, you've been warned. I'll send the visa and someone to collect the intel."

He read the in-flight magazine to learn about his new home. First stop after checking into the hotel would be a tour of the Orchard Road shopping district for sundries and dinner.

He heard the landing gear drop and looked out the window at the city skyline below. With about five million people, including over fifty thousand Brits and American ex-pats, not to mention tens of thousands of tourists, he believed he could lose himself there.

Safe at last!

As he exited the plane, he heard his real name called over the loudspeaker system. He gulped, worrying about the bank enforcers. When he picked up the white phone he'd been directed to, he heard a voice tell him there was a package waiting for him at the Singapore Airlines ticket counter. Must be the visa. He walked through Changi Airport toward baggage claim. This terminal smelled different. It seemed cleaner, somehow.

He grabbed his suitcase and went to the ticket counter. A man smiled and handed him an envelope. The man asked, "You have something for me?"

Jon handed him the thumb-drive. He tucked the envelope containing the new visa into his jacket pocket and walked toward the terminal exit. At a currency trading booth, he traded US dollars for Singapore dollars. His rate was about two American per three Singapore dollars.

So far, so good.

He turned on his new disposable cell phone. No message from Crane. His next stop would be the hotel. He needed a shower and a change of clothes.

And soon, he'd find an apartment, buy a car. Maybe he'd do some consulting work. Just for fun, not for the money.

Exiting the terminal, he was hit with a wall of hot humid air. The taxi line was short and he popped into one. "Mandarin Oriental, please." He settled in, smug in the belief he was safe at last.

The cab pulled into the semicircular driveway and stopped under the overhanging awning. He paid the cabbie and found the fragrance of growing flowers intoxicating. Jon took a deep breath and strolled into the air-conditioned paradise.

He waited in line until he faced a clerk with an accent similar to his own. "I have a reservation. Jon Sommers." It felt good again to use his real name. He handed over his real passport and the visa gifted him by Crane. "Deluxe facing the bay, please."

The clerk handed him a set of papers and he filled them in, passing them back along with his documents. "Business or pleasure?"

"Vacation. Absolute pleasure." Jon smiled.

The clerk nodded. "How long will you be staying with us, Mr. Sommers?"

"Figure ten days." Plenty of time to get him an apartment and find a cobbler to forge a driver's license.

He took the room key and rode the elevator up to the twenty-fourth floor. He was surprised by the spacious room and its exotic Asian furniture. Red colors abounded.

After dropping his suitcase on a stand, he exited, placing a thread in the doorjamb. He pressed the elevator button.

Time to go shopping. Clothes, a new cell phone, and sundries for my new life.

In the center of his head, he heard Lisa's voice rattling on, asking if he'd abandoned her and her quest for justice.

As the sun hit its zenith, Sommers returned. His tongue had slipped several times when he handed his credit card to a store clerk to pay for things, not responding to "Mr. Sommers" as fast as he should. His own name was now foreign to him. All his names were.

He walked off the elevator and checked the thread. Still there. Jon opened the door.

As he closed the door and turned to face the view, his face fell. Four men grabbed him, Middle Eastern men, all in dark suits. One of them held his arm and yanked him into the room's leather chair. Their leader was Aziz Sambol. And next to him was Zamid al-Ramen. The other two were enormous, muscled men. Men he'd never seen before.

As the shock of discovery faded, Jon found himself somehow at peace with his impending death. But Lisa's voice wasn't willing to accept his demise. She wailed at him, an incoherent noise, forcing him to cringe and hold his hands against his head.

Sambol's smile said it all. "Welcome to Singapore, Mr. al-Muhammed, or should I call you Michael O'Hara, or Jon Sommers?"

"Smith," was all Jon could think of to say.

Al-Ramen slipped on a pair of brass knuckles. "We can make your death swift. Just tell us what we want to know. Or, my preference would be for you to refuse. Our Singapore Enforcement Division has kindly offered us two of their staff. Their special talents will serve to entertain Mr. Sambol and me." His voice shifted from slow and soft to a more fervent tone and pace. "What did you steal?"

"Paper clips." Sommers clenched his eyes shut, just before Al-Ramen slammed his face with a brass covered fist. Jon felt his jaw crack. An echo of pain vibrated though his skull.

"You will tell us, sooner or later. Open your eyes. Now!"

Sommers shook his head. "No bloody way." With his eyes closed, he noticed his palms were sweaty. There was absolute silence in the room.

"Since you prefer not to watch as we tear you apart, I will grant that wish." Al-Ramen sneered. "Tape his eyes shut."

Sommers opened his eyes in panic, just in time to see one of the goons with a roll of duct tape, ripping a large piece. Seconds later his world went dark.

"Again, Mr. Sommers, if that is truly your name. It matters not, for there will be no stone to mark your grave. What did you steal?"

Sommers shivered. "The bank's phone directory." He felt the blow to his stomach and his lunch spewed forth. He gagged on the soured remainders of imperial rolls that had tasted wonderful just an hour ago.

He wondered how long he'd hold up. Not long, that was sure. He knew sooner or later he'd give up and tell them something.

And, he then realized the one thing he had control over was what to tell them. "Wait. Stop. I'll talk. I copied some letters of credit transactions." He tried not to flinch, but no one hit him.

"For whom?"

"The Russians. For the FSB." He waited, but no blow came.

"Why? What did they want to know?"

"Dunno. They paid me to find trade transactions funded by the United States government." He realized this might be true from their perspective, and there was no way they could determine with any certainty if it was.

And with that thought, he knew they had gotten what they'd come for. Soon they would murder him. Very soon.

He found himself willing to believe in God. He began to pray.

CHAPTER 22

Jon felt distant and somehow disconnected from his pending fate. His eyes remained taped shut. He forced himself to focus on the tiny noises around him. Footsteps. Whispering, but he couldn't make out the words. A flushing toilet. He heard Aziz Sambol chuckle. "You've been so patient, Khalid. Now you can have him."

Someone ripped the tape from Jon's eyes and the first thing he saw was one of the enforcers nodding back to Sambol. Jon's eyes stung, his eyebrows ripped from his face. Khalid was a huge man, missing most of his teeth as he smiled, his face tilted toward Jon.

Khalid pulled a corkscrew from his pocket. "Mr. Sommers, in Egypt I studied to be a surgeon before I was accused of being a terrorist. You couldn't tell to look at me. The interrogation sessions I suffered through included using a hammer to break my teeth. And now I practice surgery. You will be my newest patient." He flashed his broken teeth again, and Jon gulped.

Khalid held the corkscrew right in front of Jon's eyes. "I could use this to pull the eyeballs from your head. But, painful though that might be, I think I'd rather do that later, just after I use the corkscrew to castrate you. First things first. Do you know the many ways I can keep you from dying while I pull your small intestines from your body?"

Jon remembered his circumcision surgery and how painful that had been. But nothing like what he was about to face.

Khalid sneered. For the first time, Jon noticed the odor of decay coming from his torturer's mouth. "I've been told it's more painful than any other kind of torture. But soon, you can tell me. I'll leave them attached inside you at one end so they stretch out several yards along the floor until we're ready to we hang you. While I work, you will feel such pain as you never believed possible with one end of your gut still inside you. I will stretch the cut end around your neck and then bind it tight to the chandelier."

Jon stared into Khalid's eyes. The eyes of death. He wanted to live, to fulfill the promise he'd made Lisa. But he had no plan and no power to change the equation. "Please. Don't."

Khalid smiled. His left hand reached out for Jon's belt buckle and pulled it open. "Help me with his clothing."

Al-Ramen thrust his elbow hard into Jon's face as he unzipped the pants. "His small intestine first? Why not start with castration?"

Khalid sneered. "Intestines first, yes. Castration isn't nearly as painful. I'll use the corkscrew to pull his penis from him, after I gut him. I'll be careful to keep him alive while I do my work. Then each eyeball. We can hang him when we're done with our entertainment. All with this." He held up the corkscrew.

Jon could hear Lisa howl as he struggled with his bonds. He couldn't budge the knots.

Khalid laughed out loud.

Ben-Levy read through the intel Jon had sent him. At first he yawned, bored by the data stream. But as he waded deeper, his jaw dropped. His face turned red. "God help us!"

As he approached the final page, he gasped and picked up the landline phone, a secure line. "It's Ben-Levy. I must speak with the Prime Minister. Now! It's urgent, a daylight priority."

The Prime Minister was a battle-hardened former IDF sniper. Ben-Levy didn't like the man, thought him far too blunt in a time needing subtle gestures and lies to control world opinion. "Yes? Yigdal, I'm busy so make it brief."

Ben-Levy took a deep breath, marshaling his argument. "Sir, I just found out what Tariq Houmaz wanted to do with the cash."

"Can't this wait? I have a state function to prepare for."

"If we don't act soon, there may be no state!"

Silence on the other end of the line. It went on for seconds. "Yigdal. Cryptic as usual. All right. Tell me."

"One of our covert assets sent me intel stating Houmaz is buying two nuclear submarines from the Russian mafiya in Vladivostok. For delivery to the Muslim Brotherhood. Each sub contains twenty ICMBs, each with a twenty-megaton nuclear warhead."

"What?"

"I need your authority to commence a mission."

"What's the rush? He'd need trained crews. That'll take months."

"He paid the Russian mafiya to have two crews trained several months ago. They're led by Aziz Tamil and waiting in Vlad for him to arrive and make final payment so they can take delivery of the subs."

This time the silence was longer, and Ben-Levy noticed the Prime Minister's breath coming fast and hard. "Done. Get those subs out of the Brotherhood's hands before he blows up Israel and triggers the Jericho Sanction."

Ben-Levy heard the call terminate. *The Jericho Sanction. Something no one who knows about ever mentions.* If a radioactive device exploded within Israel's borders, or if the sanction wasn't deactivated every day, over seventy-five ICBMs, each carrying twenty-megaton warheads, would be sent to destinations from Libya to Pakistan. Every Middle Eastern country would cease to be habitable for the next two thousand years.

The Jericho Sanction was why the United States was so close to Israel. They needed oil, and if Israel was attacked the globe's major oil sources would be obliterated, hopelessly contaminated with radioactivity. The price of oil from the remaining sources, outside the Middle East, would spike off the charts.

He punched another number into the landline. "It's Ben-Levy. Get me the head of IDF. Urgently."

Khalid brought the corkscrew into contact with Jon's navel and smiled as he twisted it into his belly, as if Jon himself was the tip of a persistent wine bottle waiting to be decanted.

Jon screamed. The flare of pain was worse than anything he'd ever experienced. He could feel his gut ripping. His vision dimmed as he drifted away into a world where Lisa held his hand, waiting for him to die. She cooed to him, drawing him past his fear of death. The pain grew ever more severe until he lost consciousness.

Jon's mind swirled into a nightmare where the smiling face of Lisa Gabriel morphed first into Yigdal Ben-Levy and then into Charles Crane. Crane hit him hard in his gut and then the face morphed once more, this time into Khalid. The voice of his torturer asked him, "Why did you stop loving me, Jon?" He tried to speak, and as he opened his mouth, thunderbolts of pain rattled in his belly.

He came to, with Khalid holding smelling salts under his

nose. The Arab smiled. "Good. Conscious again. Ready for more?"

Jon could see his blood pulsing from his navel, pooling down his torso into his crotch. A thumb-sized piece of his flesh throbbed, red. He shook his head and pulled harder against the knots of rope holding him in the chair. He tried to think of something to help him but nothing came. "No! Please. Stop!"

"Mr. Sommers, I'm not sorry for you. And with this next step, your life will be over."

Jon had to see. He opened his eyes to slits and watched the enforcer shove the end of the corkscrew into the pulsing bubble of flesh that was his small intestine. He could feel the puncture, feel the pull and screamed in pain. *Death can't come fast enough!*

Out of the corner of his eyes, he saw the door explode and disappear. Several men entered holding handguns, their weapons spitting bullets into his enemies. Pain blackened his world and he dropped back into unconsciousness. He was beyond the reach of nightmares.

When Jon's eyes popped open, he saw the two Brits who'd hustled him into Crane's car back in New York and another man he'd never seen before.

The gun in the mystery agent's hand emitted a trail of wispy smoke, and Jon could smell the cordite. Sommers looked down and almost fainted at the sight. The long finger of red flesh torn and hanging from his gut was still pulsing with his heartbeat, bubbling blood from his belly.

The mystery agent examined Jon's wound. "We need to get him to a hospital."

American accent.

Jon guessed CIA. "Who are you?" The mystery agent was in his early forties, overweight, and wearing a cheap business suit. Jon knew he was falling into shock. He lost his ability to focus as the intense pain ripped through his gut.

"Hey, Jon. I'm Bob Gault, and I work for one of the US intelligence agencies." The man moved closer and examined the wound. "Damn. He's dying. Let's get him out of here. Where's the nearest hospital?"

Jon lost consciousness again. This time, he dreamt he heard Lisa's voice telling him to have faith. She'd protect him while he slept.

Yigdal Ben-Levy watched Shulamit Ries and her team leave his small office. He placed her folder on the bottom of the short stack and removed the next one from the pile. Opening it, he scanned its contents to be sure nothing in it would give away any facts he wanted kept secret.

Ben-Levy watched the elevator doors open, through the small glass window in his office door in the Office's basement. He saw IDF Captain Avram Shimmel emerging from the lift, smiling as he passed Ries. Mother watched her smile back, but saw her eyes drawn to the wedding ring on his left hand. She turned, staring at the ring as he walked away. As the elevator door closed, her group disappeared. Ben-Levy nodded, thinking what he'd believed about Ries was true. She had a crush on the captain.

A second later there was a knock on the steel door and he looked up. "Enter."

Shimmel walked in, nodded, and sat in the folding chair across from Ben-Levy. He was at least six-foot-seven, maybe taller. Ben-Levy watched him squeeze into the chair. "I'm here as you requested." The big man's frame made the chair look like a footstool. His eyes, an intense sky-blue, stared at the spymaster.

Ben-Levy nodded. "The mission I told you about. If you choose to take it, I'll remove you from the IDF, promote you to major, and assign you staff from the Institute. You'll work for me in SHABEK."

Shimmel shook his head. "I haven't any interest in killing terrorists one-by-one when I can kill them by the scores. A tank is more direct and brutal."

Ben-Levy nodded. "This mission is vital to Israel's continued existence. It's urgent. What I want you to do might end the lives of many more enemies in a single strike. Possibly millions. Interested?"

Shimmel shrugged. Maybe he didn't believe what Ben-Levy said to him. But he nodded and faced Mother. "Sure. Tell me more."

The older man shook his head. "I can't do that unless you join me in SHABEK. National security."

Shimmel's hands dropped to his sides. He frowned. "National security? Hah." But Mother could see the wheels turning in his head. Shimmel had a reputation as the smartest tactician in IDF. "Very well then. Make this official."

Ben-Levy nodded. "As you wish."

When Ben-Levy laid out the mission parameters, Shimmel's eyes bulged. He read the contents of the yellow file folder through, end-to-end, several times. "This is unbelievable. Are you sure?"

The spymaster nodded. "I think you're the only person we have who can do this. There's a team in the third-floor conference room waiting for you to brief them, right now. The team must be in place in under twelve hours, before they are ready to launch the submarines. How soon can you leave?"

"Now. No time to waste." Shimmel rose and smiled. "Thanks for this."

Leaving the basement, Avram clutched the slim file folder in his left hand. He saluted a major as they passed, and pressed the elevator's call button.

He pulled his cell phone from his pocket, but halfway through entering the number, he stopped. No one could know where he was going or what he'd be doing. Not even his wife. Instead, he sent her an email:

Darling Sharon,

I will be gone on business for at least three weeks. Can't tell you the details, but this is a rather mundane assignment. Take care of yourself and little Golda until I return. Lovers always.

Avie

Shimmel approached the room Ben-Levy had sent him to. He opened the door, and stood in the entrance, absorbing the mood of his team. There were over fifty men and women in the large mission center, all seated, talking and joking with one another. It looked just like any IDF briefing, but with one difference. These people weren't just out of uniform; they all looked like Arabs. Most had served in deep cover in countries like Jordan, Saudi Arabia, and Syria, and all were dressed in Arab garb.

Many stank of stale perspiration. Only three women were present, all in Western garb of jeans and blouses.

He walked to the podium and opened the yellow folder. The silence was sudden. "You will refer to me as Aziz Tamil. We will be traveling together to Vladivostok. We will locate and steal two nuclear submarines from the Muslim Brotherhood after they pay the Russians for them. Each of you has a skill set making you essential to this mission. I will further explain our mission after we are in control of the subs. Until then, talk to no one but yourselves or me. Should anyone ask you questions, answer them in Arabic. Each of us should seem to not know the others. It must seem as if we're all traveling alone on business. Once we arrive at our destination, reform by baggage claim. We'll travel separately by taxi to the Hotel Visit, where they speak several languages, not just Russian. After we check in, find my room. We'll gather there and Mother will update us on the mission. Any questions?"

Shimmel knew there would be none. From the folder, he removed a rubber-banded stack of travel billets, each in its own envelope, including tickets, cash in three currencies, and requisitions for handguns and ammunition, to be honored by the armory in the basement. These he handed out, calling each of the team by name. Within an hour all of them were in a school bus rolling toward Lod Airport.

CHAPTER 23

Knevichi Airfield,
Vladivostok International Airport,
Vladivostok, Russia
September 16, 5:42 p.m.

Sitting at the front of first class, Tariq Houmaz was the first person hurrying off the Aeroflot plane from Moscow. He took a deep breath and coughed from the foul-smelling air that polluted Vladivostok. The terminal looked brand new, but it smelled like sneakers left to ferment for months in a moldy garbage bin. And having traveled several days almost nonstop, Houmaz felt filthy. His own stench was obvious, even to himself. His shirt stuck to his back as he moved toward the terminal's exit.

He took a taxi to the center of the city, where he found a branch of the Bank of Trade. He entered and waved to a bank officer. The man smiled and led him to a desk in the back of the branch. "How can I help you, Mr., uh…"

"Tariq Houmaz. I have an account at your bank in New York and wish to arrange an internal transfer of funds to an accountholder whose account is at this branch. Can you do this?"

"If you have proper identification, of course we can." The man held out his hand. Houmaz pulled some papers from his pocket. "How much do you wish to move?"

As he sought a taxi, Houmaz pulled a piece of paper from his pocket and unfolded it. He got into the back seat and read its travel directions to the cabbie. His next stop would be the wharf. On one of the piers where the Russian mafiya had a warehouse. There, a man named Nikita Tobelov would arrange delivery of the submarines to him.

He'd wanted to meet the crew Tobelov had trained, before meeting the Russian, but the Aeroflot flight had taken an extra day to arrive and now he'd have to postpone meeting his submariners.

Their commander, Aziz Tamil, was one of the most notorious and feared terrorists in Mohammed's Martyrs' Brigade. No one had ever seen him. At least, no one still living claimed they had. The honor of meeting the man who'd murdered scores of Jews brought a smile to Houmaz's face.

He pulled his cell phone from his pocket. Earlier this day, he'd sent a coded message to the legendary Tamil using the Al Jazeera blog to reschedule the meeting with him. But when he visited the blog, there was no response from Tamil.

He'd have to ask Tobelov about it.

And he'd also need to pay for the new electronic countermeasures the Russian had promised. They were as expensive as the subs, but the new technology made them undetectable.

He felt a wave of heat as he left the terminal. And as bad as the air was in the terminal, outside the odors of petrochemical effluent had him coughing. He decided he hated Vladivostok.

The taxi let him out at the shoreline. He could see the warehouse and the office on the top floor where he expected Tobelov to be waiting for him.

As he reached the wharf, he stopped to study it. Fear made him cautious. He noticed two guardhouses, one on either side of the pier about fifty feet away. Soldiers emerged carrying AK-74's, the newest upgrade to Kalashnikovs. The men demanded his identity papers.

Houmaz held up the backpack that had been resting between his shoulders. He was slow removing it. He unzipped the top compartment, held it open so they could see inside it. A surge of adrenaline boosted his pulse and narrowed the focus of all his senses. He reached in with two fingers, keeping the remainder of his hand where the armed men could see it. He removed a tiny satchel, its tag wound around his fingers, and handed it to one of the soldiers.

In seconds, one of them spoke to him. Even with his hearing dimmed from the adrenaline rush he could tell they were speaking Russian, a language he didn't understand. He raised both hands, palms up, to signal his lack of comprehension. The bigger of the two slapped the ID back into his hand and grabbed him by his shoulders, pushing him further along the pier until they all reached the warehouse door.

The other soldier knocked on the rusty door. When it opened, a man inside flashed a predatory smile at Houmaz. "Welcome."

He spoke English, and Houmaz relaxed his shoulders, since he also spoke English. "Who are you?"

The man extended his hand. Houmaz shook it, waiting for the man to speak again. "Come inside where it's cool." The man pointed inside. "I'll make us a pot of tea." He turned and led Houmaz inside. "I'm Nikita Tobelov." The Russian was in his mid-forties, bald and thin, his lower face covered with a Van Dyke beard.

Houmaz nodded and followed him up a metal staircase into an office. As promised, there was a tea kettle boiling over a sterno stove. One of the soldiers served them cups filled with the beverage as they sat.

"Tea will make our business dealings more civilized." Tobelov smiled, but it looked more to Houmaz like a sneer.

He tried to keep the Russian from noticing he felt wary and ill at ease.

"I have transferred the remaining funds in US dollars as we agreed. I have the confirmation." Houmaz reached for the pack and unzipped its side compartment. He pulled out a single sealed envelope. "Two hundred million."

"And the payment for training your crews?"

"Twenty million. It's confirmation is included in the envelope as a separate internal transfer."

"What about the cash for the state-of-the-art electronic countermeasures?" Tobelov sipped his tea.

Houmaz raised his brows. "Are they installed in the subs?"

"*Da*. The devices make the water around the moving submarines appear to flow with the tide. Brilliant, and worth much more than I agreed to. The irony is that the Israelis developed the counter-surveillance masks at their Ness Ziona research facility in Tel Aviv." Tobelov laughed.

Houmaz chuckled as he discovered this new detail. "It's in a separate transfer." He handed the other sealed envelope to Tobelov. He sipped his own cup of tea. It was lukewarm. "Where and when do I meet Tamil and the crew?"

The Russian's eyes focused on a faraway spot. "They are currently on the beach, twelve kilometers west. But you should just come here, at the warehouse, at dawn, the day after tomorrow. I'll send you instructions for the countersign using a dead-letter drop. Old rules. Moscow rules. A tree slick at the railroad station. Details on a note. Midnight, tomorrow night. Tamil will bring your crews to the beach. When we signal from one of the subs, they'll paddle out on rafts. Our crew will exit the subs and take your rafts to shore. Your crews will board both subs with Tamil and take over. Clear? I assume you will return to shore with my men and travel home by yourself. Yes?"

Houmaz didn't answer, worrying about letting the Russian know his plans. Instead, he rose to leave.

Tobelov touched Houmaz's sleeve. "One more thing you should know. There are some political machinations in Moscow Center that will make any future dealings we have more costly for you. The government wants to take back control of all major weapons sales from us. They claim some sort of national-defense emergency is brewing. I think they're behaving like old women. But it is what it is. So, consider this sale a gift. I pushed it through before they revoked our power to sell." Tobelov's eyes were downcast. "Sorry."

Houmaz wondered why the Russian was telling him this. Would this truly affect his future operations? Possibly, but there was nothing he could do about it. He focused on his present objective: get the subs. "No problem. You have sold me what I need." Shaking Tobelov's hand, he rose and walked down the stairs, exiting the warehouse.

As he walked off the pier, his mind drifted to other consequences. *So close now. Soon, Israel and all it represents will vanish from the earth in a scorching blast of radioactive missile fire. Every Jew there, all dead.*

CHAPTER 24

National University Hospital,
5 Lower Kent Ridge Road, Singapore
September 17, 7:11 p.m.

When Sommers opened his eyes, the room was spinning. He tried to rise off the bed using his elbows for leverage, but stretching his stomach muscles caused the breath to leave him in a gasp. He dropped back, moaning.

"Clyde, he's awake." One of the Brits, the blond one, moved closer to him. Sommers wondered, *what's the other's name?*

The stranger who'd shot the bank's enforcers moved next to him. "You probably don't remember anything, but my name's Bob Gault. I work for one of the US intelligence agencies. I received the request to reinforce your MI-6 buds, and was available when the rescue mission commenced. They invited me in. How you doin'?"

Sommers blinked. What he saw shifted out of focus and then back in. He swallowed. "Belly's a bloody wall of pain. My mouth's parched. Water, please."

Clyde moved closer. "Sir Charles asked us to follow you. We were in the lobby of your hotel. We'd placed a camera in your room, and when those Arab blokes broke into it, we wondered at first if you'd invited them. We called Sir Charles for guidance, and he ordered us to help, but he believed we'd need additional assistance." Clyde pointed to Gault. "We all returned just when they were starting to screw with you."

"You followed me all the way from Manhattan?" Sommers realized that in his hurry to escape the bank's enforcement arm, his counter-surveillance tradecraft had been deficient.

"Actually, sir, we've followed you everywhere you've been for the last seven weeks. Including Sorab's apartment in Karachi. Everywhere."

Jon shook his head. But, of course. He'd been their puppet. And his tradecraft would never save him if he couldn't even tell there were two king-sized brutes on his tail for this long a time. His formulas hadn't anticipated any of this.

Clyde pulled a cell phone from his pocket. "Sir Charles wants us to get your statement. To corroborate with what we've reported. Everything you've done, everyone you've seen or talked to. In return, we'll provide Sorab with her visa. He still hasn't sent it on to her."

Jon nodded, hiding his rage. He took several breaths. "I thought you sent her the visa weeks ago." He guessed if they'd lied to him about this, they'd lied about more.

He felt his face grow hot and faced Gault. Another liar. Studied the man's face. And heard Lisa's voice, warning him. *He's not trustworthy. I just know it to look at him.* He made a decision. "I'll talk. But not with him in the room. Your deal with me doesn't include the United States."

Gault's face went from placid to red. He shook his head. "Right. Fuck you very much. You're an idiot." As he reached the door, he turned toward Jon. "Just to let you know, it was me that shot your ragheads. Clyde and Wilbur couldn't hit the broad side of a barn. So, for all my help in saving your wretched ass, I come away with *nichevo* to show my handlers. Thanks for nothing."

Jon frowned. "I just don't trust you. The Yanks have treated Mossad like dirt since time began."

Gault shook his head. "You don't understand. We can help you. I suspect you're not done yet and you'll need every assistance I can offer. How about it?"

Jon looked from Wilbur to Clyde to Gault. "No. I'll pass.

Gault muttered a curse and marched out through the door.

Clyde slammed it shut. "Right, then. Your statement."

When he slept he dreamed of Lisa. She smiled, but then reminded him he wasn't finished yet. And next she was touching him, telling him she loved him.

When he woke, he thought about his situation. Once again, his cover here was blown. There might be others from the Bank of Trade hunting him. Singapore wasn't safe, and Gault was right. He wasn't finished.

The next morning a doctor visited his room and handed Jon a bottle of antibiotics. The doctor told him not to eat solid foods for at least two days. The stitches would dissolve within a week. The doctor begged him to stay for at least two more days in observation, but Jon shook his head. "Don't think so. Not safe here. Besides, there's something I need to do." But after the doctor left his room, Jon collapsed onto the bed as the room spun.

Three hours later, the doctor released him from the hospital, after first stating it wasn't safe for him to leave. Clyde helped him up from the wheelchair.

Wilbur walked into the street to flag a taxi,

Clyde told Jon the room at the Mandarin Oriental was sealed by the local police, "so, you needn't check out."

Along with the two Brits he was now thinking of as "the twins," he rode a taxi to the airport.

The twins sat on either side of him. "Where to, brother?" Clyde was beginning to annoy Jon.

Jon remembered the intel he'd sent to both Crane and Mother. He conjured a plan, this time avoiding the mathematics that had failed him. The intel featured Vladivostok. Submarines. It was like a nightmare. "First get me Crane."

Clyde punched a number into the cell and handed it to Jon.

"Crane."

"It's Sommers. Have you delivered Sorab her visa?"

"Yes. Our embassy sent a foreign service officer and picked her up. She's in the embassy now, and she'll be in London the day after tomorrow."

Was this another lie? "Thanks." He terminated the call and handed the cell back to Clyde. "I think Vlad is the best place to start. Take me to the airport."

Wilbur tapped on the cabbie's glass. "Changi Airport."

Jon imagined Houmaz, meeting with a merchandiser from the Russian mafiya and sailing off in the conning tower of one of the subs, the other trailing close behind. He frowned and struggled to make a better plan, one that might actually work.

Israel might not have much time left before everyone there was incinerated.

CHAPTER 25

William Wing's apartment,
Ascot Heights, Block A, 21 Lok Lam Road,
New Territories, Hong Kong
September 18, 10:23 p.m.

William Wing read the latest useless email from Lieutenant Chan and cursed in Mandarin. He doubted the efficacy of using Chinese hackers. It had been his father's decision, in order to keep the border skirmish problem under wraps. But William felt his own complicity, never arguing that better talent might be available. And, it was.

He knew several in North Vietnam and a few in Riyadh he thought were much better hackers. And then he remembered the best one, Brown. *Betsy "Butterfly" Brown.* He mumbled her name with unintended reverence, as if she was a goddess. It made him laugh. But, he needed the best. And, he thought, *she is the best.* He reached for his cell phone and punched in her number.

He counted the rings. One, two, three. Damn. She used a cell phone. Had she decided to assign him to voicemail hell? But, on the fourth ring, he heard her say "What?"

"Butterfly, it's Wing." He sighed and braced himself for the onslaught of imagined insults he was sure she'd hurl.

"Little Wing. Why are you calling?"

"I have another problem. You might be better at this

than those who've been helping me." William realized too late that he'd worded his request in an insulting way and prepared for her diatribe.

"You stupid shit. First, you call me on an unencrypted line. Then you tell me your first choice of talent wasn't me. And, of course, that didn't work, did it? Some defective ass-hole you are. And you assert you managed them? Idiot, you couldn't manage an insect, let alone someone with half a brain."

He flinched. "Uh, you're right. On all counts. Please forgive me. Will you help?"

"And what do I get for being your hacker slave?" He could hear the half-laugh in her voice and winced.

He had only one thing to offer. "Another favor owed. To be claimed at the time you choose, and for anything you desire." *Ouch, another mistake. Maybe I should have had another cup of coffee before I called the little brat.*

"Well. Well, well, well. Let's see, I think that's a total of six solids you'll owe me if I agree to do this one. Maybe I'll have you be my very own house slave. You can dress in an apron, with nothing else underneath it, of course. And you'll cook my favorite dishes for me, vacuum, and clean my cat's litter box. Or maybe I'll have you stud in person for me. No more phone sex. Hmmm? Lemme think. Oh, I have a really good idea. I think I'll just—"

NO! He flinched. "Right. Well, I agree to whatever."

"Then call me back using a secure Internet phone connection." She gave him details for a temporary Internet sanctuary and terminated the call.

It took William less than five minutes to set up the new connection.

Her voice was all business. "So?"

He steeled himself, thinking. "What I need is a traceless hack of the Chinese and Russian government servers. A third party has inserted data into their computers. The hacks state that each country attacked the other. Border attacks, But they never happened. Phantom events. I need you to find out who placed the reports there. So, when you have the data strings, you'll need to figure out how they got there and who put them there. Can you do it?"

"A very trivial pursuit. Of course I can."

He took a deep breath. "Good. How long? For something so easy?"

"Dunno. It's been a while since I was deep inside the Ruskies' kitchen. And your folks' mainframes? Not for at least a year. It'll take me a few days just to see what the current state of their computer security is. I've heard both countries have enhanced their cybercrime units. Ever since the US power grids were infected with super viruses from some hacker, everyone is spending the bucks on finding and fucking with us. So, uh, figure a week to be safe. Okay?"

William nodded, smiling. "Yeah. The power-grid infection. Well, everyone knows about that."

"One more thing. This will cost you. I want fifty thou."

He stopped himself from gasping and took a few seconds to settle himself. "No. I'll give you twenty."

"Thirty-five."

He sighed. "Thirty."

"Done."

"Thanks, Butterfly. You're the best." As the words emerged, he realized he'd made another mistake.

"But of course I am. And thanks for finally saying it. So, I'll tell you what. As one of the favors you owe me, I want to you post your evaluation, the one you just gave me, on all the hacker blogs and in all the hacker newsgroups. *NOW!*"

Ouch. He knew it would hurt. *A lot*, he guessed. "Okay! Lemme know when you have what I need."

He heard her terminate the call. *Shit. There goes my own reputation. CryptoMonger is no longer the best. Now I'm just second best. Butterfly is the best. CRAP!*

The next morning, William found an encrypted email on his personal web page. It had taken Butterfly less than twelve hours to do what he couldn't do at all. He felt excitement for the intel he could send to his father, but it was tempered with disappointment for the damage to his own reputation.

It took him twenty minutes to decrypt the email. He read the contents and their attachments, his brows furrowing several times.

The text went on forever, offering myriad details. But, the bottom line was obvious. The computer hackers who did the Chinese and Russian government computers were from the Mossad, and they'd covered their tracks well.

He poured himself a cup of coffee and sat in his kitchen, thinking as he sipped. *Should I tell father? What will he do if he finds out? What if I don't tell him and the hare-brained lieutenant somehow finds out? But if he realizes the Israelis hacked his government computers, what would he do in retaliation? And if, after that, they ever found out I've worked for the Mossad as a stringer, what would the Chinese government do to me, and to father?*

He let these thoughts cycle through his brain like a computer program stuck in a buggy, endlessly looping logic routine. As he swallowed the last gulp of coffee, he stared out the window at the busy harbor below his apartment.

William decided not to tell his father. Not yet. Not until he knew why. He'd need to talk to someone in the Mossad. Someone careful. He knew only one Mossad case officer he could trust.

Michael O'Hara. He owes me.

CHAPTER 26

Jon walked into Changi Airport, one of the twins on either side of him. He held a can of cola in his left hand and answered the cell phone in his right. "Sommers."

The person on the other end of the line was silent for a few seconds. It seemed like hours to him. The voice sounded like a growling dog. "I heard you were treated poorly by our enemies."

So, Jon thought, *Mother must be receiving intel from MI-6.* It was the deal Crane had first proposed to Jon in Manhattan. And, of course, Crane was sourced by the Brits, who had offered intel from the Americans. He felt dizzy just thinking about it. He was still strung between the three intelligence agencies like a puppet whose strings were tangled.

Jon could hear the sneer in his own voice. "They bloody well tortured me and would have executed me if my friends from MI-6 hadn't intervened. Not to mention a Yank named Gault. No thanks to you after what I did to help Mossad. Who is Bob Gault?"

"He works for Mark McDougal. McDougal is one of the Ass Dires in Gilbert Greenfield's intelligence agency. That agency has no name. You didn't tell Gault anything, did you?"

231

"Don't be stupid, Mother. Just the smell of him put me off. I didn't call you to chat about the bloody Yanks. What are you doing about Houmaz?"

The laugh on the other end of the line was chilling. "Why should I give you intel? You're not Mossad anymore. At best you're a stringer now." Silence for a few seconds. Jon could feel the man thinking. "Wait. You're not intending to hunt Tariq Houmaz, are you? That would be suicide." Mother's voice was shrill now.

"Just tell me. I know where he is, and what he intends. Either you let me help, or I might get in your way. I want justice for Lisa Gabriel, and I won't stop until I'm done with him. What's it to be?" Now, Jon felt his palms go sweaty, fearing what Mother could do to him. Yet, his face was hot with rage at what he wanted to do to Houmaz.

The protracted silence was a good sign. Mother must be juggling the potential outcomes. "I have a team in Vlad. After he pays for the subs, we'll decide what to do with him. No decision until he pays the mafiya for them. We don't want to incur the wrath of Russian organized crime. They can bury Israel faster than any Arab nation, given the weapons they sell to anyone who can pay for them."

"What are you planning?" Jon's eyebrows scrunched.

"What will you do if I tell you?"

"If you tell me everything I want to know, I'll help out. You orphaned me from the Mossad. As an independent agent, it's safer to use me. I'm just a former NOC. I can give you deniability." Jon prayed Mother would comply.

"Well. Yes. There is that." Silence. "But you screwed up your last *kidon* assignment. I've no reason to believe you'll fare better this time."

"Mother, you owe me. All the intel you have, you got from me. If I screw up, it'll likely end with my death. If so, we'll be done." He took a deep breath, steeling himself to the secrets Mother held. His voice grew louder. "Give me the intel."

Ben-Levy said nothing for a while. "I sent a new Mossad recruit, an IDF major, Avram Shimmel, with a battle team from the Israeli navy. Shimmel is one of our most talented military officers, a legend in tactics from IDF. He's done work for SHABEK and also has extensive covert training. He isn't good at playing politics though, or he'd be the head of Aman by now. In Vlad, he and his squad will hunt and find Aziz Tamil and the crew trained by the Russians to man the subs. They'll execute the crew and take their places. Shimmel's crew was chosen because they can pass for Arabs, and we trained them to operate Russian submarines, using the manuals we hacked off the Russian government's servers. We learned that Houmaz has never met any of the crew his brother bought. They came through an intermediary in the Syrian government. When Houmaz hands the subs over to Tamil, he'll be giving them to us."

Jon felt a rush of surprise mixed with pride. "And then I can have Houmaz."

"No, you idiot. Patience! As a result of your work, I have a deal with MI-6. And they'll stop the flow of intel when Houmaz dies. He's part of the deal now. Executing him isn't an option."

Jon was thunderstruck. This was proof positive Mother had concluded the deal Crane had asked him to make with Mother. "But—"

"No buts. My man in Vlad. Shimmel. I'll send you contact details in an encrypted email. There. It's on its way. Don't blow this or I'll hunt you personally.

The line went dead.

Jon faced the twins. "Guys, we need to buy our tickets for the first flight out to Vlad. Have Crane's cobblers get us visas and deliver them ASAP." They both smiled and walked behind him to the Aeroflot ticket counter.

The next flight to Vlad wasn't for two hours. Jon paced, while the twins read *USA Today* online, using their cell phones. When the line cued for departure, he felt exhausted.

A messenger appeared with an envelope and handed it to Clyde. They had their visas.

After finding his seat, he'd tried sleeping, but it wasn't happening. He was primed for the next step.

Jon's belly ached, but the shooting pains were less frequent and less intense. He scratched the itchy spot under his bellybutton where his belt squeezed the stitches.

When the flight steward offered a snack, he decided to try solid food. The potato chips tasted delicious, and he drifted off into sleep. He saw Lisa, felt her hands on him, her lips kissing his, her voice whispering into his ear. And felt joy for the first time in as long as he could remember.

But when he woke, the plane was descending though a grayish brown sky to the airport runway in Vlad. The pain in his gut was wrenching. He should have heeded the doctor. He asked for a glass of water and swallowed a sip with another pain killer and an antibiotic.

Inside the terminal, the petrochemical odor of the city made him queasy. He bolted for the restroom and threw up the chips he'd eaten. Clyde asked, "You okay?"

Jon nodded. "We need to find a hotel."

Clyde shook his head. "No, brother. Been here before. We want the Hotel Visit. No electronic shit. They have an old-fashioned pen-and-paper registration book. And, they speak English there. No place else does. But, no speaking about our business in the rooms. Every room in Vlad is bugged by the Russian mafiya."

Once again, Jon was grateful for the twins. He followed them to a car rental counter.

In less than an hour, they were driving into downtown. Leaving the car, Jon scanned the area. The Hotel Visit sat on the hill overlooking the wharf. And the piers below held warehouses. Did these house the weapons sold by the Russian mafiya? Everything was as Mother had told him.

As he handed his Salim al-Muhammed passport to the registration clerk, he had a chance to think.

He needed to make another plan. A perfect plan.

PART III

CHAPTER 27

"It's Gault." The spy shifted his pear-shaped body until he stood silhouetted against the window. He shifted behind a pillar and watched the three coverts as they queued to board the aircraft. Gault watched, remaining motionless, listening to his handler's reply.

The spy nodded. "Yes. Right now, they're boarding an Aeroflot flight to Vladivostok. My guess is, they think Houmaz went there." As his targets disappeared into the aircraft, he found a seat in the waiting area.

"No, sir," Gault said. "I don't know what his orders are. But I think he's following Houmaz because the terrorist must be buying something there. Nope, don't know what. But the Russian mafiya owns the city. And they sell everything from howitzers to nuclear weapons."

The voice on the other side of the line spoke for a long time.

Gault sighed and rose from his seat. He paced around the gate area. "I understand that. But, what is it you want me to do?"

This time his handler uttered just one sentence.

"Right. I'll get on it. Literally on it." When his handler

terminated the conversation, he walked to the ticket counter. "Get me on the next flight to Vladivostok."

While they processed the ticket, he looked out the window and watched Sommers's flight disengage from the gate. The aircraft rolled along the tarmac toward a runway. Gault shook his head. *Too late for that one.*

The earliest available seat was on tomorrow's flight. He wanted to track the twins and their charge as much as he wanted a fatal wound. Yes, a night off would do him good. Maybe some female company, too.

Houmaz could wait.

The next day, Gault was the first passenger boarding the plane. He found his seat and sat rigid as the plane rose through the clouds while he considered his options in Vlad.

By the time the aircraft landed at the airport late in the evening, Gault had a plan and a bellyache from the snacks.

He debarked into Vlad's terminal, deciding which cover identity to select and how to play it to gain advantage. He smiled; the plan was good. He'd need backups, none of these identities would be washed. No time for a legend and not even time to backstop the passports or other documents. He'd be walking the line without a net, and just the thought sent a chill up his spine. A good chill.

Gault called the research desk at his agency. "I need the name and address of a cobbler in Vladivostok who forges ID's for us." He listened and wrote nothing down. The name he was given was a forger on the payroll of the Russian mafiya. He walked from the terminal to a taxi stand and gave the cabbie an address two blocks away from his destination.

The cobbler's shop was covered by a clothing store that served as its front. He found the man whose description he sought. "I need several sets of passports, drivers licenses, and gun permits. How much?" Gault noticed his own Russian linguistic skills were rusty from the old man's reaction.

The bald, thin man had a birthmark shaped like a handgun on his right cheek. He smiled as he appraised Gault. "Twenty thousand rubles each. And cheap at that price."

It was. He removed an American Express card with the name "Wesley Amanpour" from his wallet. The card was washed, of course. "Four of them. Kiril Sarkovsky, Russian. Herr Henrik Schmidt, German. Sayed Abedi, Pakistani. And Ahmed Samsir, Saudi. How fast can you produce all the documents for each identity?"

The old man stood silent for a few seconds. "One hour. There's a restaurant across the street. Give me your cell phone number. I'll call you when I'm done."

"No. I'll just check in with you from time to time." Gault looked at his wristwatch. 4:45 p.m. He chuckled. *No way I'm giving the Russian mafiya my phone number.*

He left the cobbler's shop. *What do I need to prove to earn my next promotion?* Although his handler would never admit it, what he was doing now was off the books. Either it succeeded or Gault would be taking the fall. *What will I do with the rest of my life if I fail and get my ass fired?*

While he waited, Gault found a drug store and purchased cosmetics so, if need be, he could disguise his face. Then he went to a clothing store and bought appropriate clothes for each passport. *Semper paratus*, he whispered to himself. "Always Ready," the motto of the US Coast Guard. When he checked in just before 6 p.m., all the documents were ready.

Gault had never been to Vlad, but he'd done his research during the plane ride. He took a cab to the Hotel Visit, the only lodging place which offered an English-speaking staff.

Standing at the hotel's registration desk, he scanned the lobby for threats. Nothing. While the clerk processed his identity documents and generated an electronic room key, he read the registration book. He read several lines above where he was requested to sign, and smiled. There were two lines signed by the Brits whom he'd met up with to rescue Michael O'Hara. Right above those, someone else signed in, probably at the same time. He scanned the name and smiled. Now he knew the cover name of the man he'd rescued: Salim al-Muhammed. Bingo! Gault smiled. It made sense for them to lodge here. Everything was all working out.

After dawn the next day, Gault watched the elevator from an armchair in the lobby. He held a newspaper and used it to cover his features every time the elevator doors opened or he heard someone coming down the stairs. He figured his targets would go out to commence their assigned operations within a few hours.

He waited for five long hours before he heard the elevator doors creak open and saw the three covert operatives leave. The two British coverts, Wilbur and Clyde looked out of place in this pisshole of a city, but Salim al-Muhammed looked to be at home. He waited several minutes more, and then took the elevator up to the fourth floor. Slipping his credit card between the door and the jamb, he opened the door of Wilbur's room. Before he entered, he saw a gray piece of thread fall from the door jamb inches above the floor. Idiots! Their tradecraft was so Cold War. No one had done that for ten years! He picked up the thread, walked in and shut the door.

Gault placed several bugs within the room. These were new technology, just developed for the NSA and the CIA by DARPA, the R and D agency of the Defense Department. They were much harder to detect than anything the other intelligence services were using. He hummed Gilbert and Sullivan's "Modern Major-General" while he worked, putting one bug inside the room's air vent, one under the bed, and one within the telephone's plastic wall cover for its cord. Within ten minutes, he'd replaced the thread and was gone. He repeated the process in Clyde's room and then in Jon's. When he was finished, Gault took the stairs up one floor to his own room. He thought how they must have swept for bugs before they left and wouldn't do it again the same day. But even if they did, they wouldn't find any. And that meant they'd talk freely.

He hummed a tune from Tosca as he closed the door to his room and set up the voice recorders. The batteries on the bugs would last about forty-eight hours. Much more time than he'd need. *If I pull this one off, I'll get the promotion to team leader. Finally!*

He hooked a voice alarm to the recorder and placed his headphones on the nightstand by his face. He reviewed his work to ensure all the connections were solid.

Gault napped, knowing that as soon his quarry entered any of their rooms, the shrill alarm would wake him. He slept soundly, dreaming of the office that would replace his cubicle as a result of this operation.

It was dark when the howl of the alarm woke him. Salim al-Muhammed's room. Three voices, so all were there. The record function switched on automatically. Clyde MacIntosh was speaking. "Are you sure, Michael?"

He heard al-Muhammed say, "Not sure. But all the details point to Houmaz sending the subs to somewhere in the Middle East. My guess is a deep-water bay between the coast of Oman and Somalia. It could be anywhere between the Gulf of Oman and the Gulf of Aden."

Could this be true? Houmaz buying submarines?

He left the recorder on but pulled off the headphones. And picked up his cell phone. "It's Gault. Get me McDougal. I'm in Vlad. It's urgent!"

CHAPTER 28

Trans-Siberian Express terminal,
Vladivostok, Russia
September 19, 11:45 p.m.

Tariq Houmaz sat on a wood bench waiting for the Trans-Siberian Express to arrive from Moscow. He'd taken care coming here to ensure he'd not been followed. It was deadly quiet; he could even hear the sole oak tree's leaves stirring in the breeze. He stared at the tree, twenty-five meters away on the other side of the tracks. Its trunk was what he continued to focus on as the time passed.

He tugged on the sleeve of his white bespoke-collared shirt and straightened the red silk tie that complemented his blue pinstripe business suit. Carrying a user manual and a catalogue for Cisco Systems circuit boards, he held them where they were visible so his cutout would know he sat where he'd been told to. He felt safe in his disguise as an electronics trader.

He heard the train's whistle and watched it slowing as it entered the station. Vlad was the final stop on the Orient Express. The tree was no longer visible; it was on the loco-motive's other side. He waited, as he'd been told, until the train emptied, then refilled and prepared to leave. Houmaz wanted to pace but remained sitting, watching. He scratched his beard, worrying about the next steps in his plan.

When the train reversed direction, crawling back toward Europe, he glanced at his wristwatch. Then back at the tree. He could see it now, the entire trunk. It was too dark for him to make out the hollow of the tree. If all had gone as he was promised, their message would await him. Any second now, he could leave this wretched bench and see what they'd left in the slick. As the train chugged out of town, he rose.

At just past midnight, he darted across the now-empty tracks. There was a single sheet of paper placed within the slick. He glanced at it, but the words were in pencil and it was too dark to read them.

First, get back to the shack where he was staying as fast as he could. He stashed the note in his pocket and dashed off.

Sommers replaced the infrared field glasses in his jacket pocket. He followed the bomb maker at a discreet distance, ensuring his target's counter-surveillance routines wouldn't pick him up. As he walked, his fists kept clenching, his knuckles tight. The twins also followed, but well behind him.

As the stream of coverts neared the center of the wharf area, Houmaz ducked into a ramshackle building. The door squeaked shut behind him.

Jon beckoned the twins to close the distance. He pointed to Wilbur's mission bag, with the barest essentials for immediate evacuation when necessary. "Gimme the listening scope and set it for shallow metal walls and about twenty meters." Wilbur punched a few buttons on its tiny keyboard and handed the device to Jon.

They scrambled across the street into a dark alleyway. Jon aimed the antenna of the device toward the shack and plugged in the wireless headphone transmitter, a small box with a red blinking light. Each of the three donned headsets and listened.

They heard the bomb maker moving around. *He must*

be alone, Jon thought. No other sound for an hour. Then snoring. Jon faced the twins. "We need to get that piece of paper, if he hasn't destroyed it."

Clyde nodded.

Wilbur shook his head. "What if he wakes?"

Jon found himself calculating the odds of different outcomes. "Kill him." He was sure it was the only way. And he'd wanted an excuse to send Houmaz to a better place. *Let me be his judge.*

Clyde pointed back at Jon. "No. We can't. He's our asset. Sir Charles has to approve sanction of any asset."

Jon looked at his wristwatch. "Call him. Now."

Clyde pulled the cell from his pocket and punched in a number. He turned away from Jon and spoke in hushed tones. Then he turned to Jon. "We have permission to enter and search for the paper. We aren't sanctioned to terminate him. Seems he's now the asset of an associated intelligence service." Clyde shrugged. "But, Mr. Sommers, if you wake him to force our hand, we're ordered to shoot both of you. Please hand me your gun."

Jon shrugged. He'd guessed as much. Would killing Houmaz and then being killed by the twins be a trade worth making? He wasn't sure. There was more at stake now than just revenge for Lisa. The subs must not fall into the Muslim Brotherhood's hands. "He's dangerous, you know. It might be better for all three of us to be armed."

Clyde shook his head. "Give it to me." Jon pulled the Beretta from his pocket and handed it to Clyde.

"And, we're not to take the paper. We read it and leave it where we found it. He's not to know we were ever there. Is this clear?"

Jon nodded.

Wilbur disassembled the listening device and packed it into the mission bag along with the headphones. Wilbur dug into the bag and removed two plastic-composite 9mm

Berettas and two plastic clips of plastic bullets. He handed one to Clyde and kept the other.

Jon remembered the last time he'd used a gun and what had happened to that team. Houmaz had killed everyone except him. He'd sworn under his breath it wouldn't happen again. Never again. But, this time he'd be unarmed. There'd be no way he could protect even just himself.

Clyde pulled a spray can of lubricant from the mission bag and coated the door's hinges. He replaced it, nodding to Jon and Wilbur. Then he cracked open the door and the three entered, spreading out into different sectors of the room. Houmaz rolled over inside a sleeping bag, and now he faced them with his eyes closed. Still snoring.

Jon worried the bomb maker was faking sleep and might have a pistol in his hand, covered by the sleeping bag. He approached and found Houmaz's pants on a wooden chair three meters behind their target. He stared at Houmaz, while he searched the man's pockets.

Jon removed a yellow page and unfolded it. The words printed on it named a location, a beach a few miles southwest of the city. And a date and time. Six hours from now. But there was something more important: the instruction to use a verbal call sign, "strangelove." *So, the Russian mafiya has a sense of humor*. He replaced the refolded sheet and motioned to the twins.

Time to leave.

The three interlopers walked without making a sound to the door. Clyde and Wilbur pointed their guns at Houmaz as they backed away. Clyde reached his left hand to the door and turned the knob. He pushed it open.

But at the end of its traverse, the metal squeaked.

As the Brits and Jon turned to face Houmaz, three shots popped through the sleeping bag. The sound startled Jon, and he dove for the doorway.

Small holes in both twins' foreheads dripped red. Jon

felt a burning sensation in his right hand where a gun should have been.

His brain felt sluggish despite the jolt of adrenaline. But one thing was clear: without a weapon, he'd have no chance if he didn't run. Too far away to charge at the man. Only one way out. As he crawled through the door, he heard Houmaz chamber another round. He covered the back of his head with his forearm and saw another flash from the sleeping bag. His left shoulder felt the burning bullet rip into it. Jon bolted through the door, crawled, and staggered to his feet.

He raced for his life looking for cover down the street.

About twenty meters more to an intersection. He sprinted left around a corner, back the way they'd come. Kept running, taking twists and turns away from where his team lay dead. He remembered the team in Manhattan. He'd failed them, too.

Houmaz climbed out of the sleeping bag and checked for pulse on the two Brits. They were both dead. He paced the room. A cold autumn breeze hit his shirt, and the perspiration from his excitement gave him chills. He'd recognized the face of the man he'd wounded. Mossad. It was the *kidon* whose team he'd murdered a few months ago in Manhattan. *So, they are still hunting me. He shook his head. I must kill that man. How can I trap him? The presence of a single* kidon *means there may be others.* He examined the pockets of the two corpses. One of them had a cell phone. The last call had a London country code. They were British. He wondered if he'd been burned and set up. Were the Brits now working with the Jews? They'd never done that before. Maybe the Brits knew what he was here to do. But how could they? If they did, had they told the Jews? Very likely they had. He grimaced. So close now to showing his father the man he'd become. *I must not fail!* Who was responsible for this complication?

But in Vlad, the Russians ruled. There was something he needed to find out fast. Were the Russians the glue that held together this failed attempt on his life?

CHAPTER 29

Russian mafiya warehouse on the wharf terminal,
Vladivostok, Russia
September 19, 1:28 a.m.

Nikita Tobelov threw a handful of coal into the stove that heated his warehouse office. He grinned, celebrating the biggest deal of the twenty-three years he'd been running the Eastern Branch of the Russian mafiya. He removed a jar of Beluga caviar and a bottle of Stoli vodka from the fridge in his office. Then, he grabbed a tin of crackers from the bottom drawer of his desk and spread the rich black roe onto a saltine. As he raised it to his lips, his cell buzzed. "*Da?*"

"It's Houmaz. Why did you send MI-6 after me?"

"What?" The cracker fell to his desk.

"They were here. I shot two of them dead, but the third one escaped. I may have wounded him. Tell me, why?"

Tobelov looked at the cracker. "I didn't compromise you. It's not our way. You must have been careless." He scooped up the saltine and popped it into his mouth, savoring the rich salty flavor of caviar.

The line went dead. Tobelov grabbed the bottle by its neck and gulped down a swig. Then he punched in the number for his security force. "Vasili, send a team here. We might have an angry customer visiting us soon." *But*, he thought, *it's more likely the raghead will flee the city if he's worried.*

Crickets buzzed the night sky. Aziz Tamil and the twenty-six submariners Houmaz had the Russians train sat on the shoreline, just southwest of the city. He watched his team members as they smoked cigarettes and talked. Tamil wore a balaclava over his face. He had lifts on his shoes, and there was padding in his shirt making him look fat. No one who'd tried to photograph his face had ever lived to tell about it. No one even knew what his voice sounded like.

He scribbled a note on a piece of paper and beckoned to his second-in-command. The man took the note and read it, then ripped it into shreds and tossed it into the campfire. Tamil watched as the man ordered two perimeter guards to tighten up the southeast edge of their camp.

He stared at the rafts sitting on the shoreline. Four more hours and they'd be on the subs and gone from this pisshole of a city. He couldn't wait.

"What do you mean, you don't know where they are?" Avram Shimmel could feel the sneer creeping across his face. "What do we do now?"

"You wait." The voice hissed back, just above a whisper. "What is your GPS?"

Avram scanned his location off the screen of the secure satellite phone and read off the numbers. The beach where they were camped was just northwest of the city.

"I'll call you back soon." Yigdal Ben-Levy terminated the call.

Avram shook his head. The mission seemed doomed.

Jon reached the western outskirts of the city. The bicycle he'd stolen left his legs feeling rubbery. He felt blood, warm and wet, spreading from the hole in his left shoulder. His right hand stung where the bullet scored his palm. His breath came in spurts.

As he sped away, he knew he'd had enough. Twice he'd been close enough to kill Tariq Houmaz, and he'd failed both times. He was no *kidon* and there was no way he'd ever be one. He'd failed twice, and now he needed to get away. All he could feel was fear as he pedaled as fast as he could.

Lisa's voice screamed at him to go back and kill Houmaz. He owed her that for her love. Jon whipped around another corner. Her voice screamed, *you can't go. No!* He shook his head, his mind echoing back his own *no! Bitch, leave me be!* He doubted he could win the war in his mind, but he knew he had to fight.

He made a decision, and as he made it, he knew it was one he'd regret. He dropped the bike in an alleyway and removed his cell phone from his pocket. Moving his arm sent a bolt of pain through his shoulder. He ignored it. "Get me Mother. It's Sommers. And it's urgent." He waited and went through the usual security procedures.

"You woke me. What's so urgent?"

"I know where the subs will be and what we need to know to steal them." Jon realized he was shouting and tried to control his voice. He fought the dizziness surging through him.

He heard his former handler sigh. "Really? Go on. Tell me." Mother's tone sounded sarcastic to him, and he felt his own mouth turn down. He was dizzy and realized he couldn't stand up much longer. He looked for something to sit on. Nothing there. He braced himself against the building.

Jon told Ben-Levy about their operation, the fate of the twins, and ended with the fact that Houmaz was still alive.

Then he read the note from his memory into the phone. He knew the conversation would be recorded. They always were.

"You say the countersign is 'strangelove?' Hah. Funny. Jon, you did well tonight. You have our gratitude."

Jon felt his left arm and right hand on fire where Tariq Houmaz's bullets had ripped into him. "Just one question, Yigdal. If I see him again, may I kill him?"

It seemed to take his former handler forever to consider his answer. "Jon, I like you. I adored your parents. Your father was our most feared covert. But, we are running a state here. Feelings, yours or mine, they don't count. Our adversaries' motto is 'convert or die.' Ours is 'by way of deception thou shalt do war.' If you can't help, if you become an obstacle, we'll deal with you as an enemy. Israel must survive."

Jon gripped the phone so hard his hand hurt. "Just tell me the bloody answer. May I kill Tariq Houmaz?"

He heard Ben-Levy's voice grow terse, just above a whisper. "Bring him in intact. Let our Intelligence Division interrogate him. We have some new toys from the biochemistry team. He still has valuable intel. And, Jon, killing Houmaz won't bring Lisa back."

"I have the intel you need."

"Ready. Where are the subs?" Avram used hand signals to get the attention of his lieutenants and they surrounded him. He listened to Ben-Levy for another thirty seconds. "It'll be tight. We're twenty kilometers away and if we drive fast enough to be there before they launch their rafts, they'll hear us."

He heard Ben-Levy's scowl.

Avram took a deep breath to calm himself. "Stop acting like a teenager. We will find a way." He terminated the call, smiling. It was the first time he'd ever hung up on Ben-Levy and it felt good.

He turned to his lieutenants. "Into the trucks. Follow mine." He boarded the passenger side of the lead truck and gave the corporal in the driver's seat directions.

Fifteen minutes later, the stolen trucks coasted to a nearly silent stop. The team Avram brought with him formed a double line and waited.

Avram scanned his wristwatch. They had eleven minutes remaining to terminate the sub's crew. He used hand signals to move them down the road adjacent to the beach. He scanned the map as they neared their objective. Now he could barely discern voices in the distance. He called his men to a halt.

He mounted the dune and counted the targets around the distant campfire with infrared field glasses. Using hand signals, he gave silent orders to the IDF soldiers he commanded. They spread out along the flanks of their targets.

He reviewed his plan against his mental checklist. All was a go. Pressing the button on his ear bud, he whispered. "Snipers, ready. On my signal. No prisoners. Infantry, commence firing. Go, go, go." By the time he finished his last word, the targets were all on the ground, most of them dead. Shimmel thought, *one of them must be Aziz Tamil, the famed terrorist no one's ever seen. But, which one?* He ordered his second-in-command to photograph each dead face.

In several minutes the man returned, smiling. "Sir, we found him. The only one whose face was covered. And he's still breathing."

Avram considered whether this might prove useful to him tonight. "Let me see him, Moshe."

The man's head was covered in a ski mask with a hood atop it. He'd been shot in his shoulder, but the bullet had sheared his arm off. Shimmel saw no way to staunch the bleeding. The man would surely die soon. Shimmel removed the scarf and ski mask covering Tamil's head. He said, "We know who you are. We know your password to acquire the submarines. Your team is dead. Every one of them. I intend to kill you. Before I do, you have one chance for a reprieve. Tell us everything you know and live your life in a prison cell. Make a choice now."

The wounded man spit at Shimmel. "I am dead already You are a fool if you think I will listen to your lies."

Shimmel nodded. "I understand. I'll give you time to pray. Is that what you want?"

The terrorist shook his head. "I die a martyr. And I'll go to heaven. You will go to hell. Get it over with."

Shimmel nodded and chambered a round. He pointed the Beretta at Tamil's left eye. "Last words?"

The terrorist screamed, "Death to all Jews!"

Shimmel shook his head and pulled the trigger. He ignored the coppery odor of the man's death, mixing with the smell of his fear and the after-death smell of his feces as his muscles went limp.

He mouthed the words Tamil had said until he could mimic the terrorist's voice. He smiled and placed the terrorist's scarf in his pocket.

He noted the paunch and raised the dead man's shirt. A pillow to make a thin man fatter. "Ah." He removed a shoe and examined it. The heels made Tamil three inches taller. Tamil was full of surprises. But his tricks had made him similar in size to Shimmel. But no one had ever seen Tamil, so he could easily assume the man's identity. He smiled as he walked away from the corpse.

Jon's sight and hearing returned to normal, but he felt his shoulder going numb. Dizziness threatened to cause him to black out. He opened the buttons on his shirt and pulled the shredded bloodstained fabric off his wound. He examined the area. The bullet puncture was shallow and no longer bleeding much. But he knew he'd need a doctor before too long. He used his cell phone's Internet connection to find a local surgeon, three miles away. He staggered toward downtown, planning to arrive at the doctor's home office just after dawn. With enough money, nothing would be reported to Vlad's police.

The surgeon took the equivalent of two thousand dollars for treating his wound and promised not to report it. Jon left the doctor's office with dissolving stitches in his left shoulder and a bulky bandage underneath his shirt. There was another bandage wrapped around his right hand.

He needed a change of clothing but there was no way he could risk going back to his hotel. *Where to go?*

When this plan failed, another team had died. Now, he had no plan, but there was no plan which could fix his situation. He felt useless. Rage mounted within him as he paced downtown. He wondered if Houmaz had alerted the Russian mafiya about him. But, of course he had. And, given that, he knew he had to leave Vladivostok now. Before they searched for him. *Where to go?* London, maybe. And do what?

No, there had to be a way to uncover Houmaz's next move. But exhausted, Jon couldn't figure these things. He took a taxi to the airport, his mind reeling. He bought fresh clothing at a store in the terminal and sat to think. *What should I do now?*

The sunrise deepened as Major Shimmel rushed his preparations. Near the shoreline, the submarine's new crew awaited, ready to load into the rafts, on his orders.

About a hundred yards out, the lead sub rose from the depths, water rolling off its sides.

"Time to go. Arabic only from here on out." Shimmel donned Tamil's scarf and a caftan he'd taken off another one of the dead. He made sure the scarf covered his mouth and nose.

He dropped into one of the rafts lined up on the beach. The others filled their rafts and pushed them into the cold Sea of Japan. Gray fog whooshed past them as they paddled.

As they reached the lead sub, its original Russian crew tossed ropes down to them. Before they closed the distance, a second sub broke the surface. Avram scanned the rafts, calling out in Arabic to send his crew to cover both subs. "Sayed, take rafts three and four to the other sub. Stay in the conning tower so we can use our satellite phones to coordinate the two submarines' movements."

"Sayed" was Moshe's call-sign. It took Moshe a few seconds to reply. "Okay."

Avram's team climbed onto the conning tower. He faced the sub's Russian crew. "Who's in charge?"

A bearded, dusky-skinned man climbed up the bridge. "I am. What's your countersign?"

Shimmel smiled. "Strangelove."

The other man nodded. "Come below. I am Tariq Houmaz."

Avram watched Moshe's team climb onto the other sub's conning tower. He pointed down into the sub's interior and Moshe nodded from about sixty yards away.

Avram made his way to the ready room. His immense size made it necessary for him to bend his neck to avoid the ceiling. "I am Aziz Tamil, captain of this vessel. We received your orders. We're ready."

The bomb maker nodded back. "We'll take your rafts."

As Shimmel pointed to one of his own crew, the scarf fell open, away from his face. He turned and replaced it, but the bomb maker had seen him. Too late. "Give him the rafts. Now."

In seconds, Tariq Houmaz and the Russian crew were gone from the bridge and paddling toward the shoreline.

No longer Aziz Tamil, Major Shimmel removed his caftan and the scarf. He shook his head. Through the periscope, he watched the terrorist's raft disappear, followed by the Russian crews of both subs. His second-in-command, Emil Schmidt, touched his sleeve. "Major, why didn't we just kill him?"

Shimmel's fists clenched at his missed opportunity. He faced Schmidt. "Orders from Mother."

As Houmaz led the crew, paddling away, he committed the facial features of Aziz Tamil to memory. Dragging the raft onto shore, he pulled his cell from the inner pocket of his jacket. He punched in a number, waiting while the wavelets hit the shore in incessant rhythm that gave him a headache. "Pesi, it's Tariq. Do you have a photograph of Tamil?" He paced the beach. "Yes, I know the story we've read. No photo of him? You sure?"

The voice on the other side became shrill.

"Our first time using him? Why are we doing business with a stranger?" Tariq's brows furrowed. "Brother, there's too much riding on this. See if you can dig out anything about him."

He pulled a pen and a piece of paper from his pocket and drew a rough sketch of the face of the man who called himself Tamil. He noted the height of the man was well over six-foot five. After folding the paper and dropping it in his pocket, he walked off the beach and hailed a taxi to the airport.

Getting out of Vladivostok as fast as possible would be his top priority.

Houmaz thought about what had just happened. Something didn't seem right. Tamil's accent and behavior, his gestures, were all Arabic. Probably Saudi. But his face looked European. Houmaz wondered if he might have made a mistake. Who were the men he'd given his submarines to?

Shimmel mounted the conning tower and waved to Moshe on the conning tower of the other sub. He had both his navigators set course for Oman, the first stop on their way to Haifa. He wondered if Houmaz would remember his face. Shit. Of course he would. "Moshe, let the sub's underwater antenna drag out with the communications array. I have to call Mother. Time to dive."

Shimmel ducked into the sub and closed the hatch. He dropped down one level and gave orders to the communications officer. In a few minutes the officer met him in the ready room. "Done, major."

Shimmel placed headphones over his ears and punched in the secure number.

"Status?" The gruff voice was filled with impatience. Shimmel could taste Mother's frustration at having to wait.

"It's Avram. I think your decision to let Houmaz live will come back at us."

The raspy voice chuckled. "Nonsense. We'll get more intel from him by tracking who he contacts and what he says to them. Besides that, he's now property of one of our allied intelligence services. So, for the time being, he lives. When he ceases to be of use to our allies, we'll send him to a better place. By then, we'll know everyone in his network."

Shimmel frowned. "He saw my face."

"So what? When word of this debacle makes its way onto Al Jazeera, he'll become a pariah to his people. What can one lonely terrorist do?"

"One lonely terrorist can figure out who I am and murder my wife and child. Please put a protection detail on them."

Ben-Levy changed his tone. "Major Shimmel, Israel is too small to have available resources just waiting to help us whenever we request. Everyone is assigned and busy. I have no way to do that. As for Mossad, our ventures are aimed outside Israel only. If you want protection within the country, you'll have to deal with Aman, not SHABEK."

"Then get them to help." Shimmel realized he was shouting.

"It probably won't work. I know what they'll tell you. If we did that for everyone who's at risk, the entire population of Israel would all carry guns to protect each other." The spymaster's voice got softer still. "Look, I'll call them for you. Give them a chance to reassign some resources. Maybe they can. But don't count on it."

Shimmel cursed to himself.

Ben-Levy's voice sounded calmer. "How is the crew working out?"

Shimmel paced the ready room. "The training we gave them on the Russian sub replicas, and the operations manuals Drapoff hacked from Russian military intelligence did the job. Our men are handling both subs well, and with practice drills, I expect their performance to improve fast."

Ben-Levy's voice became quieter, just above a whisper. "Tell me about the submarines. What technologies do they offer?"

Shimmel closed his eyes. Shook his head to clear the fear for his family in Tel Aviv from it. "The comm array is beyond what we've developed. The prize here is the missiles. Twenty nuclear-tipped ICBMs in each sub. Each missile is equipped with a twenty-megaton warhead. And something unexpected. The sub's countermeasures. They use the hydrophonic decoy system we developed to trick underwater sonar microphones that track submarines. This technology was stolen from Ness Ziona."

"Are you sure?"

"Yes. Moshe inspected them. We were hoping for another source, but the Institute's trademark is stamped on their cover. They've been adapted for underwater use, but the originals are also there."

"So, we have a mole."

"Absolutely. Look into that before more products find their way to the mafiya and terrorists."

"I will." He could imagine Ben-Levy's frown.

But, what Ben-Levy asked next told Shimmel how his new handler's concerns were prioritized. "How soon will you reach the Gulf of Oman?"

Not for the first time, Shimmel wondered what he'd gotten himself into. He wondered what would happen if Houmaz was able to identify him. He worried about his family.

CHAPTER 30

Trans-Siberian Express terminal,
Vladivostok, Russia
September 20, 6:29 a.m.

For the second time in less than eight hours, Tariq Houmaz sat on the same bench in the train terminal. He felt the urge to pace but didn't want to draw attention to himself. He didn't want to use the airport since, if his suspicions were true, he'd been betrayed. The train would be safer. At worst, jumping off a moving train didn't require a parachute.

The incoming train would take him west to a station where he could transfer and head southeast into Chechnya. From there he planned to take a plane to Kabul, Afghanistan. His driver would meet him at the airport and take him to Upper Pachir in the Nangarhar. Back to his lovely mountain caves.

Remembering the face of the shooter in Vlad he'd wounded, he considered how he'd failed. In the old days he'd have sent a bullet into the man's brain, not his shoulder. He'd find out the man's name and kill him as soon as he could. The shooter must be crazy, trying to kill him twice. *No one tries that with me.*

He could hear the train before he saw it. The rattle of the tracks, the smell of oil burned by grinding steel, then the headlight beam coming off the locomotive. He rose and found his body creaking and stiff. He hadn't slept well for two days. The only time he'd fallen asleep, the Brits and the Jew had visited him. Now, he was bone tired. No backpack to carry this time; the money it had held was gone.

Passengers exited the cars of the arriving train. When the crowd had thinned, he climbed on board and watched through the windows to see if anyone he recognized approached or surveilled the train.

He had a clear view of the platform. Watching, he saw fewer than twenty people board after him. The train jolted and then gained speed. He closed his eyes and drifted off, his hand on the Beretta inside his jacket holster, covered by a coat on top of his lap.

Every noise woke him. People entering the car, the train turning as it twisted around a mountain, the whistle as it neared a crossing. By noon he couldn't take it and gave up trying to sleep. He caught his reflection as the train ran through a tunnel. *I've aged so much this year*, he thought. *This too comes with the job. But I'm not yet ready to die.*

There were things he needed to do now, urgent tasks. He made a plan as he waited for the train to arrive in Chechnya.

CHAPTER 31

Sea of Japan
September 20, 3:45 p.m.

The two subs had names that Avram Shimmel translated from Russian as "Buttercup" and "Thor's Hammer." He chuckled as the he read the names off the covers of the manuals. Fluent in Russian, he noted differences from Michael Drapoff's hacked translation of the operating procedures, stolen from the Moscow Center computers. Drapoff was the best hacker in the Mossad.

So far, nothing was amiss, and the new countermeasures seemed to be working as advertised. He projected they'd arrive at their initial nesting facility near Muscat, Oman in two weeks. When they at last signaled their arrival, Shimmel would disembark back to Tel Aviv and be debriefed. He imagined the sweet faces of his beloved wife and daughter, and yearned to hold them again.

But Houmaz had seen his face. With every passing day he grew more certain the bomb maker would find out who'd stolen his property. Avram wanted to be back in Tel Aviv with his pregnant wife, Sharon, and little Golda.

He hated submarines. And after his trip there, he hated Vladivostok. He was still coughing from the rancid air. Avram swore he'd never go back there. Never again.

Lester Dushov stood up high enough so he could see across the mountains into Dongning, China. "Not really much of a city." The sun was setting bloody red against the mountain ridges.

Michael Drapoff watched the senior operative scan the valley below them. They'd been crisscrossing the border between Russia and China for seven weeks now. He turned toward Shimon Tennenbaum. "Sleepy, yeah. But at least they have wireless router connections. Let's do what we came for."

Shimon nodded and began wiring landmines across the road. While he completed his chore, Drapoff entered new data into the Chinese computers in Beijing, piggybacking on the town's wireless.

Ari Westheim and JD Weinstein stood guard duty with Dushov.

The trip here, east from Korfovka, Russia, had taken four days. They'd traveled after dark, using the daylight to set up Claymore mines. Then they'd hack the position of "enemy troops" sent by whichever country was supposed to have initiated the border incursion, into the "attacked" provincial capital city's government computer. They'd hide, watch troops arrive, and trigger the explosives.

Theirs was a false flag operation. The irony, as Michael thought about it, was that a Chinese general, Sun Tzu, had invented this type of tradecraft about twenty-three hundred years ago. And he'd done it to deceive other Chinese.

When they landed in Vladivostok twelve weeks ago, they'd stolen a boat and motored northwest through Amurskiy Bay to Ansan, Russia. There, they'd posed as Chinese troops, covering their faces with scarves against the cold weather. They wore sunglasses during the day so no one could see that they were *guilou*, or round-eyes.

They'd repeated their border intrusions, posing as Russians in Luozigou, on the Chinese border. Then they'd traveled several klicks west to Xinkai, China. Here they crossed the border and trekked northeast to Poltavka, Russia, and then west. Again they crossed the border, to Sanchakou, China. From there they'd marched southeast to Korfovka, Russia, then east to Dongning, China, where they were now. At each destination they stayed as long as it took to set up the mines, hack into whichever government's computers they targeted, watch the mines explode and soldiers die, and then journey to somewhere safe where they waited for darkness.

Drapoff found the list of destinations dizzying. It was a cook's tour of the border towns of both countries. Mountainous dirt roads covered with razor wire, deep majestic valleys, where he could see tiny villages and larger cities. They stole vegetables from the fields to complement their diet.

Now, they had one stop remaining, south in Daduchan, China. When they were done, they'd use their secure satellite phone to check in with Mother. If they'd created adequate confusion and anger in both governments, as intended, they'd head southeast into Russia's Primorye Maritime Territory, find the boat they'd camouflaged and hidden, and take a series of planes back to Tel Aviv from Vlad.

If Ben-Levy told them it wasn't good enough, they'd signal for an air drop of additional weapons and food, and continue disrupting the China-Russia border.

Drapoff raised his arm, drawing Dushov's attention. "Ready now, the data have been inserted."

Lester nodded. "Let's get out of here. I found a good place to observe, one klick west." The five covered their tracks behind them as they left the area.

As they moved away, a border patrol began scaling the hill where they'd had their camp.

The train crossed the Northern Caucasus Mountains, heading toward Grozny, Chechnya. Tariq Houmaz watched the landscape creep by. There were enough abandoned, rusting, crippled tanks to fill a museum. He peered through the window of the train as they passed landmine markers, dense forests, and dark lakes. The train climbed along a ridge and he saw the Sunzha River.

Beyond, he could now make out Grozny. He remembered the name of the city meant "fearsome." Houmaz chuckled. The Russians had put down a massive rebellion here just after the fall of the Soviet Empire. *Not so fearsome now, eh?*

The train slowed, rolling past Severny airport as it neared the station. All he could see was an old aluminum-sided building. He cursed fate as he waited for the train to stop. There'd be nothing here, he guessed. No food vendors, and possibly no restroom. He debarked past the ticket counter in the small station house. *Was I deceived by Aziz Tamil? Paranoia*, he thought. *Comes with the job.*

There was a restroom, and it surprised him how clean it was. As he used the sink to wash his face, he planned his next series of operations. He would have his force in the caves near the village of Upper Pachir, Afghanistan, build several big bombs, dirty bombs. He'd arrange to have them transported for detonation in the largest cities of America. He'd use the new hard-to-detect explosive materials his mole at the Ness Ziona had poached for him. Houmaz stifled a laugh, remembering the fool thought he was from the CIA.

But his mind pushed back, obsessing about Vlad. What had happened to the subs? Had they been stolen? He needed to know if his suspicions were correct. He'd planned for two years to buy them, and he prayed to Allah they were in the hands of men his brother had arranged to ride them back to Palestine. But, if they'd been stolen from him, he'd want to find another way to complete the mission he'd started two years ago. And, he'd have to make many adjustments to accommodate his failure to acquire them. Without the subs, how could he eliminate Israel first, before he attacked America?

He found a wrecked car the people of no other place would call a "taxi." The car was almost as old as its ancient driver. He paid the man to take him to the airport.

His next destination would be Kabul, Afghanistan. So close to his mountain camp. Soon, he'd be united with his mujahidin. He always felt safe there, sheltered in the cool limestone caves.

The airport was a set of old brick-and-mortar ramshackle buildings. He found the ticket counter and purchased a ticket to Kabul, then used the urinal. In the station building, he looked for a food vendor. There were none open at this hour. Glancing at his wristwatch, he pulled the cell phone from his pocket and punched in a number. "Pesi? It's your brother. You told me Aziz Tamil had never been seen. You said he always uses cutouts. What did you find out about the face I sketched, photographed, and emailed to you?"

The voice in Riyadh said, "No direct hits. Not enough data. When you get to the village, I'll transmit the faces and names that are close matches to the drawing you sent me. But Tariq, there are close to a thousand in our records."

Tariq Houmaz saw the jet begin loading passengers and he made his way to the line. "No matter. Thanks. Send my driver to the airport. I'll be touching down sometime tomorrow, Allah willing."

He still wasn't sure if he'd failed or succeeded. If indeed the man he'd seen was Aziz Tamil, he'd have a new piece of intel he could use to force the man to do his bidding. But if he'd been tricked...His rage escalated and his clenched fists turned white.

He took his seat on the plane and counted the hours until he was safe. He'd pay them all back. An eye for an eye. Israel first. Then, the United States.

CHAPTER 32

MI-6 headquarters, London
September 20, 4:15 p.m.

Sir Charles Crane stood at attention, forcing his face slack to disguise his sense of frustration. "Sir, we have no proof."

"Then get it." The Associate Minister of Foreign Intelligence rose from behind the oak carved desk that had once been a door to the galley of a tall ship. He smiled, examining his fingertips as if the favor he asked was trivial. He was ancient, portly, and it seemed to Crane that the man was more interested in his orchids than the spies he commanded and the intel business.

He was a man no one outside the inner circle of government knew. Even his name was false, and he'd never had his picture taken. Unlike the others in the department, he ran operations that were strictly off the books.

Crane shivered in the warm office. *God, I fear this man.* He took a deep breath. "We've tried. But after the loss of our two coverts in Vladivostok, there was no one nearby who could help us in time."

The other man walked to the windowed wall and watered several orchids. He held the small pot in left his hand and brought its flower to his face. After sniffing it, he faced Crane. "That's too bad. What do you want me to do with these unproven allegations?"

Crane stiffened. "A mission. We need to bring Sommers in. He's the only one who knows for sure what happened."

The minister turned from the flowers to face his servant. "And what if he isn't of a mind to cooperate?"

"I recommend we get the intel from him any way we can."

The minister's face swiveled sideways. "Chemical interrogation? Waterboarding? You mean torture."

Crane almost bit his lip. "Ah, well, yes. We could call it something less heinous, but that's what I suggest."

"Let me see if I get this. You bloody well want us to rip open someone we've invested time and money in. Someone we've lost coverts to protect. Because you believe he's still working for the Jews. And you think he might have masterminded the theft of two nuclear subs from the Russian mafiya?"

Crane shook his head. "No, not exactly. We think his team stole them from the Muslim Brotherhood."

The minister's face went crimson. "I don't care if they stole them from bloody Santa Claus. The point is that Israel might have the subs now, and use them to implement the Jericho Sanction. If so, the genie has left the bottle. And you can't even tell me if that's true."

"Uh, yes. But we can find out. If we mount a recovery mission for Sommers. Sir?"

"Absolutely not. We're in past our hip-boots in a bucket of shit. No way I want us in past our chins. Pass your assumptions on to US intelligence and let them go wankers on it." The minister picked up another flower pot and held it close to his face, scrutinizing its orchid.

Crane winced. Once the Americans got started on this, it would all be out of his control. He raised his hand in protest.

The minister shook his finger and turned away.

The meeting was over and Crane had his orders. As he left the office, his head fell.

Bob Gault stood at attention, blinded by the sunlight coming in from the window. Washington was way past hot, and it was a sauna on the street. Just the walk from the cab to the lobby of the agency's headquarters had left perspiration marking Gault's underarms. Mark McDougal looked like he'd been up all night. He hadn't invited Bob to take a seat. A bad sign. "You wanted me, sir?"

"Yeah. Bob, I just got this cryptic message from one of our British counterparts. Says you were involved with the rescue of a Brit in Singapore. We never gave you any rescue assignment. You were just in Singapore as a courier. Explain."

Gault's brows arched. "Well, uh, two of their coverts called and begged assistance. And in the name of improving foreign relations, I helped them retrieve one of theirs. We saved his life. I called you first but it was the middle of your night and, uh, I was sent to your voice mail. No way I could leave a message, and they claimed it was urgent, so I—"

"Shit, Bob. I don't care if it was urgent. You overstepped your bounds." McDougal's face glowed red.

Gault knew no one ever claimed to have seen his boss lose his temper. He swallowed hard, realizing he couldn't tell McDougal what else he'd discovered. There just wasn't enough proof that the Israelis stole a set of subs from the Muslim Brotherhood and were planning to assassinate Tariq Houmaz. It would just provoke McDougal even more. For all Bob knew, McDougal might be aware of these things. He took a deep breath and prepared for whatever his boss would say next. "Sorry, sir."

"Sorry? Do that again and you'll be posted to cover a Girl Scout troop in Antarctica." McDougal shook his head. Then he seemed to stare right into Gault's soul. "You ran an off-the-books mission. My contact in MI-6 is in a foul mood. He claims the man you helped save was present when the two coverts you helped to save him were murdered. Don't yet know if the Brit you rescued is the killer but I'm guessing he was."

The blood drained from Gault's face and his knees grew weak. "You mean Michael O'Hara murdered the two MI-6 coverts?"

McDougal continued staring at Gault. Shook his head. "Yes, Bob. And you played the star role in this mess."

McDougal took a single sheet of paper from the manila folder on his desk. "The Brits think the Israelis stole two submarines from a Muslim Brotherhood bomb maker named Tariq Houmaz. The Israelis have some far-fetched plan to nuke the entire Middle East if they're ever wiped out or if a nuclear device ever explodes in Israel. I told Director Greenfield and he spoke with the President. POTUS wants those subs. The United States couldn't survive if the entire Middle East became radioactive." The man scratched the top of his head. "Look, I'm gonna give you a chance to regain face with me. I'm assigning you a team. This is top priority. Get on it right now." He handed the paper to Gault. "Read it and leave it."

Gault scanned the page he held. He braced himself, fists clenched around the single sheet. An impromptu mission with no planning and little probability of success. His promotion was gone in the toilet now, and his career might follow it down. He nodded. "Yes, sir. Right away."

McDougal handed him another page, a roster with twelve names on it. His team. The only one he knew was a hacker he'd had problems with in the past. He'd never gotten along with Lee Ainsley, and he suspected the man would see this as a chance for payback.

Here it is, Gault thought. *My new assignment. The*

mission from hell. In his mind he named this black operation "Project Shitbag" as he left his boss's office.

Yigdal Ben-Levy walked around the chalkboard in the tiny basement office, scratching his chin though his beard. He drew a schematic of the problem. Sort of a Venn diagram, but using roughly drawn boxes in place of the usual circles. The lines connecting some of the boxes indicated the relationships among their events. The text in some of the boxes contained descriptions of missions he'd initiated.

He sketched Jon's new intel into its own set of boxes alongside the ones that had been there before.

Box one was labeled "Weapons Source." The Russian mafiya sold weapons to anyone who had enough cash. The source of this intel was Mossad's Intelligence Division.

Box two was labeled "Cash Source." The Muslim Brotherhood was receiving large payments from someone unknown, and using the cash to buy weapons of mass destruction from the Eastern District of the mafiya in Vladivostok. The source of this intel was Amos Gidaehl, Jon Sommers's predecessor, now presumed dead. Ben-Levy hadn't learned who was funding them but suspected either MI-6 or the United States. Iran couldn't spare enough cash for this operation, and he'd also ruled out the Saudis since it would have taken several princes to afford it, and he believed such a large group wouldn't be able to keep this secret. Whoever it was had assassinated Gidaehl before he'd had the chance to complete his mission and relay the details to Mother. *Why would a Western intelligence agency fund the Muslim Brotherhood?*

Box three was labeled "Leverage requires proof." Of course, if he could prove either the Brits or the Yanks had funded the Muslim Brotherhood, he'd have untold leverage.

The edges of this box intersected boxes for American intelligence and MI-6. But now, he didn't have the proof.

Box four was labeled "Steal Subs." He'd found a way to stop the sale of the subs to the Brotherhood—if Shimmel and his team succeeded in delivering the subs to the Gulf.

Box five was labeled "Border War." His mission was to shut down the Russian mafiya's ability to conduct their arms-sales business. If he was correct about the Muslim Brotherhood's source of funds, any alternative course of action he took would soon make things sticky for their funding source. He'd designed Operation Bloodridge to shut down the mafiya's export sales forever. He hoped the mission might be enough to convince the Russian government that the mafiya's weapons were needed at home just in case the border war with China escalated into a full-scale hot war.

He'd mounted Bloodridge as an off-the-books operation without the consent or even the knowledge of either Oscar Gilead, Deputy Director of SHABEK, or the Prime Minister. His team of coverts, Lester Dushov, Ari Westheim, Shimon Tennenbaum, JD Weinstein, and Michael Drapoff were now on the border between China and Russia in what the Mossad called the Bloodridge Mountains, causing trouble for both countries, and keeping the confusion in Moscow escalating.

He referred back to box two. How could he stop a foreign intelligence agency from funding terrorists off the books? He needed proof. He smiled with a new thought.

He drew another box, labeled "Proof," overlapping pieces of each of the others: If he couldn't find it, maybe he could manufacture fictive proof. He'd done as much before. After all, it was Mossad's motto: wage war by deception.

As he stared at the overlapping portions of some of the boxes, he wasn't so sure that Houmaz was necessary now, after the sale of the subs.

Moving back to take in the full picture, he thought, *no one has any idea what I've sacrificed. My own blood, my*

family. Maybe Houmaz is more trouble than he is worth?
What if Jon is right?

Within minutes of the time his driver stopped the armored Hummer in front of the Tora Bora caves, Tariq Houmaz was jogging through the vehicle's dust trail and into his home, a shallow cave partitioned into several rooms with plaster walls. He grabbed the secure satphone from a desk drawer and a folding chair from his makeshift office and walked back outside where he could get a signal. He retrieved his email, containing a huge file of photos sent by Pesi Houmaz from Riyadh. Excellent. Now he could find out who the man calling himself Aziz Tamil was. He took a deep breath and examined the first image.

The photos of Tamil candidates were endless. As the afternoon faded and cooled, he considered one picture after another, rejecting each and moving on. At dusk, he stopped for a break and scanned the mountains. He cursed. One of his militia brought him a dinner of smoked lamb shoulder and bulgur. He ate it fast, but savored the flavors of home cooking. When he finished, he took out a flashlight and was back to the photos of suspects.

Houmaz was up all night. Just before noon the next day, he saw one that made him frown. An IDF captain, Avram Shimmel. A tank commander. He scratched his head. Not Mossad. But the photo was the same image as the man called Aziz Tamil. He had his proof. His face reddened. The Jews had stolen his submarines.

He shook with rage and took a deep breath to settle himself. Rising, he walked to the officer who'd served him dinner last night. "Khalid, call my brother in Riyadh. Have him send me a washed Israeli passport and an air ticket to Cairo. And have him get me personal intel on Avram Shimmel and his family. Everything."

Yigdal Ben-Levy's phone rang. He walked from the chalk-board to his desk, taking an extra second to clear his head. Then he answered. "Ben-Levy."

"It's Avram Shimmel. We're off the coast of Muscat and I just left the subs. They're submerging and in seconds they'll be undetectable. All the provisions from your supply boats were loaded. The subs will be patrolling off the coast of Yemen until further notice, as you ordered. I'm done here."

"Good. I have an exfiltration team waiting for you. Look for them along the Muttrah Corniche, outside the entrance to the Muttrah Souk. They'll be in a moored fishing boat named 'Shariff's Smile.' Make your way back to Israel. We'll celebrate when you arrive."

"Whatever. Should take me a few days. Shimmel out."

Ben-Levy frowned. He'd need to find a way to push this man more. He wanted not just success for his new recruit but also respect from him. And Shimmel wasn't giving him any. He was sure the major's attitude was due to his failure to provide a protection detail. But surely he understood there was no way he could share intelligence with Aman or cross their lines of authority. He picked up the phone. At least he could follow up for Shimmel. "It's Ben-Levy. Give me General Nemirovsky."

The voice of the other man was oily smooth. "Yigdal. Can't this wait until Friday, before the department heads meeting? Say at noon for ten minutes?"

Ben-Levy's hand clenched. "Just tell me the status of my request for a protection detail for Avram Shimmel's family?"

He heard voices in the background. Then silence. *Nemirovsky is figuring out his excuse*, thought Yigdal. "We're, ah, in the process of seeing what we can do. Give me two more days."

Ben-Levy grimaced. "Let me know when it's done." He terminated the call. Whatever they did provide would come at least a week from now.

He pulled the old creased folder from his desk: "Project Bloodridge." Placing his reading glasses atop the bridge of his nose, he went through the details and checked off the phase labeled "Obtain two nuclear submarines without paying for them."

He waited for another call. From Lester Dushov. He hoped this phase of Bloodridge would also be successful, so the subs would never have to be used.

Ben-Levy took another deep breath. His next move would be critical. *Yes*, he'd decided, *Houmaz is no longer necessary*. He pulled up the Al Jazeera website and keyed in the User ID and password Michael Drapoff had hacked for him. He found the blog on Israel and entered the following:

I have heard Israel has a plan called the "Jericho Sanction." Should we drive them into the sea or explode a nuclear device on their soil, there is a computer program set to launch ICBMs into every Arab country, killing us all. Can this be true? Is there no way to stop it? I have heard that there is not!

Ben-Levy smiled. That would do it. Now for the final straw. He keyed another entry into the blog, labeled "failed mission":

I have heard that Israel has two nuclear submarines with enough guided missiles to make the Middle East uninhabitable forever. I heard the Muslim Brotherhood paid for them, and the Israelis stole them from Tariq Houmaz. If this is true, we should find and kill this traitorous son of a goat.

CHAPTER 33

Upper Pachir, Nangarhar Province,
Afghanistan
September 21, 9:12 p.m.

Houmaz watched the practice skirmish rolling out in the valley below him. Over seven hundred men used rubber bullets, painful but not lethal. Houmaz had stolen Israeli technology from the Ness Ziona to mask the valley from surveillance satellites.

His next operation would have to make up for the recent failure. Thanks to Allah, it was a private failure, known only to him, his brother Pesi, and the Israelis. And his brother would hold his tongue. As for the Israelis, publicizing this would cause as much grief for them as it would for him. Everyone suspected Israel had nukes. But they'd never made their achievements public. If the theft ever became public, the United States might feel uncomfortable with yet another member of the nuclear-weapons club announcing itself to the world.

The next operation had to please Allah. But as of now, he had nothing. While he thought, the satphone buzzed. "Yes?"

"It's Pesi. Go to the Al Jazeera website. Do it now."

"No. I'm too busy to read all their gossip." His thumb moved to terminate the call.

"Tariq, your failed mission is public news everywhere. It's the biggest blog discussion on Al Jazeera in the history of the website."

He dropped the phone as the breath left him. He picked it up, his hands shaking. "What?"

"They have your purchase of the subs, the theft by the Israelis, everything, including something called the Jericho Sanction."

"I was named?" His palms were sweaty.

"Yes, brother."

He shook his head. But something else Pesi said perked his interest. "What's the Jericho Sanction?" He felt his eyebrows furrow.

"Go to the blog section. Read for yourself. Some mullahs are calling for you to be beheaded. Leave camp before your soldiers heed the call and plot to end you!" The call terminated.

He headed to the Hummer, still carrying the satphone. From the driver's seat, he found the blog and read the entries. His face reddened and he pounded the dashboard with his fists.

The skirmish was still on and men were shouting orders to each other in the valley. No one was watching. Houmaz started the engine and drove off. There was one more task he'd have to complete before Allah took him.

"Your father will be disappointed with you when he sees what you did to the library." Sharon Shimmel pointed to the pile of books Golda had spilled off the shelf in their small living room. There was fresh scribbling in red crayon on the pages of several.

The little girl cried, stomped her feet, and ran from the room.

Sharon shook her head. The growing soul in her belly

kicked hard and she smiled. Two more months. She'd wanted to name him David, but Avram insisted he be called Isaac.

She picked up the books on the floor and placed them back on the shelves. She knew their locations by heart. Avram had studied American football and used the plays to construct military maneuvers. He had over fifteen books on football tactics. He'd used them as research for the one he'd written. This one she'd read. It had bored her to tears. But he was proud, using it to teach courses at the IDF college. She touched its spine with fondness.

Her watch chimed and she looked at its face. *Time to go pick up Avram*, she thought.

She entered the nursery and grabbed the blond child's tiny hand. "Come. Time to go get poppa."

The girl stopped crying and ran toward the door, pulling her mother down the stairs and outside to the car. "Take me to poppa!"

Sharon smiled. Golda's misbehavior was to be expected. Her beloved poppa was gone most of the time and now she was faced with the arrival of another baby.

She pushed the key into the car door and turned to her daughter. "Get in the back. I'll buckle you into the seat." She bent over with difficulty and pushed the belt into its holder. Then sat in the front and adjusted the steering wheel to accommodate her pregnancy.

She turned the ignition key.

A ball of fire erupted from under the car, sending scorched metal, melted plastic car parts, and her burning flesh and bone in all directions.

Two blocks away, on top of a building's roof, Tariq Houmaz saw the mother and her toddler die. He tapped the button on his cell phone's-movie recording function to stop it and save the file. He smiled with satisfaction as his busy mind turned to how he'd reach the Gaza, where he could find safety.

He'd planned to place the video of his revenge on the Al Jazeera website within the hour, hoping that might cool the fanatics who called for his death. He rose and snuck down the steps to the street.

As he hurried off, he thought about the blog entries on Al Jazeera. Who had done this to him? When he found them, he'd need another bomb.

Avram Shimmel waited just inside the terminal. They were overdue now by fifteen minutes. He dialed Sharon's cell phone for the third time but once again heard the message indicating that the party he'd called was outside the calling area. He guessed Sharon had turned it off or forgot to recharge its battery.

He shrugged, pacing around baggage claim, worrying about traffic. When they hadn't arrived and a half-hour had passed, his mood darkened with worry. He grabbed his bag and sprinted from the terminal where he flashed his Mossad credentials and cut in front at the taxi line. "Take me to Meier Road, corner of Yahuda."

The cabbie nodded and pushed Shimmel's bag into the trunk. Climbing in, he started the car and maneuvered the roads onto the highway. "That was some explosion this morning. Did you see it?"

Avram's eyebrows rose. Bomb explosions were no longer common in Tel Aviv. But his gut wrenched as he worried. "No. I just got here." He leaned forward. "What happened?"

"At the very intersection where I'm taking you. A woman and her daughter were murdered. A car bomb."

Shimmel's jaw dropped. "How did you find out?"

"It was on Al Jazeera news this morning. I saw the film made by the bomb maker who posted it."

His heart was pounding. He needed to find out, but the echo in his head told him he already knew. "Were the two who died a black-haired pregnant woman and a blond-haired little girl about six years old?"

"So, you saw it too?"

Once he started wailing, Avram Shimmel couldn't stop.

Just after dawn the next morning, Shimmel appeared at Ben-Levy's door in the SHABEK section of the Office, before Mother arrived.

He waited outside, in full military dress, holding a single sheet of paper. His flesh was red around his eyes. He paced the small area around the door, his fists clenching and unclenching.

When Ben-Levy arrived, he saw the piece of paper and frowned. "Avram, I'm so sorry."

Avram's eyes began to tear. "I told you. He saw my face. Why couldn't you get Aman protection for my family?"

"They were in process of arranging a detail." Ben-Levy shook his head. "I know Mossad rules kept you from warning your wife while your mission was in process. But, you could have broken protocol and done it anyway."

Shimmel's mouth dropped at the accusation. His voice dropped to just above a whisper. "Our orders prohibit that. It would have been treason." He turned away. When he swiveled and faced Mother, his face was a war of emotions. "This is my resignation. Don't try to stop me." His face stiffened as he marched down the hall away from Ben-Levy's office.

Jon Sommers's cell phone buzzed. He looked at the screen. "Yes, Mother?"

"I have news you might be interested in."

"Shit, man, you bloody never give up, do you?" He moved his thumb toward the button to end the call."

"Wait. Tariq Houmaz murdered Avram Shimmel's pregnant wife and child with a car bomb yesterday evening. Shimmel resigned, and I believe he's also out to hunt the bomb maker."

Jon stopped, stock still. "Out to hunt?" He wondered, could he trust anyone Mother sent him. "Is this Shimmel the one who stole the subs for you? Can I send Houmaz to a better place? And what's Shimmel's cell phone number?"

CHAPTER 34

Near Ben Gurion Airport, Tel Aviv, Israel
September 22, 8:24 a.m.

Sitting in coach class of the Sun D'Or flight from Bratislava to Ben Gurion International Airport, Jon dug his cell from his pants pocket and dialed the number. It rang once and dumped him into voice mail. The language was Hebrew, so Jon just waited until the beep. "I'm Jon Sommers. Mother sent me. Tariq Houmaz murdered my fiancée. I'm hunting him. Call me back."

The plane aligned to the runway as it descended. He made another call. "William, I have another assignment for you. Oh, and in appreciation of the intel you gave me about Bloodridge, I wired the cash payment we agreed to into your numbered bank account this morning. Now the other task. We need to track a terrorist. He's probably in Israel now, and so am I. It's an even bigger payday for you. Meet me in Tel Aviv. Call me back when you arrive at the airport and I'll give you further instructions." Jon logged into his bank account using his cell. He sent Wing thirty thousand pounds.

The aircraft's wheels bounced on the runway, rolling to a stop at the terminal. Jon gathered his go bag and followed the other passengers from the plane.

He flagged a taxi into downtown, tapping the Plexiglas

partition to give the cabby directions. He scratched the itch deep within his shoulder, where it was stitched together.

Tel Aviv continued to astound him. It was so unlike the other cities he'd been to. Its mix of the ancient and the ultramodern skyscrapers flashed by, and Jon felt reverence for the place. *This must be what keeps Mother going.*

The cab drove along Ayalon Highway, exiting at Hashalom. It made a right into the Azrieli Complex and stopped at the Crowne Plaza Hotel at 132 Menachem Begin Road. This was the upscale part of the city. Jon paid the driver and took his bag with him to check in. While waiting on line, his cell buzzed. "Hello?"

The voice was deep and held a thick Israeli accent. "I'm Avram Shimmel. How do I know you're who you say you are?"

"Call Ben-Levy. He gave me your number."

Jon motioned to the registration clerk. "There's an envelope for me from the Assistant Minister of Foreign Affairs." He held out his hand and ripped it open, emptying it and handing the clerk his new Israeli passport. It bore the name "Jon Sommerstein." At their first meeting so long ago, Mother had told him it was his great grandfather's last name. He pocketed the new debit card along with a scribbled note stating it held two hundred thousand shekels. At under four shekels to the dollar, the US dollar equivalent amount was nearly $47,000. He waited while the clerk processed his registration.

Speaking into his cell, Jon said, "Call Ben-Levy. Then, call me back."

"I will. Where can we meet?"

Jon nodded. "Where are you now?"

"I've just left his office. I'm in the armory of the SHABEK section, picking up some gear."

Jon smiled. "Give me an hour. I'll meet you there." A plan was forming in his mind.

ation forms and
dropped his bag in his room, Jon headed for the taxi line.

While he waited, his cell buzzed again. "Sommers."

The voice on the other end was Asian. "I'm starting to dislike you a lot. I thought your name is O'Hara. Which is—"

"Enough, William. I work mostly for Mossad and have several names. What I'm offering you is a real plum. If you succeed, we'll reward you. It's the big time." He got into the cab. "Corner of Hasadnaot Street and Hamenofim Street, Herzliyya, please."

"Who's 'we'?" He could hear the disbelief in Wing's voice.

"William, Mossad's been generous to you. Listen, the man we're tracking murdered my fiancée with one of his bombs, and dozens of others. And my partner, well, his wife and young daughter died yesterday in a car bomb built by the same man. The Mossad labeled our target a danger to all of Israel. Not human, not fit to live."

"You mean Tariq Houmaz? The man you had me help you with?"

"Yeah. He knows about me and my partner. Not about you. We'll need to track his whereabouts electronically, and we're offering you the opportunity to prove you're the best there is. Will you?" Jon held his breath, hoping.

"The best? Oh, fuck." Silence reigned. "Well, I am the best there is, so, okay. Yes! But keep my name out of this. Where are you now?"

Jon glanced at his wristwatch. 9:50 a.m. "In a taxi on my way to the Mossad armory. I'm staying at a hotel in Tel Aviv. How long will it take you to get here?"

"I'm in San Jose, California. Helping a high-tech startup recover stolen secrets. I can be with you tomorrow morning if I leave now."

"Then come as fast as you can. I'm in room 412 at the

Crowne Plaza in Tel Aviv." The taxi approached his destination and he pulled his wallet from his pocket.

"Right. Okay, I'll come. But, in addition to the cash, you'll owe me a favor of my choosing. Anything I ask. Okay?"

"But of course." Jon wondered what the hacker would want in return. But he took a deep breath. Whatever he'd need to do, it was worth it.

The two men eyed each other with obvious suspicion. Avram Shimmel was so much taller and more muscular than Jon, but when he extended his hand, Jon smiled. "I believe we share the emotional glue to bind us into friendship. We both lost loved ones to Tariq Houmaz."

Avram nodded. "Come with me to the commissary. We can talk over a cup of terrible coffee." He smiled back.

Two floors above, the elevator doors opened and they seated themselves at an empty table. Avram said, "I want the bomb maker dead. How can we find him?"

Jon tried to smile but found it impossible. "I also want justice served. Vengeance, really. I know a hacker who may be able to help us."

"Do you have a plan?"

Jon froze. All his plans had failed to produce their desired result. "Not yet. It will take the three of us together to craft one that works."

"Where is your hacker?"

Jon closed his eyes, seeing Lisa's face, the battle where Houmaz murdered his team in Manhattan, shot the Brits in Vlad, and then he thought about Avram's wife and daughter. "He'll be here tomorrow. Tell me about yourself. Who are you?"

For the first time, Avram relaxed. "I'm a soldier. A patriot. A mourner."

Jon saw a tear bud and roll down Avram's cheek. "As am I."

William Wing used his cell to check his bank account as the aircraft landed, rolling down the runway. The twenty thousand dollars was now part of his available balance. He reached up, grabbed his suitcase and walked into the busy terminal.

Another hour passed before he was at Sommers's room in the Crowne Plaza. He knocked and two men cracked the door open, both holding handguns. Wing's eyebrows flew up. "Don't shoot me!"

Sommers held up his hand and pointed to Shimmel. "Avram Shimmel, meet William Wing."

Shimmel flipped the safety on, tossed the gun into his left hand, and extended his right. They shook. "Welcome."

Wing closed the door behind him. "Listen, Sommers, or should I call you O'Hara? No guns."

Sommers reached out for William's shoulder. "Thanks. Call me Jon Sommers. It's the name I was born with." He motioned to the table in the corner of the room and pulled a third chair to it.

"What's the plan?" William pushed his glasses back up his nose.

Jon placed copies of a single sheet of paper in front of each. "Right, then. William, we want you to stay out of harm's way. You're too valuable to put at risk. Your task is to track Tariq Houmaz. Backtrace his cell phone voice and email signals. Find his source-point and keep us informed, real-time." Jon looked at Avram. "We'll go hunting Houmaz just as soon as you can find him. Avram's a former IDF major. His specialty is tactics. Logistics, battle planning, setting traps. That's what his primary role will be. Our former handler has delivered cash and weapons. He's promised additional help if we need it. Any further intelligence that requires someone to go to someplace dangerous will be my job to go onsite and spy. So, you see, I'll be the one most at risk here."

The three discussed the specific details of just how they'd work together.

William sat at the table, munching a kosher Twinkie. He watched the screen of his notebook flash lines of data, white on blue background. Nothing interesting had happened for several hours, and the other two men slept, Jon on the couch and the goliath named Avram on the bed. William yawned. His eyes closed and his head went slack.

The notebook beeped. All three woke. "I've got him!" The two would-be assassins closed the distance and peered over his shoulder. William shook his head. "Shit, guys, he's not in Israel. He's, well, he's in Muscat, Oman. Rats! We'll need a plane and visas."

Avram nodded. "Let me have your cell phone. I can get the visas in less than an hour."

The corporate jet William Wing rented landed and taxied down the runway at what used to be called Seeb International in Muscat, Oman. The aircraft headed toward the corporate terminal hanger. William, Avram, and Jon picked up their bags and waited by the aircraft's door as it stopped. An airport worker popped it open and stood aside to let the team pass down the stairs.

They were dressed as tourists, wearing Hawaiian shirts. But these shirts were special, coated with stress thickening fluid, or STF. The liquid-armor shirts were gifts from Ben-Levy to Avram for this mission. There was one unfortunate detail about them, however. Each had the image of Jimi

Hendrix burning his guitar at the Monterey Pop Festival on the front and back of the shirt. The shirts might be bullet proof but their drawback was that the three now were marked as a team. It was too hot to wear something over them.

All walked toward the terminal.

Once within the terminal and out of the sun, Jon felt comfortable. He led them to one of the Western-style restaurants. The menu looked like one from Denny's, but without any pork products.

They ordered food while William set up the notebook computer and searched for backtraces since they'd left the plane. Jon knew his teammates felt the pressure of not knowing where Houmaz was.

William's eyebrows arched when he saw the results. "Got him. Well, not exactly. But, I know now right where he was yesterday." He blew out his breath in a huff. The others looked at him, but he said no more. William's face reflected excitement and urgency. "He was in Muscat, but not at the airport. Downtown, possibly at a hotel. And the last phone call he received was from Riyadh. From Pesi Houmaz. I assume that's his brother. It was made yesterday, around noon. But his cell is off right now."

Something happened in that instant. Jon felt a camaraderie towards these two he'd never felt before about the teams assigned him by the Mossad and MI-6. He couldn't put his finger on it, but it just felt good. It felt right.

Without Houmaz's cell signal, William couldn't place Houmaz's current location. The bomb maker's cell phone was primitive, without GPS. Using special programs he'd hacked off DARPA, he could locate the cell through triangulation of the phone's transmission signal against cell phone towers. The Defense Agency Research group had a collection of what were the most sophisticated hacking tools William had ever used. But, using the last known point of origin wouldn't be good enough. He'd need to wait until the cell was turned on again before he could triangulate the bomb maker's current position. William faced his companions. "I'm hacking all the cell phone providers searching for the one matching Houmaz's phone number. The holder's name certainly won't be 'Tariq Houmaz.' This'll take a few minutes."

Muscat was a city with over 650,000 residents. Hacking might be the only way to find their target.

As the minutes passed, his eyes shifted focus from the computer screen to his team in the room. "Nothing." He took a bite of an egg omelet filled with feta cheese.

As he swallowed, his notebook computer chirped and he almost choked at the sound. He smiled. "Yes! He's turned it on. Making a call right now, to someone in Riyadh. Probably his brother. I have a fix on him. He's still in Oman. In Muscat, at the Bustan Palace InterContinental near the souk at Muttrah. A long taxi ride from Seeb. And he's got a new smartphone. Backtraced his new number. CryptoMonger is the best!"

Jon's eyebrows arched. "CryptoMonger? What's that? Is it a hacking utility?"

William shook his head. His smile vanished. "Well, uh, no. It's my call sign."

Jon laughed. "Ah." He turned to Avram. "Let's get Houmaz now. We can eat dinner after he's dead."

William touched Jon's sleeve. "I want to come."

Jon's eyebrows rose. "I thought you wanted to avoid anything dangerous."

Wing's face fell and he seemed to focus on his hands. "Yeah, well, things have changed. I'm coming."

Jon paused in thought. "What changed?"

"I can't explain. I want to be part of this."

Jon nodded. "So be it. We'll all go together." The team grinned back at him; faces split in greedy smiles.

Tariq Houmaz sat in the lobby of the Bustan Palace Inter-Continental, looking at his purchases from the souk. When he'd arrived, he was out of cash. Using any bank account with his name on it might mark him. But he'd solved the problem, stealing money and other documents from a tourist by picking the man's pocket. Houmaz patted his jacket pocket, reassured that the man's passport was still there. He wore the straw Panama hat he'd bought. When he'd checked in, he shaved his beard and cut his hair short. He'd done his best to make himself look European and sophisticated. The bag in front of him held a few changes of underwear and several inexpensive dress shirts in a shopping bag. He'd need to fix the passport by having a forger insert his photo before he could use it, but that was easily taken care of.

Noise from a group of guests entering the hotel snared his attention. His smile faded and his head snapped up. He was still nervous about the possibility he was being stalked. He looked toward the entrance, and what he saw made him shudder with surprise.

Houmaz recognized the Brit from Mossad and the man he knew as Shimmel. Their tradecraft was sloppy. There was a third person with them; a short Asian wearing fishbowl eyeglasses. This man he'd never seen before wasn't built like a killer. No, he was dumpy and had greasy hair. In Muscat, he wouldn't easy to forget. He must be their hacker.

The Brit led them, walking toward the marble check-in counter. *Oh shit.* In desperation, he pulled the hat down to cover as much of his face as possible, and also reached for the Arabic-language newspaper that someone had left on the ottoman in front of him. Holding the newspaper in front of his face, he pretended to read it while he watched from around its edges.

He focused his attention on the Brit, who stood at the reception desk. Just loud enough for Houmaz to hear the words, the Brit said, "Begging your pardon, sir, we're looking for our business associate who is staying at this hotel. We're here to meet with him." The Brit pushed a picture and a stack of unconcealed money toward the clerk. "Could you tell us which room he's in?"

How had they gotten a photo of him? Then he remembered the cameras on every corner in Tel Aviv. Shit! He flinched. He was unarmed. His heartbeat accelerated. The lobby seemed to become smaller and warmer. His vision scoped and his ears buzzed. Perspiration bubbled on his upper lip. He wanted to bolt, but his body wouldn't obey, leaving him frozen in his seat.

He forced himself to conceal a scream of rage as the clerk gave his room number to the Brit. He watched the group head toward the elevators. He could see the bulges made by the weapons stuck in the waistbands of the Jew and the Brit. Unlike the Chinese restaurant in Manhattan, the lobby was wide. No real kill zone. He realized he'd die if they saw him.

As the elevator doors closed, Houmaz forced himself up from his seat. His legs wobbled as he left the hotel lobby carrying the shopping bag. He staggered into the first taxi in the line at the hotel's entrance. Forcing a smile, he stared at the driver in front of him. "Take me to Muscat International. To Seeb."

At the airport, he bought a ticket on the earliest plane leaving, a flight bound for Paris. The city was home to many Islamic fundamentalists and would be a dangerous place for him now that he was blamed for arming Islam's enemy. But he'd need to flee Muscat now. He had no weapon.

Houmaz ran toward security and stood in line. Behind

him, a fat, balding American in a suit and tie closed the distance to within a foot.

Houmaz faced him, considering whether he was a threat. The other had no luggage with him, and there was a bulge in his shoulder. Only police could carry a gun in an airport. *Shit.*

The man bore a sleazy smile. "I'm Bob Gault. We need to talk." Gault held his hands out where Houmaz could see them. "I'm unarmed. American intelligence. I can help you."

Houmaz stared at the man. *The man is lying. I can see the outline of the gun under his suit jacket.* Gault grabbed his shoulder and pointed further into the terminal.

They left the line and Gault pushed him to the darkest area of a snack bar. Houmaz faced the spy. "How did you find me?"

Gault pointed to the bomb maker's pocket. "Your cell phone. I've been tracking you for weeks using NSA's ECHELON network. We've got your cell hot-miked and I've been listening to every conversation you've had for the last month."

"But it has no GPS!" Houmaz pulled the device from his pocket, handling it as if it was cursed.

"Yeah, well, as long as there are cell towers to work the phone, we'll know where you are." Gault shook his head. "Too bad for you."

His ignorance of technology had made Houmaz unsafe. Tech knowledge hadn't been a priority until now. *But*, he wondered, *how did the assassination team track me?* His eyes popped. The little Asian bastard was tracking by hacking. He'd been too confident. Sloppy. From now on, he'd need to use prepaid cell phones, and he wouldn't be able to use computers until he learned how to disguise his location.

Gault held out his hand. "Gimme the cell." Houmaz handed him the phone, and the spy pulled its battery out. He dropped the unit into a trash receptacle, and then the battery. "So, I have an offer you can't refuse."

Houmaz felt confusion. He wrung his hands. "You want me to work for you?"

"We want to know what the Muslim Brotherhood cells you're in contact with are planning."

"But I work for the British."

"Uh, no, you don't. They put out a burn notice on you. In fact, if they see you, they'll kill you. It's a terminate-with-prejudice burn."

Houmaz rubbed his sweaty palms together. "What are you offering?"

Gault smiled. "We'll fund you, but only for operations we approve in advance. To sort of keep our hand in. Maintain the balance of power, and keep the voters in the United States motivated." He shrugged.

"What about my problem with the fundamentalists?"

Gault frowned. "Yeah. There is that. But I think with the proper application of money and public relations, we can turn it around for you." He stared into Houmaz's eyes. "So, if I walk away without enrolling you, you'll be hunted and killed by those you served. Brits. Mossad. Fundamentalists. Or those who you've hurt. It doesn't matter. Dead is dead. If you're willing to work with us, well, there may be a bright future for you."

Houmaz thought for a few seconds. "I'll want something from you. To prove your interest. And sincerity."

Gault smiled. "What?"

"I want the assassination team following me dead. The Israeli major, Shimmel. The Mossad *kidon*. And the Asian hacker."

Gault shook his head. "No can do. If we kill our allies, there'll be hell to pay. Might even get noticed by our politicians."

"No deal then." Houmaz started to walk away. He suspected this American was lying to him and somehow setting him up. *But, if this man has the power to help me, maybe I can make it work. Just maybe, if I'm careful.*

"Wait. We won't kill them. But maybe I can make it easier for you to do it." Gault's brows twisted with thought.

Houmaz nodded. "What do you propose?"

CHAPTER 35

The Bustan Palace InterContinental
near the souk at Muttrah, Muscat, Oman
September 22, 1:56 p.m.

The self-appointed assassination team took the elevator up to Tariq Houmaz's room. Jon slipped a credit-card sized-room key attached to an electronic device into the room's card reader. The LEDs on the device cycled until the lock popped open. With their handguns pointed into the room, he sprang the door. Jon and Avram entered in shooting stances.

They searched the room while William stood at the front door, holding his breath.

"Crap." Avram beckoned William to enter the room. "Empty. We wait here for him."

Jon nodded, closed the door, and sat at the desk, his Beretta aimed at the entrance.

"What if he doesn't return?" William paced near the window. "What if he's on his way to somewhere else?"

Avram said nothing but kept his handgun trained on the door.

Jon shrugged. "Set your notebook up here, now, and see if you can backtrace his location."

As the sun set and the room darkened, Jon listened to the

muezzin from the nearby mosque calling the faithful to prayer. He'd read the Koran and studied Islam. How could such a beautiful religion incite such heinous murderers?

His stomach growled, and he realized they hadn't eaten for a long time With his Beretta Px4 subcompact Storm 9mm still in his hand, he woke his two companions. "Let's get dinner."

William picked up the hotel directory and pointed to a page. "This hotel has an Italian restaurant. I want to get out of this room. Hope the restaurant's good."

Avram shrugged.

In the elevator, William's head hung. He said, "Somehow, I don't think I'm gonna find him again."

Jon could see the pain in William's eyes. "You hate to lose."

William nodded. "I'm the best. Least I was. Now, not so sure." His brief smile faded.

Jon sought a table in the emptiest part of the restaurant.

Their server brought menus. As the waiter moved away, Jon saw a man standing off in the shadows. He glimpsed the face of the person and realized it was someone familiar. But he couldn't remember where he'd seen the face before. Was the man a threat? He nodded to Avram and both men reached into their jackets for the guns in their shoulder holsters. Each pulled their guns but kept them under the table.

The man walked closer and raised his hands. "Easy now. Remember me? Bob Gault. I saved your life, Jon."

Jon holstered his gun. He frowned, looked to Avram and William, and in a voice just above a whisper, said "Yeah. He did. He's with American intelligence. But I don't trust him."

Avram nodded back and pointed to the empty chair. "Hungry?"

Gault shook his head. "No. But, listen, I found Tariq Houmaz. I know where he's going."

William smirked. "Yeah, right. And, tell me how you did what I can't."

Gault stared back, shifting his eyes from one of them to the next. The seconds ticked by. "Okay, well, if you aren't interested, I'll just go." He rose from the chair.

Avram touched his sleeve. "No, we're interested. But we're not fools. Answer William's question, please."

Gault sat down again. He faced William and spoke as if they were alone. "The agency I work for. We've been tracking him for weeks. We use ECHELON." He turned to Avram and smiled. "Maybe you've heard of it? It's the system Mossad's spies stole a copy of, the one Mossad now calls PROMIS, which they updated and placed trapdoors into. Mossad's been selling PROMIS to other intelligence services. Of course *you* remember." He shook his head. "We used ECHELON to locate Houmaz. I found him at the airport. I've convinced him to become my agency's asset."

William shook his head. "You mean you threatened him."

"Didn't have to. The Brits burned him, and we think your spymaster convinced the ragheads at Al Jazeera to want him dead. So, he's on a short tether. He really had no choice."

Jon's eyes half closed as he considered this. "What did you offer him?

Gault smirked but didn't reply.

Jon tried again. "And you're here to help us?"

Gault nodded. "Well, Israel is our ally. So—"

Jon swiveled his head toward each of his companions. "See what I mean?" Avram and William nodded back at Jon.

Avram shook his head. "This is starting to sound incredible. You can't expect—"

Gault rose and took several steps away from the table. He stood, facing away, waiting.

Avram touched Jon's shoulder. "Just listen first."

Jon muttered, "And hear more lies?"

Avram shook his head. "Wait. It won't hurt for us to listen."

Jon clenched his fists.

Gault returned to the table and sat back down.

Jon pushed his chair farther from the table, preparing to get up. "I don't believe half of what you tell us. Go now, or we will."

Gault smiled. "Just listen before you decide." He looked at each and waited. "I set him up for you. All you have to do is be where I tell you he'll be, and then..." He rose from his seat. "I'll call your cell, Jon, when it's time. Probably in a day or two." Gault rose and disappeared from the restaurant.

William frowned. "Now I know why you don't trust him. He's as sleazy as they come. Lost my appetite. If he found us, it's not safe here. We'll need to find another place to stay. He probably intends to tell Houmaz he saw us here."

Jon nodded. William, Avram, and he worked well together. All seemed to have the same thoughts at the same time.

The three walked from the restaurant in lockstep.

Gault boarded the United Airlines plane bound for Washington, DC. After finding his seat, he flagged down the flight attendant and ordered a black coffee and a stack of snacks. While he waited for the food, he punched a number into his cell phone. "Mark? It's Bob."

Mark McDougal, the agency's Assistant Director, Middle Eastern Operations, asked, "Did it work?"

"I believe so. Congratulations. Either way, we win. How long before I move the next piece on the board?"

"Not yet. When you get in, go home and get some sleep. Be at my office tomorrow afternoon. Say, 2 p.m." The call terminated and Gault smiled. Maybe this would be enough to earn him the long-overdue promotion to team manager. He hated black ops.

He closed his eyes and tried to imagine the alternative outcomes. *Yes, either way, we win. I win.*

The Golden Tulip Seeb Hotel on Exhibition Street was just obscure enough to quell Jon's sense of paranoia. If necessary, they could sneak out a door from the stairwell, exit the garage, and walk to Seeb in less than fifteen minutes.

And it wasn't exclusive or sought after. As they stood at the registration desk waiting for a clerk to check them in, Jon scanned the area around them. Not crowded. Well, that might be a problem. They'd be seen, and probably remembered, every time they walked through the lobby.

They walked toward the elevator, passing its restaurant, the Côté Jardin. French. Good enough.

They'd taken three rooms on the fourth floor. Jon stood in front of one of their rooms and pointed to the door. "Whenever we first enter a room, we all go in armed and ready."

William shook his head, not buying into using a gun.

Jon raised his palms. "Better safe than sorry."

There was no one in Jon's room and they left it with a gray thread in "armed" position. They repeated this process for Avram's and William's rooms.

Within a few minutes, they were all gathered around the desk in Jon's room.

Avram said, "We need to make a new plan that assumes Gault is setting us up."

William opened his attaché case and set up his notebook computer. "I have a wireless signal here. Let me find out what Gault knows and what he was told to do."

Jon smiled. "You're going to hack his agency. Aren't you?"

William nodded. "Duh!" And he started keying, faster than Jon imagined anyone could. "Hey, Jon, Gault knows we're in the city and I'm sure he'll find a way to track us if we go out. So, order room service, will you? Figure this will take at least a few hours."

It took all night and half the next day. As William came across facts of interest, he read them to his team members. "Here's one. Gault reports to Mark McDougal, an Assistant Director. Did you know they're called 'Ass Dires'? And here's the log of their conversations. Well, guess what?" He stared across at Avram, then at Jon. "An email from Greenfield, the Dire, to McDougal. It orders our good friend Mr. Gault to set up Houmaz, and also us. If Houmaz kills us, he'll owe his life to Gault et alia. And if we kill Houmaz, Israel will owe a favor to Gault and his friends. Either way, they win."

Sandwiches arrived. Wing chewed while he keyed. He said, "Hot damn," and both companions rose from their seats, but he held up his hand. He took a deep breath. "Look at what I found deep inside Gault's agency. Wow! I could never have guessed. The setup of us and Houmaz? It's just a diversion. What Gault's primary mission is, well, it's to steal the subs from Israel."

Avram's brows arched. "Are you positive?"

"Hell, yeah I am." William pointed to the notebook's screen and turned it around so they could see it.

Jon pounded his fist on the desk. "Bloody fuck! I'm calling Mother."

CHAPTER 36

Gilbert Greenfield's unnamed intelligence agency
headquarters building, K Street, Washington, DC
September 23, 2:26 p.m.

McDougal paced the room, the phone against his ear. "Sir Charles, we understand you put out a burn notice on Tariq Houmaz."

Crane confirmed this.

"I'm just calling to tell you we picked him up. Please comply. Drop your execution order for him."

The voice asked a question.

"I understand your concerns. But the problems he created are now ours. We'll take care of everything. How do you contact him?"

McDougal listened. "Yes, of course. I'll get you a seat at the table. Everything ECHELON finds regarding Europe and Asia will be escalated to MI-6 with top priority."

Crane wanted more.

"Be reasonable, Sir Charles. Getting that intel will raise the entire posture of our relationship past the deniability level. Please, now, I've offered you something significant. How do you contact him?"

Crane's voice sounded cooler. Something about coded blog entries in one of the Al Jazeera website pages. McDougal scribbled notes on a pad. "Thanks. We owe you one." He terminated the conversation and thought for a second about Gault's plan. The entire concept of running their own terrorist might have some merit.

McDougal placed another call. "Bob, what's your status with the 'Three Stooges'?" He always found the call signs Gault assigned to opposition ops teams a hoot. Bob had given the Israeli assassination team a nasty call sign, and thinking of what he'd designated for the individuals themselves had him chuckling: Moe. Larry, and Curly! "Sorry. Status?"

He held the phone to his ear, listening. "Good. Commence the op. Here's how to contact Houmaz." He repeated what Crane told him.

After his morning prayers in one of the café restrooms, Tariq Houmaz read the Al Jazeera blog website from a rent-a-computer within the Muttrah Souk. The souk had grown into a huge labyrinth and was now the largest indoor market in Oman. Houmaz had found several ad hoc entrances in addition to those most tourists used. Tourists and native customers walked its halls buying food, clothing, and tourist items. To get to the café he'd had to dodge rolling garment hangers wheeled by merchants shouting warnings as they spun around its corners. He admired the ceiling of the indoor section, ancient carved wood and peeling plaster.

The blog he found on the Internet contained over two hundred entries calling for his beheading. It was the Sharia punishment for murder. His hands clenched into fists, taking deep breaths to keep from throwing the coffee cup he'd been holding. The hotel where those hunting him were staying was a short taxi ride away. The American spy, Gault, was tracking them for him.

But he wasn't ready yet. He took the last sip from his coffee, rose, and exited the café into the long hallway. Roaming the souk, he found a cell phone store and bought several for cash. In an hour, they might be traceable. But he could use each once and then throw it away.

He walked into a distant corner of the store and punched a number into the new cell phone. "Pesi, it's Tariq. I need you to place a few messages into the blog. I can't. It would take too long and I don't want to be in one place for more than ten minutes. The first one is most important. Explain what happened to me in Vlad. Say it's not my fault, the Israelis posed as my submariners. Tell them we were infiltrated by the Mossad. Say we have found and executed the mole in our organization. Pesi, I believe there is at least one, but maybe more. Probably some Mossad deep coverts. Find out who they are and detain but don't kill them. I want to question them myself, when it's safe for me to return."

He listened to his younger brother for a few seconds on the burner cell. "That will work fine. I have obtained a new sponsor for our future operations. The man is a professional spy and a poor liar. He may be testing me, or he may be setting me up. Either way I have no better alternative. I'll just have to do his bidding."

He heard Pesi urging him not to risk his life and he chuckled. "I make my own choices. This is an opportunity for me to send a message back to the jackals at Mossad, so I'm using the opportunity. But I'll need your help. I need you to recruit a team for me. No one who's seen my face, so you can't use my training ground near Upper Pachir. Your best bet is one of the mosques near you in Riyadh. Figure at least five or six, and have them dress as businessmen. I'll meet them at the Zilo Café in the Muttrah Souk in Muscat tomorrow evening after prayers. Tell the team my name is Aziz Tamil. Yes, that's correct. So far, the Israeli's haven't made a claim. Make your men believe it."

It was well into the night. Ben-Levy was in the back seat of his limo, being driven toward his home near Haifa. He scanned his notes from the Research Department concerning developments along the border between Russia and China.

He saw the caller's name and pressed the Receive Call button. "What?"

"This is a daylight alert, Mother," said the voice, using the term for the highest-priority alert. "I have intel you need." Ben-Levy was about to terminate the call when he heard Jon say words that chilled him. "Seems the bloody Yanks are going to steal the subs."

"How did they find out about them?" Mother sank into the car's seat as the air left him.

"Dunno. But, I've recruited a hacker into my team. One you mentioned once. We hacked the Feds' systems."

"You hacked—"

"Yes. Don't know what you can do to keep the subs, but whatever it is, don't wait too long. There'll be SEAL teams on their way soon."

Ben-Levy thought for several seconds, his breath sounding in the phone. "Thanks. I've something for you. Consider it a trade. I know how Houmaz's handlers communicate with him."

"What?"

"Go to the Al Jazeera website and follow the link to blogs. One of our resident hackers, Michael Drapoff figured this out before we sent him out on assignment two months ago. They use the blog named 'Israel.' Coded messages. I'll send the configuration they use to your cell phone as an email attachment. Their code words, their countersigns. Happy hunting." He terminated the call and crafted and sent the email from his cell.

The car trip home took over an hour. Ben-Levy sat still in the back seat. *Will the United States become Israel's enemy? What steps can I take if this is true?*

Within a few minutes he came to a realization: he

already knew that the funds to acquire the submarines came to the Muslim Brotherhood from a mix of the Saudi royal family and MI-6, and that the Brits hadn't realized what the money would be used for.

But the Americans hadn't been duped like the idiots in MI-6. What if the Americans had compromised the original setup of the Jericho Sanction? What if the Americans had found a way to circumvent its functioning? The subs were the newest and closest to foolproof piece of the plan. But if the Americans managed to steal the subs from the Israelis, what would happen? What if the subs were now the only way the Jericho Sanction could be implemented?

As Avram closed the door to the bathroom, William looked up from the notebook's screen. He closed the lid and faced Jon. "Jon, there's something else important here. For the longest time, I wasn't sure what to do with this intel."

Jon stopped pacing the room. "What?"

"Before you called me the first time, I'd been doing some work for my father. Rummaging through the computers of Russia and China. I had some help from the Chinese government's cybercrime unit, but they were useless. Anyway, I found it was Mossad. A false flag operation. They've been hacking into Russian and Chinese government computers, trying to start a border war. I'm not sure why. You have the connections within Mossad. Can you confirm it for me? Can you tell me why?"

Jon reached out for a chair to steady himself. "Are you sure?"

"Shit, Jon, I had the help of an expert, the best hacker on the planet. She did the heavy lifting. What I told you is irrefutable."

Jon scratched his chin, thinking. "Betsy 'Butterfly' Brown.

Correct?" He thought hard. This would be trouble, of that he was sure.

He remembered what he'd been taught about Israel's national policies. No, he didn't know enough or understand what the changing imperatives could be. He knew little of the people involved. What about Mother? Was Ben-Levy behind this?

Wing's voice was just above a whisper. "Yes. Betsy Brown. Well, Jon?"

"Uh, shit. Do us both a favor, William. Keep this to yourself until we figure it out together. You and me. No one else. And tell your super-hacker not to tell anyone. Got it?"

"She won't. But don't you betray me. Don't tell anyone I was the one who told you. And don't hang me out to dry. I've got an insurance policy. All the secrets I've ever hacked. Everything worth anything. Much of it involves my work for the Mossad. If I disappear or die, if I don't or can't enter a specific ever-changing password into a specific website every so often, the computer where I've stashed the pile of goodies will vomit forth everything. Send all the stuff to everywhere, from Al Jazeera to the *Washington Post* to *Sixty Minutes*. Understand?"

"Yeah. We're good." Jon realized he needed something just like this for his own protection. He smiled. "Thanks, William. What's your father's name?"

"Xiang Wing."

Jon considered the impact this intel could have on Chinese relations with Israel. "Please don't tell him what you know until I tell you. Okay?"

Wing frowned, his eyes unfocused for a moment. "Well, okay. Sure."

Jon remembered the last word that Rimora mentioned in her dying breath: Bloodridge. Did it have any significance here? Jon wished he knew. This was all so Byzantine, it was just possible the spymaster had designed it. If it was true, Jon now had a tool he could use to level the playing field with Ben-Levy. He leaned close to William. "And, come to think of it, I need yet another favor."

"Shit, Jon, I don't have time for—"

"Please. Just listen. I'll pay for it." When William said nothing, Jon nodded. "Okay. Can you create a similar life insurance policy for me? Website and password?"

Wing nodded his eyes questioning. "You don't have one? Hah! Sure. Easy."

Jon thought about the secrets he'd place within his "insurance policy." He took a deep breath. "Thanks."

CHAPTER 37

Yigdal Ben-Levy's office,
basement of Mossad headquarters,
corner of Hasadnaot and Hamenofim Streets,
Herzliyya, Israel
September 24, 2:33 p.m.

Bone tired, Ben-Levy paced the small room, stopping to stare at the chalkboard. I've been over this so many times. Still haven't got a usable plan and time is running out.

A knock on the door pulled him from his private world. "Come."

The tall, thin man with black hair and a moustache cracked the door open and smiled at Mother. "We're back. Lester, Ari, JD, and Shimon went directly home. Lester sent me to check in first." Michael Drapoff's eyes wandered to the chalkboard. "Oops. You're busy. Uh, call Lester when you want to debrief us and he'll get us all here." He turned away.

Mother took a step toward Drapoff. "Wait, Michael. I could use your help. You're the best hacker we have in house. Maybe you can tell me what will happen if I try each of these alternatives." Ben-Levy pointed to the other chair in the room, then sat in his own.

"Sure." Drapoff walked to the board. He ran his finger just above the chalk lines several times in multiple directions, and pursed his lips. "Your best alternative is this one."

"Why? Why hack MI-6 and plant the message there? Why not just talk to Sir Charles on the phone? Or send it as email to McDougal?"

Michael sat. "McDougal? That won't work. He'll never forward it up the chain of command. I'm sure his op is off the books. And if you talk to Crane, the verbal message might be garbled in transmission. Hell, Crane may even decide to ignore it. But if you leave Crane a text message he can forward on to the White House, it puts the message in over McDougal's head. The email leaves a permanent, indelible mark within the British government's servers. Evidence. Creates a fait accompli. Crane has to follow through."

Ben-Levy closed his eyes. "I think you're right. Thanks for a second set of eyes. I've been staring at this for over an hour and I'm brain-blind."

"Uh, do you want me to plant the text?"

Ben-Levy smiled. "Yes." He pointed to the computer behind his seat, and the message on screen he'd typed into it an hour earlier. "Just find the right place to put it." He walked out the door. Michael sat behind the desk. Once again, he read the message on the screen:

As you know, Israel has two nuclear submarines it captured from Tariq Houmaz, one of MI-6's former Muslim Brotherhood assets. We also have hard evidence indicating the United States funded the purchase of those subs through its bank accounts at the Bank of Trade, and that the terrorist who purchased the submarines was an unlisted covert agent of both the British and the American intelligence services. Even if you could find some way to prove the evidence is untrue, were it made public, Congress would be forced to investigate, creating a messy scandal for the President and the British Prime Minister.

If any attempt is made to take the submarines from us, the evidence will be released to every political blog and website of importance, and to the global press.

Of course, should Israel ever be subjected to attack, the Jericho Sanction commences, making every oil-producing country in the Middle East radio-active, whether or not we have the subs. Not including the forty ICBMs with twenty-megaton atomic warheads present on those subs, Israel still has over two hundred fifty nuclear missiles of its own. The safest disposition of these submarines is with us, unless you wish Israel as your enemy.

Before today, Israel has always thought of itself as America's ally and has shared intelligence with our American intelligence partners. Attempting to take possession of the submarines could create terrible public press and diplomatic turmoil, with myriad unforeseen consequences.

The message wasn't signed, and the steps Drapoff took to insert it into MI-6's computer system left no way to track back its actual sender or point of origin. He pressed the button and transmitted the message.

As Michael rose from the seat, Ben-Levy returned to the office and touched his shoulder. "I have another mission for you and the team. How soon can you all be ready to travel?"

Drapoff pointed to the go bag he'd dropped on the floor, containing the barest essentials for immediate departure. "Ready now. Where to?"

As his plane crossed the Mediterranean toward Kuwait, Bob Gault's cell phone buzzed. He scanned his cell's screen and frowned. McDougal. It must relate to one of his two assignments, either the set-up of the Three Stooges or the sub-theft, "Project Shitbag." His team for the latter assignment was on its way to Yemen.

He pressed the Receive Call button. "Gault."

"Bob, I'm calling off your submarine-theft operation. Your SEAL team is returning stateside from Yemen as we speak."

Gault wanted to ask why, but remained silent, thinking, *somehow, the gods have saved my ass. That mission was never going to succeed, and its failure would have ended my career*. "What about the Three Stooges?" This one was a mission he desired.

"Proceed on that one. When will things be set up?"

Gault focused on the PERT chart he conjured in his head. On the timeline, everything was on schedule. "Very soon. I sent messages to Houmaz through blog entries just before my connecting flight left Paris. I expect him to post a reply within hours."

"Good. Call me when it's over. McDougal out."

Gault thought he'd name this part of the operation "Gunfight at the Muttrah Souk Corral." He chuckled. When he landed in Kuwait City, he'd need a flight to Oman. He called Yemeni Airlines and cancelled his flight from Kuwait City to Aden, Yemen. His next cell phone call was to Kuwait Airlines. Although the two countries were both on the same peninsula, it was too far and too dangerous to drive. But, he was in luck; they had a flight leaving less than two hours after he landed. He booked himself a seat.

Gault set to work as the aircraft descended toward the runway. Now he could be present to oversee the slaughter. He had no hatred for Houmaz. The man was just a chess piece. While he admired the Israelis for their toughness and resiliency, the events to follow were his best hope of being promoted. After over ten years as a case officer, he was tired of working the field.

If I've got to run a black op, it's always best to be part of one where every outcome was a win for me.

Life is sweet.

Jon's cell phone buzzed. He scanned its screen. Gault. He pressed the Receive Call button. "What've you got for me, Mr. Gault?"

"I've set it up. Tonight at ten at the Muttrah Souk. Houmaz may be alone, but I doubt it. Our intel indicates he'll be there to receive an arms shipment. So his helpers might be there just to tote the crates. The delivery is to Al Fursani, the rug merchant, close to the entrance from Al Wadi Al Kabir Market. By that time of night, it should be empty as a ghost town, except for them."

Jon's mind automatically generated equations modeling the alternative outcomes, the many ways Gault could set up him and Avram in a labyrinth as full of twists and turns as the souk. "Thanks. I'll call you when it's over." He terminated the call, sure that Gault would now call Houmaz to set up the other side of the skirmish.

Jon heard a knock on the door. He pulled the safety off his Beretta and walked near the door. When he peeked through the peephole he saw several faces he didn't know. The man in front was tall and had black hair and a moustache. He turned and whispered to Avram. "Visitors. No one I know."

Avram drew his handgun and moved to the other side of the door. He looked through the peephole and smiled. "They're friends." He opened the door. "Shalom, Michael. What brings you here?"

Michael hugged Avram. "Shalom. We're all sorry for your loss. She was a wonderful woman, putting up with all your bullshit. And your adorable little daughter. We also miss them. We just returned from the border between Russia and

China. A mountain range the residents of both countries call the Bloodridge, due to the wars they've had over the centuries. Mother thought you could use some help."

Jon's mind snapped into focus at the mention of Rimora's last word. *If this is it, why is Mother trying to keep China and Russia at each other's throats?* And, as he thought the question, a possible answer occurred to him. The Russian government was filled with *siloviki*, a gang of former KGB agents who now occupied the Kremlin. *And, the same* siloviki *also run the Russian mafiya. I wonder if Bloodridge was designed to keep the mafiya from selling the Russian arms because they might need them in an imminent war with China? Could this be it?*

Drapoff entered the room. Behind him, Lester Dushov walked in, carrying a black satchel and his go bag. When all five had entered the room, Avram closed the door. Dushov grinned at William and Jon. "We're in the SHABEK division. When we were in IDF years ago, Avram was our commanding officer. I know you, Jon, from your photo. Who's he?"

William answered. "I'm their hacker. William Wing. Who are the rest of you?"

Dushov dropped his satchel and go bag on the floor. "I'm Lester Dushov. I'm the group leader for my team. My special area is poisons and interrogation chemicals." He pointed to his crew. "Michael Drapoff, our hacker and tele-comm specialist. Ari Westheim, martial arts. JD Weinstein, explosives and guns. And Shimon Tennenbaum, our sniper." They walked in behind Lester.

Weinstein closed the door and pointed to the satchels. "Claymores and flashbangs, night-vision goggles, guns, and ammo. It's a good way to carry nasty things in public and still be undetected." He faced Shimmel. "Sorry about your loss, Avram. Sharon was a great woman. And your daughter. A tragedy."

Avram frowned. "Thanks." Tears formed in his eyes. His face went rigid. "I want to see Houmaz die."

Jon nodded and patted Avram's shoulder, but all the time he was thinking about Bloodridge.

Michael pulled open his bag and removed a stack of fabric. "I brought us all Hawaiian shirts treated with Liquid Armor. These are new, no more Jimi Hendrix. These have different scenes on each." He scanned the room, and walked to where he could see the screen of William's computer. "Uh, what's the plan?"

Avram shook his head. "With you to help us, we can design a better plan."

Jon looked across the table at Avram, feeling the man's grief echo against his own. "We've just enough time to change the plan. But we'll still need to arrive with all our equipment no later than one hour after sundown, so we can set up."

Dushov nodded.

Jon faced William. "And, as for you, it's now time to pack your bags and fly back home to Hong Kong."

William frowned. "Change in plans for me, too." Jon felt surprise and stared at William. His face seemed somehow both harder and softer. Jon couldn't tell what his friend was thinking, but something had refocused and changed in William as he spoke. "No way. You two and me, we're a team. Shit, man, I never thought I'd find myself saying something like this. But, I've been thinking about what I stand for, and what my life is worth." He seemed to focus on something deep within himself. The words came out slow, but filled with purpose. "Look, guys. I'm probably the worst shot on the planet. Doesn't matter. You're going to need every hand. So give me a gun. I'm going with you."

When he picked up the gun, he looked at the Mossad team. "Uh, can any of you tell me how to make this work?"

CHAPTER 38

Along the Muttrah Corniche,
Muscat, Oman
September 24, 6:54 p.m.

It was a short walk from their hotel to the objective. As Jon and his team drew near, he realized the Old Muttrah Souk projected a more menacing presence after nightfall. Each carried a map of the place, although the minor alleyways were missing. They approached from Al Bustan Club, where they'd eaten a quick meal.

Walking north on Al Fursani Street toward Al Wadi Al Kabir Park, they passed along the Muttrah Corniche on their left flank. Jon located the main entrance, just past the doorway to a silver and jewelry shop. He faced William. "Look, I can't let you join us. You've had no training. It would be suicide."

William opened his mouth but Jon cut him off. "Sorry. I can't have your death on my hands. I've been responsible for too much death."

William clenched his teeth. "I'll wait here. Outside. If things go south, I can help you escape. I won't go inside. You have my word."

Jon stood still, thinking. "All right. I have your promise."

William smiled. "Yeah. Enough. Go hunting."

Jon nodded to the others. He pointed left. "That way."

William stood outside, looking in. He paced for a few seconds. Then he scanned the souk as he entered, looking at the map. He traced his finger over their route. It was a labyrinthical path through the narrow corridors, through six intersections to the point where the hallway widened just in front of their destination: Al Fursani rug merchant. As he stood staring at the map, he memorized the path.

Jon had divided them into two teams. Jon, JD, and Michael were team one. Avram, Shimon, and Lester were team two. For the trip to the rug merchant, they marched as a single group. Framing the entrance to the passageway into the souk was a tall tiled arch, flaked with gold and silver. According to the notation on their map, its roof was built of ancient wood. It was a flammable labyrinth.

As they walked single file inside, Jon's eyes darted around the corners of the narrow hallways and twisty passages, filled with shoppers. Business was just now starting to wind down for the night.

Merchants were hawking their exclusive baskets, traditional wool carpets known as *kilims*, wall hangings, clothing, spices, and jewelry. The souk's interior hallways were close and well lit. And, the air was thick with the heady fragrance of perfumes and aromas of burning frankincense.

Jon scanned the path in front, between the flanking merchants stalls, looking for threats. As they approached an intersection in the maze, he peeked around at both directions of the choke point. He took a breath and stopped. So far, nothing threatening.

Jon had marked their destination on the tourist map with a neon-colored permanent marker. He led them northwest to their next site, an intersection studded by a café and a spice shop at opposite corners.

His wristwatch indicated it was now 8:54 p.m. "We're

close now. Let's find a place where we can conceal ourselves for forty minutes until we're sure Houmaz and his team has had time to enter the rug merchant's shop."

Avram pointed to a clothing dealer who was locking his stand. As the merchant walked away, the three in Jon's team and the three in Lester's moved behind the closed stall.

Soon, silence reigned.

At 9:30, Jon saw movement on his flank. He dropped the safety off the Beretta and took aim. Staring at where he'd seen the movement before, he started to squeeze the trigger expecting Houmaz's men, but realized it was William.

He lowered his weapon and stared at his friend. "William, your word is crap! Why?"

William's face was a frozen mask. Jon could smell the hacker's fear. "I can't let you do this without me. I want to freakin' help!"

Jon shook his head. "All right, follow me. And follow my orders, or I'll kill you myself." Jon watched William stare at him in fear and it echoed against his own fright. He was sure Gault had led them into a trap. Were Houmaz and his men here and ready? There was no way to tell.

By 9:35 p.m., the souk was empty and silent. Jon pointed to his wristwatch. "Time to plant the Claymores." He pointed to the map, his finger touching the spot near the top center where the rug merchant was. "These intersections, as we agreed. Around the entrance to the rug merchant, at the first set of intersections."

Ari and Shimon divided up the mines. Each was a military gray rectangle, about ten by eight by five centimeters, and weighing about one kilogram. The fuse was electronic, with a red USB port for a timer and a green LED for its cell phone trigger.

Jon touched William's shoulder. "Wait here. If we need you, I'll yell."

William's face fell. "But, Jon, why—"

"My orders, William. Follow them. Sheesh!" Jon skirted away from the merchant's stall, motioning for Lester, Ari, and Michael to follow him.

William crouched behind the stall by himself. "Fuck."

Avram nodded at Shimon and JD. They followed him, circling the intersections surrounding the rug merchant. JD crisscrossed between the groups, deploying a network of infrared tripwires.

William remained crouched behind the clothing dealer's stand. He held a 9mm Beretta in his right hand, its safety on.

At 9:58 p.m., Jon returned. "Listen, William, it's still not too late. You can still get your ass out of here. Save your bloody life."

William responded by lowering the Beretta's safety. He stared back at Jon.

Jon nodded. "Well, there it is. You're in now, up to your bloody neck. Follow about ten feet behind me. If trouble finds me, I'll move fast and you'll need to go pace for pace where I do. Don't fuck this up for me. Clear?"

"Yeah, Jon. Clear as mud. Where's Avram and his team?"

"They're on the other side of the rug merchant. The Claymores are set and all he needs to do is place the final wire into the arming mechanism. After that, anyone within the rug merchant's perimeter will be trapped. All we need to do now is wait for Houmaz and his friends to make their entrance at the party. Once they cross the infrared tripwires for the Claymores, we'll arm the mines and rain hell on Houmaz and his team." Jon motioned for the rest of his team to spread out and take cover.

William noticed an ear bud on Jon's left temple. "You guys are wired?"

"But of course. Just Avram and me. I didn't bring but two. Sorry. Didn't know we'd get help from the Mossad, and I didn't know you'd remain on the team. Just stay close to me."

Just then, every light in the souk went out.

Jon looked at his illuminated wristwatch: 10:01 p.m. and the souk was closing. He pressed the button on the side of his ear bud. "Night-vision goggles on now. And, ready the guns."

William heard Avram's reply even though the noise was mere leakage from Jon's ear bud: "Hand signals only. No speech from here on."

Jon nodded to William, pointing in the direction of their final destination. They inched down the hall, going from darkness to darkness.

While they walked, Jon wondered if there were hidden flaws in the plan. He knew Gault had set them up. Still he had no choice if he wanted another chance at Houmaz. He ran the measures and countermeasures through his head as he pulled the infrared binoculars from his pocket. So many things could go wrong. He scanned the rug merchant's booth.

There was no one. Jon wondered if they'd somehow misunderstood what Gault told them. Were the spy's lies accurate? He felt doubt and confusion, and found himself shaking his head. Would it all come down to the quality of his plan? A shiver of fear ran down his spine. What if Houmaz's plan was better than his own? He couldn't help himself. "Status?"

Shimmel's voice through the ear bud was a whisper. "Silence. Either they're late for the pickup, or—"

A silenced shot tore into the booth behind Jon. He flattened to the floor. *Shit!* Jon fought the adrenaline spike. He took a deep breath and examined the entry point of the bullet and tracked its general direction back toward its point of origin.

He felt a sinking feeling in the pit of his gut. The adrenaline rush bloomed, narrowing his vision, dimming his hearing. He felt his ability to reason fade into the dusty air. *Shit!* He thought about their position relative to that of the rug merchant's store.

Jon shouted into the ear bud. "Avram. We've messed up. They're way outside the perimeter of where we laid the Claymores, not inside! They've surrounded us! Don't turn the Claymores on yet. Can you close the distance between us?"

A hail of bullets rained on them.

Jon felt a mix of fury and disappointment. He struggled to relax, knowing he needed to clear his mind. But it was no good. The voice in his head was babbling non-stop. He wanted to rip his head off. He closed his eyes and let the rush fade. *Okay. I'm over it.*

Avram's voice came through the ear bud. "Jon, we're on our way right now. Don't shoot us. Twenty feet away, on your right, moving to you." His tone seemed calm but Jon knew it was just Avram's battle experience. He hoped Avram could make this work.

More shots pierced the booths of the souk, and most were silenced rounds, making it difficult for Jon to tell where they'd come from. He scanned the area and saw nothing. Perspiration drenched his palms.

He saw Avram close the distance and nod to his team member, Shimon. Jon said, "Turn the Claymores on now." He motioned for them all to move away from the perimeter and take cover. They moved thirty feet away, behind the merchant stalls and locked containers.

They were still just inside the perimeter of the Claymores. Now, when Tariq Houmaz and his men came for them, they'd cross the infrared tripwires coming inward.

They all waited.

Jon realized he had no idea where Houmaz's men were. The implication rocked him: the plan he'd made might not work. Too late. He scanned the area, his gun hand cramping. Seconds passed and there was an explosion. *Must be one of the Claymores.* Flesh and blood spewed into the air, coating everything.

Jon swept his gaze left, then right, looking for a tactic

that could reverse their fate. "Avram, I don't see them. How can we fight when we don't know where they are! Is there any military maneuver that'll work for us?"

Jon waited for a reply while William found a target and pointed his Beretta at it. The hacker's shot went wild, but many of their attackers moved away as they shot back in William's direction.

From the muzzle flash Jon could see where they were. "They're at my two through my four." With that, everyone in both his teams fired back and three of their attackers fell from behind a booth, less than ten feet from them. Too close. How'd they get this close?

Now he knew precisely where they were. "Avram, I have a plan. We're surrounded but the Claymores might work for us if we turn them off until we retreat back through the intersection we came from. It doesn't appear guarded. Then we draw them after us until they're within the perimeter. We leave the mines where they were, we just move ourselves and draw the targets within range of the mines. Then turn them back on, trapping them within the perimeter. Turn the mines off right now, then move your team southeast, back the way we came, following me and my team."

"Right."

Jon touched William's shoulder. "Follow me." Jon and William retreated, laying down covering fire to slow their attackers. He remembered the old military saying, *no battle plan survives first contact with the enemy.*

Jon's two teams were closely grouped now, and Avram stopped them. "Wait." He flipped the switch to disarm the mines and led them across the perimeter. "They'll follow right behind us."

Jon nodded. "Set up twenty feet past our current position, on both sides of this hall." He waited twenty seconds before he told Avram to rearm the Claymores. "When they trigger the mines, it'll kill a few and show the locations of the remainder. It's our signal to open fire and try to take down the remnant."

Avram nodded and they waited.

Jon took deep breaths, trying to recover his ability to think. A shattered perfume bottle from one of the vender stalls scented the air. Lisa's scent. He tried to focus but all he could see were olive-colored eyes in a splash of red hair. He shook his head. And saw Houmaz, smiling, ten feet away, aiming a handgun right at him.

Jon knew he should duck. Houmaz grinned, a nasty twitch at the corner of his mouth. Jon took aim at the bomb maker who had murdered his fiancée and sucked in a deep breath.

He squeezed the trigger, just as Houmaz did. He felt a round pierce his chest. He strained through the pain to keep his eyes open, pulling the trigger again and again, and saw blood arc from Houmaz's torso in several places before the bomb maker hit the ground.

The souk revolved around Jon as he fell. He bounced on the ground and saw his own wound pulsing blood. Laying there, gazing at the carved ceiling of the souk, he felt his head grow light as though he rode an out-of-control merry-go-round. A set of equations depicting what had just happened swirled in his head and abruptly disappeared.

Jon's consciousness swirled away. *Lisa!*

CHAPTER 39

20 meters east of Al Fursani Rug Merchant,
Muttrah Souk, Muscat, Oman
September 24, 10:54 p.m.

William's eyes had adjusted to the dim light. If he could see, he was sure the darkness wasn't an obstacle for any of the terrorists either. He looked around at the continuous stream of muzzle flashes. Both their teams were firing at Houmaz's men. And the Arabs were shooting back. *Shit!* The firefight made so much noise he couldn't tell if anyone would hear him.

Less than three feet away, he saw Jon fall, his chest soaking in dark liquid. Jon's blood. He touched and sniffed it, to be sure. *Yes, blood.* Then he realized the liquid on his own face wasn't perspiration. *It's Jon's blood. All over me! I'm not CryptoMonger here.* He pulled the ear bud from Jon's ear. "Avram! Jon's hit. It looks real bad. What should I do?"

He heard Avram's voice. "Keep shooting. And try hitting your targets for a change."

William saw six Middle Eastern men break cover and charge them. He heard shots from the Mossad weapons just in front of him.

Avram counted their targets as Jon's team hit them. "Six. Seven. Eight."

William heard Avram shout, "JD's hit." Seconds later he

325

saw one of their attackers launch himself between him and Jon's body, holding some kind of automatic weapon.

The man was just a few feet away when William pulled the trigger. His first shot went wild, and his target smiled as he pulled the trigger, but his shot went wide. William aimed fast and fired until the clip was empty. Two of his shots hit the man, and one blew a small hole in the man's forehead. William watched the man's body fall. He felt dinner coming back up his throat. *Jon was right. I'm in over my head.*

He picked up the dead man's automatic.

He looked forward and saw another of Houmaz's men emerge from behind a corner passageway, holding a similar weapon. William sneered and lifted the gun, aiming it into the target's body. He was surprised when the bullets came from his gun before he even realized he'd pulled the trigger. His shots went high, but one opened a large hole in the attacker's throat.

Another loud explosion indicated a Claymore had found its mark. William heard Avram yell, "If Gault told us the truth about how many men Houmaz brought, I think they're all down. William, we must leave now. Just in case I miscounted or Gault lied about this, too. Hurry. I'll circle back and pick up Jon. I've turned the Claymores off. You just head out as fast as you can."

William was shocked to find he could only see what was directly in front of him. He felt something wet in the crook of his elbow. It was blood. *My blood!* He touched the spot and it didn't even hurt. *Rats!* The blood seeped so it must not be critical. But seeing it made him dizzy. He turned his head left and right around him. He seemed to be alone. He bolted, sprinting for the entrance and the safety of the street.

As he breached the souk's exit, William could hear sirens closing on them. Reaching Al Fursani Street, he turned south onto the Muttrah Corniche. Avram caught up, sprinting, and William could see Jon laying slack across Avram's shoulder. Four of the other coverts from Israel trotted several feet behind, one of them helping JD, who was having trouble walking. One of the Israelis walked backward, facing the souk with his weapon pointed back just in case.

"Avram, is he breathing?"

"Yah, but not for long if we don't get him to a doctor. Get us a cab!"

William ran out into the street and stood in one of the traffic lanes. He pointed his gun at the driver inside a car. He used his other hand to motion for the driver to stop. As the car halted, he signaled to the driver and the man opened the door and fled from the vehicle. William yelled and the team members converged on him.

As the light of sunrise filled the private room of the doctor's office, Avram and William stood around the bed. The bandage strapped around Jon's chest still leaked blood.

The doctor opened the door and walked in holding an iPad. He stared at William. "I was told you are all family."

William stared back with defiance. "Brother-in-law."

"Ah, well then. Your family member is no longer on the critical list. He'll be out for a while longer, and there's still a chance that he could worsen, from a blood clot or infection. If we can get him to a hospital, he'd have a better chance." He checked Jon's vitals and made a note in the iPad. "At least he's young and strong." With that, the doctor left the room.

But, they weren't safe yet. Would Jon be okay without a hospital? Was Houmaz dead, or still at large?

The SHABEK team that Ben-Levy had sent said goodbye and left to travel back to Israel. Before leaving, Lester Dushov paid the doctor in cash and threatened his life if he told the authorities about his wounded patient. Lester promised Avram an exfiltration team for Jon, William, and him.

But, as the doctor and Jon's two team members stood at

his bed, the door burst open and two burly men entered holding guns. They announced themselves as detectives from Muscat's local police force. One of them examined Jon and nodded to the other. "Get an ambulance here now. He'll go to Royal Hospital and these others to the station."

Avram asked, "What are we charged with?"

One of the men pointed his gun at Avram. "Place these on your friend's wrists. And then, do the same for yourself." He handed Avram two sets of handcuffs.

"The charges?" Wing's voice was just above a whisper.

"Damaging merchant stalls at the souk, for starters. But more important, there are twelve dead bodies you left lying among the ruined merchant stalls. Murder."

CHAPTER 40

Royal Hospital, Muscat, Oman
September 24, 2:32 a.m.

Jon could see her now. She reached for his hand. *You did what you promised. I still want you. Come to me now.*

Jon reached out. Dying, he realized he still loved her. Even though he hated her. Both feelings raged at each other in the tempest of his mind.

He yearned for her. Touched her outreached fingers. *Yes.* It was time. It would be so easy now, to give up what he'd become. A murderer whose way was to seek revenge. And become something else.

But the tone of her voice rose. *He is dead, Jon, isn't he?*

Jon's smile vanished. *Don't know. I shot him. Several times. But I wasn't able to confirm the kill.*

She withdrew her hand. *Then you can't. I won't let you come to me.* He was alone again.

Jon's eyes cracked open. "Whazit?" He coughed and a bolt of pain shot through him from head to toe. He tasted his own blood. "Where am I?"

"Easy now." The detective touched his shoulder. "You're in a hospital bed. Looks like you'll live." He pointed to the other detective behind him. "You have to answer our questions."

"Get me something to drink first. And get my doctor."

The two detectives faced each other and shrugged. One left the room.

Jon modeled the scene in a series of formulas. *I'm in an Arab country, albeit an enlightened one. But it's not a democracy and murder here is still punishable by death.* Jon looked at the remaining detective. "Where are my friends?"

"In jail. What happens to them depends on what you tell us. Clear? We don't torture prisoners in Oman. But if you fail to tell us what we need to know, it will look bad when you are all tried in court."

Jon was certain the police detectives would pass this case to military intelligence very soon. The Oman government would use torture to get every last bit of intel from them, if they had enough time. Given that, he was sure Ben-Levy would send an exfiltration team. If the timing was poor, he, Avram, and William would be caught in a crossfire. He'd have to get his teammates released from jail before a team arrived.

He stared into the detective's eyes. His throat was so dry he found it difficult to speak. "Release my friends or I won't tell you anything. Bring them here." He couldn't keep his eyes open. He drifted into sleep.

It was dark outside when he woke. The two detectives were still there. One of them, heavy, with long, oily black hair, asked his name. In the back of the room, he could see William and Avram.

Jon remembered that when he'd gone out hunting Houmaz, he carried no passport. He remembered that Avran and William cleaned their hotel rooms before they all walked to the souk. He was sure they wouldn't have given his name to the detectives. He wondered, *which identity would evoke the least suspicion? Michael O'Hara, Jon Sommers, or Salim al-Muhammed? Not much of a decision.* "My name? I'm

Salim al-Muhammed. Born in London. Live now in Karachi, Pakistan."

The older of the two detectives nodded and used a stylus to scribble onto the screen of his iPad. "What about the bodies you left behind in the souk? Shot to death."

Jon shook his head. "Listen, I murdered no one. It was self-defense."

The detective entered more notes into his iPad. "You claim you shot all of those men in self-defense? This story of yours is unbelievable. You have no identification, and no permit to carry a gun."

Jon stared back. "They must have stolen my wallet. I don't own a gun. Uh, listen. We were attacked while we were leaving the souk. Those men tried to rob us. My friends fled. They must have thought I was right behind them. But one of the robbers caught up to me and I wrestled his gun from him. We fought and I shot him. Then another came after me and shot at me. I used the first man's gun to kill him. I shot all the others."

The detective frowned. "Your friends didn't return to help you?"

Jon took a deep breath to give him time to think. "No. My friends fled. By the time they returned, I was wounded and dying. They found me a doctor and saved my life."

The detective shook his head. "You're saying you killed twelve men?"

Jon gawked. What happened to the thirteenth? Hadn't the three slugs he fired ended Tariq Houmaz? This was something he couldn't ask. But now he knew someone had helped the bomb maker, just as his team had saved him. Probably Gault. And Houmaz might have survived his wounds that night. "I didn't count them. It all happened so fast."

He closed his eyes, bitter tears rolling down his cheeks. "I'm tired now. What happens next?"

The detective pulled out a tape recorder. "Repeat everything you told me, but don't leave out any details. Start with the moment you entered the souk." He turned on the unit and motioned toward Jon.

Jon told the story. A complete piece of fiction. He thought as he spoke, making sure everything he said made sense. When he was done, the detective switched off the recorder.

Jon asked again, "What happens next?"

The detective motioned behind him. "We go and file our report. Soon the crime scene reports, ballistics and finger-prints, will come to us. We'll decide then what to do with you. Your friends can stay in the room with you, but the hallway is guarded by a team of detectives. And this part of the hospital is empty now, occupied only by us and your friends. No one else here. Very quiet. The guards will hear everything you say when you speak."

The detectives walked out the door, and Jon heard it latch.

PART IV

CHAPTER 41

Royal Hospital, Muscat, Oman
September 26, 5:29 p.m.

As the sun set outside his hospital room's windows, Jon tried to sit up in the bed. The excruciating pain drove him near to unconsciousness. He tried rolling on his side instead, and felt his insides twisting within him. He worked to hoist himself into a sitting position.

Avram and William both slept in chairs near his bed. If what Avram whispered to him after the detectives left was true, an exfiltration team would arrive within hours. William had tried the door but it was locked from the outside.

He needed to be ready to leave with them. He wondered if his blood-stained clothing had been taken as evidence. *No doubt, yes.* He touched the hospital gown. He was naked underneath it. *Can't travel like this.*

When the pain had subsided, he braced himself and dropped to the floor. As his feet bounced on the linoleum, pain roiled through him. But, with clenched teeth, he stood and tried to take a step. *Not too bad. Another. Yes, I can do this.* He took tiny steps, walking to the dresser. Were any clothes within? Could he bend over without losing consciousness? As he bowed, the world spun. *No.* He took some deep breaths.

The door behind him burst open but the light didn't go on. "Jon, don't move. We'll help you." It was the voice of Shula Ries. "Grab his arms, Harry, Samuel. Esther, put the bag of clothes on the bed and undress him."

Jon tried to smile but his pain forced it out as a sneer. "So pleased to see you, Ms. Ries. And aren't you sweet, bringing friends to visit." Jon's visual field began to stipple. "I, ah..."

When he regained consciousness, he was sitting in a wheelchair, dressed in jeans and a blue-and-white-striped oxford shirt. He scanned in front of him and saw four unconscious uniformed men on the floor, gagged and bound.

Esther led the way, dressed as a nurse. She swung her head left, then right. The other members of Shula's team flanked Jon.

Shula pushed the wheelchair. Avram and William were gone. He wondered what had become of them. They walked through the emergency entrance and loaded Jon and the chair into an unmarked white van. No one tried to stop them or even asked who they were. He winced as they pushed him into a seat. Avram sat in the driver's seat and William was parked in the shotgun seat.

The ride along the Muttrah Corniche was bumpy. Every twist, pothole, and rut in the road shot bolts of pain through Jon. He replayed the scene where he was hit and still continued pumping bullets into Houmaz. How could the bomb maker still be alive?

His plans, every one, he thought, had been watertight, yet all of them had failed. And the last plan, so haphazard, had worked. What was the difference?

A sudden realization shocked him. All the teams before had been assigned to him by someone else. By Mossad. By MI-6. The last team, William and Avram, had worked so much better with him. The difference was his faith in his team, not his faith in the plan! The team had formed with a common purpose, to seek justice for what they'd lost.

The key ingredient was trust in each other. He smiled against the pain echoing through him as the van stopped at the edge of the water and its doors sprung open.

Shula and her team loaded Jon into a boat. William and Avram jumped aboard. In seconds, they were all headed into the Gulf of Oman. Jon wondered, *where is the boat going?* And smiled as he understood. No math was necessary.

They must be headed toward the two stolen submarines.

CHAPTER 42

Mediterranean Sea,
6 kilometers east of Crete
October 10, 12:14 a.m.

Almost three weeks later, the submarines entered the Mediterranean, settling off the coast of Crete.

When one of the subs surfaced, Avram, William, and Jon climbed the ladder up the conning tower and stood on the deck in a stiff breeze. William smiled as if this was the greatest adventure of his life. Jon thought, *perhaps it is. For all of us.*

Avram's face remained a mask of sadness.

Jon felt somewhat distant, immersed in a world of his own, struggling to keep his attention on the real world and not his conflicted feelings about Lisa. He'd found it was possible to ignore her voice, but when at last he did, it faded away.

The sub's commander jumped off the conning tower and joined them on the deck. "We can't stay on the surface for more than a few minutes without being detected. Please hurry. Get in the motor-raft."

They climbed down the side of the sub, dropping the last five feet into the raft. Within minutes they were speeding toward one of the island's beaches. The ride was bumpy, but

Jon felt little discomfort. *My body is healing. As for my mind, well, not so bloody much.*

Avram remained silent and moody as they called a taxi using a new burner cell phone the sub's captain had given them. Tickets to Tel Aviv were waiting for them at the El Al ticket counter.

The plane ride from Crete to Tel Aviv was smooth. Jon spent the time in silence, thinking about what he'd say when Mother debriefed him. He wondered if the secrets he held had any power.

Avram sat in the seat next to him. He faced Jon. "I can't believe you hit him three times, and he's not dead."

Jon frowned. "Yeah. Anyway, well, I'm just not sure, is all. He might have escaped the souk and bled out. But according to William, there is no hospital record of anyone else wounded that day or the next."

"So you think he walked away."

Jon shook his head. "No way to know." But, he knew he'd failed. And he was sure this was his last chance. Ever. He sighed.

Avram asked the flight attendant for a cola.

William sat on Jon's other side.

Jon faced him. "Avram told me you shot three of them. Didn't know you could handle a gun."

William shrugged. "Neither did I. It was the first time I ever held one. And, if I never see one again, I'll be much happier." He touched Jon's shoulder. "What should I tell my father?"

Jon stared into the space in front of him. "If he ever finds out what Mossad did, it'll be bad for Israel. And if he finds out you lied to him, it'll be worse for you. Can you destroy the Bloodridge data in the Chinese and Russian servers?"

William shook his head. "Not easily. And I think any hack I try will leave traces behind. A trail of bread crumbs back to me." He shook his head, then sat rock still, and seconds passed. "But there is a way." He smiled. "Remember the Butterfly? I'll need cash for this favor. I don't think she'll settle for phone sex this time."

Jon's brows rose. "Really? Phone sex, eh? Well, how much money? Whatever it is, I know I can easily arrange it."

"And what do I tell my father?"

Jon frowned. "You'll just have to take the risk and lie to him. Can you do that?"

Wing's face fell. "I've done worse, but never lied to him." He shook his head. "Maybe I can figure something out, but don't count on it. At least I think I can get Betsy to destroy the evidence."

Jon remained silent. He'd had enough deception to last a lifetime.

William pulled his cell phone from his pocket. He got out of his seat and headed to the aircraft's restroom.

After William returned, he smiled at Jon. "Done. Here's what it'll cost you." He handed Jon a slip of paper on which he'd written a number.

Jon's eyes widened. "So be it." Jon saw the bank codes for Betsy's intermediate numbered bank account, also written on the scrap. He pocketed it and shook William's hand. "Thanks. I'm grateful for your friendship. I'd be honored to work with you again."

William glowed. "I hope there won't be a next time." He extended his hand.

Jon took it. "Friends and secrets forever."

Bob Gault stood at the foot of the bed in the military hospital at Incirlik Air Base, Turkey. The army doctor scratched instructions on a clipboard for the patient, George LeFebre, and hung it at the foot of the bed. He faced the bulky spy. "He's making progress every day. I think it'll be another week, maybe ten days. It's likely he'll regain consciousness. If and when he does, Mr. Lefebre can start walking soon after that." The doctor scanned the top page of the clipboard, without bending over. "He is strong and healing fast. I'll check in later, in the afternoon."

As the doctor moved to the next bed, Gault counted the tubes coming into and leaving the torso of Tariq Houmaz. It occurred to him that the terrorist was the reincarnation of Mary Shelly's Frankenstein's monster. He thought of screaming, "He's alive." And with that thought, the spy chuckled.

He had no intention of spending another ten days, or perhaps even more, with a comatose terrorist. But orders were orders.

The bomb maker was the ultimate toy for McDougal. A worthy prize, useful in so many ways.

Gault still believed the bomb maker held the trump card to gain the spy his long-overdue promotion. He decided to call his work with Houmaz "Project Frankenstein." He thought, *wake up, you useless piece of flesh. Wake up. I am your master and I have a world to give you!*

CHAPTER 43

William Wing's apartment, Ascot Heights, Block A, 21 Lok Lam Road, New Territories, Hong Kong
October 14, 2:37 p.m.

William rolled his suitcase through the door of his Hong Kong apartment. His mind was filled with a swirl of alternatives so contradictory and so dangerous, he couldn't decide what to do. If he told his father he couldn't find the perpetrators of the computer intrusions, his father might dismiss him and once again bar him from ever returning. No good. But his father might detect the lie in him and do worse. Would he? Was he ruthless enough? He thought and concluded, *yes, he is.*

If William never called, it might alarm the old man more. He might send an exfiltration team. Would he torture his own son? William didn't want to find out.

He tried sleeping the first night he was back. But his mind kept cycling through the dismal alternative Jon had left him. Damn! Maybe he should just tell his father the truth? What was the worst that could happen? Maybe China had already hacked the truth from the Russian computers? If so, any lie would mark him with his father. And this would no longer be an issue of saving face.

In the middle of the night, he gave up trying to sleep. He

plucked his cell phone from the bed stand. After dialing the number, he waited for her to pick up.

"Little Wing! You know, I was beginning to miss you. Let me take off my dress and we can begin. I'm horny. Really—"

"Uh, Betsy, I need another favor."

"Crap. I need another orgasm. And after all I—"

"Yeah, I know. And we'll get to you right after."

"You're a miserable piece of shit, you know that? Fuck. Okay, what now?"

William steeled himself to the task. He formulated his request with care. "I need to see you. Even an encrypted phone connection won't work for this."

"This sounds dangerous. You know the rule. No danger!"

He clenched his fists, even though one gripped the phone. "My father is involved, and his helpers are good at what we do."

"Your daddy? You have a daddy?" He heard her snort.

"Butterfly, listen. This isn't dangerous if it's done right." And then he remembered Jon saying those words to him. He sighed. "I know this is a break with our arrangement, but, please?"

The silence was painful to endure. "Okay. But, if we're to do this, there will be major changes. I'll own you for a month. And you'll do whatever I ask for this simple favor I grant you. Clear?"

He grimaced. "Yeah."

"And, well, I lied about my appearance. I took a few liberties."

William chuckled. "Well, I did too."

He heard her sigh. She asked, "Okay then. What next?"

"I need to know where I'm going."

"I'm in Woodbine, Iowa. A real hole. You'll love it. For excitement, the locals watch the train go through town. Fly to Omaha and rent a car. Then call me for directions."

He nodded to himself. "Are you still horny?"

"Well, duh!"

He closed his eyes. "Okay, then. I can help. Listen. You're lying on a blanket at the beach. An obscure, empty patch of sand in Hawaii. Near Waikoloa. No one else you can see, so you decided to go swimming nude. Got it? Okay, then, take off your suit and walk into the warm water. You drift floating on your back. Are you there?"

"Yes." Her words came to him in a hiss.

"Suddenly, an Asian man, young and strong, floats nearby on a surfboard. He admires your body. See him?"

"Yes. Yes!"

William felt his own arousal, imagining the scene he painted. "You turn your head to inspect him. He removes his bathing suit and smiles."

"Oh, god. Yes."

William smiled. "And he reaches across the tiny gulf separating you from him. Touches your breast with one hand as you both glide on a wave onto the beach. Can you feel his fingers?"

"Uhh uhhuh."

William unbuckled his pants. "His hands are on both your breasts, your hands are guiding him inside you. The waves, he rocks you in their rhythm. Can you feel it?"

"Ahhhhhh. Oh, god, yes. Yes!"

When they were done, he thought seeing her might not be a good thing after all. He felt misgivings about how he'd lied to her and cheated her.

But, it would be good to be done with their lies. He was surprised to realize that lying disgusted him. With that thought, he finished packing his bags.

Before he could leave, he had one more call to make.

The building in Herzliyya always amazed Jon at how obscure

it looked. He walked through the garage to the guard's booth. "Jon Sommers for the SHABEK trainer."

The soldier picked up a cell phone and checked a list. He shook his head. "You're not on the list."

Jon nodded. "Yeah. I know. Please call Yigdal Ben-Levy. Tell him I'm here. He'll want to see me."

In minutes he wore a visitor badge and was accompanied by an armed guard. He knocked on the basement door.

"Come," boomed the voice inside.

He entered, but Ben-Levy continued reading a page from a yellow file. He turned the file over and pointed to the seat opposite him. "Welcome, Jon."

Jon sat.

Mother smiled. "Someone sent you a message." He handed Jon an envelope. Heavy, expensive paper, and the return address was printed: Phillip Watson and Jennifer Stolworth. The techno-weenie prince and his fiancée. Jon placed the envelope in his pocket.

Mother's smile disappeared. "I've been reading Shula's debrief report. You did some excellent work. For the record, I never doubted your quality."

Jon frowned. "Really? Then why did you try to have me terminated?"

Ben-Levy leaned closer. "I felt it was necessary to motivate you. And, it worked."

Jon held back the anger he felt. "Motivate me? You sent a hit squad to motivate me?" He took a deep breath. "Tariq Houmaz lives."

"Yes, I've read the reports. But he bought us such wonderful toys. Excellent gifts." Ben-Levy's lips half-formed another smile.

Jon frowned. "And, you think this was all about some toys? Shit, man. People died." Jon started to rise.

"Sit! We're not done yet."

Jon stared into the spymaster's eyes. He took a deep breath. "Do you have any further business with me?"

"No. But you have business with me, don't you?"

His formulas predicted Ben-Levy would want closure. Jon could see it in the old man's eyes. Both knew they weren't through with each other. Lisa's voice in his head whispered, *now, Jon. Tell him. Ask him.*

Jon said, "I know all about Bloodridge." He saw the spymaster flinch. "My hacker's father is Xiang Wing, your counterpart in the Chinese government. The elder Wing had my friend search for the cause of the border skirmishes. I had William promise not to tell his father. It was inevitable it would lead back to you. And, it's inevitable they'll find out. So, consider this a bit of advance warning from me. I'll keep your secret. So will my hacker. But if we go missing or when we die, all secrets will become public. You understand?"

Ben-Levy stared at the floor. "A life insurance policy? Well, done, Jon. And, thanks." He smiled.

Jon ticked that one off his mental list. "My hacker knows another who may be your best shot at eliminating all traces of Bloodridge within the Chinese computers. This hacker can plant evidence within the records of the Beijing supercomputers pointing to the United States. But Moscow Center's servers will continue to point to China, so Moscow may keep their hold on weapons sales. It'll cost you five million USD. Interested?"

Mother sat motionless for a second. He looked away, but when his gaze returned, he nodded.

Jon handed him a piece of paper with the bank account information written on it. "Make sure you wash the sending account and make the transaction description read 'Uncle Yig's Will.' Okay?"

Mother's smile was momentary. "But I sense you want something from me. And, given what I do for a living, I'm a good judge of talent."

Jon moved his seat closer. "But of course. Several things. First, answer my questions. My parents. Who really killed them? And why?"

Ben-Levy's eyes focused on his hands. "We believe Yassir Arafat ordered their deaths because of the operation they were involved with at the time. In return, we had him assassinated using an undetectable poison Lester Dushov developed at Ness Ziona. Arafat's death was officially a heart attack."

"Is that all you can tell me?"

"Unfortunately, I've told you more than I'm authorized to. But, well, they were important to the state. And they were my friends. It was a simpler time then. Before the mission that caused both your parents' deaths, I promised your father, if anything ever happened to him, I'd look after you. Jon, I'm your godfather. He wanted you to become Mossad. I make few promises. So in return for their service, I had Israel fund your education and keep you safe. As I told you once before, I keep my promises."

Jon's eyes widened. "So the attempts to have me killed, they were just orchestrated moves by Shula and her team?"

"Yes. And I made the deal with Crane to have MI-6 get you from the safe house in East Meadow."

Jon nodded. "All of it was an act. Tell me, was it you who delivered the envelope to Phillip Watson?"

Mother shook his head. "Michael Drapoff noticed the feeble attempts someone had made trying to penetrate our network firewall. He backtraced the datastream to Watson and I decided to deliver a message."

Jon nodded. "Did you send Ruth DeWitt? Is she one of yours?"

Mother frowned. "Who?"

Jon saw the empty denial for what it was. He tensed. "Is she back in Israel?"

"I have no idea who you're talking about."

Jon shook his head. His resolve peaked. "I want something. Something important. I want a job with Mossad."

Ben-Levy shook his head. "Jon, you've proven you're not a killer. I can't use you in SHABEK."

Jon's brows furrowed. "I know that. But I've worked here and experienced the passion of this country. I feel a part of it now and don't want to lose it. I want to protect it. Look, I've been well-trained, and the best way for you to let me keep your secrets is have me within the Mossad. I don't want to work for you. I want to work in traditional espionage. In the Collections Department. Turns out, that's what I do best. Find things out. Work with teams to turn them to the task. But no assassinations."

The spymaster smiled. "Ah. Let me think. Yes. I can make that happen. We can place you in Collections."

Jon's breath left him in a rush. "Please. And something more. I want citizenship. I've given enough to prove I'm worthy."

Yigdal Ben-Levy nodded. He pulled a cell phone from his pocket. "Let me start the process right now."

Jon remembered the last time he was with Lisa Gabriel. He conjured her voice, from the last time he'd ever seen her. The last time he'd held her hand: "I'll bring you there. I want to show you. You'll be proud." He felt his eyes grow moist.

He finally had a home.

Twenty minutes later, Mother had done all he promised. A courier entered the basement office and handed Ben-Levy an envelope. Mother passed it across the desk to Jon. "Our computers will reflect your citizenship by the end of tomorrow."

Jon ripped it open. His passport and citizenship papers. He shook hands with Mother. "I'm sure our paths will cross again. Maybe some of my assignments will produce actionable intel for you."

Ben-Levy nodded. "Welcome home, Jon."

Jon left the basement office and walked to the elevator, on his way to Mossad's Intelligence Operations Division, which housed the Collections Department. The lift's doors opened and a tall, willowy blond walked out passing him. Jon did a double-take. "Ruth DeWitt?"

The woman walked on, but Jon was sure it was her. Maybe she hadn't heard. Or, more likely, it wasn't her real name. He caught up with her and touched her shoulder.

As she turned, the question on her face altered to a sunshiny smile. "Jon!"

"Ruth DeWitt. What's your real name?" He found himself lost in her perfume.

"When you left me, I got the idea you never wanted to see me again." She cast her eyes down and to the left. A lie.

"That was long ago. Things have changed. Look, can you just tell me your name?" He tried to smile back but his mouth wouldn't work.

"My name is Ruth Cohen. I'm one of Yigdal's *bat leveyhas*. But you knew that, didn't you?" Her eyes lifted to his face.

Jon nodded. "Yeah. Well, Ruth, I'm pleased to finally make your acquaintance." He smiled. "Were you telling the truth when you met me?"

Her smile fell away. "I wasn't under orders. I came on my own, worried that Aviva might have left you in a dangerous position. I knew she'd been sent to recruit you. I was curious, wanted to get to know you."

His lips tightened. "But you almost let me seduce you. Was that what you were told to do?"

She shook her head. "You just looked delicious to me. If I've offended you—"

He reached out and touched her shoulder. "No. Listen, I'm new in town. Do you know any blues clubs in Tel Aviv?"

She laughed and it melted his heart. "As a matter of fact I do." She pulled a card from her purse, scribbled on it and handed it to him. "I'll take you there. Let me know when you're free."

Elizabeth Rochelle Brown wondered what to do when he arrived? Kiss him or punish him?

He'd been a pain in her ass in every way. Cheating her when they competed. Slamming her on blogs after he'd faked winning. Asking her for favors, with payment in the form of favors to be granted in return at some distant later date. Arggghhhhh! Kiss him or punish him?

He'd also been sweet to her. He'd guided her to nirvana on the phone, often spending hours as she climaxed and drifted and climaxed again. Kiss him or punish him?

But this would be different. It was obvious Little Wing was deep into dangerous terrain. It was a place she feared. Would she find herself compromised? Hackers were often sent to prison if they were caught. A few corporations already had her on their hit lists. She feared walking in public, let alone being stranded in captivity. If they met, would the danger transfer to her? Of course it would.

Kiss him or punish him?

No, it would be better if she was never in the same room with him. He was becoming dangerous. She wondered if it was too late to cancel their date.

She picked up her cell phone.

"Father, it's your son." William wondered if his father could detect the petulance he tried to hide.

"I have waited for your call. Have you been successful?"

"How are you?"

"I'm well. What progress have you made?"

He closed his eyes and took a deep breath. "There is an American intelligence agency without a name. Its budget is hidden from Congress. Gilbert Greenfield runs it. The man responsible for setting up the hack is Mark McDougal. His covert agent Bob Gault ran the project, paying DEFCON independent hackers. The hackers had no idea what they were doing or who was running them. It was their action that caused the border war." William held his breath.

"You have done well, son. You have my everlasting gratitude. Please come home now."

"No. I have things to do before you see me. But soon, I will visit. Soon. Until then, father, know I do love you. Give my love to mother." William terminated the conversation, frowning from his lies. He'd have to call Jon, so Sommers could coordinate with his Mossad masters. And he'd need to visit Betsy as soon as he could, to coordinate all the additional hacks.

Yigdal Ben-Levy pressed the Enter key, approving the funds transfer to Betsy Brown's numbered account. Soon, it would be over, and his Bloodridge black operation would be untraceable. He exhaled. How had Jon discovered the operation? Was it through Rimora? She'd done the analytical work and the setup of the project for the spymaster.

As an IDF sniper years ago, and then as a Mossad *kidon*, Yigdal's soul was drenched in the blood of Israel's enemies, and he felt no remorse for their murders. He knew, more than most, how Israel's precarious fate was no more settled than a leaf floating in the breeze.

He remembered how proud he'd been of Jon Sommers, his godson. He'd visited the family in London several times, but there was no reason for the young boy to remember what had happened so long ago. He thought of his promise to Jon's parents. He'd had great expectations for the young boy, following his life until the tragedy of his parent's death. And from then on, he took a role arranging Jon's life until the young man was ready for first contact. After training, Yigdal felt Jon could hunt Houmaz.

When the mission had gone badly, Yigdal was ready to forgive Jon. But when Jon told him about his recruitment to work as a double for Sir Charles and MI-6, the spymaster knew it would be a death sentence. Oscar Gilead hated Crane and the Brits for what they'd done during the years preceding Israel's independence.

To keep Gilead from ordering a terminate-with-prejudice order for Jon, Yigdal had sent a *kidon* team headed by Shula Ries to find and hold Jon, while Yigdal called Crane and offered a deal to trade intel. The spymaster hoped if he brought the deal to Gilead, the Deputy Director would assume it wasn't Jon who'd been recruited. If Gilead declined the deal, Yigdal would tell Jon to stay away from the Brits.

But, he'd convinced Gilead of the value the Brits could provide. To keep Gilead from discovering Jon was working with the Brits, Yidgal kept Jon from returning to the Mossad while he sought a way to fix the problem. And Jon's work over the months had provided evidence he'd become an effective *katsa*, or case officer.

The Brits had done what they'd promised. After Mother convinced Jon he'd been captured to be sent to a better place, they'd rescued him and made him one of their own. And, Jon had performed, just as his father said he would. A perfect spy, without whom, Israel would have been rendered to dust. Yigdal had kept both his promises, to Jon's father and to the state.

He smiled with pride.

But he felt empty and hollow. Something else disturbed him, kept him awake every night.

He removed a yellow folder from the locked, hidden drawer at the bottom of his desk.

Opening it he stared at the photograph of Aviva

Bushovshy, his sister's daughter. He wiped a tear from his eye.

She'd smiled at him as she entered Yigdal's office in mid-December. He remembered how she took her time getting to her reason for the meeting. "Uncle, I need permission from you and Mossad for something. If you can't grant it, well, I'll resign."

No one ever resigned from work at the Office. Mother had sighed. "What?"

"I want to marry Jon. He proposed, and I accepted." Her face had glowed.

Mother remembered shaking his head. "I'll speak with Oscar. If he agrees, you have my permission. But, you cannot resign. You know that. Right?"

He'd seen the anger in her eyes. Her voice had raised up an octave. "It's my life. I want Jon in it." She'd seemed defiant. "Let's hope Deputy Director Gilead agrees." She hadn't even smiled at him.

He remembered taking the elevator to the top floor to see Gilead. As he'd neared the office, Oscar's door had swung open, and he seemed to be in a controlled state of rage. "Yigdal. I was just coming to see you. Please come in. Shut the door."

Before Yigdal sat, he'd told his boss of her intention to marry Jon. Gilead looked at the floor and shook his head. "Aviva Bushovsky. She's what I was going to see you about. I just learned something disturbing. One of our surveillance teams had some trouble tracing her. Several times she ran counter-surveillance detection routes when she knew we were ghosting her. The day before Sommers took her to the airport, we saw her with Sir Charles of MI-6. She's become a double."

Ben-Levy's lips had moved but he couldn't produce a sound. He'd never suspected, blinded by the love of his niece.

"I'm sorry, Yigdal, but you know what I have to do."

Gilead had opened the door. "Wait here for me. I have to see the Prime Minister."

Stunned, he'd stood in Gilead's door as the Deputy Director rushed out past him. Why had she worked with the Brits? They must have known about her budding relationship with Sommers. Had they threatened her with Jon? There had been no way for him to know.

When Gilead returned, his face was red with rage.

Gilead was the only man alive whom Yigdal feared. He ordered Mother to authorize the mission terminating her life as a warning to other Mossad agents and MI-6 as well. Ben-Levy argued with every bit of passion he could muster to have her dismissed from the service or put in prison. Anything but a terminate-with-prejudice order.

But the Deputy Director had shouted back a single word: "Orders!"

The rest followed like a clockwork mechanism. Yigdal lied, telling Aviva there were pressing matters and he couldn't see Gilead until tomorrow. They argued and she'd left his office, slamming the door.

While most of the Mossad took its lunch break, Yigdal called Shimon Tennenbaum for an urgent task. The *kidon* took a tiny bomb from the weapons locker and followed Aviva's car to the parking garage. Tennenbaum placed the device in the gas tank, and wired it into the ignition just before she'd arrived. He watched her start the engine and blow apart. It was all in the report Ben-Levy had removed from the yellow folder.

When Tennenbaum returned, his face was ashen. "Was it really necessary to do this?"

Mother clenched his fists, fighting for control. "Orders." His voice cracked.

Tennenbaum nodded. "It wasn't a clean kill. She thrashed as she burned to death. I'm so sorry."

Mother's voice was weak. "We have to find a suspect.

Find a Palestinian student. Shoot him several times but don't let him die. I will interrogate him." A week later, he visited the hospital and placed one of Dushov's undetectable poisons into the boy's IV. He wrote a report indicating the boy carried a bomb made by Tariq Houmaz.

Then he'd had Michael Draper hack the servers of the newspapers, placing the name "Lisa Gabriel" into the stories of the terrorist bombing in place of Aviva's, hoping Jon Sommers would see it.

Mossad intel had indicated the terrorist was planning something big, and Amos Gidaehl had been sent with a team to find out what it was and stop it. But Gidaehl's entire team had vanished. After his recruitment and training, Ben-Levy had sent Jon to track Houmaz.

He stared at the photograph of the young redheaded woman with olive-colored eyes. Tears formed and fell as he clenched his fists. The sound coming from him was just above a whisper. "Oh, God. Forgive me!"

Across the desk from him sat the ghost of Aviva Bushovsky. The ghost laughed back at him. *Never! When Jon finds out what you did to me, and someday he will, your life will become a real hell.*

CHAPTER 44

Mount Hebron Cemetery, Tiberias, Israel
October 20, 3:11 p.m.

The sun gleamed off marble tombstones placed on the earth in fond remembrance of passed loved ones. Most headstones had several stones placed on them, the traditional marking placed by a Jew who'd visited a grave. A stiff wind blew as Avram Shimmel and Jon Sommers left the car at the curb.

Avram walked to where Jon stood. "I'll always consider you my friend." He extended his hand.

Jon shook it. "Yes. Friends and secrets forever." He smiled. "What will you do now? Where will you go?"

Avram shrugged. "I hadn't had time to sit *shiva* and properly mourn them. After visiting their graves, I'll sit in our apartment with the mirrors covered. Maybe some of my friends and comrades from IDF and Aman will pay their respects. After that, I'll think about what I'm going to do. I think I may wander for a while until I figure it out. I have to think some things through." His voice cracked. When Jon stepped forward to get closer, Avram stepped away. "No. Please, leave me be." He shuddered, then faced Jon. "Uh, what about you?"

Jon stared off into the cemetery. "Dunno. I'll work with

Mossad, but I'll never trust them again. Or any other intelligence service, for that matter."

The big former soldier stiffened as the breeze hit his face. "Can't blame you. I'll be here for about half an hour. I can give you a ride back."

Jon wondered if Avram wanted his company. Probably not. He shook his head. "I'll be here a bit longer. Perhaps you'd best leave when you're done. I can find a taxi. I know our paths will cross again. Here's hoping it's better times."

Avram just nodded and hiked away.

Jon closed his eyes for a second. Who was it that had long ago written the lines, "He who seeks revenge must first dig two graves?" Shakespeare? *Today I'm here to visit two graves, and remarkably, neither is my own. But neither belongs to Tariq Houmaz, either.*

He watched Avram shuffle toward the other end of the cemetery to visit the graves of his wife and daughter.

Jon walked on in a different direction, seeking the stone marking the first site he was here to see.

The grave's grass was brown but the headstone was clean and elaborately carved. No stones were left on the headstone. He could smell flowers in the breeze.

As he took another breath, the aroma of ozone from a brewing storm hit his nostrils. Grew clouds moved in on him, but he felt nothing beyond a twinge of pain in his left arm and others in his gut and his chest, remnants from his recent escapades.

The stone read, "Lisa Gabriel. Born February 18, 1994, Died September 12, 2014." He murmured, "Lisa, I never knew you, but I'm here to thank you for loaning me the name of the woman I loved."

All the nearby graves had small stones on them, but Jon had come with a bouquet, wanting to mark this visit with something temporary. He dropped a single red rose from the bouquet, and stood for a minute in silence.

Examining the cemetery map, he searched for his final destination today.

It seemed like he walked on forever, into a remote area of the graveyard where the markers were naked white posts with numbers painted on them, each topped with a star of David. No tombstones with names for the dead spies of Gideon.

Jon read the numbers, searching. As he neared the one he sought, rain clouds moved closer and the wind picked up. Finally, the number on the page he held was a match to the one on the post. He stopped and stared at the grave of Aviva Bushovsky. He folded the map and dropped it into his pocket, then placed a small rose close to the gravepost.

"There was something I asked. Marry me and be with me forever. But I didn't know then who you really were. Your lies, your terrible deceptions. You crushed my heart and destroyed my life. I did your bidding after you died. Your voice in my head compelled me. Will you free me now?" Jon paced the turf in front of Lisa's grave.

There was just the sound of the wind. Her voice in his head, his constant companion since her death, was silent.

He felt somehow lighter as the wind grew fierce, blowing drizzle into his face. He smiled.

The sky opened and rain poured heavy on him, mixing with the the salty tears from his eyes. He'd come here to say farewell. But now, with her voice absent, he felt alone. "Good-bye, darling." He dropped the remainder of the bouquet on the soil where she rested.

His hands empty, Jon Sommers turned away and walked toward the cemetery road. He had no plan to guide him, no voice compelling him. His friends were headed to their homes.

He wondered what lay ahead, knowing he could survive under the most difficult and dangerous circumstances.

Jon reached into his pocket and fingered the envelope

Ben-Levy had given him. It was Phil Watson and Jenny Stolworth's wedding invitation. In two weeks. It would be his next stop.

He wondered where the Mossad would send him and what cover he'd have for his work. He might even be a banker for them.

Jon thought once more about the woman who would always be "Lisa" to him, and smiled as rain washed away the tears that had streamed down his face. He remembered her lies, but they no longer disappointed him. What did hurt him was the realization he could lie to the next woman he found interesting. What else could he do if the calculus of the situation demanded it for his survival? For his people's survival?

He was now capable of anything.

So be it.

Appendix A.

<u>Glossary</u>

- Aleph – lead *kidon*, the assassin leading an execution mission
- AFI – intelligence branch of the Israeli Air Force
- Aman – intelligence branch of the IDF; also called Israeli Military Intelligence
- *Ayin* – tracker (surveillance)
- Backstopping – fake identification papers
- *Bat leveyha* – female agent
- Better place – euphemism for murdering an enemy agent (thus sending him to a "better place")
- Blind dating – meeting place chosen by an agent to meet his or her handler
- *Bodel* – courier
- BP – Israeli paramilitary Border Patrol
- Collections Department – Intelligence Department abroad
- DARPA (Defense Advanced Research Projects Agency), the research arm of the Department of Defense, defunded from a development shop to a project-management office by President George W. Bush
- Daylight alert – highest-priority alert
- Dry cleaning – counter-surveillance techniques
- Exfiltrate – retrieving an agent from hostile territory
- *Heth* – logistician
- False flagging – an operation falsely made to appear mounted by another country

- Fumigate – sweeping an area for electronic bugs
- Honey trap – sexual entrapment for intelligence purposes
- IDF – Israel Defense Forces; the Israeli army
- *Katsa* – case officer
- *Kidon* – operative specializing in assassination
- Krav Maga – Israeli martial art developed by Aman and used by IDF and Mossad. Now taught to many of the global spy agencies
- MI-6 – also known as Great Britain's Secret Intelligence Service
- Mossad (the) – the Institute for Intelligence and Special Operations, Israel's national intelligence agency
- *Neviot* – surveillance specialist
- NI – intelligence branch of the Israeli navy
- NOC. – Non-official-cover; an intelligence operative not employed by an intelligence agency, usually a subcontractor in black or gray ops.
- *Qoph* – communications officer
- Safe house – apartment or house used covertly for base of operations
- *Sayan* – a helper (plural *sayanim*)
- SHABEK – also known as GSS or Shin Bet; responsible for internal security and defense of Israeli installations abroad, including embassies, consulates, and other organizations.
- Slick – hiding place for documents
- Tze'elim – Israel's Urban Warfare Training Center in the Negev desert

- Va'adet Rashei Hasherutim, the Committee of the Heads of Service in Israel's intelligence community; Mossad is a prime member.
- Wahhabi – Puritan doctrine of Islam, founded by Muhammad ibn Abd al-Wahhab (1703–1792) in Saudi Arabia
- Wash – recycling of a valid passport obtained by theft or purchase
- *Yahol* – a covert computer hacker, or cybercriminal working for the Mossad (plural *yaholim*)

Appendix B.

Russia and the Russian Mafia

- *Cyber War: The Next Threat to National Security and What to Do about It*, Richard A. Clarke and Robert K. Knake, Ecco Press, 2010

- "Russian Mafia," from Wikipedia, the free encyclopedia, en.wikipedia.org/wiki/Russian_Mafia

- "Wikileaks Demonstrates Even Russia Not Immune," Dec 02, 2010, by Robert Weller, http://www.allvoices.com/contributed-news/7494949-wikileaks-demonstrates-even-russia-not-immune

- "The Global Reach of the Judeo-Russian Mafia," by Gordon Wagner, http://open.salon.com/blog/gordon_wagner/2010/02/25/the_global_reach_of_the_judeo-russian_mafia

- "Are criminals in Russia sending missiles to Iraq?" by Lucy Komisar, *Sacramento Bee*, Feb 23, 2003, http://thekomisarscoop.com/2003/02/are-criminals-in-russia-sending-missiles-to-iraq/

- "Eastern European Arms Sales to Rogue States," by Sam Vaknin, 12/25/2005, http://www.globalpolitician.com/21506-arms-sales-eastern-europe

- "Russian Mafia Abroad Now 300,000 Strong," March 2, 2010, http://mafiatoday.com/other-mafia-orgs/russian-mafia-abroad-now-300000-strong/

- "Russian Mafia - Politicians - Mogilevich and Birshtein," http://www.telusplanet.net/public/mozuz/crime/lemieszewski20001103.html

Appendix C.

Novelsisterhood.com Interview with D. S. Kane on March 15, 2009

NS: So you have a special ops agent in your story, what does he/she do? You want to make it believable!

Special Guest D. S. Kane: That's the deal I made with the Feds when they remotely searched my computer to see if I was writing a nonfiction account of my activities. And, no, I'm not. Now I write fiction to keep them happy. And they no longer threaten my life. Of course, I'm no longer doing dirty work for the ubers. Google both my names and you'll see who I am and who I was, missing the bits about my covert activities, but you can see where they'd fit. I may be one of the few thriller writers who write in self-defense. By itself, it's a pretty good story, one I can't tell. [Visit his website: http://dskane.com/.]

NS: Thank you for agreeing to interview with us and share all of your knowledge. Before we start with the questions is there anything you'd like to add to your bio?

D. S. Kane: I've been published and quoted ten times in nonfiction, mostly in financial textbooks and the financial trade press, including *U.S. News and World Report*. And, I did some work for the federal government. But when my former "handler" told me I couldn't tell my story, I had to learn a new trade. A week after that conversation, all my work products were reclassified.

Fiction is a tough mistress. It took me two years to master it enough to complete a salable manuscript. If I was telling my own story, I could have done it well and fast.

It'll take a trilogy of novels to tell the story. Many non-fiction writers underestimate just how complex fiction writing is.

NS: What mistake do you see authors make the most when using a special ops agent in their story?

D. S. Kane: Fiction is all about escalating tension until the story's resolution. Most writers forget to think about how much can go wrong just because of how intelligence agencies are organized. In designing your story, think of the following:

There are sixteen agencies that I know of in the United States (CIA, NSA, FBI, DIA, NCIS, ATF, DEA, NRO, ONI, US Marshals, etc.) and over a hundred on the planet for other countries: FSA and SVR Sluzhba Vneshnei Razvedki (the Foreign Intelligence Service) in Russia; Mossad and ISS for Israel; Germany's GSG9 and BFV, their Foreign Intelligence (like our CIA), and BKA, their Federal Office of Criminal Investigation (like our FBI); the Dutch security service AIVD; the Egyptian secret police or SSI, also called the Mukhabarat or General Directorate of State Security; Milli Istihbarat Teskilati, for Turkey; and so many others.

Many of the intelligence agencies have a paramilitary arm as well as an espionage arm. CIA's paramilitary division is known as the Special Activities Staff.

And of course, the terrorists have their own networks. In the Middle East, for example, there are the Fatah Revolutionary Council, or FRC, and Jihaz-el-Razd, their intelligence arm, and Islamic terrorist organizations including Hamas, Hezbollah, the al-Aqsa Martyrs' Brigades, the remnants of Al Qaeda, and the Muslim Brotherhood.

Every intelligence service is divided into five functional areas. Administration and policy wonks have *never* been in the field and they think like basic accountants. Analysts are either uninterested in field work because it's dangerous, or living vicariously. The field agents are sub-divided into espionage (gathering and sending back intelligence, but no killing) and black ops (enforcement, including killing). Then, there are contractors to an agency, giving the administrators deniability. Contractors are the wild card. Not subject to government oversight as agency employees are, contractors do whatever it takes to get the job done. They have "non-official cover" and are called NOCs. That means they pretty much walk naked in this world. Finally, there are the geeks that provide hacking services and data security for our intelligence agencies. These people, once the back-office urchins, are now vital to everything that goes on in any agency. If you watch the Fox TV series *24*, think of Chloe O'Brian.

Making it more complex, the CIA, for example, has its analysts divided up into "country desks" with each head of country running both operatives and NOCs (the contractors). Valerie Plame, for example, was an analyst running the Iran country desk's Weapons of Non-Proliferation program. And I believe she was outed to remove her and the knowledge her NOCs could provide on Iran. Not Iraq. So, there's a story underneath the story we were told in the press. The administration wanted to invade Iran after Iraq was occupied to give us presence in Iran, Iraq, Afghanistan, and Israel. Plame was their only obstacle and they set her husband up. When he (Joe Wilson) wrote his op-ed article in the *New York Times*, it gave them their excuse.

Intelligence agencies compete for budget dollars and therefore screw with each other continuously. There is also misunderstanding and jealousy between the administrators, analysts, and covert operatives.

All this raises an important question for thriller writers: *Quis custodiet ipsos custodes*? Who spies on the spies?

There is a strong temptation to lie in this business. Telling the truth can get you killed. And the best gems of intelligence are easily salable to competing agencies of your own government or any other country's agencies. While administrators and analysts tend to sell their own country's secrets, analysts and operatives tend to sell the intelligence they've unearthed from other countries to those of still other countries.

Most thriller writers don't use these sources of tension enough in their stories.

NS: Do you have a book or a website you can recommend when an author is doing research for a special ops agent/ story?

D. S. Kane: Read thrillers. Lots of them. Daniel Silva, for example. His series with protagonist Gabriel Allon is a wealth of knowledge on Israeli intelligence and politics. From my time dealing with Mossad, I believe his thrillers contain a real view of the Israeli perspective on black ops. I recommend *The Kill Artist*.

Chris Reich writes about the financial end of espionage and his thrillers are excellent in their use of facts and fictions about the funding of terrorism and weaknesses in the global banking system. I recommend *The Devil's Banker*.

Barry Eisler, who's been a friend since before he had a literary agent, is former CIA in the Directorate of Operations, Far East section. His series about John Rain is six books and hit the best sellers list. His protagonist is a hit man working for the Japanese mafiya, the Japanese FBI, and a group he calls "Christians in Action," or the CIA. His female contagonist is from Mossad. A good read. I recommend *Rain Fall*.

Jim Rollins' Sigma thriller series is about a fictitious (I believe) covert paramilitary arm of DARPA. It mixes science and covert activities. One of his "discoveries," Liquid Armor, a clear STF (Stress Thickening Fluid) that can stop bullets, was invented by the US Army about five years ago. It's far superior to Kevlar because it can be used to coat normal clothing, making a Liquid Armor-treated Hawaiian shirt virtually undetectable as bullet-proof clothing. Good science is a key element in thrillers. I recommend *Map of Bones*.

Watch television shows that rely heavily on covert ops to glean details of their tools and tradecraft. *Burn Notice* is one of the best. Also, *24* is absolutely essential.

Listen carefully to the evening news. There's a larger story behind most of what you hear coming out of Washington. The place is a powder keg. Most wars are designed there before the intelligence is gathered.

For a veritable how-to on NOCs. read *Confessions of an Economic Hit Man*, by John Perkins, one of my competitors back when I was active. There are plenty of "conspiracy theory" websites. On my blog (at http://dskane.com/) I have one entry that could easily provide the concept for a great thriller. I haven't used it because, when I discussed it with a literary agent, he told me it was far-fetched. In fact it's real—you can't make this stuff up! Also, try http://www.crooksandliars.com/ and http://www.fromthewilderness.com/

The best of all, I believe, is the history of Irangate. Very real, and start by Googling Oliver North and John Poindexter. Wikipedia (http://en.wikipedia.org/wiki/John_Poindexter) has a wealth of information. Most interesting of all is Poindexter's recall to public service after being pardoned for his role in Irangate. Most of those involved in Irangate have been "recycled" and are now working in the intel biz. As the Eagles sang in "Hotel California," "You can check out any time you like but you can never leave."

NS: What is the biggest misconceptions authors/people have of special ops agents?

D. S. Kane: There are some simple, ugly realities about the character of people in covert ops. Working in black ops requires a person to have maximum distrust of others and a desire to kill for pleasure. I believe no one does it out of patriotism. Espionage, on the other hand, is either driven by patriotism or a desire to possess and sell valuable intel.

With operatives, there are safety procedures they adhere to religiously. When it comes to the location of clandestine meetings, operatives use a procedure with the acronym "PACE," standing for primary, alternate, contingency, and emergency. And, there is always a backup to the backup.

When moving on foot or in a vehicle, we use a maneuver known as an SDR—surveillance detection route. In other words, we make sure no one is following us. But, by having men placed in different locations, people can follow the spy without alerting him to the fact he was being followed.

NS: I'm going to show my ignorance here, what agencies actually have special ops agents? Military or government?

D. S. Kane: Uh, both! CIA has a paramilitary SAS branch—the Special Activities Staff—for example. DIA is the Defense Intelligence Agency and also runs covert ops. The Navy has NCIS investigating criminal activities in the military. And of course, the secret police agencies themselves have spies spying on other spies. Finally, I believe the White House has its own little group, mostly for ad hoc ops.

NS: How much leeway would you say an author has when writing a special ops agent story? I have this conception of special ops as being so secretive I could basically make up any type of James Bond–type action story and be within the realm of possibility, as long as I have the correct agencies involved. Is this true?

D. S. Kane: As thriller readers became more sophisticated about the actual intelligence community, the margin for error has continuously eroded. When we leave the service, we can't write about our lives as coverts, so we write fiction. John LeCarré, Barry Eisler, the list is endless. All former coverts. And each of us has his or her own special focus within the industry. For example, LeCarré had to reinvent himself when the Cold War ended, since that was what he'd written about. Eisler is a friend of mine, and when I had a "problem," I met with him and asked his advice on counter-surveillance. He couldn't help. Told me his focus is martial arts and assassination. I found help from another friend who opened with the line: "Sheesh. Your tradecraft is so 1980s. It's a wonder you're not dead." He helped me in that area, with tip after tip. For example, when you meet with someone and don't want the government to overhear you, be sure to remove the battery from your cell phone. They can turn your cell on remotely without activating the screen and listen in. Didja know that? I thought not.

My own current interest focuses on counter-surveillance tradecraft and tech toys used by the covert community. Some of my friends have worked to develop toys for our country, and before DARPA was mostly defunded, their careers led them to produce some amazing things. Think of Q in the James Bond movies. I've found out about a few of those toys and altered them so I can use them in my own novels. One of the best is that it's possible to recode the programs in multiplayer online games to enable a player to plant a document within the game that another player can pick up with no one the wiser.

When I was covert, my function involved a mix of banking systems and hacking. I traveled out of the country and visited banks where I...well, I can't tell you what I did or I'd have to kill you. But, by writing about a fictive protagonist, I can tell these stories. They're hidden in my novels. And since I wasn't officially an employee of any intelligence agency, I never signed a non-disclosure agreement. My first novel, *Swiftshadow*, is out with agents now. Errr, that's literary agents, not covert agents. And I have others planned in a series for those characters.

NS: Can the government really spy on people, especially if they consider them a threat of some kind?

D. S. Kane: Before 9/11, yes, but only with a FISA [Foreign Intelligence Surveillance Act] warrant. Then came Bush and no FISA warrant was needed. Now, and even after Uncle George's "retirement," yes, the government can spy on you. FISA court will give a wiretap permit to any agency citing "national security interests."

NS: Writing, whether it's a screenplay or a book, still needs to be accurate, mostly anyway. What movie would you say depicts the best/true representation of a special ops agent?

D. S. Kane: My current favorite is *The International* with Clive Owen. It's similar to my own covert experience. And one of my friends is an investigative reporter. She worked at getting a French arms dealer thrown into a Swiss prison. The guy worked out of the BCCI (Bank of Credit and Commerce International) office in Fort Lauderdale back in the day. It's amazing we never crossed paths until we both moved to California.

Television does a decent job on tradecraft with *Burn Notice* and, as I stated before, with *24*. Many people fault *24* for its use of torture, and many in our government believe it doesn't work. I believe torture can be effective if there is a hope in the victim that they might be set free if they cooperate.

NS: How can an author incorporate the skills of special ops in their civilian character?

D. S. Kane: Best to give your protagonist a streak of paranoia and a technical bent. And make them at least marginally qualified in martial arts. My characters run the range from mercenaries to policy wonks to technology geeks at intelligence agencies. Don't try to put too much into any one character. Have them work together in teams: a hacker, a black ops agent, an analyst with political and economic training, and a traditional "spy" who can do dead drops and drop ins.

NS: Where does a special ops agent train? Quantico?

D. S. Kane: Quantico is the FBI's home. Not a training arena for coverts. There are several places for coverts in the United States. Best known, Camp Peary is the CIA's spy school, better known as the Farm. It's located at Harvey Point, North Carolina, just south of the Virginia coastline. They teach all the US intelligence agencies hard-core paramilitary training.

At Camp Peary, Harvey Point itself is just that—a stubby finger of land curling out into the murky water where North Carolina's Perquimans River meet the Albemarle Sound. The CIA's facility sits on over sixteen hundred acres of mosquito- and poisonous-snake-infested swamp with thick-trunked cypress trees overgrown with heavy Spanish moss. Nine miles southwest of the town of Hertford, the road ends at a sign that reads, "Harvey Point Defense Testing Activity." It opened in 1961. Helicopters land and take off at all hours, and blacked out transports roll through town in the middle of the night. All sorts of old cars, buses, SUVs, and limousines can be seen entering on flatbed trucks, and are carried out later either riddled with bullet holes or burnt to nothing more than charred hulks.

The Point is where the CIA's hard-core paramilitary training takes place. Personnel are schooled in explosives, paramilitary combat, and other clandestine and unconventional warfare techniques. While the Farm at Camp Peary is where CIA personnel earn their stripes and learn their tradecraft, the Point is where a chosen few received a PhD in serious ass-kicking. The personnel invited to the Point aren't only limited to American CIA operatives. Recently, the CIA provided counterterrorism training to several American Special Operations groups, as well as foreign intelligence officers from more than fifty countries, including South Korea, Japan, France, Germany, Greece, and Israel.

And, there are others worthy of note:

One of the most secure counterterrorism training facilities in the world is in a remote corner of North Carolina's Fort Bragg—Delta Force's Special Operations Training facility. The facility has many different nicknames. Some call it SOT for short. Because of the original stucco siding, it's also called it the Fiesta Cantina. Some refer to it as Wally World, after the amusement park in the Chevy Chase movie *Vacation*. Some call it the Ranch, because of early Delta Force operatives' penchant for chewing tobacco and wearing cowboy boots. It boasts a wide array of training areas. There are large two- and three-story buildings used for heliborne inserts and terrorist takedowns; indoor and outdoor live-fire ranges; as well as ranges for close-quarters battle, combat pistol, and sniper training. Delta's Operations and Intelligence Center has staging grounds where mock-ups of structures in different terrorist scenarios can be constructed. It has a host of other facilities and training areas too numerous to list.

The Navy's SEAL Team Six's training facility is located in Dam Neck, Virginia.

And remember Blackwater? Although I've heard they've relocated from the United States and changed their name to "Xe." If you go to their website and use this URL—http://www.blackwaterusa.com/—you'll see the four locations within the United States where they (used to?) train mercenaries.

NS: For my last question, everyone likes a kick-ass heroine, so here goes: Are there any women in the special ops? If so, in what capacity?

D. S. Kane: Definitely, and there have been for over a hundred years, starting with Mata Hari, whose real name was Margaretha Geertruida. She was Dutch, and spied for the Germans during World War One. The French caught her and executed her by a firing squad at the age of 41.

Valerie Plame was a covert agent for our country, working the Middle East to gather intelligence about nuclear weapons.

I can't point out any others, for obvious reasons. But Hollywood and the New York publishers seem to love female spies.

Nora Roberts, writing as J. D. Robb, has a successful "In Death" series, getting close now to thirty books. One of the characters in Jim Rollins's Sigma series is a mysterious female assassin.

And Hollywood worships hard-boiled female protagonists. For example. a television series called *Alias* featured a female spy. It was popular for about five years.

As part of my agreement with my handler, I'm writing a female. One of the folks I worked with was from Mossad, decades ago, and told me she'd been an Israeli tank commander during the Six Day War. I know, Israel claims women weren't allowed into combat roles until recently. Maybe she was lying? It's what spies do best. I met her when she was running the global non-credit services area of a New York bank. I believe she was there to launder money for Mossad, but I've no proof of that.

The example I'm offering you is my protagonist from my novel, *Swiftshadow*: Cassandra Sashakovich. She earned a PhD in economics at Stanford and was recruited to work as an NOC at one of Washington's intelligence agencies. Her family immigrated to the United States from the Soviet Union just before it fell. Her mother was a commissar for the KGB, her father an economist working for the Central Committee, and her uncle a KGB operative. She speaks most Middle Eastern languages and is a computer hacker with basic tradecraft and weapons skills when my story starts. In Riyadh, her cover is blown by a mole within her agency and she's hunted by terrorists until she discovers why the terrorists are interested in her and who the mole is, and figures out how to recover her life. By the end of the novel, she's a crack shot, a master hacker, and the CEO of a mercenary company with a hacker division.

Writing women characters is tough for a guy. Luckily, my wife Andrea has a publishing background, and she reads my material before anyone else does. She pushes me to think in ways a male brain isn't designed to. By the time my critique group at ActFourWriters.com gets the material, it's close to a publishable draft. She's helped me learn how to write fiction.

One more thing: If any of your readers would like assistance on the tradecraft for their character who is a covert agent, or feedback on potential plots for a thriller, they can contact me at dskane@dskane.com.

NS: Thank you so much for your helpful insights into the world and mystery of special ops agents.

Acknowledgements

So many people were crucial in preparing this manuscript for you, the reader.

My critiques were provided by the ActFourWriting.com group, including Dennis Phinney, Linda Rohrbough, Janet Simcic, Brenda Barrie, Aaron Ritchey, Caryn Scotto, Liz Picco, Julia Reynolds, Daniel Houston, Steve Eggleston, Juliann Kauffman, Teri Gray, Carl Vondareu, Claudia Melendez, Megan Edwards, and Judy Whitmore. I also received valuable feedback, especially concerning military tactics and strategy, as well as inside information regarding sites where conflicts have occurred or are now occurring, from several folks from the Drink of the Month Club, a group consisting mostly of Naval Postgraduate School administration and faculty, including Ron Nelson, Martin Metzger, Fred Drake, Lee Scheffel, and Gary Ohls. Also, my friends and family contributed critiques, including Barry Groves, Michael Spicer, Frances and Elliot Spiselman, and Dana Gorman. And finally, Andrea Brown, my wife and the CEO of the Andrea Brown Literary Agency, Inc., is the best and final voice for judging what I create.

Several best-selling authors have contributed to my efforts, including James Rollins (for his discussions with me on Liquid Armor), Barry Eisler for his advice on self-publishing, Holly Lisle for her coursework on world building, and Greg Bear during our discussion on craft after the graduation ceremony at Northwest Institute of Literary Arts.

I want to thank my publication team, consisting of my editor, Sandra Beris; copyeditor Karl Yambert; graphic designer Jeroen Ten Berge; my website designer and host Maddee James of xuni.com; my publicist Brandi Andres; and Paul Marotta and Megan Jeanne of the Corporate Law Group, who incorporated The Swiftshadow Group for me.

I also want to thank my literary agent, Nancy Ellis, and my film agent, Brandy Rivers, for all their hard work on my behalf.

I am grateful for all the suggestions and advice I have received but I alone am responsible for the resulting work.

About the Author

D. S. KANE is the name the author has chosen to write under. He worked in the field of covert intelligence for over a decade. During that time, he traveled globally for clients including government and military agencies, the largest banks, and Fortune 100 corporations. One of the banks he investigated housed the banking assets of many of the world's intelligence agencies and secret police forces, including the CIA and NSA. Much of his work product was pure but believable fiction, lies he told, and truths he concealed.

Now, he's a retired spy, still writing fiction. Through his novels, he exposes the way intelligence agencies craft fiction for sale to sway their countries and manipulate their national policy, driving countries into dangerous conflicts.

He's been published under his real name many times in financial trade journals on topics including global banking, computer fraud and countermeasures, financial forecasting, global electronic-funds transfer networks, and corporate finance, including one book on finance published by a major publisher. He has been a featured speaker at financial conferences and conventions. His children's book, *A Teenager's Guide to Money, Banking and Finance*, was published in 1987 by Simon & Schuster. He was once the CEO of an eBook publishing company and writes a blog (http://dskane.com) on topics that include new technology, politics, and the future of publishing.

He has been adjunct faculty at the Whidbey Island MFA program, and also teaches a course at the Muse Online Writers Conference entitled Covert Training and Covert Operations for Fiction Writers, and one on a similar topic at California libraries, funded by a federal grant. He has taught a thriller-writing course at the Pikes Peak Writers Conference and was a featured speaker at a dinner meeting of the California Writers Club. He taught finance at the Stern Graduate Business School of New York University for over ten years, and is one of the co-founders of ActFourWriters. com, a unique email-based novelists' critique group (http://www.actfourwriters.com). His website can be found at http://dskane.com.

Made in the USA
San Bernardino, CA
29 July 2014